G000153325

John Steele was born and raise
In 1995, at the age of twenty-t
States and has since lived and w
cluding a thirteen-year spell in J
been a drummer in a rock band, an illustrator, a truck driver
and a teacher of English. He now lives in England with his wife
and daughter. He began writing short stories, selling them to
North American magazines and fiction digests. *Seven Skins* is
his second novel and the second Jackie Shaw book. The first,
Ravenhill, was published by Silvertail Books in 2017. He is currently writing a third, set in northern Japan.

SEVEN SKINS

John Steele

SILVERTAIL BOOKS • *London*

For Mum and Dad,
with love

CHAPTER 1

Saturday

Somewhere beyond the reaches of the Square Mile, at 11.15 on a Saturday night, London rages, but the man and woman sit in the quiet seclusion of an eight-pounds-a-glass City wine bar, twitching with anticipation. The man is in his later years, a solid but unspectacular career behind him, and the woman is at least forty years his junior. She has an eager smile that verges on greedy and the man thinks she wants to be with him in the mistaken belief that he is worth something substantial.

He has refined the anecdotes and crafted the cues. Snippets tossed into conversation: 'When I was in Zimbabwe – of course, it was Rhodesia back then...' a rueful smile, '...or off the coast of North Korea...' then a few operational titbits and a shallow sigh. 'But I shouldn't go on: I signed the *Act*.' And, for those too clueless to understand, 'You know, the Official Secrets Act.'

He has the look, too: just enough calibrated dignity and the world-weary confidence of a man who has trod the darker roads of human existence and seen a world only glimpsed by others when the body of some foreign diplomat or oligarch washes up in the Thames, or lies broken in a Knightsbridge apartment. The whole package is good for a couple of free drinks from the younger City boys, and it reminds him that once he had, indeed, been a trusted operative with the British intelligence services.

The blank but polite look on the girl's face reminds Len Parkinson-Naughton that she is too young to know what or where Rhodesia was, or to have any interest in Korea. She has finished her Prosecco after taking an age to sip it – he has finished three gins in the time – and is fingering the stalk of her glass with slim, spidery fingers. Her cheekbones and slim, angular nose say Slavic, possibly Serbian, making a mockery of the name she gave him: Beatrix. He can't quite place her accent. The bar is striving for post-industrial chic; it is almost empty as the financial quarter slumbers between business days. The harsh fluorescent spotlighting, like the lamps in an old-school interrogation room, serve only to heighten the brilliant sheen of her coal-black hair. To all intents, despite her diminutive frame, she appears brittle and beautifully cruel, and he wants her with a restless desperation. The fact that this seems, somehow, all wrong enhances his desire all the more. After all, wrongdoing has been his forte for the last few years.

I'm a fool, he thinks. An old, proud fool who doesn't know when he's beaten. At this age, I should be gardening and building models of the North Atlantic Fleet in '43.

The Rhodesian and North Korean cues are, like many of his conversational hooks, vicarious. Giles Reid, a HUMINT man in MI6, had met Mugabe back in the seventies and related the story at a conference in the States. In over thirty years with MI5, Parkinson-Naughton had never learned much of the tradecraft, even during his stint in Northern Ireland. He'd attended the lectures and heard the gossip in the canteen, but Senior Recruitment and HR officer at Thames House hadn't been seen as a high risk position in need of fieldcraft training. There was a brief spell of responsibility for running logistics in Ulster, but only because they were short-staffed and he was already in Lisburn doing performance evaluations. No, not much chance of being 'spotted' back in the old days, seduced by some Russian GRU 'swallow' girl in a honey-trap, and even less now. This woman before him sees a lonely, older man in a good suit with the right accent, and smells money. And that is fine. He's been paying for it since Pat left him and he'll make sure Beatrix earns her fee.

They leave the bar and he catches her gazing at the glowing steel and glass bullet of 30 St Mary Axe, all 41 storeys. He lights a cigar, the tip flaring in the dim light, and glances at Mitre House directly opposite, pleased to see there are no lights in the cramped offices of the consultancy where he works two days a week as a favour to an old Oxbridge friend. A former intelligence agency officer is worth the salary of a non-executive director when it comes to tenders for Home Office or military contracts. The fact that Parkinson-Naughton had been an administrative manager for most of his career is immaterial. He talks a good game. To be seen on the street with an unknown young woman in heels and short skirt, however, would never do.

Then there is the handsome civil service pension and the savings from some other, secretive dealings. For a moment his eyelids flutter at the thought of that third income – what he considers his retirement fund – and he wets his lips with a booze-coated tongue. Then his eyes widen at the thought of Pat discovering the undisclosed cash, how she would revel in ruining him, and he determines to work the delicate girl beside him that little bit harder in lieu of his poisonous ex-wife.

Beatrix takes his arm and steers him towards the larger thoroughfare of Aldgate and a taxi to his home in Twickenham. But after a couple of yards she edges him to the left past Mitre Square, where Jack the Ripper eviscerated Catherine Eddowes, and into the narrow alleyway of St James's Passage. He lets her lead him and feels a vague spark kindle in his belly. The passage is a dim trench at this time and, like much of the financial district at this hour, devoid of life. She stops him twenty yards from the far entrance of the passage, the empty avenue of Duke's Place beyond, with a gentle shove against the alleyway's wall.

She'll pay for that later, he thinks, and feels the flame below his gut burn a little brighter.

Her kiss is strong and frantic. He feels a flicker of disappointment at the clumsiness in her embrace and surprise at how angry her tongue feels in his mouth. But he draws her to him nonetheless, crushing her small body hard against his, stooping, his shoulders still broad despite his years, to lock his mouth onto hers. He feels her bony knees stab at him as he closes his eyes, and her muffled, 'No. Not like this,' only serves to goad him on. He is so inflamed, so lost in the struggle for a few seconds, that it takes him a moment to register that she's been wrenched from him and that his hands are left clawing the musty air. He hears a short, stifled cry and then his world is filled by white heat and the angry bite of stinging fragments of brick. He sees a young man, pale and terrified, holding a pistol with a long, cigar-like suppressor. He smells the heavy musk of brick-dust and hears, distorted and far away, a hiss, 'Get out of the way, youngster.' Disorientated, he barely registers the harsh Irish accent.

A wiry, bearded man, perhaps in his late forties, takes the gun from the younger man and aims at the left side of Len Parkinson-Naughton's head. The ex-MI5 man feels the beginning of a dull, excruciating ache and realises that part of his ear has been shot off. Then he hears the tinny clack of the suppressor doing its job – a sound cut off as abruptly as if someone had slammed a door.

#

The three of them had been waiting long enough for the kid, Padraig Macrossan, to get a bad case of the jitters, and for the veteran, Harris, to get bored. Alex Morgan knew what could happen when men with guns had too much time on their hands and that's why he'd insisted that only he carried; he'd give Macrossan the pistol when the time came. Besides, he'd already decided Harris was enjoying himself a little too much to be given a gun.

The girl was taking her sweet time but they'd been assured she was the older man's type: short, scrawny and young.

Each to his own, thought Morgan. He preferred a woman with some meat on her bones but if the whore could get the old man where they wanted him, he had no complaints.

At around 11.45 they heard the couple in the passageway, her stilettos telegraphing their approach. The empty stone tunnel of the passage was an echo chamber and he worried for a moment about the noise of the shot, knowing the suppressor would mask only around 30 per cent of the report. He hoped that Macrossan would get the job done with one bullet. They stood on Duke's Place at the entrance to St James's Passageway, glancing up and down the thoroughfare for traffic or pedestrians. It was deserted. Not even a taxi. Harris smoked beside him as he took the Beretta M9 from his pocket and screwed the suppressor in place. The kid, Macrossan, stared at the weapon. The silhouettes of the couple, when they appeared, were almost comical, one tall and lanky, the other short and petite.

The shadows merged and he heard muffled grunting as he handed the gun to Macrossan and followed him into the alleyway. Morgan grabbed the girl, slapping a hand over her mouth to smother her cry and for a moment it looked as though the kid would do as he'd been told. Stride up to the target and adopt the Weaver stance: double-handed grip with forward pressure on the drawing hand and slight rearward pressure on the second hand to control recoil. But Macrossan stopped too close to the target and Morgan realised that the kid was holding his breath. Macrossan's hand trembled as he fired and the bullet clipped the side of the old man's head, ripping part of his ear off. The round tore into the brick behind and struck like steel on flint, sending a shower of fragments into the bloodied conch shell of the ruined ear and hurling the ricochet at a crazy angle, forcing Morgan to duck on instinct and hurl the girl behind him. The

5

old man stood wild-eyed, his hands beginning to shake, while Macrossan cowered against the wall. Then Harris appeared, wrenched the Beretta from the kid, clouted him behind the head as he said something in an irritated tone, and shot the target twice in the head, just below and to the right of the shredded left ear.

The old man folded in on himself. He hadn't hit the ground as they caught his body and made their way back out of St James's Passageway, Harris unscrewing the suppressor from the pistol-barrel and Morgan and Macrossan dragging the corpse. The girl had already fled into the dark, vacant heart of the City.

#

It is one of a row of unremarkable, well-tended semi-detached houses on the dark street in west Belfast. Even the twenty-five-foot Peace Line wall, separating the street from its parallel neighbour, tapers off a few yards from the row of semis. Instead, the corrugated iron fence of a small industrial complex stands opposite number 85, albeit with a stencil of a gun sprayed on it with the scrawled legend *You are here* with an arrow pointing from the muzzle to the angry lettering.

But number 85 is distinguished from its neighbours thanks to the store of three Glock 17 handguns, an SA80 assault rifle, two Mossberg 500 shotguns, and ammunition wrapped in sacking and hidden in the loft insulation. Behind the closed curtains, the three men sitting in the small living room watching reality TV and drinking strong, bitter tea, are hard men with prison records and blood on their hands. They don't know each other. If lifted by the police, they'll have minimal information to give under questioning, should they break. All three have been diligent in maintaining a low profile in order to keep the house and its residents in good stead with the locals: the area is close-knit and gossip spreads fast, particularly when strangers move in, so a minimum of attention is vital.

The street is silent and empty. It is almost midnight and most people are at home, drinking in one of the bars on the larger road nearby, in an illegal shebeen, or in one of the city-centre clubs. A thick veil of cloud hangs over Belfast, as though someone has stretched a blanket from the Black Mountains in the west to the Castlereagh Hills in the east, and the sodium streetlights of the city below lend a flame-like glow to the overcast sky.

The three tea-drinkers don't hear the low grumbling as ten Police Service of Northern Ireland Land Rovers cough to life at the rear of the industrial complex opposite. The sound, and the whine of the PSNI helicopter hovering three miles away, is drowned by the wail of a mannequin-like celebrity wife in conflict with a glamour model over a pad of eyeshadow on the TV. One of the men rises to stretch and another lights up his fourth chained cigarette.

'Turn that down, Marty. We don't want the neighbours giving off.'

'Sure the walls are thick.'

'Not as thick as your head. Turn it down. I saw the woman next door with a wee child yesterday. You'll be waking it up.'

The tap of Marty's finger on the remote control seems to amplify as the soft clatter of men and equipment running towards the front door drifts in from the street. The third man, sitting nearest the living room door, spills his tea at the first shout of 'Armed police! Armed police!' punctuated by the heavy thump of a battering ram on the front door. Light floods the room despite the closed curtains, infused with blue flashes, throwing bogeyman shadows of the three men on the walls. The thin, insect-chatter of the helicopter above fills the air like the whine of a migraine.

Marty and his companions hear the dull explosion as the front door gives way. The men drop to their knees and place their hands behind their heads before the first officers enter the room, Heckler & Koch submachine guns at the ready. The man on Marty's right takes a look at the PSNI men in full body armour, wearing balaclavas and goggles, helmet-mounted cameras and mics, and clutching the ubiquitous H&K MP5s, and says, 'Sorry lads, we finished playing *Call of Duty* a couple of hours ago.'

The boot on his neck keeps him quiet while he is cuffed along with his companions, and one of the forced entry team reads their names.

'Philip Cross. Robert "Sav" Savage. Marty Catterick.'

Twenty minutes later they are separated, Philip Cross in the back of a Land Rover on the street, Robert Savage in the forensic tent which has been set up in the front garden, and Marty Catterick in the living room, face down and kept company by two officers wearing chequered baseball caps and their enmity on their sleeves.

A tall sergeant, his face slick with sweat after finally peeling off his fire-retardant balaclava, enters the cramped space clutching a shotgun and sits on the sofa.

'Mr Martin Catterick. So, what's on the shopping list, eh?' says the sergeant. Another policeman enters the room and gives him an official-looking form then exits again. 'Three Glocks. Not any of ours, I hope.'

Marty says, 'Fuck you.'

'No thanks, I'm on duty. One SA80.' The sergeant winks at one of the other officers as he writes something on the form and says, 'Take the paperwork up to McMahon. He's in the loft going through the ammunition now.'

The officer leaves with the document. His companion shifts position slightly, getting a better grip on his sub-machine gun.

The sergeant says, 'And, finally, two Mossbergs: check.' He pats the shotgun. 'I believe the Yanks were fond of using these, although that's changing now. We prefer the Remington 870 ourselves. Still, I suppose a shotgun's a shotgun, at the end of the day.'

He smiles at Marty and stands, lifting the black, murderous Mossberg. Behind his back, Marty Catterick's hands fidget. He needs to piss.

The sergeant says, 'Unless they have one of these in the barrel.' The tall policeman tips the shotgun muzzle-down and a small, plastic, rectangular object falls out, landing on the beer and fag-ash-stained carpet. The cop drops to his haunches in front of Marty and picks up the black and green memory stick. As Marty stares at the device, held between the tall sergeant's thumb and index finger, the policeman leans closer to him, his Kevlar flak jacket straining against his chest.

'Let's you and me go up to Serious Crime in Antrim, Marty, and have a wee chat about this.' The sergeant sniffs, like a bloodhound, his nose in the air. 'And we'll give you a change of clothes to wear, seeing as your jeans are covered in piss.'

CHAPTER 2

Monday

Jackie Shaw scratches his arse, places the shotgun in the back of the Range Rover and straps in for a bumpy ride. He starts the vehicle and begins the drive down the stubbled lane leading to an eight-furlong grass gallop that will be pummelled by several thoroughbreds later in the morning.

Neither the gun, nor the car, is his. Nor is the land he now crosses or the bed he woke up in twenty minutes ago. Jackie doesn't own much at all, but the bad dreams are his and his alone. Sometimes he wakes moaning, emerging from a veil of panic to the dim, sparse contours of the stone-walled room and functional wooden furnishings in his small flat, the loft of a converted barn on the farm. At others, the upper half of his body springs forward, like the blade of a flick-knife. The flat is his cocoon, his solace. It contains a large wardrobe with a mirror on the door, kitchenette, shower cubicle, sofa and coffee table. There are two photographs propped on top of the chest of drawers: his mother and father, both buried back home in Northern Ireland, and his sister with her husband and kids. The quiet purity and solitude of the bare, whitewashed walls calms him and there are no curtains on the windows. He doesn't want to feel entrapped: there should be no veil over the world outside.

At the end of the lane, the car's headlights pick out a sign, wreathed in a gossamer mist: *Garbella Hill Farm*. He's been working as a nominal security guard on the farm, with its racehorse stables, yard and training facilities, for a couple of years now and enjoys the seclusion the location in the Cotswold Hills affords. He remembers years ago, staring out across the Irish Sea, a beautiful woman sitting next to him. He'd told her he could never live in England, it could never be home. But that was a long time ago. He's always liked hill country and he feels as at ease here as anywhere he's been in the last twenty years. And he's been around.

Life has begun to cloud the open-featured countryman's face he sees each morning in the mirror, his brow knit like the knotted skin of the large scar on his right forearm. Since last year, there is a little more salt in the dusting on his dark crew-cut.

The Range Rover begins to lurch on the lane, the ground puckered by man, machine and beast. In the glow of the head-lights, the lane is a shattered spinal column of loose stone and muck. After sixty yards it splits and Jackie takes the left branch, heading for the gallops rather than the main road. He wills the sun to rise, to bleach the night shadows.

As he approaches the gallops, Jackie can discern the small stone rectangles, sprouting at crazy angles from the ground on the left of the lane, of the graveyard. All thoroughbred winners laid to rest on this spot on the one thousand acres of Mack Stevenson, racehorse trainer extraordinaire. The millions of pounds now stirring in the stables is a fraction of the fortune buried in this patch of long, grasping grass. It's still too dark to read the names, the cobalt sky still some time from dawn, but he knows many of them from memory. Flashing Blade. Call for Empties. Duke of Windsor. Ernie's Cat.

'Sickbag' Simpson. Another name; a very different animal.

'Ruger' Rainey; 'Big Dog'; Billy Tyrie. Killers, abusers, pushers, terrorists. The victims, too, and friends shot down or blown to bits: a lifetime of memories from a couple of years in the RUC.

He pulls over onto the grass verge and lifts a shotgun, wrapped in a leather cover, from the back of the Range Rover.

Locking the vehicle, he sets off on the mile-long course used to give the thoroughbreds a workout. The Beretta semi-automatic is mostly used for pest control, and is light for a shotgun. Jackie holds it crooked in his arms, patrol-style.

As Jackie strides across the dark plain of Hogg's Hill, the world around nothing more than a shadow, he takes comfort from the gun in his arms, its weight and finality. He hates firearms, and yet he can face down the dark with his finger on the trigger, an ounce of pressure and the terrible bark of the weapon; its savage discharge.

The open space, ringed with the black husks of the Gloucestershire hills, is a world away from the terraced streets and fierce, tribal murals of his youth. Then the ground becomes clogged with thick, unruly grass and clumps of bracken, and he's forced to concentrate on threading his way through the thicket. He can see the mass of the copse beyond, the trees like black storm clouds anchored to the earth. The sky is a lighter hue and sunrise will be upon him in another twenty minutes or so. He unwraps the Beretta.

Jackie doesn't like guns, but he respects what they can do. He knew men in the Army who obsessed over them, studying makes and models, comparing calibre, magazines, sight radius, muzzle energy and trigger pull. Many of those in paramilitary groups had a terrible fascination with weaponry and the damage it could inflict. Jackie is repulsed by it. But, on days like this, when he awakes with the shadow of his past looming over his bed, he comes out here to shoot.

He's already loaded the shotgun and creeps into the copse, sighting on some targets he fashioned out of rusted iron left lying around the yard. Mack gives him free rein on the land and has insured him for all the vehicles. Ian Sparrow, the gamekeeper who owns the gun, is fine with him using it so long as it is back in the cabinet, cleaned and oiled, by mid-morning and

Jackie pays for the ammunition. Tight oul' bastard, he thinks with an affectionate grunt.

Sparrow, a Londoner by birth and twenty years Jackie's senior, served in the Gloucestershire Regiment back in the eighties and feels a profound, if sentimental, kinship with Jackie thanks to his service in the Royal Irish Rangers. Both men know their regimental history: the ferocious fighting of the Royal Ulster Rifles, while the Gloucesters clung to Hill 235, at Imjin, Korea. A battle long past in a war not yet over, fought a world away.

There is no cloud and the day is going to be a beauty. The ear-protectors block some of the morning chill and Jackie finds his grip on the moulded chequering of the stock and fore-end of the shotgun, breathing evenly as he does so. This is why he comes out here to fire off a few shells: the concentration drives all other thoughts, whether good or bad, away. The repetition, too: sight, breathe, squeeze; absorb the buck of the weapon, and start the sequence over again. For a while, at least, he can stop living in his head.

The first shot sends a murder of crows soaring. It also tears the iron trowel target out of the soil thirty yards away. Jackie works steadily with the gun, alternating a sequence of slugs at distance with double-ought buckshot at larger, closer targets. Each heavy blast, still deafening despite the ear protection, takes a little edge off his morning. Each punch of recoil on his shoulder works some more tension out. The mechanical cycle of fire and reload drags him from the violence of his past into the cold, crisp light of the present just as the daylight chases the dark from the Cotswolds hills. As the weapon spits each spent cartridge out the side of its ejection port, each flashback of his brutal past spins away.

After thirty minutes he has almost finished the ammo and, for today at least, has settled his soul some. The target shooting is both a workout and a purge. He wraps the Beretta in leather and searches the ground for the spent cartridges, feeling a chill graze his back. He has worked up a sweat and his T-shirt and sweater are not enough protection against the fresh bite of early-morning country air. Working quickly, he takes a plastic bag from his pocket and fills it with the empty cartridges then walks back to the Range Rover. Once at the vehicle he places the bag of spent cartridges and the semi-automatic on the back seat. Fishing in his pockets for the keys, he realises that he has forgotten his mobile, left back in his flat at the farm, then smiles. He has no one to call. His sister, Sarah, is in Australia with her family, a long-cherished trip. A year ago he wouldn't have known she was out of the country, they communicated so little. Now they speak regularly. One of the better outcomes of the trip home for his father's funeral last year and he is glad that some good came of Samuel Shaw's passing.

The colours hang limp on the tall spike of aluminium rising from the champions' graveyard. Rifle-green and scarlet. Mack Stevenson's racing colours, the silks worn by the jockeys when his horses run at Aintree, Newbury and Cheltenham. As the vehicle sways along the worst of the lane, a young woman on a chestnut mare canters towards him in the field beside the track. He recognises the wiry brush of blonde hair erupting from under her riding helmet: Kelly, one of the stable staff. She is fit, her thighs strong and lean in her jodhpurs, and he can see her working to boss and steer the horse. She wears a tight-fitting cream sweater which accentuates the pale pink of her face, now flushed with the sting of morning air. An open and simple face. An English face, with an elegant nose and well-set lips, almost prim. She is also, in Jackie's eyes, obscenely young at twenty-five and he has kept his distance, despite her attempts at flirtation. She is like this countryside: gentle, uncomplicated, perhaps a little raw and privileged. He, by contrast, is tainted.

As Jackie pulls up next to her, Kelly leans over in the saddle and says, 'Mack is looking for you. He's been calling your mobile for the last half hour.'

'Is there a problem?'

'Only some dark, handsome Irish guy brooding about the yard. What are we going to do about him?'

'If I see him, I'll let him know you were asking for him.'

'You do that. You let him know *the craic*,' she says, her voice deep with an exaggerated rise in tone at the end of the sentence.

It's an abysmal attempt at a Belfast accent but he smiles as she canters away and he puts the Range Rover in first. The smile stays with him until the farm buildings and stables appear around the bend in the lane. Mack stands in the yard, hands on hips in a checked shirt, mud-spattered quilted vest, corduroys and Wellingtons, flat cap on head. Ian Sparrow stands beside him, his brow knit in a frown, a warning in his eyes. Behind them sit two BMWs and, standing in front of them, four men in jeans and spotless suede boots wearing new-looking Barbour jackets. They all sport short, ordered haircuts and are clean shaven, a uniform of sorts. And, as he pulls up a couple of yards away, Jackie can clearly see the bulge of a shoulder rig and handgun under one of the shiny green waxed jackets.

CHAPTER 3

Monday

Better late in one place than early in the next, thinks Ruth Dodds. It was a favourite phrase of her mother's when Ruth was a child in Pretoria, and it is a phrase she lives by. Not that there is much chance of her rushing, or of her arriving early in the next world during the commute under the river from Chiswick Park on the District Line, but the truth, which she knows but steadfastly refuses to acknowledge, is that she is always late for work – if she bothers to turn up at all. The privilege of position, she thinks as she drags herself up the steps leading to the exit of Kew Gardens tube station, and she enjoys exercising it to the full.

Ruth has worked hard to get where she is today: office manager for a small translation and interpreting agency with a two-bedroom flat in Chiswick despite not having a qualification, or even second language, to her name. And then there is her evening job, most lucrative of all, in the northern reaches of the Borough of Camden.

The first step had been crafting a persona. Her parents had afflicted her with not one, but two accents that she detested. The first was broad South African with its thick, clotted vowels and unaspirated plosives; the second, the glottal soup of Geordie. Her parents had wrenched her from Africa to Newcastle upon Tyne when she was nine years old. But with time, effort and hours of Merchant Ivory films, she managed to approximate a decent imitation of received pronunciation.

She is sweating hard, an oily rivulet caressing her beak-like nose, speared between close-set eyes in an oval, dough-like face, and trickling down to the ointment smeared over the explosion of eczema on her neck. She reaches the crest of the steps and sees the quiet, residential space of Layton Place through the station exit, the vast spread of the Royal Botanic Gardens somewhere beyond. She is short, squat. She enjoys a bottle of wine and a rich meal on the company credit card; not a help to the eczema. And she served for five years in the British Army, at which time she built considerable muscle mass for a woman of her height which congealed to fat over a period of years and now stubbornly refuses to burn.

The street has a quiet buzz as she steps onto the paving in front of the station building and checks her watch: ten past nine. The rest of the staff will have been in the office for forty minutes already, no doubt bemoaning her constant abuse of position in turning up at some point before ten, locking her office door with blinds drawn, and beginning her daily trawl through internet shopping sites. This was the second stage of her climb to a modest sports car and the odd dinner in Kensington or Chelsea: a thick skin and shameless duplicity. She had learnt from the best in the military and applied the same rules. The staff do the work and she positions herself, square and immutable, between them and the absentee owner of the business. While the Africans and Asians and Arabs and the rest toil in the purgatory of the daily grind, and the Managing Director sits in his mock-Tudor kingdom in Herefordshire finalising his third divorce, she basks in intercessory sainthood, filtering, disseminating and deceiving as she sees fit.

She turns left and, with resignation, begins the climb up the west steps of the Grade II Listed Kew station footbridge, passing an idling Peugeot parked next to a black Suzuki motorcycle. As Ruth begins her laboured ascent, a slim, pale, fair-haired man wearing sunglasses eases himself out of the car and flicks the motorcycle's ignition switch, before returning to the Peugeot's driver's seat.

A smattering of people are crossing the bridge, and a gaggle of schoolkids walk towards Ruth as she reaches the concrete deck at the top of the steps. They walk in an orderly line, a shepherding teacher at either end. Ruth takes in the children as she approaches them, perhaps seven or eight years of age, and considers their future. Some are white, some black, some Middle Eastern or central Asian, and a couple are delicate-looking oriental children. Some might be successful; some will probably marry; some may live quiet, productive lives; some could even be famous. And she wonders if some of the girls might end up in a decaying townhouse, in their late teens or early twenties, a sweating, heaving Russian or Serb or Saudi or Chinese or Brit pounding away while she, Ruth Dodds, shepherds them, goads them, dominates them through the long working night. Just as she will do tonight on the silent lane, in the shabby, hidden nook in north London.

And that is the third and final step of her three-point plan for success: complete and unstinting amorality.

Ruth's second job, three, sometimes four nights a week, is to manage and run a 'stable' of up to twelve girls. Some are trafficked, some are British strays and one, whom she plucked from the translation agency, is a statuesque Romanian who had thought the work was simply hostessing in a private club. Ruth learned to park any moral sense when working with the spooks and Military Intelligence, and employed the same strategies she'd absorbed from some of the NCOs in the forces with the girls. Aggression, emotional bullying, humiliation. Above all, fear.

And her own fear begins as a faint unease, escalating to a mounting dread, and pinnacling in stunned horror at the realisation that she is going to die in this quiet, suburban corner of London under a bright, cloudless sky. The two men in jeans, leather jackets, and wearing motorcycle helmets are wrong from the off. They walk with purpose, one rangy with a mobile phone in his hand, the other solid and relaxed, right hand resting inside his jacket. Despite the visors she knows they are spotting her. The children and teachers are the only other people in their sight range. Behind them walks a man in a suit and two pensioners with a young woman. As the stockier man's hand emerges from the inside of the jacket with a black handgun, Ruth develops something she thought was lost to her: a conscience. She acknowledges, for the first time in many years, that she has done bad things, treated numerous people with contempt, and facilitated the ruining of multiple lives. Not that she can manage regret or repentance, only a sharp terror at the razor-stab of the 9mm rounds tearing into her chest and the sudden loss of control over her body. Her legs give way, the right limb folding as her ankle snaps, and she begins to register a burning sensation in her left breast. The shooter appears above her and fires at the moment she spasms in shock, the first bullet sending a small cloud of dust and concrete into Ruth's face. He curses, just audible over the screaming that has erupted on the bridge, then takes aim again, calm and deliberate, and shoots her twice in the head.

#

Harris was raging with the kid as they climbed the steps of the bridge. They'd left the bike with Morgan on the other side of the tracks and walked a long, circuitous route to get to the east side of the bridge. The woman worked on that side and they'd decided to hit her on the bridge as she made her way over the tracks to work, always late, according to intel. Morgan sat in the car and surveilled the station while Macrossan waited for his call to let them know the target was approaching.

Harris thought Morgan was all right, although a bit fucking superior at times. Typical of his kind, mind. But the kid was a waste of space, in Harris's opinion. He'd botched the oul' lad on Saturday night, forcing Harris to step in. Then, as the mobile had chimed and he'd read the text, the youngster had said, 'Are you sure you want to do this? I mean, a woman?'

It was lucky their visors were already down as his look might have dropped the kid on the spot. He took the gun from inside Macrossan's jacket and hurriedly shoved it into his own, handing the kid his mobile.

'Fuck's sake, what difference does a pair of tits make? And it's not a question of want, young 'un. Now get your bony fuckin' arse up those steps, before I kick it up.'

Still seething, he saw her before Macrossan confirmed the target. The timing was perfect, too. The kids were already almost past her, the other civilians behind himself and the kid. He breathed easy and kept a rhythmic pace, even with the spike of adrenaline as she saw them and her face creased in horror. Then her expression went slack as he fired four into her a little above centre mass. Not a word from the bitch, she just gave in to gravity and folded. Just to be sure, he'd walked up to her and loosed off another round; besides, the kid had wound him up and he was in love with the gun at that moment, its quieting anger. But the whore jerked and the bullet gouged the concrete, spinning away and he caught the high-pitched yelp ahead and to his left. It was enough to bring him back from that other place, and he put two in the dying woman's head for good measure.

Now Macrossan is whining again, because the useless wee shite is already running, yelling, 'A kid! A fucking kid!'

And there is the boy, a wee black ragdoll, a small smear of blood on his temple and a crimson liquid halo spreading around his head on the dirty concrete. It's like a spectacular own goal in a football match: the ricochet couldn't have found the child more cleanly than if he'd been aiming for the boy, a one-in-a-million shot. Harris keeps moving, following Macrossan across and to the other side of the bridge, where Morgan is already pulling out of his parking spot in the Peugeot. Harris carries the gun in a loose grip by his hip, ready to shoot Macrossan if the useless wee shite tries to do a runner on the Suzuki. But the youngster climbs on the pillion and waits, a jerking scarecrow figure with his gangling, shaking limbs, until Conal Harris mounts the front of the motorcycle and kicks the stand up into the belly of the bike.

It's a sweet, merciful release to have the revs drown Macrossan's hysterics, 'Shit, shit, a kid, a fucking kid!'

Yes, a fucking kid, thinks Harris, but a job well done on the target, Dodds.

A job that had to be done. It isn't a question of want.

#

Marty Catterick is exhausted. They'd brought him up to Antrim Serious Crime Suite in the wee small hours and he hasn't had a minute's peace since. He doesn't know where Robert Savage and Philip Cross are.

He hadn't been lifted in years and didn't know what to expect. He'd never been in Antrim Barracks before and discovered that Serious Crimes was an annex to the main buildings, where two detectives escorted him to a custody sergeant, a small man but solid, not like the big bastard who'd raided the house.

The doctor was new. Back in the day, the RUC weren't obliged to consider health and safety, and he'd laughed as the doc had advised him to drink less and knock the fags on the head. Then it was more familiar: his belt, keys, comb and watch were taken away and he was shown into a room with perforated walls, like the old recording studios he'd seen in documentaries about Elvis. The sergeant fucked off, probably for a brew, and a custody superintendent walked in, introducing himself as Conlan. Catterick had passed the time of day with the sergeant, who he took to be a Protestant and, therefore, a cunt, but it was expected that a Prod would serve in the Crown forces. With a name like Conlan, Marty was disgusted that this tall streak of piss before him would wear a badge with a crown. The sop of not using the St Edward's Crown, the symbol of the British Sovereign, on the PSNI crest was meaningless. A crown was a fucking crown, an indication of monarchy. Besides, the harp on their badge wasn't the Brian Boru harp either. The whole lot of them were neither one nor the other, neither here nor there. And this bastard was a disgrace to Irish Catholicism and nationalism.

The superintendent briefed him on why he'd been lifted and the charges against him. Membership of a proscribed organisation, possession of firearms and ammunition with intent, possession of a firearm and ammunition in suspicious circumstances and possession of articles for use in terrorism. Catterick thought it must have been a slow day in the admin office, but why issue one charge when four would do, he supposed.

Now, hours later, the woman is at it again.

'You tired, Marty? I know I'm tired, and Davey here has been on for over twenty-four hours now.'

Davey rustles up a scowl, but Catterick can see that the interviewer's heart isn't in it.

'We have you on possession, no question. Through association with other dissident republicans and intel from a CID source, I can't see you walking on membership either, which means the "use in terrorism" charge is a given too.'

Catterick stares straight ahead at one of the tiny perforations behind the female peeler's head, not that easy to do for a sustained period as she's blonde and his type.

'Our job's done, Marty. With one exception.'

The fucking memory stick, he thinks. He hadn't even known it was there. His commander, Donnelly, had fitted the chokes to the Mossberg muzzles before they'd wrapped and buried them in the insulation. He hadn't met Cross before that night, but Donnelly had vouched for him. Savage, himself and Cross had been paid to do nothing more than sit in for a couple of evenings with the weapons, until someone from the east of the city came over to give further orders. When the big sergeant had tipped the barrel up and the stick had dropped to the floor, Marty Catterick had been as surprised as the PSNI bastards standing over him.

The fucking memory stick.

'The memory stick,' says the woman. 'Like I say, Marty, our job is done. But that stick takes things to a new level. Hold on.'

She glances at her male companion, and then rises from the table and leaves the room. The other detective, Davey, lets the recording equipment run and sits in silence. Catterick can see him fidgeting with the edge of the table, his leg shaking. Like Marty, he's probably cursing the laws on smoking in public buildings. In the old days, whether you got a slap or not, the RUC would spot you a fag once in a while.

The door opens and the blonde detective takes four strides to the table and stands, arms crossed. 'People have had a look at the stick, Marty. People well above our pay grade. Do you know what they found?'

Catterick picks out another perforation and focuses.

'A cipher. There's just one document on the USB, and it's coded. I'm out of time, Marty. Davey's out of time. This is your last chance to tell us about the contents of that stick.'

He's fuming. He'll kill Donnelly for this. A fucking code. And nobody had told him what he was sitting on. Bastards.

'They have people who will crack it, Marty. But before that, there's others who'll want to talk to you. Branch, maybe MI5.

23

Sentencing will go a lot harder on you if you don't volunteer information to CID.'

Information he doesn't have. Bastards.

'Fair enough. We're done. I hope you had a good look out the window on the drive from Belfast, Marty. You'll not be seeing the outside world for many a year, mate.'

CHAPTER 4

Monday

The glass and steel monstrosity of Government Communications Headquarters appears on the left as the BMW swings into the sprawling car park in west Cheltenham. Seen from the air, the GCHQ complex appears as a great, grey ring, nicknamed 'the Doughnut' by locals. But from ground level, Jackie thinks it resembles an overblown car dealership.

After passing checks by two bored-looking G4S security guards, Jackie, flanked by the four men who waited for him at the farm, enters the visitors' lobby of the intelligence service buildings. It could be a five-star hotel, all modern sculpture and minimalist sheen, with a tastefully lit crest of the service carved in Cotswolds stone. If the decor is corporate gloss, the thin man with short-cut spiky hair and thick lips stretched in an awkward grin is pure librarian.

'Welcome to our facility, Mr Shaw. My name is Dee-K, thank you for coming.'

Jackie, peering at the man's lanyard, says, 'Dee-K?'

'An abbreviation: my father is Chinese-Malay. You would struggle to get your tongue around my real name.'

Condescending bastard, thinks Jackie. 'I didn't think you people dealt in real names, *Dick*.'

'First names are fine.' A shallow smile. 'If you'll follow me.'

The bookish man has a colourless Home Counties accent and a stoop, despite his limited height. He leads Jackie and the four heavies up a flight of slatted steps to the first floor, then into a sparse, windowless room containing a table, two chairs and a thin, musky stink of damp. A smudged whiteboard is mounted on one wall. The table carries the ghosts of errant black biro strokes.

Dee-K says, 'Can I get you tea? Coffee?'

'An explanation wouldn't go amiss.'

'Not my department, I'm afraid. Make yourself comfortable and someone will be along shortly.'

As the door shuts, Jackie already regrets not taking the man up on his offer of coffee, if nothing else, to occupy his hands while he waits. He takes off his jacket, hanging it over the back of a chair and sits at the table opposite the whiteboard, smoothing the front of his T-shirt across his chest before picking at a hang-nail. The four strong-men in the room stand silent in the corners; the clock on the wall above the whiteboard displays the time: 09.18.

For twenty years, Jackie had lived a world away from the business of intelligence and the security services. Even back in the nineties, when he'd been embroiled in the insanity of the violence in Belfast, he'd distanced himself as much as possible from the spooks. He'd managed to get out by the skin of his teeth and he rubs his broken nose with his trigger finger as he remembers the trip home last year, and the new nightmares it brought. But he works, pays tax, calls his sister and sends emails. All normal, all traceable and recordable. They had been watching him all the time, monitoring him like a criminal on parole. And now, here he sits, back in the vacuum of the sordid world of secrets and intelligence, intrusion and cloaked brutality.

The door opens. A well-groomed man enters with a laptop and a plastic cup, and sits with care in the chair opposite Jackie. He looks to be in his late twenties and places the laptop and cup on the table between them. He doesn't wear a lanyard.

'Good morning, Mr Shaw. My name is Agir.'

'And your surname?'

'We deal in first names here.'

'So everyone says, yet nobody uses mine.'

Agir sits back in his chair and opens the laptop. He pushes the cup over to Jackie and says, 'I know you refused, but I thought you might be thirsty anyway. It's coffee, or at least what passes for it in the café.'

'Do you people read minds as well, or is there a truth drug in it?'

Agir's fingers begin flickering across the keyboard. The four men, still in their Barbour jackets, continue to stand impassive in the corners of the room.

'You were a policeman,' says Agir, 'and a soldier.'

'Not in that order, but, yes. I joined the Army young and left early. Then I served in the RUC in Northern Ireland.'

He wonders if Agir knows much about the RUC. He looks too young to remember Northern Ireland as anything more than a neglected, troublesome corner of the United Kingdom. Jackie feels old.

'You lived for a spell in Hong Kong, too, I believe.'

'Yes, after I left Belfast back in the nineties. Royal Hong Kong Police Force. I left before the Handover.'

The man closes the laptop again and stands, leaving the PC on the table. He says, 'Nice to meet you, Mr Shaw. Take care,' and leaves. Before the door closes Jackie hears Agir greet someone, unseen, out in the corridor. He considers asking what is going on but knows there is no point. They have him isolated, guarded and, they hope, off balance. Right where they want him. He has to sit it out, keep calm, and wait.

The door opens and another voice, familiar, rich and plummy with a faint nasal burr, says, 'Jackie, you look well. Even leaner than last we met.'

Jackie shifts position on the chair, straightening, and catches a tension in the two Barbour jackets in his line of sight.

Clenching his jaw and relaxing his hands, he turns to the open doorway as a tall man enters the room. He has a smooth nub of chin set between two fleshy jowls. The eyes are large and shining with something more than dislike and less than outright malice and the wiry brown hair has receded another inch or so on the scrubbed, pink scalp since Jackie last saw him. The thin ridge of the man's nose is slightly off-centre, broken, the result of a disagreement with Jackie, who smiles when he sees it hasn't set as straight as his own.

Stuart William Hartley says, 'Welcome to GCHQ,' then glances around in mock panic. 'Did I say that? They're a bit touchy about using the real name of this place, always calling themselves "The Sister" or "The Office". As if the bloody building isn't conspicuous enough.'

'And MI5 aren't backwards about coming forwards, I suppose,' says Jackie.

'Oh, we're as security conscious as this lot. It's just that they're a bunch of civil servants sitting in a glorified call centre, so they frighten easily. Ourselves and the tourists across the Thames don't even class them as real security services.'

'The tourists being MI6?'

'Of course. This isn't America. We only have a couple of agencies at the sharp end.'

'You having been at the sharp end yourself,' says Jackie. He taps his nose and smiles again.

'Charming as ever,' says Hartley, trailing thumb and forefinger down the crooked bridge to the flared nostrils. 'Still, it's less conspicuous than a tattoo, I suppose.'

Jackie glances at the scar on his right forearm, the discoloured, gnarled skin where once there had been a loyalist paramilitary tattoo. A permanent reminder of his time undercover.

Hartley produces a small crumpled paper bag from his

pocket, opens it and takes a plastic-wrapped cherry-coloured boiled sweet in his fingers. He unwraps the sweet with some ceremony, pops it in his mouth and offers the open bag to Jackie. There is a strong scent of menthol; Jackie declines. Hartley looks at the bag before shoving it back in his pocket and says, 'When were you last in Belfast?'

'I'd have thought the curtain-twitchers in here could have told you.'

'Let's say I'd like you to confirm it.'

'Since I reset your face, I've been back twice. The last visit was two months ago, to see my sister.'

Hartley nods. He sits on the chair opposite, heavily, as though carrying an invisible weight and says, over his shoulder, to the Barbour-jacketed men standing behind him, 'Our Mr Shaw has a propensity for violence. He's entirely civilised to a point, then tends to lose control, like many of his countrymen.'

Jackie meets the Five man's gaze and says, 'I'd give you a nasty look, but you already have one.'

Yet Hartley is right. There is a point when he loses control, like a tilt switch in an explosive device: then, detonation. It had happened a number of times in the old days. And it happened last year.

Hartley says, 'Have you been to London recently?'

'A couple of times.'

'How many?'

'In the last six months, maybe three.'

'When were you last there? Where did you stay, eat?'

'I don't keep a fucking diary.'

Hartley turns theatrical with a long, deep sigh and a shake of the head. 'This hostility is very worrying. We are on the same side, you know.'

'I've got nothing against brown people and I don't play golf.'

'And you've become so cynical since last year.'

29

'Ach, fuck off.'

'I see you've held on to the local vernacular.'

Jackie is tired. He thought he'd left seedy offices with amoral men, double-talk and squalid secrets behind, and isn't enjoying the refresher. He says, 'I've been to London twice in the last three months: six and ten weeks ago. The first was to visit the British Horseracing Authority with my employer: his business, not mine. The second was to catch an exhibition at the London Film Museum. I didn't stay overnight on either occasion.'

Hartley opens the laptop again, checks the screen, and says, 'Did you ever meet a Miss Ruth Dodds?'

'Can't say I have. Look, I know it's like asking a dog not to lick its balls, but could you cut the cryptic nonsense and come to the point?'

The room goes quiet and Jackie realises that it's sound-proofed. There's no background noise and the voices in the corridor were smothered when the door closed. They are sealed off in an airtight cell. Then he thinks what they could do to him here and now, and flexes his fingers under the table.

'Very well,' says Hartley. 'What I tell you is, of course, classi-fied. I could have you sign the Official Secrets Act, but I think a man like you understands the ramifications of repeating what is discussed within these four walls.'

Jackie listens.

'A woman, the aforementioned Ruth Dodds, was shot dead at Kew station in London this morning. A seven-year-old boy was also hit by a stray shot. He's in intensive care, but it doesn't look good.' Hartley's face rearranges itself in a pained expression. He looks like an actor searching for the right air of sorrow in a dressing-room mirror. 'In the early hours of Sunday morning, PSNI raided a house in west Belfast after a tip-off that there were weapons being kept there. They found handguns, an assault rifle and shotguns. Hidden in the barrel of one of the shotguns, secured by a choke, was a memory stick. The stick contained only one file, which was uploaded and sent to us in Thames House and here at GCHQ.' Hartley clears his throat and glances at the laptop screen again. 'I've been sent here from London to liaise on this. I arrived in Cheltenham five hours ago, before the shooting at Kew. It's rather raised the stakes in this whole affair. We think Miss Dodds' assassination and the contents of the file may be linked.'

'Assassination? What's to say it wasn't a mugging gone wrong? Gang related or mistaken identity?' Hope springs eternal, thinks Jackie.

'Ruth Dodds served with the military for five years, some time ago. For a period of six months, back in the early nineties, she was seconded to Military Intelligence.'

Jackie squeezes the bridge of his nose with callused fingers and breathes a low, weary sigh. He knows what's coming, feels the cool shiver of its terrible inevitability and braces for his world to list madly once again.

Hartley says, 'She was stationed in Northern Ireland.'

And there it is. The never-ending chain of violence and re-crimination, the flame of sectarian grudge kept alive by men of older generations who can't, or won't, let it go.

'I see I have your undivided attention,' says Hartley. 'Allow me to brief you on where we are. The file was encrypted, but it didn't take long for the programmes here to break that. The contents looked like this when HQ, here, received it.' He turns the laptop to give Jackie a clear view of the screen, a cluster of letters, nonsensical, in the centre of a plain Word file.

c11ad11einccaeineincte1111daeareincaa11daeineincactead11 cadacad1111etedteaaaacccac11aeinceindcaeincteadeind1111da dac11d1111d11dteeintecc11teinein11aac11cteeineinaca11a

Hartley says, 'It's a cipher. A VIC cipher to be exact, further secured with a second, substitution cipher employing the Modern

Irish alphabet and a numerical system of the Roman alphabet. Once the cryptologists had finished with it, it looked like this.' Hartley punches a key and the screen changes. A different stream of letters are slashed across the bright, white space.

sevenskinslenparkinsonnaughtonruthdoddsjamesmcveap-atrickfergusonsamuelmclellandkennethbannister

Hartley pauses for a few seconds, then hits another key and the letters are gone, replaced by a list of words.

Seven Skins
Len Parkinson-Naughton
Ruth Dodds
James McVea
Patrick Ferguson
Samuel McLelland
Kenneth Bannister

'You'll notice the second name, Jackie, and the title: Seven Skins.'

'Sounds like a pub.'

'It isn't. We've checked and can find no pubs with that name in the UK or Ireland. It could be a reference to the Inniskilling Dragoons, a former British regiment from your neck of the woods; the regimental nickname was "The Skins". However, none of the names on the list served with the Inniskillings. Perhaps the title refers to human targets, similar to claiming "scalps"; a pejorative term for those to be executed. Or it may have significance beyond our ken, or no significance at all. It's a code within a code, deliberately obtuse.'

'What about the others? Anyone dead other than Dodds?'

Hartley says, 'Not that we know of. The Met are checking up on the others, although Parkinson-Naughton isn't at his home or place of work at present, and we're beginning to fear the worst; and McLelland is of no fixed abode – a vagrant. He could be on a friend's sofa, waking up in a park somewhere, or have been dead for some time. We are pretty sure he's in London, however.'

'Where does Ruth fit in, her being a secretary?'

'Guilty by association. Unlucky for her, but no one ever said life was fair. She replaced a Corporal Denny Walters for a spell in Ulster, and continued the work he'd been doing over there. Walters died of a coronary two years ago.'

Jackie focuses on the table-top and says, 'There are six names on the list. I know your average hard man isn't the sharpest tool, but most of them have mastered basic numerals one to ten, so why *Seven* Skins? And why am I here?'

'To decrypt a cipher,' says Hartley, 'one requires a key. The key, or "hat", is usually a word, sometimes a number, occasionally both. The software took a while to come to a conclusion on the key as it wasn't an English word. It wasn't Irish either. Indeed, it wasn't written in its proper script, but Romanized from Japanese Kanji.' He peers at the keyboard and searches for the appropriate key. Jackie sits forward a little in his chair, while the four Barbour-jacketed statues remain immobile but resolute in the corners of the tired, cell-like room. Hartley's once strange, nasal accent has all but gone, and Jackie realises that the Five man has had his teeth fixed, so that they present a smooth, white shield to the world. The upper lip seems to have to strain to cover them, and he hopes the dental work is a result of the brief beating he handed out last year.

'Ah,' says Hartley, prodding a key with his index finger. 'There we are.'

The word *Katana* appears on the screen.

'Katana, as you know, is the curved sword of the samurai in feudal Japan.'

Jackie nods, a slow, deliberate dip of his head. His mind is far from Hartley's teeth, the bodyguards in the corners. His mind is in the terraced-brick rabbit-warren of east Belfast, the alphabet soup of Ulster terrorist killing machines, and the fear and adrenaline-spike of Special Branch operations.

'Katana was also a call sign,' says Hartley. '*Your* call sign, when undercover for SB in Belfast. We believe Katana is Jackie Shaw.'

Jackie's head continues bobbing. He's afraid that, if he stops, he'll somehow slip back to the life he fled over twenty years ago. It has been snapping at his heels the whole time, took a bite out of him last year, and has caught up to him once again.

'Congratulations, Jackie,' says Hartley. 'You are lucky number seven.'

CHAPTER 5

Monday

Harris says, 'I never shot a black kid before.'

Morgan keeps his counsel.

'Felt the same as shooting a white kid, really,' says Harris. 'Never let it be said I'm not an equal opportunities gun-for-hire.'

Padraig shoots a look at Morgan on his left, then stares at Harris on his right, almost uncomprehending. The man crosses his legs, his wiry frame compact, and scratches his beard. A loose strand of his black hair is trying to make a run for it in the riverside breeze.

'Gallows humour,' says Harris. 'Coping mechanism, you know?' He slides a sideways glance at Morgan then locks eyes with Padraig.

'Besides,' he says, 'we did a lot worse back in the day. Sure, your da must have told you.'

The Nine Year War and the Flight of the Earls; the Plantation of Ulster; Cromwell and famine; the Easter Rising and War of Independence. Padraig Macrossan had learned all of these highlights from over three hundred years of Irish misery and conflict from his father, Terence Macrossan. If he closed his eyes, he could almost smell the warm, copper scent of blood spilled on Bloody Sunday. He could see the glowing fire of rebellion, the yearning to free a people from centuries of discrimination and right the wrongs of internment, of British military oppression, of vicious Protestant bigotry. But children dying by republican hands had never been a feature of his father's stories and he refused to believe Harris, whatever the man's pedigree.

'He was a County Louth man, your da, wasn't he? A Leinster man. Did he ever set foot in Ulster? In the north?'

Harris knows well. Padraig's cheeks flush scarlet and he drops his gaze from the sluggish brown broth of the Thames, slithering past before him, to his feet. His elbows totter on his knees as he sits on the hard concrete in front of the Tate Modern on the South Bank. He had worshipped his father and was devastated when he finally lost a long battle with coronary heart disease three years ago. Terence Macrossan had been a man of modest means in Dundalk, a carpenter by trade, who had been sponsored by a friend of his mother, Padraig's grandmother, to settle in Birmingham and work in a furniture shop near the Jewellery Quarter. He was living in Deritend before a shot was fired in the Troubles.

'No need to blush, youngster,' says Harris. 'No doubt he did his bit for the Cause. Sure, he spread some good 'oul Irish seed with your ma, produced the fine young freedom fighter we see before us today.'

Morgan takes a sip of coffee from a huge paper cup and says, 'Enough. Stop riding the boy and keep your voice down.' His eyes continue to drift along the path which separates them from the metal railings and river, and the great lead helmet of St Paul's beyond.

The problem for Padraig, the conundrum he wrestles with most waking hours, is balancing awe of Harris with his hatred and fear of the man. The primal element which keeps the hatred in check, and maintains the balance of their current relationship, is the fear. For Harris is terrifying, in a way that eighteen-year-old Padraig has never encountered before. The man has no compunction about killing, and is good at it. It's not that Conal Harris lacks human feeling. He'd laughed, scolded and raged in the weeks and months prior to the cell going operational. But the strongest emotion he's seen the Irishman exhibit is pleasure at a job well done, a target downed. It had been there on Saturday night, trumping his irritation with Padraig's botched shot at the old man, and it was there in the tension of the body, the mad dance in his eyes after they sped away from Kew on the motorcycle a couple of hours ago, leaving two bodies lying on the concrete of the footbridge. One, the stout, bent husk of a bad woman: Padraig takes some comfort from that. But the other, the delicate frame of a beautiful child.

'What the fuck is that all about, anyway?' says Harris. He points across the oily swell of the Thames, the colour of weak coffee, to the child's toybox of the City of London on the other side, off to their right, huge building blocks randomly scattered across the skyline like the aftermath of a giant toddler's tantrum. He singles out the Walkie-Talkie, 20 Fenchurch Street, a squat, blunt mass of ribbed steel and reflecting glass. 'It's like somebody shoved a slipper in the ground and left the heel sticking up.'

Padraig loves it. He loves the Cheesegrater, 122 Leadenhall Street, with its sheer slope like some crazy extreme sports ramp. And he loves the Gherkin, 30 St Mary Axe.

'And that giant dildo we were near on Saturday night,' says Harris, as if reading his mind. 'We gave youse a chance to put something decent in there when we blew the fuck out of the old place back in ninety-two, and youse built that monstrosity. Sure you can't even see it from here because of the slipper blocking the view. Probably cost millions to build the fucking thing, then you shove another building in front of it to obscure the view.' He shakes his head with a snort. 'Only the fucking English.'

The hackles rise momentarily before fear smooths them back down again. Padraig looks to the pale blue sky, free of the tobacco-stain taint of London's pollution today, and sucks in the air. After the hit at Kew, Padraig and Harris had dumped the Suzuki at a garage near Richmond Park. It would be driven out of the city and burned later. Morgan had driven the back-up vehicle, the Peugeot, to a lock-up near Mortlake station. It would be cleaned, the plates changed and then driven north, again to be burned. Then Padraig, Morgan and Harris had taken the London Underground to Waterloo, Southwark and London Bridge stations respectively. They had all strolled along the river, finishing up at the Tate Modern where they bought drinks at a nearby café and sat on the wall in front of the gallery facing across the Thames to St Paul's.

Then a man appears about one hundred yards away on their right and all three go quiet.

Harris looks left to Blackfriars Bridge while Morgan, who raised the coffee cup to his lips a couple of seconds before, takes a long sip, peering over the rim as he does so. Padraig stares for a moment before scratching the back of his head with his right arm, trying to hide his face with his sleeve. The man came from the Millennium Bridge and, prior to that short walk across the Thames, Mansion House tube station. As he passes them, Padraig glimpses a slouched figure with a shock of dirty-fair hair wearing jeans and a light jacket, a sports bag slung over his shoulder. James McVea, on his way to a double shift at the Maruyama restaurant on Park Street. He passes them and makes for a small kiosk to their rear.

'At night, this is a good spot,' says Padraig, in an almost stage whisper, 'to slot him.'

'Slot him? That's a Brit term,' says Harris. He laughs, a hollow cough. 'Oh yeah, you were born in bloody Hounslow.'

Morgan says, 'This is a terrible location. We don't have a three-sixty escape route because of the river, and we're forced into a bottle-neck by the bridges if the cops respond quickly on this side: it's too open, no side-streets or alleys.' He turns to Padraig. 'And don't raise your hand like that again. Big, sudden movements attract attention in peripheral vision.'

Padraig's cheeks redden. He folds his arms and seems to withdraw into his body. The two older men ignore him, speaking to each other while staring at the river.

'Better to do it outside the restaurant or at Mansion House,' says Harris. 'Escape routes with both options. Even the tube is a possibility.'

Morgan says, 'If we hadn't lost the girl with Naughton we could have used her again.'

All three go silent and a palpable tension seizes Harris. Air whistles through Morgan's nostrils in soft, slow trills. Three men begin crossing the space from the Millennium Bridge towards the Tate Modern. They wear casual clothes, jeans with brand T-shirts and leather or canvas jackets. All three wear trainers and are in good shape. Their hair is cut short and two wear wedding rings. The shoes are a sign: no heavy soles, which are more difficult to run in. The cropped hair is another. But it's how they walk with purpose, as a unit, a study in casual, two of them scanning the area with bored eyes while the third keeps his gaze fixed on the target up ahead, that alerts Padraig, Harris and Morgan to the fact that the men are possible undercover police. Before they reach McVea and take him by the elbow, the three men sitting on the concrete have dispersed. Padraig heads for Blackfriars Bridge and the City across the river. Morgan makes for the back streets of Southwark, beginning a wide arc to the rear of the Tate Modern. Harris, cursing softly, strides left along the South Bank, losing himself in the milling crowds of the curious, the idling and the lost.

#

London terrifies her. The scale, the constant sweat and heave of humanity, and the awful, crowded isolation of being alone in the huge city. People of every creed and colour, the cacophony of traffic and construction, the towering buildings, so densely packed. Constant noise and motion driving the metropolis forward. The first time she saw the streets, blinking and high on some poison they had fed into her veins, she was frightened by the sprawling, grey monotony of the architecture. Tirana, in contrast, is a shabby potpourri of colour, the result of a programme of aesthetic improvements to the city by a former mayor who had been a painter before taking office.

Yet Beatrix, cold, hungry, suffering from lack of sleep and hollow with shock at the violence of Saturday night, marvels at the streets of Kensington as she wanders the district. She found Harrods thanks to tourist maps displayed on the busy streets and, from there, began to search for Kynance Mews. Her large eyes, the black pearls of her pupils set in corneas the colour of a lion's mane, are on the move, darting to and fro. She moves as fast as her skinny legs can carry her. This is hopeless, she thinks. The tall rows of buildings seem to link arms, blocking her view and hemming her in on the narrow streets. There are no mountains or features to help her find her bearings. She is utterly lost.

Tirana is home: she is Albanian. She is proud of the city of Skanderbeg Square – the Fortress of Justinian and the great bulk of Dajti Mountain rising to the east. Too young to remember the years of communist Diktat, Tirana was a vibrant playground for her. She had attended the Universiteti i Tiranës, excelling in French and English. But even then, she saw her future abroad. She had been young and callow, sheltered by a warm but cloying upper-middle-class upbringing, her father a banker with political connections. Upon graduation, Beatrix secured a place at a summer school in Paris and was accompanied by her mother to the French capital, and her boarding accommodation in a respected international school.

Paris was a grand confection, buildings rising like tiered cakes from the boulevards and avenues, and she met someone while there, in a café, and let the romance of the city seduce her into a passionate affair. Her lover was much older, had money, and paid for a dream trip to Switzerland, although he couldn't accompany her at the last moment due to business commitments. She was chauffeured through Zurich and chaperoned by a bodyguard, a silent Corsican, at all times. Beatrix returned to the apartment in Arrondissement de Passy to find her lover gone and two large men waiting for her. They crowded the room with their bulk and she could see the contours of thick arms, bursting with potential violence, straining against their tight-fitting Italian shirts. She felt small, corralled into a corner of the room by their physical power and heavy silence and, worst of all, she was helpless. It was like two attack dogs rounding on a child. One produced a knife and they both advanced on her.

Hours later, she did not know how long, they drank coffee and waited for her to clean herself. She had not been a virgin but the pain, while intense, was nothing to the loathing she felt for them and herself. When she had finished vomiting and dressed, slow and stiff, like an old woman, she was shown photographs. They were of her family. Her father and mother sitting in their garden, taken with a telephoto lens. Her older sister walking on a street, a mobile phone to her ear, then another of her inserting a key in the door of what, she knew, was her sister's home in London. She was told to pack and call the summer school to inform the registrar that she would be leaving due to ill health. If she refused, her family would suffer.

They drove her to Calais where she was given a fake passport and walked past the ramshackle camp, the 'jungle' of desperate migrants with their hungry stares clustered at the roadside or clasping the chicken wire of the camp, seeking passage to the UK. Some were darting for the back of articulated lorries in the hope of a dark nook to hide in until making port at Dover, and keeping the immigration officials occupied in the process. Her chaperone accompanied her to the foot passenger terminal of the ferry. There, she was met by a hard-looking, soft-bodied Englishwoman, short and fat, who never left her side, even to go to the toilet, until they docked at Dover.

The immigration officers at both ports were swamped with the task of monitoring and apprehending the Eritreans, Sudanese, Syrians, and other lost souls seeking passage to Britain. A young woman on a French passport, accompanied by an English citizen, mustered only a cursory glance from the official who checked her document. Once in the car park, the fake travel documentation was seized by a man and woman, both Albanian, the second time in three days she had lost a passport. They drove her to a flat in Southend-on-Sea where, for the first and last time, she was drugged. She drifted in and out of consciousness in the back-seat of a car and finally awoke in a small room with thick, stale air, stacked ceiling high with boxes. It was the storeroom of a strip club in Soho, in London. A large man, his head shaved and nose splayed flat across his broad face, entered. He had a large belly hanging over his jeans and an ugly black gun jutting from the waistband at the rear. His name was Bashkim. He named her Beatrix. Then he took the gun from his waistband and used her for an hour, sometimes with the muzzle in her mouth.

From that moment, she was gradually broken. Isolated, vulnerable and terrified for herself and her family, she worked as a whore for a well-organised gang. She knew where her sister lived, as she had moved to the city while Beatrix was a student in Tirana. Flori was ten years older and, like Beatrix, had a flair for languages. But Beatrix never tried to find her and run. She knew what might happen to them both, and her parents. The gang, the *Fis*, would find and kill them all.

So, she endured. At times, if she did not make enough money, a knife was held to her throat but she was never beaten. It would drive down her worth. She was ferried from Soho to Camden to Hackney. The other girls despised her for her privileged upbringing and because she was old to many of them, a crone at nineteen.

Then she had been told to seduce the old man in the wine bar and take him to the narrow passage nearby. The man, Morgan, had spoken with Agon, the most senior underboss. They had shaken hands and money had been passed. She had found the old man sipping gin alone in the bar, had talked with him, and giggled and smiled, and led him to the passageway. And the men had grabbed her, and the sharp smack of the gun had sounded. There had been blood; she had thought she would die and so had run.

Her parents might be dead already. Her captors may have come in the night for Flori, her body floating in the filthy river that snaked through London like a drunk's piss on a city pavement. But she cannot countenance that thought and it is too late to go back. It is useless to brood. She had panicked, had bolted, and now she must try to find Flori and warn her. They have to run, together. Now Beatrix walks the Borough of Kensington and tries not to attract attention while she searches for her sister. The people march past, dressed with opulent restraint, and work hard not to stare at the thin, shivering girl in miniskirt and tottering heels, her face a shambles of red-rimmed eyes and melted mascara. And, for the first time since her flight took-off from Tirana International Airport Nënë Tereza, named after the beatified Albanian missionary, Mother Teresa, she prays.

CHAPTER 6

Monday

It's the kid, Christopher Martins. He can't get the boy out of his head.

Incredibly, they didn't have a photograph to hand at GCHQ – 'collateral damage' was the phrase Hartley had used – so all he's seen is a blurred family snapshot on the flat screen in the waiting lounge at Cheltenham train station, the muted morning news reporting the shooting as he killed time before the 11.15 to London Paddington. But Christopher is with him nonetheless, another phantom to accompany him to the shady copse of a chill morning and watch as the shotgun slugs and shot tear into the trees and targets. Assuming he will ever see the farm and horse training grounds again.

And something else is with him. The phrase Hartley used to describe Dodds, why the office worker had been targeted on the list: *guilty by association.*

#

MI5 had sprung for a First Class seat and paid for the one next to him. It would remain reserved but empty, privacy a factor as he studied the files on the mobile they'd given him. Crown property, of course, to be returned to the officer waiting when Jackie reached the safe-house in Victoria, along with the train tickets, to be handed in and claimed back later as expenses. He dumped his backpack containing a change of clothes and toiletries on the spare seat.

He'd said nothing when Hartley had told him of the code key: *Katana.* He knew they wanted something from him, that they weren't warning him and sending him back to Garbella Hill Farm with a promise of protection and an armoured Jaguar parked by the farm buildings. But he was damned if he would make it easy for the bastards. It was Hartley who had broken the impasse.

'Do any of the names mean anything to you?'

'Not one. If they're Army intelligence or your crowd, I wouldn't have met them. In Belfast, I worked exclusively for RUC. Even in uniform, I met lads from the infantry but never any of the intel guys. Due to undercover work, I didn't know many of the other Branch men either.'

'Samuel McClelland?'

'Nothing.'

'He was a colleague of Gordon Orr.'

Jackie couldn't disguise the flicker of surprise when he heard his old partner's name. 'He passed some time ago,' he said. 'Natural causes.'

'We are aware. However, he served with McClelland on the E3A desk, monitoring the republican side of things. After your time.'

'If it's after my time, it's hardly relevant to me.'

Hartley eased back in his chair a little, putting a few extra inches between them. He began fishing in his pocket for his bag of sweets.

'I called Rebecca Orr this morning. The good widow hasn't heard from McClelland for quite some time. After Gordon's death they kept in touch sporadically, then McClelland fell on hard times and, last she heard, he was living rough in London.' He rolled the small, hard ball of sugar between thumb and forefinger and grimaced. His absurd dental work stretched his upper lip until it appeared to disappear. 'She did give us the address of a mutual colleague, however: Derek Bailey.' Hartley slipped the cherry-red sweet into the wet seam of his mouth.

Jackie shook his head. He'd never heard of the man.

'We're alerting the other names on the list to the threat via the Metropolitan Police,' said Hartley. 'They all live in London which makes the task considerably easier. McClelland, however, is a challenge. He's homeless and we have no idea where to find him. He may not even be in London any more. But Bailey could be in contact with him. Old veterans' network and all that.'

'And all that,' repeated Jackie. 'So, contact Bailey.'

Hartley smiled. It was a strained, failed effort.

'Mr Bailey is currently under investigation. He is an Ulster loyalist with links to other, less than salubrious, racist and right-wing groups both here and abroad. An official approach from the police or security service may hinder any surveillance or investigations currently being conducted. In addition, he is unlikely to be receptive to our requests for help in locating Mc-Clelland, if not outright obstructive.'

'So you thought an old veteran might reach the spot your lot can't.'

'Something like that,' said Hartley.

'And it gives you a man on the ground with some built-in history, moving in circles you could take a long time to infiltrate, who can feed intel back to you.'

'There are fringe benefits, yes.'

'And who's supposedly on the list himself, prime bait to draw the triggermen out.'

Hartley pushed his chair back further and spread his arms wide, hunching his shoulders.

Jackie said, 'Why are these people being targeted, myself included?'

'Presumably, the connection to the Province. McClelland and McVea are from your neck of the woods and both served in the

Royal Ulster Constabulary. Dodds, Ferguson and Bannister were all Army in some capacity, and Parkinson-Naughton was one of ours.'

'Did they work together? I don't recognise any of the names on there.'

'They all worked in and around Belfast, yes. Dodds was admin at Thiepval Barracks, Lisburn. Parkinson-Naughton and Bannister both worked out of Palace Barracks, Holywood, and Ferguson was based at Lisburn with Dodds but had more of a role on the ground. They were all focused on PIRA and INLA activity. As you were concerned with the loyalist side of things, it's hardly surprising that you never met.'

'It is surprising that my name's on a dissident republican target list, though.'

Hartley fiddled with his tie, his eyes hooded. 'Not necessarily. If I recall, an attempt was made on your life by PIRA back in 1993. You wounded two of the hit team and all three were apprehended by security forces. Someone may harbour a grudge. One of the team, a Declan Connolly, died in Long Kesh, killed by loyalist inmates. You put him there.'

Jackie looked up at the ceiling, exhaled a long, slow breath and said, 'You have no idea who the triggermen are?'

'No. The PSNI have been questioning the men who were sitting on the weapons stash in Belfast. It looks very much like they didn't know the memory stick had been hidden in with the arms.'

'Were the weapons to be used in taking out the names on the list?'

'Apparently not. They were headed for east Belfast, presumably Short Strand area.'

Jackie's pulse spiked for a moment. East Belfast. His home. 'What are you going to do if the hitters come looking for me and make an appearance? Hereford's just up the road from here.'

Hartley frowned, the concerned schoolmaster. 'Heavens, no. SAS running around on UK soil confronting republican killers? Far too risky.'

'You weren't so squeamish in the old days, back home.'

'As I have told you before,' said Hartley, rubbing his nose, 'that was before my time.'

Jackie leaned forward, placing his forearms on the table and forcing a nervous glance from the Five man to the Barbour-jacketed bodyguards behind Jackie. He studied Hartley for a moment, heavy silence hanging between them. Then, his voice flat and quiet, he said, 'Is this about collusion?'

'Be careful what you imply, Jackie.'

'I'm not implying anything. Some squaddie or peeler with a hard-on for the loyalists setting up republican movers, supplying names, dates and places to loyalist gunmen so they can take out a few republican players, achieve the result that due process can't; is that what this is about?'

'Remember who I am and where we sit.'

'You have a list with ex-Special Branch – on the republican desk – and Military Intelligence personnel, based in Northern Ireland back in the eighties and nineties, found with a dissident republican arms cache. You don't need a join-the-dots book to paint the picture. Somebody's holding a grudge.'

'I, and the organisation I work for, are unaware of any such operations or activities on UK soil –'

'And why would I be on the list? I was trying to put the fucking loyalists away, not placing an address and a semi-automatic in their hands and wishing them well.' Jackie leaned back and ran a hand through his hair. 'Thanks for the offer, but no. A tussle with the IRA back in '93? I don't think that's enough to earn me a spot on a hit list with the next generation of republican homicidal maniacs. This is somebody else's problem now, and I'll take my chances. Katana? You really think I'll swallow this bullshit that it signifies my old call sign? No: maybe some nutcase likes his Japanese comics, or his Kurosawa films, or has a sushi fetish. You're reaching, Hartley, and I've had enough of running around, playing cowboys and Indians.'

'I see.' Hartley pushed his chair back another fraction, putting more space between himself and Jackie, and less between himself and the two bodyguards behind him. 'When you were, "running around, playing cowboys and Indians" last year, a couple of people met a rather nasty end.'

Jackie tilted his head a fraction. His shoulders squared.

Hartley glanced at one of the men in the corner behind and said, 'Of course, they were of a bad sort. I doubt many in the PSNI shed a tear when they shuffled off this mortal coil. It is strange, though...' His voice trailed off for a moment. 'You looked pretty banged up the last day I saw you. Almost as though you'd been in a rather brutal fight.'

Jackie shook his head. More in resignation than denial.

Hartley said, 'Then the Detective Chief Inspector who took charge of the investigation into the deaths of a couple of local gangsters was transferred out to Newtownabbey and pathologist reports were lost. Some fool of a constable handled the bodies at the scene before any forensic work was undertaken, compromising the evidential value of any fibres, hair or DNA found.'

'You seem to know an awful lot about the investigation. A layman would think you'd orchestrated it.'

'Well, as you know, the local colour in Northern Ireland was something of a hobby of mine, as were you. I'd like you to be again.'

You always pay the piper at the end of the day, thought Jackie. He'd gone home, back to Belfast, for his father's funeral. Hartley had found out and played him, setting him up to clear the way for his own prize asset to sit at the top table of east Belfast UDA. Now Hartley was using the threat of imprisonment to coerce him into working on the ground for MI5 again. At least this time, he knew he was being used.

He said, 'Are you blackmailing me?'

'I'm merely doing my job.'

'I'll take that as a yes.'

But, he thought, finding McClelland, playing a role in stopping these killings, might bring him a little peace, no matter how fleeting. Not redemption, but something. Then there was the little boy on the bridge at Kew: he could help stop any more innocents getting caught in the crossfire. And he wasn't ready for three square meals and the uniform of a prison inmate.

So he had said, 'I'll make contact with Bailey, and I'll try to find McClelland. That's where it ends.'

And Hartley said, 'Good enough, Jackie.'

#

His fieldcraft is a little rusty, but Jackie still spots a possible surveillance operative at the entrance to the short tunnel leading from Victoria station main concourse to Buckingham Palace Road. A couple of homeless men sit a little distance from one another in the tiled burrow, asking passers-by for some spare change. A gaggle of Spanish school students chatter in an erratic line, a few couples wander and a bald, heavy-looking man in jeans is swearing at volume into a mobile phone. The ammonia stench of piss is all-encompassing, and the pedestrians, in perpetual motion, occasionally betray their disgust with a wrinkle of the nose. Only the homeless men are stationary, inured to the stench. And one other, in a hooded top and black jeans, playing with a mobile, as though texting. He looks around twenty-six or seven, and the angle of his head to the device is wrong: he peers down his nose as though struggling to focus on the words, despite his age. The angle affords a better range of peripheral vision.

The man continues texting as Jackie hoists his backpack on his shoulders and walks up to him. He says, 'Excuse me, mate, is there a post office nearby? I have to pick a package up at Box 500.'

A small, scarlet inkblot spreads across the man's cheeks at the mention of Box 500: civil service and security forces slang for MI5. He says, 'Sorry, no idea. I'm just a visitor.'

Jackie says, 'You looked like you belonged, my mistake.' Then he strides out into the scuttling masses of Buckingham Palace Road. He's sure that his hunch was right. Hartley is innately suspicious and will want eyes on Jackie until he reaches the safe-house on Lupus Street. It will send a message if he can spot the team. He picks his way through the traffic and makes for a café on the corner of Eccleston Street, diagonally across from the station entrance. As he enters the café, he turns to a chalkboard menu propped against the window and scans the street outside.

In counter surveillance, identifying 'marked' behaviour – behaviour out of the ordinary – is a challenge in a city with the diversity of London; instead, he turns to uniformity to give him an edge. Around 11 per cent of the Metropolitan Police is comprised of ethnic minority officers, and around 23 per cent are women. The Security Services are stretched keeping tabs on the current crop of Wahhabi maniacs, so there is a strong possibility that SC&O 10, the Specialist Crime and Operations Covert Policing unit, will be monitoring him until he reaches the safe-house. This probably skews the demographics a little, but he still looks for white men and women.

He discards the groups of foreign tourists and students first, then the tattooed-and-pierced crowd. Similarly, the old or infirm and families. He buys a small coffee and steps out onto the pavement with four possibles: three males, one female, all white. One of the men hails a taxi and jumps in, leaving three possible operatives. Jackie walks along Eccleston Road, calculating a vague surveillance detection route through memories of coach trips into

Victoria station from the West Country. He turns right onto Eccleston Place. The street is a dead-end, fronted on the right by a long steel and glass office building; the left side comprises a long brick wall with railings and a ramp to a car park. There are only five people in the street when he enters.

As he walks, he glances to his right and squints, as though trying to peer through one of the floor-to-ceiling windows of the office block, and catches two of the possibles stopping at the entrance to the street in the reflection. One loiters, checking his pockets, while the other begins sauntering some distance behind Jackie. There are now four people ahead: one has entered the office building. Another then walks up the car park ramp. Of the remaining three, one is a delicate-looking young man in a business suit. The other two are women also in business suits, chatting as they clutch manila folders. Jackie drifts towards them and brushes his shoulder against the older of the two, tipping his coffee over himself, so that the arm of his jacket is soaked.

The woman says, 'Oh, God! I'm sorry!'

'You fucking will be!' shouts Jackie. 'This jacket cost a fucking fortune! You going to pay for the cleaning?'

His voice echoes around the narrow street and the young, slim man begins walking over, shouting at him to back off. Jackie rants, shaking his head in disgust, and eyeballs the possible standing stock still for a beat, then hugging the railings opposite. A flicker of confusion crosses his face. It is 'marked' behaviour and the possible's expression says that he knows he's been blown as he takes out a mobile and makes for the car park ramp.

Jackie begins backing away, apologising to the woman and calming the young businessman, who begins attending to the woman once the threat has passed. Reassured that chivalry isn't yet dead, Jackie reaches the entrance to the street again and spots the possible who had been loitering there. The man is now standing in front of an Italian restaurant opposite, checking his mobile.

The area is a confusion of traffic and wandering pedestrians, the constant roar of traffic amplified by the close-packed buildings. The surveillance team will have more knowledge of the area so Jackie doesn't stray far. He walks a hundred yards on the busy street until he reaches a strip of landscaped garden surrounded by black railings and boxed in by stucco-fronted rows of townhouses. A sign reads *Chester Square*. The houses, a millionaire's row of giant cream pill-boxes, stand either side of a large church at the west end of the square. Jackie walks towards the ragstone gothic facade of St Michael's Church. The woman he identified from the café as a possible operative strolls twenty feet behind and to his left. She is around five feet tall with blonde hair scraped back in a ponytail, wearing tight pale blue jeans. Her legs are slim but look strong and athletic and she carries a black handbag slung over her shoulder.

Jackie stops ten yards from the end of the square and crosses to the railings encircling the private gardens in the centre. He drops the mobile phone Hartley gave him in Cheltenham on the pavement and vaults the railings of the gardens, landing on an immaculate lawn. Without breaking stride he covers the twenty yards to the other side of the gardens and vaults the railings again. He walks to the church and along its outer wall, doubling back and directly opposite the end of the gardens. The girl is standing between the front door of a townhouse and a parked Bentley, muttering – possibly into a small mic – her eyes on Jackie's discarded mobile, still lying on the pavement.

She doesn't pick it up. She doesn't call to him, pointing to his forgotten phone. 'Marked' behaviour. When he passes her, the Five mobile still lying in front of the railings, he mimes and mouths, 'Call me'; her face sets in a hard stare and she strides, a little too quickly, in the opposite direction to retrieve the mobile.

The last possible operative is still standing, looking agitated, in front of the Italian restaurant when Jackie returns to Eccleston Street. The man's team is blown and he knows it, but he crosses the street for a better field of vision as Jackie turns right towards the arrival building of Victoria coach station. Now they are on the narrow lane which leads to the station arrivals building exit. Travellers haul cases and bags past Jackie as he nears the station, a covered bus shed with a narrow strip of interior corridor housing a newsagents and toilets. Jackie stops at the small brick arch of the exit. There is only one way in and out of the building on foot. The entrance to the shed is kept clear of pedestrians to allow the large coaches to come in.

He looks at a parked taxi and sees the operative standing at a row of bicycles across the street to the left. Jackie turns and walks into the station. A few travellers are milling around but the crowd is small and the station dingy and down-at-heel in comparison to the cathedral of the train station, and he doesn't have to queue to thumb his thirty pence into the turnstile and push his way through to the public pay-toilets.

A minute later he steps back onto the street and notes that the man has now moved to the corner, twenty yards away. Jackie approaches him. He has dirty-fair hair, a slight pot-belly and a light dusting of stubble.

Jackie says, 'I need to talk to you.'

'Sorry?'

'I removed the battery and sim card from the mobile I left at Chester Square. You can call your female colleague and check if you like. They are now on the floor behind the toilet in the second cubicle from the left of the gents in the coach arrivals building. I doubt you want anyone picking up that sim, so you'd better get a move on.'

Jackie takes the man's hand, opens it and drops thirty pence into his palm.

'On me,' he says.

As he turns left onto Elizabeth Street, he hears the frantic slap of shoes running on concrete echoing behind him.

#

He tosses the sim and battery onto the glass coffee table to a sigh from the man seated opposite on a white leather sofa.

Jackie says, 'Is this about collusion?'

The man, a mug of tea in his hand and a nicotine patch on his arm, says, 'Take a seat.'

As Jackie eases himself onto the sofa across the table, he takes in the surroundings. A well-appointed lounge in a Westminster flat. There are two other occupants. A tall, rangy-looking man sits next to the door reading a magazine while another, stockier in build, checks a tablet. Both wear Glock 26 handguns in shoulder-holsters. The man seated on the sofa gestures to the man with the tablet to get up and says to Jackie, 'Coffee or tea? Milk and sugar?'

'Coffee, just milk.'

The man opposite relaxes in the sofa and says, 'My name is Laurence Gilmore. It's my real name, I don't hold with the cloak and dagger bullshit when a man is working with me. And you're Jackie Shaw.'

'In the flesh. For God's sake don't say you've heard a lot about me.'

'I've read up on you. You did a good job of losing the surveillance team. We work with SC&O a lot these days, and the guys on you were pretty good.'

'But not your best,' says Jackie. 'The best are busy with a whole new breed of religious nutcase, which is why you put a small team of Met on me rather than your own people. Sadly, I'm not a nineteen-year-old gang member or a common-or-garden thug with an IQ in single figures.'

The man at the door looks up from his newspaper. Jackie doesn't want to put the boot into another copper but he isn't in the mood to make friends.

'We're working with the National Crime Agency on this. The Met aren't aware of your existence beyond the small group of specialist officers on secondment to us.' Gilmore appraises Jackie, looking him up and down. 'I have to say, I don't have much grounding in the Northern Irish office. I've been involved in more London-based affairs. Various African issues, Nigerian and Somali, some work with the NCA on Yardies. You mentioned the "C" word.'

'Collusion.'

'Yes.' Gilmore takes a swig of his tea. He looks fit and trim. He wears a simple T-shirt with jeans and desert boots, one of which is balanced on the edge of the coffee table. The circular nicotine patch, sandy-coloured with a pale pink spot in the centre, sits like a target on his ebony skin. He says, 'You looked at the files on the mobile.'

'Yes.'

Jackie had looked through the data on the mobile with mounting trepidation. Each file had amounted to a potted personality – or 'P' – file like those Special Branch had kept on known republican and loyalist players back in the old days.

Ruth Dodds, now deceased, had been a mid-level admin staff and a first-rate manipulator in Military Intelligence office politics. The file photograph showed sharp, mean features set in a puffy oval face. Her eyes were small and close together, her nose lean, cruel. An angry-looking rash crept above her collar. Not an attractive woman, but one of the few in the testosterone-led environment of Thiepval Army Barracks in Lisburn, outside

Belfast, where she'd been stationed from 1994 to '95. In that time, it had been noted that she had cultivated relationships, at least three of which were sexual in nature, with a variety of higher ranks within the military who were separated or going through divorces. She had left the services shortly after the posting and worked as office manager in a translation company in Kew, where she was headed when shot, earlier this morning.

One of her sexual liaisons while at Thiepval was Len Parkinson-Naughton, an ex-Security Service, or MI5, officer who worked out of Palace Barracks near Belfast for a three-year spell in the early to late nineties. Inept and pretentious, he had been installed in a largely ceremonial management position to keep him busy, and spent a year as liaison with Military Intelligence in Thiepval, taking a desk in one of their offices. Dodds worked and, according to her file, played under Parkinson-Naughton during this period. He was twenty years her senior and now enjoyed a position as a non-executive director at a small consultancy based in the City of London. The file photograph showed a scrubbed, sagging face with an imperious look in the watery eyes.

Kenneth Bannister, third on the hit-list, had been on the ground during his time in Northern Ireland, running assets, or informants, in the paramilitaries and occasionally undertaking surveillance work on PIRA and INLA figures. He was posted on Special Duties for thirty-six months from '93 to '96 with 14th Intelligence Company, the Det. He was based at East Det, Palace Barracks with Parkinson-Naughton and moved with the MI5 man to Lisburn. He had retired from the Army a decade ago and now worked with a private security company in a management and training role. He was a clean-shaven, nondescript man, a small nick in his forehead betraying the shrapnel he took from a blast bomb twenty years ago.

When Jackie had begun reading the file on Samuel McClelland, he had felt a vague unease fester in his gut. McClelland had been, like Jackie, with RUC Special Branch. Unlike Jackie, he had served with RUC Headquarters Mobile Support Unit, HMSU, before joining the human surveillance unit of E4A. HMSU had come to Jackie's aid when an IRA hit team had targeted him back in the nineties. But McClelland had displayed a naked hatred of republicans verging on sectarian malice, and had been encouraged to move to a less confrontational post with surveillance. In that role, he had taken bets with fellow officers as to which republican would be shot next, either by security forces or loyalist paramilitaries.

Following the republican and loyalist ceasefires, he had become deeply embittered towards the British government, considering their disbandment of the RUC as a sell-out, and had joined the Metropolitan Police in London. Unpopular with fellow officers and prone to violence, he had been disciplined on several occasions before quitting the force. His current whereabouts were unknown: it was believed he was living rough. The file photograph was old and blurry, from McClelland's RUC days. A note explained there were no recent pictures of him.

The fifth file concerned another Special Branch man, James McVea. McVea had worked closely with McLelland at E4A. He had been a quiet individual who showed none of the hatred or sectarianism of his colleague. He had, however, a young family at the time of his service, and had displayed a morbid fascination with the details of other officers' deaths at the hands of republican gunmen. He had attended counselling sessions but, thanks to his reticence, had proven an impenetrable subject for the counsellors. He had accepted a retirement package in '99 and his marriage had lasted six months after he became a civilian. He met an English girl online and moved to Essex, then London, where he had lived for six years, and had studied to be a chef. He now worked in a restaurant near the Tate Modern Gallery. Even in his file photograph, he looked nervous and shrunken.

Jackie accepts a mug of coffee from the stocky policeman, the taste as bitter as the copper's face. Gilmore takes a small packet from his hip pocket and offers it to Jackie. 'Chin chin snacks. My mother gets them sent over from Nigeria. I can't stop eating them, now I'm off the fags.' Jackie takes one and unwraps it from a tight plastic wrapper. He remembers munching on similar snacks in Malaysia and Vietnam. 'Patrick Ferguson is proving more difficult to track down. He was last seen somewhere around Aldgate last night in his taxi. Not a black cab, a minicab for a company in Camden. The Met are trying to trace him now.'

Ferguson had been with Military Intelligence in Thiepval Barracks, via the SAS, at the same time and in the same office as Parkinson-Naughton, Dodds and Bannister. He had also trained Samuel McClelland when the Special Branch man had been with HMSU. In his photo, he looked the stereotypical hardcase, all glowering stare and broken nose.

Jackie says, 'Quite the cabal.'

'It should be noted,' says Gilmore, 'that this team and others were investigated in several inquiries, none of which came to the conclusion that systematic collusion had occurred between security forces and loyalist paramilitary groups.' He glances at the two Met men in the room, takes his boot from the table and leans forward. 'What is fact, is that the operational effectiveness of the loyalist Ulster Defence Association paramilitary group increased to a very great degree while these men, and Miss Dodds, were serving at Thiepval Barracks. All had colleagues handling and running assets within the UDA: these same assets were implicated in the killings of several high-profile republican targets during this period. All had access at various levels to P Cards on known republican players, and Bannister, Ferguson and McClelland all requested Restriction Orders on security force activity in the areas where several republican terrorists were killed by loyalist gunmen. Parkinson-Naughton facilitated the requests.'

'There was some American involved too, wasn't there?'

'A fundraiser for the IRA. His body was found near Antrim. Parkinson-Naughton had been a liaison officer with the FBI before the Yank flew to Ulster. He collated data on the man and basically put the P Card together himself. We think McLelland and McVea began running the loyalist asset who pulled the trigger, although the poor Yank bastard had been severely beaten and tortured before they drilled him.'

'And Dodds?' says Jackie. 'She just typed and filed, right?'

'Guilty by association.'

That phrase again. Jackie takes another sip of his coffee and picks up the sim card, like a shard of shrapnel, fingering the slim plastic. He says, 'Nothing on me in these files, but I'm on the list.'

Gilmore says, 'Everything I read about you – even heard about you from Hartley – says you don't belong with these characters. You're the anomaly, Jackie, a wild card. Hartley says he thinks you're there as revenge for an IRA hit gone wrong back in the nineties. Whatever the truth, whoever put you on that list fucked up. I think you might just be the joker in the pack.'

CHAPTER 7

Monday

The beating starts with a sudden blow to the jaw. Morgan, primed for the violence, suppresses a soft hiss of exasperation and pops a mint in his mouth. Fucking Albanians, he thinks. All that *Besa* shit, their code of honour. And their *rakia*, a vicious brew, almost as lethal as poteen.

Morgan isn't much of a drinker but the cadaverous Leka, his eyes dark, viscous pools floating in a slack face devoid of emotion, hands him the glass and Morgan knows better than to decline generosity from a member of an Albanian *Fis*. He sucks hard on the mint as he watches the foot soldier reel from the punch, and the dazed man battle to stay on his feet. The man staggers and tenses to deliver his own punch out of reflex.

Agon, the underboss, or *Kryetar*, is occupied with business matters, Leka had said. Bashkim, the *Krye,* the godfather, is at home in Islington. Morgan has been granted an audience with the third rung on the ladder, the link between the top men and the cannon-fodder, like the poor fucker weaving around the stage and taking a second blow, aimed at his chin but grazing his left ear as he rolls with the punch. The foot soldier is the scapegoat for the girl's disappearance. Ridiculous, of course. He's probably a bouncer in the Soho strip club in which they now sit, perhaps a courier for less important messages and packages: a nobody. Ultimate responsibility for the girl, he knows, lies with Bashkim. Immediate responsibility, with Agon. But, as non-clan members – as non-Albanians – Morgan doesn't merit an audience with the top men. Instead, he's granted a meet with Leka, no more than a cockroach in the food chain of the gang which runs Soho, and most of the whores operating out of it.

They'd called a pre-paid mobile after Harris had finished Parkinson-Naughton and informed the Albanians that the girl had run. After a short, indecipherable outburst on the other end of the crackling connection, they'd been told to come to the Soho club on Monday afternoon.

The man on the stage, dancing with the impact of a welter of punches as three thugs get down to the job of beating him senseless, has been tossed at Morgan's feet as a concession. It was this man, said Leka, who had not disciplined the girl correctly. This man had shown weakness and, perhaps, compassion in handling the whore. Not yet open for business, the Gentleman's Sporting Club on Dean Street is sad and oppressive under the harsh fluorescent strips above, the soft glow of the business hours' low lighting, designed to cloak the girls' imperfections and cloud the punters' judgement, not yet in effect. The biggest of the three attackers on the stage, a man with a clear and symmetrical scar running from his left to right ear across his shaved cranium, sucker-punches the scapegoat, a full-force punch to the jaw intended to jolt the brain, hammer the mandible out of position and briefly cut off oxygen supply to the grey matter. The man should collapse like shit out of a shopping bag, job done and honour satisfied.

But the stubborn asshole stays up, and now the three are working up a sweat to put him down, a fellow Albanian, all for some *I huaj pista* of a foreigner. Morgan can see the frustration and resentment in their eyes as they bludgeon away at their countryman. He finishes the mint then knocks back the *rakia*. The sting in his throat and slow burn in his belly feel good, despite his reluctance to drink hard liquor, and the mint helps smother the fumes in his nostrils. From the stage, the dull clout of knuckle on skin is becoming a turgid, wet slapping sound.

'Thank you for your generosity in offering the drink, Leka,' he says, 'and for punishing this man in my presence. However, there is still the matter of the girl.'

Leka fills a second glass from the bottle and downs it with a thick gulp. 'She has fulfilled her purpose, no? She led the man to you. She fucked up the scene for the *polici,* their forensics; she is illegal in this country, her fingerprints are on no file. Her DNA will be on the old man's lips.'

'True, but she saw at least one of us before she ran. She's loose in London. She could go to the police.'

Leka shakes his head and giggles, a patronising hand on Morgan's shoulder. The dull, violent claps of fist on face from the stage slow in intensity.

'You do not understand this business, my friend. To make money from a girl, we must own that girl. To own that girl, we must break that girl. This, we do with violence and domination. A woman is like a horse, a free spirit. But ride that horse, whip that horse, starve that horse until it believes it cannot live without its master – lives to *serve* its master – and you can work it. You can make it earn for you. This animal, Beatrix, she is broken. She will roam London and she will stay away from the police because she is frightened of them. She has a sister here. If she goes to the police, we will kill the sister: she knows this. When she is cold and starving she will come home to us, or she will die on the streets.'

'Maybe she won't come because she knows that, if she does, she will die.'

Leka tuts, looking at the floor. Something wet and heavy hits the wooden stage.

'We will not kill her. She is young and has many more men to fuck and much more money to make. We will punish her, of course, but not in a way that damages her earning potential. She will suffer, I promise you.' He withdraws the hand from

Morgan's shoulder and lights a cigarette. 'The sister is very successful, lives in Kensington. An interpreter. We are watching her place in case Beatrix goes to her. But she won't, believe me. She will return to us.'

'Why not move on the sister now?'

'Insurance. If we hurt the sister, Beatrix has no incentive to work for us. She will waste away and we cannot make money from her.'

Morgan smiles, conciliatory, relaxed but frigid. 'You will understand that I and my friends must look for her too.' He stands, bends slightly at the waist and backs towards the entrance, the flat of his right hand against his chest in a gesture of thanks. The man at the door, a short, scrawny terrier with a bristling moustache and fat, almost obscene lower lip, shoots a glance at Leka before unlocking the door leading to the stairs and the street outside.

Leka says, 'If you find her, you will bring her to us, yes?' Then, dropping the interrogative tone, 'You will bring her home.'

Morgan offers a short nod and retreats to the landing, then takes the stairs at a measured pace until he reaches the locked outer entrance. He knocks on a side door and a janitor emerges from a small office and opens the glass door which leads to Brewer Street. It gives with a shove and Morgan enters the thrashing bustle of Soho, a sharp sun-glare off the bleached pavement. As he walks towards Shaftesbury Avenue, he pops another mint and concentrates on sucking it, soothing nerves that have been untested for years.

Fucking Albanians, he thinks.

#

'We're blown,' Harris says. 'Brother Jim had company when we went to visit this morning.'

'What kind of company?'

'The official kind. We're blown, for fuck's sake.'

Harris stands in the public telephone box at Morden underground station. It's a forty-minute tube journey from Southwark on the Jubilee and Northern lines, far from their operational area, a clean location. And now the voice on the other end of the line is arsing about.

The voice says, 'Have you been ID'd?'

'We'd hardly fucking know if we had, would we?'

'But the first two relatives have been seen to?'

'Yes, job done. But you might want to look into how the Brits knew McVea was being scoped this morning. You could have a tout on your hands.'

A sharp snap of irritation. 'You might want to moderate your language.'

'Catch yourself on, for fuck's sake.' Throughout the call, Harris's voice has been a low hiss. He is self-conscious, despite a Belfast accent drawing little or no attention for years in England. Old habits, he thinks. 'We're still on schedule, and relative number three should be sorted today. This morning we had a scout on number four; things might be held up if he has an escort for any length of time. But the Brits couldn't know who we are. Only you and the Chief have our names.'

Harris realises he hasn't had a cigarette in a while, and is suddenly gasping for one.

'Somehow, the Brits know about the targets, or McVea at least. You let us worry about seeing this through and concentrate on finding the tout and nutting the cunt.'

Before the voice can reply, he hangs up and strides to the nearby Sainsbury's for a packet of smokes. He spots a single magpie, utters a hushed obscenity, and whispers, 'How're the wife and children?' His mother had been a Tyrone woman, steeped in superstition, and would never pass a single magpie without muttering the short query to show due respect and ward off ill-fortune.

You were a great woman, Ma, he thinks, but you filled my head with nonsense.

Padraig Macrossan learned all he knew about Ireland from his father. His mother, a quiet and studious woman who had done the spadework of his upbringing, is a loved and respected part of the furniture in Padraig's world. A small world, at that: he's never been north of Watford. When his mother moved to Lancashire to be closer to her sister and brother, her husband dead a couple of years, he promised to visit. He's yet to stray beyond the northern reaches of Maida Vale.

Padraig Terence Macrossan had emerged, screaming and shaking, into the world at seven twenty-three on the morning of 12 August 1997. From that moment, he had spent the vast majority of his time with his mother. His father had set the precedent of a lifetime – Padraig's – by getting steaming drunk in the Coachman's Arms while his mother screamed and strained in agony to birth him. There are photographs, in a shoe-box in his mother's home in Manchester, of Padraig on the day he rolled over for the first time. His first crawl; eating pulverised, slimy rice; swimming in the local pool; at a picnic on Parliament Hill; his first day at school in Hounslow. In many shots, the small, fragile woman with the worries of the world etched on her delicate face sits proudly with Padraig on her knee. In his teenage years, not yet passed, she stands by his side, dwarfed by his stature and awed by the young man she raised.

Terence Macrossan, his father, appears in only a few pictures, mostly taken at home or at Gaelic matches. But Padraig and his mother had never gone wanting and, as he grew and matured, he knew this was down to his father. It wasn't an easy life for an unskilled man, providing for a family. It was only right that his dad, sweating on building sites and freezing by roadworks, should take a little comfort in a few drinks with his mates to ease the pressure.

While a young child, Padraig's mother had set about cultivating his interest in reading with the same quiet determination which she applied to most endeavours in her life. He had lain in bed listening to tales of talking lions in far-away lands, spiders weaving messages on their webs in fantastic farms, and children touring chocolate factories filled with terrible wonder. His father, when home at his bedtime, had sat next to his cot and told different stories. Monstrous lords and monarchs who oppressed simple folk, marching to the sound of terrible drums and slaughtering these honest folk before stealing their land. Imperial soldiers pillaging with impunity and protecting usurping settlers, who so tormented the decent native folk. And then there were the brave men, the freedom fighters, who struck back: ingenious, resourceful rebels.

To the young Padraig, it had sounded like a fairytale; to the older Padraig, it's a crusade. He has always believed the republican cause was for Irish Catholic freedom. The deeper conflict, beyond the struggle with Britain, is with the unionists and loyalists, a mongrel race who must be conquered and, eventually, extinguished. He can support the England football team, he can wear an England rugby shirt, and still be an Irish republican.

But, he thinks, Conal Harris despises not the political and imperial framework of England but the nation itself and, by extension, Padraig. Harris is a walking contradiction, steeped in the 'struggle' yet devoid of any capacity for empathy, or concept of freedom. Padraig hates the man for it. The feeling is mutual.

Padraig met Morgan in a pub in Kilburn, had come to know the republican networks which still existed throughout London, like the tunnels which criss-crossed below the city. Morgan had introduced him to Harris, who had trained him. The barracking, the insults, the festering animosity, Padraig had accepted as the stern bark of a sergeant major shaping his charge. But he had been introduced to another man, a man who had flown in from Belfast for a fortnight of huddled meetings with Morgan and Harris, who had shown him kindness, patience and a measure of respect. The corrosive bark of the Belfast accent was, in this man, a soothing lilt, and Padraig realised Harris merely loathed him for who he was.

Now, as Kenneth Bannister, a fellow Englishman, opens his front door and kisses his wife goodbye, Padraig wonders if he, too, would hate Padraig if he knew him. Bannister looks average in every way: height, build, nondescript haircut and styling by Gap. His wife Arlene, however, is stunning in tight blue jeans and simple T-shirt, blonde hair tied back in a dangling pony-tail.

The affection between husband and wife is obvious and the two men who spoke with Bannister on his doorstep are relaxed and at ease in his company. After McVea was approached outside the Tate, Padraig knows these men must be some form of security forces. His chest tightens for a moment as he stands at the bus stop two hundred feet away from the house on the Avalon Road, a typical Ealing street, all leafy hedges and neat, identical semi-detached homes. The nose of Bannister's Vauxhall Insignia is almost on the pavement, forced to teeter, parked at the edge of the driveway, by the wife's Mini Cooper parked between it and the house. Parked directly in front sits a large, sturdy-looking BMW.

Bannister and his wife speak for a minute or two. Padraig thinks again how good the woman looks, with two children now at school. The two security men walk around the Vauxhall, one crouching to peer at the undercarriage of the vehicle, while Bannister touches his wife's face and puts his forehead on hers.

Padraig makes a mental note of the appearance of the other two men and the time Bannister leaves the house. They had scouted the target for three weeks now, and he is holding to the pattern that emerged from surveillance. Home for lunch, parking in front of the Mini, leaving to drive back to his workplace at 14.00. He must report back on what he observes to Morgan and Harris. They will have to recalibrate their plan. The alert from the security forces will almost certainly prompt Bannister to vary his schedule. He'll take different routes to and from work. The presence of the other men will be a challenge. To get up close like they had with Parkinson-Naughton and Dodds will be out of the question for a while.

There is a part of Padraig, a small but ever increasing part of him, the part that has been cherished and fostered by his mother – the part that had ached at the thought of never getting that promised kiss from his first love in form 6G at school – that is relieved. Let Harris and Morgan handle the killing, men who see a target as an objective on a page, a box to be ticked, albeit with a 9mm bullet.

Bannister climbs into his car and starts the ignition. The two security men climb into the BMW and the car growls to life as they wait for Kenneth Bannister, and his Vauxhall. Bannister's car begins rolling onto the street. Padraig notes the licence plate of the BMW as the wife walks to the front door of the house, standing in the frame, arm raised. Harris might want to hit Bannister while he is in the Vauxhall, perhaps parked or at traffic lights. The Irishman always preaches that a stationary target is cleanest and easiest to execute. Padraig checks his mobile to make a note of the exact time just as the Vauxhall explodes, literally ripped apart by a combination of fertiliser and Semtex.

All is heat and white flame and a turmoil of flying glass and metal, the air filled and alive with a sudden roar which swells to an echoing thunder, swallowing the street in its fury. The energy of the detonation rushes towards Padraig, followed a millisecond later by a high-velocity shockwave. As his innards broil, he is flattened against the bus stop. Arlene Bannister is hurled against the frame of her front door at one hundred mph, breaking her collarbone and battered unconscious by the blunt force trauma to her head. It is a mercy. The Vauxhall's windscreen, now a grab bag of glass shrapnel, lets fly. The lacerations rake her cheeks and shred her left eye. Her skin bubbles with the furnace-like heat and her sweater and jeans meld with her red raw flesh, welded to her by the fierce, scalding embrace of the explosion. Her home becomes a maelstrom of flying glass and wood as the window-frames implode. Max, the family cat, sat dozing on the rim of the sofa in the front room, is a shredded carcass in an instant. The BMW is armoured and withstands the brunt of the blast without toppling over, but the glass in the car is too close to the point of detonation and the men inside feel hundreds of razor blades slice two-inch papercuts into their faces and arms as they reflexively cover their heads. The heat takes their eyebrows and sears their bodies as their clothing burns red hot. For Kenneth Bannister, the end is instantaneous. A sudden flash of white-hot pain, and he ceases to exist.

Then, quiet.

There is only the faint clatter and tinkle of glass and slivers of metal falling back to the concrete. There is no screaming. Arlene Bannister lies slumped in the doorway, a broken marionette, her face unrecognisable. The men in the car sit in shock, insensible to the horror of what has happened.

Padraig Macrossan vomits, terrified and shaking, his guts still swirling from the blast. Then, as the first neighbours creep out from the safety of their homes, and shouts and yells come floating down the street, he runs.

CHAPTER 8

Monday

The pub is a cavern, a small clutch of drinkers huddled at the counter. The Lily Bolero couldn't have been better named. Above the bar, splayed like a Spanish fan, are the Saltire, the Ulster Flag and, in the centre, the Cross of Saint George. A mural of the Inniskillings hacking their way through the Russians at Balaklava dominates one of the walls, with the regimental crest of Enniskillen Castle emblazoned above the carnage. A tapestry of the 36th Ulster Division wading through the mud and death of the Somme adorns another. The intricately detailed plaster ceiling, a canopy of circular leaves and features surrounding a bas-relief of a gallant trio of warriors galloping on massive chargers, is supported by several heavy-looking pillars. The pub was a haunt of cavalry officers in the nineteenth century and has somehow retained the miasma of stale tobacco smoke of two hundred-odd years. The whole is a strange combination of swagger and gravitas.

The Lily Bolero squats below four storeys of Victorian decorative brick and sash windows, squeezed on either side by a research institute and a finance company. As a rolling drumbeat plays from the digital jukebox in the corner, Jackie weaves through the tables and makes his way to the counter. He pockets a salt shaker as he passes the last table top and leans on the counter, glancing at the flat-screen TV above the bar, just below the Saltire. He recognises the music: 'The Drowners' by Suede. The punters are staring at the flat-screen, which displays a suburban street strewn with blackened, tortured metal and a collage of glass and car-fragments. Police and firemen wander around and a white forensic tent is set up in the front garden of a semi-detached. Angry shards of glass protrude from the gaping, hollow mouths of the windows. It is a scene not glimpsed for a while on UK streets, and one he knows all too well. The car bomb was one of the most feared tools in the terrorists' arsenal among RUC officers during the Troubles. He thinks of the cipher key, *Katana*, and wonders if someone really could be watching him, gun loaded or detonator readied.

The drinkers are hushed in shock, fed by booze. There are seven, all male, at the counter. A young barman leaning on the oak surface turns the volume down on the jukebox with a remote control. He turns the volume of the TV up and a sombre voice says, '...*Bannister served in Northern Ireland with the security forces. There has already been speculation that the bombing was carried out by dissident republicans...*' The second man from the end furthest from Jackie is heavy-set, a beer gut and the sag of a broad chest gone to fat showing through his grey shirt. He looks just he does in his MI5 file photo: Derek Bailey.

Jackie lays his Belfast accent on broad and thick, battering through the low mutter of the others and snapping the barman's head to the left. 'Pint of Guinness, mate.'

The barman says, 'Sorry, didn't catch that.' His voice is glottal Estuary, all sarcasm and disdain. Two of the drinkers ease their bodies back from the counter: an old-timer, all Blitz spirit piss-and-vinegar, and a leather jacketed pitbull in jeans and work boots with regulation shaved head. Bailey glances at Jackie then returns his attention to the screen.

Jackie speaks slow and loud. 'A pint of Guinness, mate. Please.'

The barman snorts and a third punter, a man with a pinched face and long, fibrous arms hanging from a brand name T-shirt, leans back from the counter. Bailey is studious in his attention to the BBC report on screen. Jackie, hand in pocket, turns to the other drinkers and focuses on the three now a step back from the counter and facing him.

He says, 'What are youse having? Can I buy youse a Guinness?'

The old-timer says, 'Bit of English heavy's more to our taste.'

Jackie stands a little straighter as his fingers work in his pocket. With a smile, he says, 'Aye, the English pish is all right, like. Just doesn't have the history – the tradition – of the black stuff. It's a bit lightweight for me.'

Bailey has lowered his head to peer at the mixers behind the bar as though he has shares in Smirnoff. The old-timer drops all pretence of civility and says, 'You paddy bastard,' spitting with venom. A fourth man turns to face Jackie, a short, stocky item in a heavy coat, jeans and trainers. Pitbull is psyching himself up; the lean man is squaring his shoulders. The short man looks indecisive. Jackie takes a couple of steps forward. He takes his hands from his pockets, splays them wide in supplication and lowers his tone. 'Look, I didn't mean nothing. No hard feelings right, lads?'

The old-timer, scenting fear, says, 'You come in here – one of *you* – on a day like this, and you order a fucking Guinness.' His head cocked to the side, he says, 'A fucking paddy Guinness. Look at the TV, you bog-trotting bastard. See what your people have done.'

Jackie reads the tele-type message running along the bottom of the screen: *Ex-security forces member killed in republican-style car bomb in suburban London*. He steals another glance at Bailey, still fixated on the bottles behind the counter. Then he shoves his hands back in his pockets and speaks to the barman, his eyes still on the four men in front of him.

'I ordered a Guinness, now pour the fucker before I knock

seven shades of shite out of ye. And you four, sit down and behave yourselves.' As eyes widen and jaws slacken, he nods to the pitbull in the leather jacket and says, 'And keep a civil tongue in your heads.' Then he walks to within an inch of the big man's face and headbutts him, his forehead glancing off pitbull's cheek. He steps back.

The big man drops his chin and shifts his weight slightly while clenching his teeth and fists. He couldn't have broadcast the punch more clearly if he'd sent a memo first, and Jackie moves forward fast, ducking under the swing. He grabs the back of the shaved head with his left hand and crushes the handful of salt from the shaker in his pocket into his attacker's eyes. Pitbull bellows and stumbles into the counter, blinded and flailing in panic.

Jackie takes a glancing blow on his shoulder and turns in a crouch. The lean man has surprising heft behind his wiry build. Jackie takes a fleck of spit across the cheek as the man spits an obscenity, and sends a sharp jab into the skinny throat. More panic, stumbling and loss of control. Jackie takes a fistful of brand T-shirt in his right hand and kicks at the rangy legs with his right foot. The man is upended, landing hard and badly on the carpet. The short, stocky man in the coat has hesitated and his eyes betray him. He's lost all momentum and stands rocking on the balls of his feet. Jackie feints and the stocky man puts his hands up, protecting his face. Jackie steps in close and takes a firm hold of the man's right ear with his left hand, then throws a strong, hard, open-handed slap against the unprotected left ear. There is a short yell, like a teenager's voice breaking, and Jackie wonders if he's burst the eardrum. Then he throws his right elbow in a short, vicious arc. The hard cap of the point drives into cheekbone with a flat slap, driving the face to the left and sending a searing needle point of pain through the already damaged ear. The man staggers backwards and raises his hands in defence and surrender, a low moan of pain escaping from clenched teeth, like a ventriloquist's dummy. The lean man is kneeling, clutching at his throat, swallowing hard despite the agony it causes. Only the pitbull, eyes a soaking tapestry of angry red veins, still has some fight in him. He holds onto the counter and roars, 'Fucker!'

He advances like a shambling Frankenstein's monster. The lean man, kneeling to the pitbull's right, gags, then hawks up a thick wad of phlegm as Jackie's boot connects with his chest, kicking him back and into the legs of the leather-jacketed pitbull. Both men collapse and Jackie takes a short run up, as though to punt a football, before delivering a full-blown kick to the pitbull's bollocks.

The man in the heavy coat stands in front of the other patrons, a shaking hand clamped over the damaged ear and a welt blossoming on his cheek. The old-timer is trembling, his rheumy eyes like pools of spittle in a face like crumpled paper. Two drinkers stand in silence, one with knuckles white against the lip of the counter, the other with arms stiff and rigid at his sides, as though sudden movement might trigger an attack. Bailey appraises him with a calm and focused eye.

Jackie places a hand on pitbull's shoulder. 'You're all right, big lad. Just breathe slow and deep. They'll grow back.' He opens pitbull's hand and trickles some salt into the open palm. 'Throw this over your shoulder, son, just in case.' He leans in close to the small, stocky man in the coat and says, 'Sit down and have a drink. It'll pass.'

The barman lifts a mobile phone from behind the counter.

Jackie says, 'Who're you calling, cowboy?'

'The police. You come in here, tearing the place up and assaulting customers.' He makes the statement a question with an incredulous tone. 'You're a fucking animal. Fucking micks.'

Jackie steps over the lean man, now lying with eyes closed in an aspect of prayer, and says, 'You want to keep a civil tongue in your mouth, son. I didn't serve in the RUC in South Armagh for a streak of piss like you to be calling me a mick.' The young man drags his finger down the mobile screen to activate the dialling keypad. Jackie presses both hands on the counter top, ready to vault over, when a voice says, 'Leave it, son. The lads've had worse on a Saturday night.'

Derek Bailey steps forward and offers a thick, callused hand. Jackie wipes a clammy palm on his jeans, breaks out a crooked grin, and clasps it in a firm grip.

They wander down Ensign Street headed for the river.

The brawl had been a gamble but Jackie had needed to establish himself as someone of interest to Bailey and proving his worth in a scrap had seemed a logical place to start. He'd expected to take a few more shots and come away with a bruise or two but the punch to his shoulder had barely registered, and he hadn't grazed a knuckle. It's simple, he knows. Read your opponent and show him you are prepared to go further than he is prepared to risk. Pitbull was all front, the other two hiding behind his size. None of them had really wanted a fight.

God forbid the kid had actually poured the pint for him. Jackie hadn't touched the booze for years, and didn't intend to start now. So when Bailey had introduced himself, Jackie had asked if they could talk outside.

Bailey lights up a cigarette as they stroll through the streets of Whitechapel to the great rolling syrup of the Thames. 'Better to make an exit. They might share our politics, but we aren't locals.' He exhales a thin stream of smoke.

Jackie says, 'But that pub is loyalist, right? That's what a mate of mine told me.'

Bailey takes another drag on the filter. 'Do they support our view on Ulster? Yes. Do they really care? No. They've nothing at stake, not like us.' He throws a thumb signal over his shoulder towards the Lily Bolero. 'They're too busy fretting over some imagined kid in Tower Hamlets plotting to poison the water supply to pay much attention to us any more.'

Jackie nods with a sympathetic grunt.

'Sorry about the mouth on the barman, too. He's a kid, just standing in for the regular, Hugh. Hugh came down with something. I don't know where they dredged that lippy wee shite up from.' He clears his throat. 'Anyway, you said a mate told you about the pub. Anyone I know?'

'Denny Walters,' says Jackie, remembering the name of the corporal replaced by Ruth Dodds.

Bailey shakes his head. 'Don't know him.'

'He was in the Army, served back home. English, but all right. Had a bee in his bonnet about blacks and Asians. You know, the whole mighty-white thing.'

Bailey drops his fag butt next to a street bollard as they turn left onto The Highway. 'I know the type,' he says. 'I've no time for them. Clowns. Running around with their crew cuts and their football chants; acting the big man with some wee Indian shopkeeper trying to earn a living, and then having a curry later with their dole money.'

Jackie frowns. Fucking MI5: intelligence agency my arse. So much for Bailey's links with racist and right-wing groups.

Bailey catches his expression and says, 'Sorry, no offence to your mate.'

'None taken,' says Jackie. He sweeps the street for suspicious cars and signs of foot surveillance. It looks clean. As they head for Vaughan Way he says, 'There was another mate of mine, Trevor McCandless. Used to work out of Castlereagh.' Jackie had never actually met McCandless but knew of him through a fellow officer at Special Branch.

Bailey slows his pace and studies the power-station-chic monstrosity of the Thomas More Square building.

Jackie says, 'He worked with Gordon Orr, on and off.'

They stop in front of a hedge so sculpted and rigid it could have been made of jade.

'Special Branch,' says Bailey. 'I heard of Orr.'

'I did a stint with Special Branch North. E3A desk, some E4A time. I met Gordon through Trevor. Both good lads, although chalk and cheese. Gordie spent all his time praying to our Lord and maker, and Trevor spent his trying to outdo Oul' Nick. A terrible man for the drink and women, Trevor, but he always had your back.'

'Do they live in London?'

'Both gone and buried. Gordon passed a few years ago, massive stroke. Trevor followed him a year later. Traffic accident. Some drunk wee shite on a joyride.'

'You're a dangerous man to know,' says Bailey.

Jackie takes a lungful of smoke in the face as the other man belches a cloud of tobacco. Then Derek Bailey's eyes crinkle as his mouth hooks in a grin. 'Your mates are dropping like flies.'

Jackie winks. 'You know what they say,' he says, 'things happen in threes.'

#

As they pass a block of council flats, they reminisce about life in the RUC. The clatter of Wessex helicopters at various barracks. Training at the Enniskillen Barracks and drinking near the town's castle with its riverside tower, the Watergate. Sitting in the sweltering pressure cooker of an armoured Land Rover while petrol bombs ignited on the steel skin.

Now Bailey works in Islington as a security guard in warehouses and office buildings. So many ex-coppers ended up in the same gig, thinks Jackie. He lies, 'I'm out of work at the minute. I lost my job in Scotland. An oil company up in Aberdeen, driving executives around and the like. The recession hit there, just like everywhere else.'

'Why not go home?'

'Things are pretty dire over there, job-wise.'

They reach St Katharine Docks and Bailey lights a third cigarette. They lean against the metal chain bordering the path and look down at the water below. It shines with a kaleidoscope of colour, slick with oil.

Bailey says, 'You were pretty handy back in the pub.' He looks at the gangs of tourists milling and business people flitting between appointments. 'But you want to be careful here. You could piss off the wrong people very easily. It's not like home where the lines are drawn: big fucking pictures on walls and flags on lampposts.'

'Do you know any other ex-Constabulary here? Maybe I could network a bit, try and get something going.'

A seagull takes up position a couple of yards away and Bailey flicks his butt at the bird. It pads a few paces away but keeps a beady eye on them. 'There was a guy, Mitchell, lived in Haringey, but he moved up to Yorkshire.'

'And there's no one else?'

'That I know of, just the one. He's not the easiest customer to track down, though. Bit of a drifter, sleeping on sofas and dossing in parks. Homeless. You see him about sometimes, in the City. I think he spends a bit of time in Soho, too. He does the odd bit of manual labour when he can find it: building sites, delivery work on lorries, off-the-books stuff. McLelland, his name is.'

'Do you think you could find him? Be good to talk to somebody from home, knows the streets.'

'Give me a contact number, I'll see what I can do.' Bailey coughs, a thick, chesty bark. 'Better keep you sweet,' he says with a hoarse laugh. 'After McCandless and Orr, I don't want to be number three on your hit list.'

CHAPTER 9

Monday

Padraig Macrossan shudders, his eyes red and raw.

'It was a mess,' he says. 'Like nothing I've ever seen. The place was just ripped apart.'

Conal Harris picks flecks of dirt from under his fingernails with a toothpick. Morgan takes a measured breath: the patient father with a slow child. They sit in a clean but spare hotel room in one of the budget chains that have colonised British cities, all chipboard and plastic. Morgan says, 'Listen, Padraig, back in the day, an IRA Chief of Staff described a car bomb as a strategic and tactical weapon. Strategically, it disrupts the enemy government's ability to administrate. It spreads terror.'

Padraig laughs, a harsh, mirthless cough. 'You got that part right.'

Morgan forces a smile. 'Tactically, it ties down security forces. And, it advances our ultimate goal of executing the list. It's another target dealt with.'

'And his wife?' says Padraig, his voice a desperate whine. 'She was next to the car. Oh, Christ.'

'It's a statement, a reminder of what kind of damage we can do. It's a calling card.'

'But weren't there warnings in the past? Didn't you call in the threat? Contact the media?'

Harris says, 'Sometimes.'

'But you picked your targets. You were an army.'

Padraig is pleading.

Harris, still focused on the black dirt wedged under his nails, says, 'The warnings depended on the target. You want to cause chaos and disruption, you call it in. You want to kill people...' He raises his eyebrows. 'Sometimes, the point of the bomb was to terrorise. Sometimes to blow some fucker up.'

'But you weren't terrorists. You were soldiers. *Volunteers*, the Green Book called you.'

Harris spreads his hands: there it is, take it or leave it. 'Listen, young 'un. I knew a fella, became Chief of Staff for a while in Belfast. One night a car bomb goes off intended for a peeler. The guy's wife gets caught in it instead. He was laid up in bed with flu or whatever, she went out to get medicine for him. She was snapped out like a light.' He takes a packet of cigarettes from his jacket pocket. 'This mate of mine, the future Chief of Staff, he turns to me in the club and says, "I hope the bitch was pregnant: two for the price of one".'

The features of Padraig's face are on the point of collapse. He breathes hard through his nose.

'Sorry if that doesn't fit with your da's bedtime stories,' says Harris.

Morgan stands and says, 'Padraig, we didn't know they'd be tipped off on the list. On a typical day, Bannister would have got in the car and driven out of the driveway while his wife sat watching some daytime shit on TV. Because the security forces show up and stress her out, she's at the door to see him off.'

'She wouldn't have been much better off inside,' says Padraig. 'All the windows were blown in.'

'Then the lazy cow should have got herself a job instead of sitting at home watching *Jeremy Kyle*,' says Harris.

'Look, the first time I killed for my employer,' Morgan says, 'I built a profile of the target, followed him around, learned his routine. When I finally pulled the trigger, it was mistaken identity. I shot a bus driver.'

'Bit of an anti-climax,' sniggers Harris.

'Not for the bus driver. The point is, there will always be casualties. But, this time, we got the right man.'

Padraig knows they are right. The objective is to take out the names on the list and if that means collateral damage, so be it. Innocents had died in the six counties, many of them. It's the way of war, and they died for a cause and a better future for the people of Ireland. Tragic but true. And yet he closes his eyes and sees an attractive woman, full of life, embrace a loving husband and a little boy, swinging a lunchbox, cross a footbridge to school. He puts his head in his hands and sniffs.

'Why me? You've done the old git and the bitch' – he stares at Harris – 'and you built the fucking device.' He turns to Morgan. 'Why didn't one of you go? Or at least tell me the fucking car was going to blow. You made it sound like a recce.' He stops himself calling them bastards: his fear of them still trumps his anger.

Morgan cocks a thumb at Harris, who is tapping a smoke on the edge of the cardboard packet. 'Belfast wanted to deal with Harris. He's one of theirs, known. They trust him. When we realised we were blown, someone had to contact them, and that someone had to be him.' He goes to the coffee maker perched on a fitted cupboard and selects a sachet of instant from a small box. 'Did you want to deal with the Albanians? They cut your throat for refusing a drink because it's a slight or some shit. The Sicilians don't want to deal with them because they're too unpredictable.'

Morgan walks to the en-suite toilet door to fill the kettle from the tap, and says to Harris, 'Don't even think about lighting that shit up in here.' Then, from the toilet, 'You want to go and talk to those animals next time, Padraig, be my guest.'

Harris watches Morgan return from the toilet and plug in the kettle with a raised eyebrow, the cigarette hanging loose from his lips. 'You should be honoured, son. You were there, confirmed the kill. You saw another imperialist aggressor of dear old Éire blown to smithereens.' He eases out the creases in the packet of cigarettes, the unlit fag still hanging from his mouth. 'Sounds like Uncle Morgan here did a grand job, too. C'mon, Alexander, tell us how it was done.'

Morgan bristles, flicking the switch on the kettle to bring the water to the boil. He hates hearing his first name and is cultivating a festering loathing of Harris. But the device, the hit, was well put together and executed. He'd scouted the site with the quiet man from Belfast and they'd agreed on a pressure-plate detonation. There was a small metal drain-cover in the pavement directly in front of the Bannister driveway and a pressure plate device was attached underneath in the wee small hours three days prior. Macrossan didn't know they couldn't have aborted if they'd wanted to once the charge was in place. A cheap digital watch for a timer, a second, 'forensic charge' to detonate a split second after the initial explosion in order to destroy forensic evidence, and they were good to go. It was amazing how, after all these years, ammonium nitrate and Semtex was still the tried and trusted go-to for an IED. The police would take days, at least, to realise the device wasn't under-car.

The kettle hisses in satisfaction at a job well done and Morgan pours boiling water over the thin grit in the plastic cup. Harris has slid the cigarette back in its packet and is fiddling with the TV controller. Padraig Macrossan's face is scarlet, as though he has been slapped hard across the cheeks. Which, in a sense, he has.

Morgan says, 'Parkinson-Naughton, Dodds, and now Bannister. We're halfway there,' and takes a sip of the bitter coffee.

#

If she could just catch a glimpse of Flori, Beatrix might be warmed a little, find respite from the bone-chilling cold. It is spring, yet her heart and soul are in the long, dark dusk of the Albanian Alps in winter.

With each day of fear, threat and relentless, soulless fucking in Soho, she had slowly chipped away at her emotions, her being, willing herself to feel less and less until – God help her – she had succeeded. She became no more than a resource for Bakshim and his gangsters to work, and a shell for the desperate, spiteful men who paid to empty their loneliness inside her.

She heard from a pretty girl busking on Cromwell Road that there was a hostel for the homeless near Earls Court but, crazily, the street people cannot stay without paying a charge and she wondered at England. Albania is a country crippled by decades of isolation and mutual suspicion with its neighbours and the Western powers. What's the UK's excuse?

The hunger was beginning to bite, but a young woman near West Brompton station, a Scot with hair like an unravelling doormat, told her of the night shelters nearby. Free food and a bed. Thin soup and a roll would be something, but she decided not to stay. She would take her chances on the street. It is not yet evening and already she has seen a pair of young men urinate on a ragged figure sleeping in a small square. The old man had awoken and muttered in what she thought was Romanian. The young men, English, laughed and walked away. Herself no stranger to degradation, she saw in the tired gaze of the Romanian that he had lost his capacity for outrage. He had simply seen too much.

It is the vast scale of the city that frightens her. So many streets, so many doors, millions of them, and all closed. Locked. It is a city of grandeur that doesn't seem to want people: they might spoil its majesty. And the thought that Bakshim, Agon and the rest could be around the next corner, standing in the next shaded doorway, under the next set of townhouse steps, terrifies her. She sees Kensington, and the city, as a giant maze like a grid in a game, herself a cursor flitting through the labyrinth pursued by malevolent, hungry monsters.

So she finds a house near the entrance to her sister's mews and settles herself in the small trench at the front of the building, the entrance to an empty basement flat, and waits. She doesn't know for how long. She doesn't know if Flori is there or shopping or dining. Perhaps she is working, staying somewhere on a trip.

Life with the *Fis* taught Beatrix to live in the now. Memories are no comfort: rather, a throbbing pain which lead to despair. But she wonders what her sister is doing now, and she thinks of Flori, smart, fierce, independent Flori; her older sister, the first-born, the success. Proficient in French, English and – the reason for the Kensington flat and the Gold Card – Arabic. Beatrix loves her desperately, wanted to follow her, even studied French. The trip to Paris was the first step. Next would have been Shanghai, Mandarin study and then, who knew? But now Beatrix has nowhere else to go. And she knows that if she wanders much longer, her terror of this metropolis, so foreign and alien and closed, will trump her dread and hatred of the *Fis*, and she will return to them. To the pain and punishment.

So she sits in her mini-skirt, flimsy and cheap, in her heels, now chipped and soiled by the dirt of the streets, and her crumpled blouse and short jacket. She shakes out her thick black brushstroke of hair. And she waits.

'Why are we sitting here? Why aren't we out looking for this *lavire*, this whore who thinks she can run?'

The underboss and the *Krye* sit in the Gentleman's Sporting Club as staff busy themselves preparing for the night's business. The barstaff and waiters work that little bit harder and chance anxious glances at the boss and his *Kryetar*, the latter sipping on his third lager.

He's drinking more than usual, thinks Bashkim. London is too comfortable? When they carved a slice of the Camorra's business in Napoli, his brother-in-law had been sharp, aggressive, hungry. Bashkim had had to hold him back, sometimes physically, from violent clashes in the Scampìa district. His sister, Drita, would never have forgiven him had her husband died on a Neopolitan street. Now she harps at Bashkim about Agon's drinking, his ambivalence towards the kids, how he's never home. Yes, London is easy compared to Tirana and Napoli but also, he can see that his *Kryetar* is agitated and furious: a girl has never run before. And he is stewing in guilt at losing her, his nerves shredded. So Bashkim says, 'Drink your beer and calm down, Agon. Where can she go? Home, to Tirana? She is lost, she is frightened. She will come back to us.'

'I love you, Bashkim. You are my family and my *Krye*. But this sends the wrong message to the *huajt*. We have a reputation, and if we do not act to find this *buce*, this bitch, the foreigners will see it as weakness.'

Bashkim puts a hand on his underboss's arm, covering the crude tattoo visible beneath the obscene pink slit of a knife scar. Agon is right: they do have a reputation. And, for now, it is important to uphold that image, the ultra-violent mafia organisation with no limits or tolerance for insubordination. But they are also a young face on the London criminal scene, despite their heady rise to lords of Soho's sex industry. It isn't wise to alienate potential allies and associates, particularly with the interest currently being shown in their operations by the National Crime Agency. And his weakness, if anything, is the slender, well-bred girl who is out there, somewhere in this huge, sprawling temple to avarice, London, ripe for the pillaging.

'Patience,' he says. 'The foreigners will not find her. Even if they do, they will merely bring her back to us.'

'Or kill her. An insult to us.' Agon shifts his thick frame in his seat, the boxer's grace still commanding his movements despite the drink.

'They wouldn't,' says Bashkim. 'Leka met with Morgan today. He said the man has front, but he was nervous. They won't risk reprisals.' He takes a sip of orange juice. 'We handled things right. We made a show with Fatmir, and we are lucky the stupid *kurvar* is so thick-headed. He stayed on his feet and was beaten to a pulp. They have their pound of flesh.'

'But we don't have satisfaction.'

'Satisfaction is overrated,' says Bashkim. 'Just ask the useless *karet* who pay for our girls. It is never enough.'

Agon gestures to the barman for another beer.

'What you need is patience,' says Bashkim. He shakes his head at the barman: no more alcohol for his *Kryetar*. 'Remember the proverb, brother. "Patience is the key to paradise".'

CHAPTER 10

Monday

Maria loves to run on the broad green mound of Hampstead Heath. Like many living in the surrounding boroughs of Camden and Barnet, nestled in ordered, comfortable streets and cul-de-sacs of semi-detached houses, she is inured to the view of London from Parliament Hill. Maria just runs with all the energy she can muster, every morning, in all weathers.

Except today. Her owner and master, Van Dimitriou, had a few too many at the office bash last night and is still suffering for it now, so Maria's run is mid-afternoon rather than first thing. Still, Darla from Creatives finally paid Van a little attention and he went home with the drunken promise of a dinner date next week. And they had won the soft drinks account, which would be huge. He trudges across the Heath and watches his four-year-old Labrador Retriever, Maria, hurl herself into the undergrowth at the boundary of Kenwood estate.

Van considers lighting up one of the cigarettes in his jacket pocket, left over from last night. He hadn't smoked in four years but, the thing of it was, Darla did. And he got so drunk, and she looked so good, that he slipped out to the Afghan convenience store two doors down from the bar and bought a pack, just so he could offer her one.

Maria is busy. The long, thin object has a ripe smell and she gives it a good going-over with her cold, wet nose before sinking her teeth into the tough, spongy flesh. She hauls at it but something appears to be holding it back and, not comprehending that the naked remains of Len Parkinson-Naughton are tangled in the thick shrubbery, she begins growling. When she hears the weary tones of her master, she turns to greet him.

Van Dimitriou takes a moment to comprehend the scene. It looks so fake, so rubbery, that he thinks it must be a joke. A scrawny, grey leg is protruding from a dense bush, a calf now once again clamped in Maria's jaws. He walks forward, in thrall to morbid curiosity. He stamps down the bushes. The day is fresh with a breeze battling valiantly against the reek around the body. He can see a torso now, colour like dirty alabaster, criss-crossed by nicks and gouges wrought by the shrubbery. As he works his way further up the body, past skin drawn so taut over the jutting ridges of the ribcage as to be almost translucent, he comes to the head. It's at an impossible angle, as if the body were turned back in on itself, and the ear has been shredded. Two bullet holes are drilled neatly into the side of the skull.

Maria looks expectantly at Van as he stumbles past her, heading back to the wide open space. Before he can get there, he empties the contents of his stomach in several sharp spasms.

#

Jackie cracks open a bottle of water and says, 'You might want to have another look at your intel.' He takes a swig while the tinny, clipped tones of Laurence Gilmore come through on the MI5 mobile wedged between his shoulder and ear.

Gilmore says, 'Surveillance shows he frequents suspect pubs on the Isle of Dogs, in Peckham and the Lily Bolero. He's been photographed shaking hands with major figures in several militant racist organisations here, in Yorkshire, and in Scotland.'

'I've been photographed shaking hands with Keith Richards. It doesn't make me a member of the Stones, does it?'

'Because he just met you, he's keeping his cards close to his chest.'

Jackie begins tracing a finger along the vast circulatory system of London on a map spread out on the bed in his sparse hotel room. His fingertip sweeps over the roads and streets of the City, then follows the sinuous blue thread of Regents Canal to Camden before coming to rest on Islington, where Bailey said he worked. He sketches a rough cross over the area with a red pen.

'I declared previous membership of Special Branch,' says Jackie. He tells Gilmore that he dropped the names Walters and McCandless for authenticity. 'And Gordon Orr.'

Jackie's finger slows as it traces the border of the boroughs of Camden and Islington. A tree-shaped patch of green lies on the northern extreme of the boundary: Highgate Cemetery. He feels a spidery scuttle of unease. His mother, a born-and-bred countrywoman from the hill country of north Down, would have seen the cemetery as a bad omen.

'Bailey doesn't come across as the white-is-right type. I can't see him at home with a fascist bible and a swastika hanging on the wall. He came across as too cynical for any of that.'

'As a trait, it seems to run in your countrymen.'

'You learn from experience, don't you?'

Jackie begins making small red circular marks on various locations on the map. Each represents a homeless shelter or hostel.

'And starting a fight, beating three men, hospitalising two of them?'

'I had to establish credibility.'

'That's about as cynical as it gets.'

'Are they pressing charges?'

'No. Two are on court bail pending further investigation into public order offences. The third doesn't want any further trouble: he works for a banking organisation in Canary Wharf.'

'There you go, I performed a public service.'

Jackie turns his attention to Soho on the map. There are no shelters: it seems theatreland prefers to ignore the harsh realities of London street-life. 'Did you have anyone on me today? I had a quick scout and couldn't see any surveillance.'

'As requested, you're on your own.'

'Aside from a couple of million cameras across the city,' says Jackie, and the phone I'm holding, he thinks. No doubt there's a constant trace on it.

Gilmore speaks to someone in the background, then his voice returns, louder and distorted. 'Parkinson-Naughton is dead,' he says. 'A dogwalker on Hampstead Heath thought he'd lost Fido in the trees. He found the dog gnawing on a scrawny, bare leg sticking out of a bush. Turns out it was Parkinson-Naughton, naked with a severed ear and a couple of bullet holes in the side of the head.'

Jackie looks at the sprawl of Hampstead Heath on the map and scratches another cross on the green space.

'Someone reported blood in a small alley in the City, near the Gherkin on Sunday morning. CCTV picked him up entering the alley with a woman. City Police were investigating, but Special Constabulary got on to the Met when word came through of the list. Seems Parkinson-Naughton worked near the site and went drinking in a wine bar opposite his office in Mitre Street.'

'Have you questioned the bar staff?'

'The barman who usually works the weekend is on holiday in Portugal. The cover staff said business was quite slow but he saw a tall, older man with a small, attractive woman Saturday night. It had to be him. CCTV footage from Duke's Place picked up three males loitering near the alleyway, St James's Passage, at 23.30. Fifteen minutes later they entered, then a female matching the bar staff's description of the girl fled from the passageway entrance in what appeared to be some distress. Shortly after, the three men emerged supporting another, fourth man, as though he was drunk. A second camera picked them up flagging down a taxi and departing the scene.'

Jackie lifts the water bottle from between his knees and takes a sip. 'Faces?'

'Covered with baseball caps and scarves.'

'Can you follow the movement of the taxi through cameras? Black cabs must have GPS systems, too.'

'The taxi was unlicensed and the reg on the vehicle isn't showing on records. It was a getaway car, to all intents and purposes. We're extending the sweep of the CCTV coverage but it takes a lot of men a long time to review the digital footage. We've tracked them as far as Holloway.'

Jackie takes a moment to find Holloway on the map. It nestles at the end of one of the strokes of the cross he drew over Islington. He traces his fingertip west across the mesh of streets, a short distance beyond Highgate Cemetery to Hampstead Heath. He lies back on the bed and stares at the clinical light fixture above. The hits on Dodds and Bannister had been very public, very brutal headline fodder. Almost a performance. Parkinson-Naughton's body had been dumped in a popular spot for runners, dogwalkers and tourists.

'What about the ear? Was he tortured?'

'It looks like it was taken off by a bullet, possibly a stray shot. Forensics is buggered. The crime scene in the City had been contaminated long before police turned up. It was hours before anyone reported the blood. The area where the body was discovered has had the dog and its owner blundering through. Not to mention the dog walker's lunch spewed all over it.'

These guys are professional, thinks Jackie. And nostalgic. A naked body in the undergrowth with a bullet in the head; a very public execution; a car-bomb. It's like a Provo Greatest Hits package.

'The shooters may not know that the list is blown. The girl

must know something: they'll be looking for her. I'd pursue that angle, if I were you. If you have any coverage of her face on CCTV, circulate it and have the Met try to locate her.'

He takes a pre-paid mobile, picked up on the way to the hotel, from a sports bag lying next to the map on the bed. 'I'm going to grab an hour or two's kip. Then I'll trawl the shelters and hostels, see if I can turn up anything on McLelland.'

He hangs up before Gilmore can reply. When he returns to the map, he notices the two crosses he sketched resemble makeshift grave markers, drenched in blood-red ink.

Gilmore looks at the mobile and tuts.

'Charming, isn't he?' Stuart Hartley collapses onto the sofa opposite in the room, the two armed Met officers brewing coffee.

'He's a liability. He put two men in hospital thanks to a brawl he started in the Lily Bolero, and he pissed off a Met SC&O 10 unit at Victoria. It's only a matter of time before he causes a real shitstorm.'

'Yes, he's quite the boy, is our Jackie,' says Hartley. He runs a fingertip along his skewed nose. Gilmore detects a note of admiration. 'Blunt but effective.'

Gilmore perches on the edge of the sofa. 'Why use him? We have teams. We can put every policeman in Central London on the lookout for McLelland as well as this girl; we have SO15 at our disposal.'

'All of which will cause ripples within all the wrong circles within hours, drawing attention to our involvement. Trust me, Jackie is the right card to play. I know. I've seen him in action.'

Gilmore sits back with a heavy slouch and looks to the high Regency ceiling. Hartley has rank, has some pull in Operations, and in the future Laurence Gilmore sees himself on embassy duty, or even one of the few who makes the trip across the river to join the glamour brigade, much reviled by colleagues, at

Vauxhall Cross. So he looks at the older man with the comical, bird-like face and says, 'Do tell.'

'Well, I have only given you the briefest of profiles on him,' says Hartley, straightening his jacket and leaning in closer, his voice dropping to a soft hum. Gilmore finds himself transfixed by the man's teeth, the upper front row of which appears to be attempting to escape the boundaries of the drawn, pale mouth. Hartley licks his liver-coloured lips and continues.

'Jackie had been undercover for RUC with the loyalists back in the nineties.' He fiddles with his watch, a Breitling. 'We also had an asset within the gang, an alcoholic idiot we turned. Special Branch didn't know, so Jackie didn't know.'

'We had an asset in play and didn't tell Special Branch?'

'Typical of the time. RUC and Military Intelligence got along like a house on fire, while we were rather suspected as being the Tarquins and Tristans who sat sipping G and T and moving men around like chess pieces on an operational map.'

'If we didn't inform them of another man in the cell they infiltrated, wasn't that kind of what we were doing?'

'Well,' says Hartley, a whistling stream of air exiting his flared nostrils, 'if you don't tell, I won't.' Bloody kids, he thinks. Probably thinks we should have drawn up a risk assessment before recruiting over there. 'Jackie was compromised and everything got terribly messy. You know the Celts when their blood's up. Our boy Jackie, being the pugnacious little scrapper he is, did some damage, got out and left Ulster.'

Gilmore edged further forward on the sofa. Bloody hell, he thinks. It must have been like the Wild West over there.

'Jackie went back to Ulster last year for his father's funeral,' says Hartley, warming to the tale, 'and two of his old associates contracted him, each to kill the other. They used his sister as leverage.'

'Jesus Christ. What a circus. And he did it?'

'Oh, let's just say he left a nice little trail of carnage.'

'And he's walking around the capital free as a bird, working for us.' Gilmore shakes his head, strokes his chin, fingers the nicotine patch on his arm. The yarn he's just heard deserves at least a couple of smokes and he's gasping for a coffee. At least Hartley isn't eating those bloody menthol sweets of his. As if on cue, Hartley produces a crumpled paper bag and offers him a cherry-red ball of mentholated sugar. Gilmore declines with a raised hand and swallows as the scent drifts across. As though reading his mind, Hartley says, 'I need these to unblock the nasal passages at times. Our Jackie broke my nose last year and my sinuses have played havoc ever since.'

No doubt Shaw would be thrilled if he knew, thinks Gilmore.

Hartley raises an eyebrow. 'Right now, we want him in play, to see where the cards fall and nothing more. If he finds McLelland, that's a bonus.'

'You think he'll find him. Maybe this hit team?'

'I wouldn't put it past him,' says Hartley. 'And if he doesn't, I bloody well hope he dies trying.'

Monday

The rain starts around seven o'clock. It greases the forecourt of the Chelsea and Westminster Hospital, sending blue flames of light skating across the asphalt as ambulances drop the battered and broken off at the Accident and Emergency Department. Inside, in the Burns Unit, the children of Kenneth and Arlene Bannister, Glen and Ceri, sit in an empty room, eyes raw as they wait for news of their mother. A fretting grandmother sits next to them, muttering in prayer and worrying over her husband, Brian. His heart medication has eased the stabbing pain in his chest. When told of the bombing, his legs had caved like folding tent poles. A ten-year-old single malt eased his troubled mind into a fitful sleep. Arlene is their only child.

#

The patch of earth and leaves where Len Parkinson-Naughton's body had lain is still dry under the forensic tent that will remain on Hampstead Heath for the night; a couple of police officers shift from foot to foot as their uniforms become clogged with the drizzle. Nine hundred miles away, in a small café in Barcelona, Patricia Parkinson-Naughton sips a strong *vi negre* and enjoys the attention paid her by the young waiter as she takes in the warm spring evening. She is unaware that her ex-husband is dead, and would drink a bottle of *cava* if she knew in way of celebration.

#

Van Dimitriou sits hunched in his bedsit, slowly running his fingers through Maria's thick coat and staring at the crack in the mantelpiece before him. He had never seen a dead body before. He had never spoken to a police officer. He has no interest in seeing Darla from Creatives now. He just wants to sleep, but the splayed white body, tangled in the bushes, will not leave him.

#

The orange brick of the Westminster Public Mortuary gleams in the soft glow of the streetlights. Ruth Dodds' body lies prone on a gurney, a coroner's officer finishing off a prawn sandwich at the desk nearby as he waits to begin a post-mortem. The Met has insisted on the coroner herself conducting the procedure. She's been held up by a body in a suite of the Dorchester. Money trumps all other considerations in London, even in death.

#

Christopher Martins's breath comes in shallow sighs, marking time with the soft beep of the heart monitor. His mother, Mary, sits next to the bed in the private intensive care unit room, willing her little boy's eyes to open in recognition. She kneads a small teddy bear in her hands, worn smooth by a child's love, and concentrates on happy memories with her son, crowding out the snapshots of terrible violence on the bridge at Kew. Her husband sits next to her, his hand on her back, drawing strength from his wife. He looks at his son, so fragile, seemingly fading in front of his eyes, and bows his head. He isn't a religious man, but Carl prays that he might take his son to another football match, watch another superhero film with him, counsel him on future girlfriends and take him to the pub for his first beer. He prays that the three of them might share more meals together, travel together, bicker and laugh together.

The ward is quiet, the nurses, for the moment, busy with other duties.

Christopher's breathing continues in time with the monitor and the insistent patter of the rain at the window, like impatient fingers drumming on the glass.

#

Three-hundred miles north, in the Newburn district of Newcastle upon Tyne, Fred Dodds wipes the grit from his eyes and finishes off a strong coffee as he gazes at the clouded night sky. His wife, Janice, has busied herself with packing and booking their hotel accommodation in London. Fred and Janice really lost Ruth a few years back. The woman who had visited twice a year, full of talk of promotion and management, a new sports car and business trips to America, was a very different person to the little girl who'd brightened their lives in early middle age.

Fred looks to the sky again and wishes it would rain as he feels the first hot, salty tears burn his cheeks.

#

In Soho, the rain discourages tourists from trawling the streets, leaving only the determinedly horny to stroll the grimy maze east of Regent Street. The drizzle has begun to soak Beatrix's hair, causing it to cling around her delicate features like a jet-black landslide. She crouches in a deep trench at the foot of a Victorian townhouse. The broken metal slats above, level with the grimy pavement, give little protection from the rain but some refuge from prying eyes walking on Lexington Street. She hugs her skinny body tight. Bashkim is right and she hates him for it. He said that he owned her, that she was an animal now and she would be treated as such. If she were bad, she would be punished.

And here she is back in Soho, a couple of streets from the strip club. She despises herself for her dependency, the fear of the unknown and the temptation to go back to the familiarity of the *Fis* that has brought her here. She hides in this filthy pit, yet she will not leave. Fear and anger and sheer bloody-minded defiance stop her giving up hope and stumbling through the door of the club into the huge, brutal arms of Bashkim. Instead, Beatrix will hide in this trench until morning. Tomorrow she will walk the streets again, back to the tidy little mews with the hope of seeing Flori, warning her and getting word to her parents.

Her parents. She has hardly thought of them, and a new wave of fear sweeps over her.

She shuffles sideways on the freezing stone as a thick wad of spit lands next to her and she hears a phlegmy cough wrack the air above.

#

Rain is nothing to Conal Harris.

Morgan has taken Kensington, sitting on the sister's home while Harris wanders the streets, hunting the girl. The patronising bastard thinks the wee bitch will turn to the sister or, like a masochist, to her pimps. The kid, Macrossan, is working a circuit from the Oxford Street end of Soho. In ten minutes they'll meet up and decide on whether to keep trawling or not.

Harris is edgy. Psychology isn't his strong point, a bonus when your one, true skill is violence: the ultimate expression of action. So he doesn't know why a man would slink through this snarl of offices, overpriced artisan shops and sex emporiums on a miserable Monday night, just to pay a small fortune to look at a pair of tits and knock one out. Not that he's a prude. Nothing soothes the nerves like a woman after watching some fucker's head explode, but he likes it simple and direct. He's seen wretched forms tonight, tottering through the rain-slicked dusk in stiletto heels, bodies scrawny and tough, like mean joints of meat. He almost hopes that he won't see the girl: he doesn't want to have to lay hands on her in case she has some disease. The men are worse. Fucking queers.

Harris fingers the hammer of the Beretta 92 FS, snug in a hip holster under his jacket. He's glad he gave the kid the revolver. He didn't fancy lugging the sturdy hunk of metal around the streets. The polymer frame of the Beretta is less effort. He's sliced the lining from the jacket pocket so he can access the grip through the material. He stops on the corner of Brewer and Lexington Streets. He slouches his way down the latter, hawking up a gob and spitting into a dark basement trench in front of a building.

#

The rain is just the latest misery for Padraig Macrossan, who wanders the blur of darkened windows and security doors of Poland Street at night. A fleet of black cars passed a while ago but now the street spreads silent and abandoned, the money locked up for the night behind thick, reinforced doors and trellised, barred windows.

Padraig hopes that the girl doesn't appear. He's had enough blood, death and misery in the last few days and she couldn't identify them clearly anyway. They've been careful, professional. The heavy revolver, its weight drilling a dull ache into his shoulder in its underarm rig, frightens him but twenty-four hours without someone being shot, maimed or butchered will give him some time to psych himself up for the next round of mayhem. How had people lived, he thought, through this shite, every day, week after week, year after year, in the north of Ireland?

Jackie huddles in the entrance of Wardour Street and studies his map. He'd begun with the shelters and hostels around the Lily Bolero. The file photo of Samuel McLelland was a few years old but all he had. He passed it around men and women, young and old, some reeking of drink, some of the street. Some were embarrassed, with stories of separation, redundancy, trauma; some bitter and simmering with anger; all raw and human.

No one recognised McLelland.

He walked the bank of the Thames, dropping to his haunches to disturb bundles of sleeping bags and ragged blankets. A pretty girl thought she knew the man in the photo. He enlarged it on the screen of the mobile, but the girl's face lost its moment of light and returned to a dark stare. No, she realised. The man resembled a teacher in her school, someone from a different life, just three short years, yet a lifetime, ago.

In front of the Tower, under London Bridge, on the Hanseatic Walk, no one recognised McLelland.

Frustrated, he decided to trawl the Soho streets and took the tube at Mansion House station. Jackie emerged from the steep stone steps at Piccadilly Circus to the pulsing light show of the West End and turned his back on Regent Street. He walked up Shaftesbury Avenue to Wardour Street.

Now he takes in a small patch of concrete and grass seeded with flowers, St Anne's Churchyard Gardens. A high fence, jutting out over the pavement at an angle at its rim, protects the grounds at night. It reminds him of the blast walls surrounding RUC stations back in Belfast. A couple are huddled opposite the locked gates. Jackie crouches next to the bundle of blankets and rags, takes out the mobile with the photo and begins searching for McLelland again.

CHAPTER 12

Monday

Beatrix can take the dull ache of the cold. She can take the hunger. But the rats disturb her. They came a short time ago, moving like soft, glistening globs of dark flesh. Vermin have always been feared in Albania, carriers of disease and symbols of corruption and decay.

She shifts her weight, trying to compress her body into a tight knot, hard against the filthy brick. But they move closer, their snouts stabbing at the air as they sniff her scent, scuttling close to the brick. Her fear has grown, seems to tower over her, and the rats burrow deep into its centre. Reason crumbles and she stands. The metal stairs out of the exterior basement lie beyond the small, slithering forms. As she picks her way through, she is thankful for the height her heels give her from the dank stone, despite the biting pain as they gouge her ankles. One of the heels is at an angle, partly split from the sole.

The street is a long canyon of steel shutters, wrought-iron railings and plate glass, barred windows: so many iron bars, like an industrial prison yard. Beatrix takes her shoes off to kill their insistent click and walks barefoot at a distance, sticking to the pockets of shadow as best she can, not knowing where she is going.

#

'The Function. Somewhere in Maida Vale, that's what he said.'

Jackie struggles to keep the underside of the map dry and balanced on his knee as he scribbles the name. His hand is frantic.

Hours of walking, sitting in shelters at long, battered tables, or crouching in doorways, has led to this. A man who looks in his seventies and is probably twenty years younger has recognised McLelland from the file photo.

'And you're sure it was the Function?'

'I'm not sure of much these days, son.' Eyes so red they seem to be bleeding. A face that has the look of modelling clay set-to with a Stanley knife. But a voice that is steady and clear.

'I didn't know this fella, Mac what?'

'McLelland. Samuel McLelland.'

'This fella McLelland very well. There was a shelter at Centre-point I saw him in a few times and we'd pass the time together once in a while.'

The eyes turn to Jackie, the sagging skin below too tired to bother moving with them.

'People turn up some stuff on the streets, you know? One girl found a laptop somewhere about Bloomsbury. Useless. Needed a password to get into the bloody thing. Good for a couple of quid from the right buyer, though. McLelland, he had a mobile phone. Didn't look all that banged up, either. Anyway, that's why I remember him. I worked the ferries from Liverpool to your neck of the woods years back and the Irish accent always sticks out to me.'

Jackie says, 'Aye, it can be hard to miss.'

A smile reveals a couple of teeth the colour of rotten apple flesh.

'Yours isn't so strong. Anyway, I picked his voice out, this McLelland fella. He was on that phone, his head lowered, but he was on about Maida Vale and the Function.' The eyes lower again. 'Maida Vale. Might as well be Monaco if you're on the streets around here.'

Jackie thanks the man, pressing a few notes into the claw of a hand and turns onto a street laden with small restaurants, warm lighting glowing and flickering through Dickens-like windows and artisan cafés. It's nearing ten. He'll canvas the area for another hour or so, return to the City, and aim to be in his hotel bed at around one.

Another turn brings him to Brewer Street and the small passageway of Walker's Court on his right. He glances up at Maurice House, the dingy concrete box acting as a footbridge between the two sides of the meagre strip of sex-shops and strip-clubs. It's a sad and squalid passageway, little more than an entry, in comparison with the 'entertainment' districts of some of the great cities in Asia to which he's been. A couple of lost-looking souls are doing their rounds in the hope of midweek business but street prostitution is no more than a token effort in Soho now. Nevertheless, one punter shifts uneasily as he passes Jackie, eyes trained on the pavement. He glimpses a hard-looking man, hair cropped short with a tended beard and a solid-looking build beneath a dark-coloured canvas jacket. The man looks angry, uneasy.

He doesn't fit.

#

Padraig is nearing Golden Square when the mobile shudders to life in his pocket. The screen burns a fierce, incandescent white as he reads the text:

Walker's Court. Now. Possible back-up. Avoid Brewer Street. CH.

Harris.

He passes a row of sceptres in the garden in the centre of the square, and a scurry of disquiet forces him to shrug his shoulders. An art installation: various disembodied body parts are arrayed on plinths in front of the stately form of George II: a twisted torso; a foot and shin planted firmly in isolation; and a great, severed head, a small hole drilled through between gaping, vapid eyes, like a bullet wound on a small boy's flawless forehead, on a bridge in Kew.

#

The man, awkward and embarrassed, turns into Walker's Court. Jackie recognises the angular, tight stance, hands straining deep in pockets. He knows the brutal features and callous stare, snapped to the right, of a man who has seen too much. He's seen it on the streets of Belfast, from a hood beating protection money from a struggling small-business owner; in the dive bars of Kowloon; he's seen it in the hardcore drinking clubs. He's seen it, at times, in the mirror.

Jackie crosses Brewer Street, passes a Thai Massage parlour and opens the door of a corner pub with a cracked wooden sign displaying an austere-looking general in a scarlet tunic hanging above the entrance. Inside, the warmth enfolds him. He makes his way through the cluster of drinkers at the bar, orders tonic water and takes in the punters, a scattering of men chatting or slouching over drinks and mobile phones. He takes out his mobile, ready to ask some if they recognise McLelland. The pub is smaller than it looks from outside, decorative plasterwork on the ceiling, fairy lights draped across the optics and tables and chairs along the wall opposite the counter. The decor is puritanical compared to the Lily Bolero. As he mingles with the punters, Jackie keeps an eye on the windows, large and wrapped around the outer wall of the pub, just as it bends to accommodate the corner of Brewer and Wardour Streets, with a view of the neon-edged crack of Walker's Court beyond.

Padraig enters Walker's Court from Peter Street and finds Harris smoking against the metal-plated wall a little before the footbridge of the Maurice House building.

105

'Took your fucking time. I thought you knew this shit-hole.'

'You told me to avoid Brewer, so I had to come around.'

'There's a fella,' says Harris, 'looks a bit dodgy. I can't put my finger on it, but he just looks wrong.'

'What, like his expression?'

'Just his look. He passed me, rangy-looking but fit. Close-cropped hair, maybe black although it's hard to tell in this dark. Black jeans, boots and a mid-thigh length coat, looks dark blue. But his eyes: he looked like he was taking everything in around him, like.'

'Maybe he's a tourist.'

Harris shakes his head, a jagged, savage movement. 'I don't think so. I had a look round the corner and he's gone into that pub.'

'It's a gay pub. Maybe he looked shifty because he's embarrassed. You know, hasn't come out yet.'

'Fuck off. He's no more an arse-bandit than I am a priest.' Harris stabs the hardened muzzle of his index finger in Padraig's chest. 'Get yourself in there and keep an eye on him.'

'Why can't you go?'

But Padraig knows the answer. The man has already seen Harris and the Belfast accent might draw attention, even now. And, plain as the price on the peep-show door opposite, Harris is scared.

#

The door sits squat in a Victorian facade brushed with the grime of over a century of city dirt and sin. Beatrix finds that she can't, no matter how she might will her body to obey, move.

She stands in front of a collector's magazine shop, sixty yards at a diagonal across from the Gentleman's Sporting Club, her shoes in her hand, the split heel now hanging at an angle from the sole, her feet filthy and numb with cold. Her hair is like a clump of knotted black hemp, her skirt and jacket soiled. She is a mess but the men on guard at the entrance to the club, low-ranking *banditë* she's seen drinking inside from time to time, have not noticed her, even though she is within clear sight of Bashkim's club and whorehouse and the bouncers in front. A neon glow lights their faces when they turn to chat and she sees the shaved heads and powerful, hulking shoulders under the leather jackets as they take drags on their cigarettes.

She cannot move.

#

Jackie received a few negative responses as he showed the photo of McLelland around the drinkers. Most helpful was the barman, Jeff, who agreed to him circulating the picture and promised to keep an eye out in the future. He assured Jackie that he'd check with the other two bartenders, off duty tonight, in the next day or two and took his number. When the young lad pushes the door of the bar open and makes his way, all gangly arms and jutting knees, to the counter, Jeff greets him warmly and, after a short chat, points Jackie out.

Jackie notes the tension in the boy's frame and, lulled by the chatter and warmth in the bar, becomes alert again. He watches the kid, around nineteen or twenty at a guess, share a joke with the bartender. Angular face, straining cheekbones, deep-set eyes lost in pools of shadow in the soft lighting of the pub.

The boy's left shoulder slouches, and the parka he wears is zipped to the neck, despite the heat indoors. As though he were concealing something weighty, as though he were guilty. Then again, perhaps Jackie's imagination is running wild. Jackie pockets the mobile and pushes past a punter in a pinstripe-suited Quentin Crisp ensemble on his way to the bar.

It's a couple of months since Padraig has been in the Duke and chatted with Jeff. He's pleased to see a familiar face as he scans the punters.

Jeff says, 'Paddy, didn't expect to see you on a Monday night. What's the occasion?'

'Just lost my mate somewhere about Shaftesbury Avenue. Came into Chinatown for a meal, somebody's birthday, and he wandered off drunk. I'm trying to phone him on his mobile but there's no answer so I popped in to see if he'd stopped here for a pint. It's Eric. You know, Asian guy with a piercing on his top lip.'

'Haven't seen him in tonight. Funny, there's another guy looking for a friend in the bar. Over there.'

Jeff nods to where a man in a coat and black jeans, his dark hair cropped close to his skull, makes his way to the bar.

Shit, he thinks. The guy. Harris's guy.

Padraig straightens his posture. He's been slouching, still imagining he's wearing the gun. His hand goes to the spot under his left arm where the shoulder-holster and Ruger Security Service revolver was nestled minutes before, now bunched under Harris's coat. He'd been pissed off at the Irishman for disarming him but, as the man in the jacket approaches, a hard stare boring through a crooked smile, he's relieved. Harris's suspicion that he'd panic and someone, the wrong person, might get killed, had seemed like a jibe. Now, he realises, it was a statement of fact.

When the man introduces himself with a pat on Padraig's shoulder he realises Jeff is standing grinning behind him.

'Paddy, this is...sorry, mate...'

'Jackie. Good Irish name, that, Paddy.'

The accent is a Belfast drawl salted with a little clipped

English and rounded in the mid-Atlantic. Padraig stiffens. He wills his body to relax while forcing the corners of his mouth into a smile.

'Yeah, on my dad's side. Jeff mentioned you were looking for someone; maybe I can help.'

Jackie produces the mobile and Padraig squints at a cropped photograph of a man, a headshot. He sees a fleshy face with a thick, chestnut-brown moustache draped over a compact-looking mouth and neutral eyes gazing directly at the camera. He glimpses the peak of a baseball cap at the top of the screen. It's a familiar face, washed-out in the grainy photo: Samuel McLelland.

'Sorry,' he says, shaking his head. 'I don't recognise him.'

'No bother. He's just fallen on hard times and I want to help him out, you know?'

Jeff says, 'Paddy has a big heart, Jackie.' The barman winks as he moves off to serve a punter further down the counter and mutters, 'It's not his largest asset, mind.'

Padraig rolls his eyes and leans back against the bar, easing his shoulders down as his elbows rest on the counter and his feet balance on the brass rail running a few inches above the floor. It makes him taller than the man and, he knows, he looks uncomfortable, awkward. The man's smile manages to stay a while longer, but Padraig can see that he's losing interest in him.

'Well…' says the man, Jackie. He leaves the word hanging in the air for a moment as his eyes park their gaze on his for another couple of beats and Padraig thinks for a moment that he will actually hit on him. Then the man says, 'Thanks for looking at the photo, Paddy. Maybe I'll see you around.' And with that, he leans over the counter to thank Jeff for his help, nods at Padraig, and walks out into the Soho night.

\#

The kid seemed clean: the pat on the shoulder told him that. Despite the slouch, there was no shoulder rig, no weapon that he could discern. It was automatic, a copper's reflex: Jackie had checked the cut of the coat and could see no tell-tale signs. No uneven distribution of weight, hitching or bulging around the hips or waist, and the kid's discomfort was probably embarrassment, like the tough-looking man he'd passed on the street.

Perhaps he's the one with the guilty conscience, slinking around the greasy streets among the tired sleaze.

He's so lost in the problems of the present that he almost barges into the girl. He has strayed across the street, oblivious to his surroundings. The girl is standing a little to the left of a shaft of light from the streetlight above, as though clinging to shadow, and she starts as he mutters in surprise at seeing her. She's small and delicate, and he has the urge to put an arm around her and shepherd her into the light: she looks cold and lost. Her clothes are a father's worst nightmare, a tight mini-skirt and low-cut blouse revealing the faint trace of her small breasts. One hand cradles a pair of painful-looking stilettos, one heel jutting at an angle like the splintered bark of a tree. On this street, at this time, the obvious conclusion is that she's working.

He begins fishing in his pocket for the mobile, ready to show her the picture of McLelland and says, 'Sorry, didn't mean to startle you. I've lost my fr– '

She screams. A throaty bawl that seems to make her very frame vibrate. Then she bolts. Dumbfounded for a second, he watches her sprint past him. Then he runs after her, catching her in a few quick steps, his longer stride out-pacing her speed.

#

It was the accent that made her scream. Beatrix remembered another voice, more harsh and brittle but with that same singsong lilt and rounded 'r', just before the old man had been shot. She has not even seen this man's face, this man who almost walked into her, so sudden and instinctive was her reaction. She just screamed and ran.

The grip on her arm is strong and she is whirled around to face a man with short cropped hair and a concerned expression. A strong set of features: eyes the colour of freshly ground coffee and a nose off-kilter a fraction. A troubled face, deep-set lines notched between the eyebrows and the stretched mouth set in a dark grimace. A hard face but not cruel.

The man says, 'I'm sorry, I'm sorry.'

He is panicked, shocked by her reaction. She can't speak, tries to wrench her arm away. But his grip remains firm.

'I didn't mean to frighten you. Please, calm down. Please.'

He is almost pleading. She looks at his hand, then up to his face again. She realises that this is the first man she has met in many, many months without a trace of cruelty, indifference or hunger in his dark, searching gaze.

#

Harris isn't convinced by the kid.

'I used to go on weekends sometimes with mates, girls as well as fellas.' The boy's voice is a thin whisper. 'People come into Soho at weekends all the time.'

'To a fucking gay bar? Catch yourself on, son.' Harris presents the revolver and shoulder rig, his voice a hoarse growl, taking pains not to touch Macrossan. 'I've never worked with a Brit before and now it turns out you might be a fucking ring-raider.'

But he isn't angry at the boy. A Belfast accent, the kid had said. A man with a Belfast accent, and a picture of Samuel McLelland: a Belfast man is across the street, a photo of a target on his phone, asking questions like a fucking peeler. He looks at Padraig Macrossan, fiddling with the revolver and shoulder-holster, and snaps at the boy, 'Stop fucking about with the rig. Hurry the fuck up or we'll lose him.'

He steps out from behind the dirty bookshop on the corner of the alley to see the man's back disappearing into the gloom about a hundred yards away. He's counted less than four cars driving down Brewer Street in the last five minutes. The street is silent and forlorn, nestled in the middle of eight and a half million people. Harris can make out the entrance of the Albanian club a little further on, on the left. Psychos. Let Morgan deal with them. The arrogant bastard deserves them. He walks, texting Morgan, telling him to ditch surveillance on the sister's gaff and get the car over to Soho.

The kid has managed to sling the rig under his coat and Harris leans over to gee the wee shite up and give him a verbal slap when he hears a scream. Short, sharp. He draws the Beretta as he sees the man from the pub turn to pursue a small figure sprinting past him. From this distance, the first figure could almost be a boy, but Harris can see the skirt, the short jacket. He can see that it's a girl. And he can see, despite the lowering dark, that it's *the* girl.

#

'Please, please.'

Jackie keeps repeating the word, like a mantra, as he holds the girl's arm. He doesn't know why, but it seems crucial that he make things right with this girl who looks so grubby and damaged. She's looking at his hand, wild-eyed. He opens his mouth to reason with her. To take control of the situation.

But he hears, 'Don't fucking move or I'll put a bullet through the two of youse.'

The girl's eyes flicker to the space behind his left ear and her mouth begins to yawn wide, another shriek building in her slender throat.

The same voice says, 'Shut up. Shut the fuck up or you're dead, you hear me bitch?'

Her eyes lower in an instant, as if the lids are spring-loaded.

Jackie keeps his gaze fixed on her face. She seems to withdraw to another place, her features as vague as a Greek sculpture. He turns and faces two men, the young kid from the pub and the hard-bitten man he passed some ten or fifteen minutes ago. The kid looks terrified, his eyes black pebbles shining under the raised, sharp canopy of his brow. He clutches something inside his jacket, looking frantic and wired. The other is a professional, easing his right hand out of his jacket pocket to reveal a shaft of dull black plastic, and Jackie knows he's glimpsing the grip of a semi-automatic. A Mercedes glides past, a glinting red bullet, before the man nods towards a dark alleyway sandwiched between a tobacconists and a wine merchant, strapped with scaffolding.

'D'you want to take a fucking picture, big lad? Move.'

The accent is west Belfast, and Jackie works to keep tension from slowing his reactions. He fights a rising anger, too, an exasperation that he behaved like a raw young copper, had failed to see the signs, interpret body language, go with his hunch. And now he has two men behind him, at least one of them armed, as he steps into the side alley. He is still gripping the girl's arm. She is docile, allowing him to lead her, the stilettos hanging limp in her right hand, her feet padding on the slick, cold concrete.

The alley is wide enough to accommodate a couple of lorries backing in and out and has a bricked-up delivery bay halfway down on the right side. It's about a hundred yards long, ending in a brick wall painted white, a flotsam of other, taller buildings tumbling behind. A few paces from the end of the alleyway the west Belfast man says, 'Stop. Turn round.'

Jackie turns, slow and deliberate, his hands hanging at his

sides. The girl follows suit. The young Englishman is a little in front of her and to her left. The hardcase, his expression as dead as the blistered wood of the boarded window behind him, stands a few feet in front of Jackie. He raises his chin, his stare boring into Jackie's face like a 9 mm hollow-point, shakes his head and pulls the Beretta.

CHAPTER 13

Monday

He can smell the tint of oil on the air and the thin veil of rain tickles his face. Jackie runs his hand over his hair, a soaking carpet cleaved tight to his skull.

'Don't move,' says the west Belfast man. He turns his head towards the young Englishman but keeps his eyes on Jackie. 'You, get your gun out of your arse and cover them.'

The kid fumbles for a moment and pulls the revolver. It's brutal and ugly in the delicate hands. The boy looks scared of its power. The hardcase orders the young Englishman, Padraig, to search the girl and the kid looks at him, dumbfounded for a moment. Jackie isn't surprised; there isn't much to search.

'Don't stand there with your face tripping you, pat the wee girl down, you twat.'

The kid bounds forward and runs his hands over the girl who stands motionless, her face cloaked by the curtain of her hair. The boy, Padraig, handles her as though she were contagious, his face and body arched back from her and his touch rough in his panic. He snatches the stilettos from her and throws them next to a large rubbish bin across the alley.

The hardcase says, 'What's your name?'

'Jackie.'

A punch, fast and sharp, snaps Jackie's head back and he curses. The bastard has hit him full on the nose, blurring his vision.

The west Belfast man says, 'Search him.'

The younger man shoves Jackie's arms in the air and pats him down, the gun awkward in his grip. Jackie blinks hard, trying to clear his vision. The punch wasn't hard but it was well placed and he can't risk wiping his eyes and being belted again. The kid takes Jackie's wallet from his inside pocket, the mobile phone from his left jacket pocket. By the time the Englishman says that Jackie is unarmed, both gunmen are in their original positions and the hardcase is studying a small pink card.

'Jackie Shaw,' the man says, then slips the driving licence in his jeans pocket. 'Well, Jackie Shaw, what are you doing wandering Soho and bothering this young lady for on a Monday night?'

'She looked to be in trouble.'

'Not as much trouble as she's in now. Or you.' The man sends another punch, left-handed, driving his knuckle into Jackie's right cheek. 'Why are you showing photographs of Samuel McLelland round the place on your mobile?'

'He's an old friend,' says Jackie. 'I'm trying to look him up.'

'It's a bit late for that now,' says the hardcase. The man runs his hand over his pinched face. 'Now, who are you, Jackie Shaw? And why are you showing this photo around Soho?'

There is silence for a few seconds. The girl is still studying the concrete at her bare feet, her arms limp by her sides, but Jackie can see her small hands are balled into fists below the cuffs of her jacket. The younger man is holding the revolver with both hands at arm's length, as though it's a bomb about to detonate, and risking the odd glance behind to the mouth of the alleyway. And the Belfast man is searching Jackie's face. Even in the shadows of the alley he can see the man's eyes, like black craters, studying him. This man with a gun in his hand and a voice from home does not know who Jackie Shaw is. The word *Katana*, on the list, is not a reference to him. Fucking MI5, thinks Jackie. I could be home with a cup of tea and the Monday-night football on telly and these jokers wouldn't give a monkey's. Instead, he's been dropped in it, and he's fucked if he knows how to climb back out. He knew that fucking cemetery on the map was a bad omen.

'Face the wall.'

As Jackie turns, the kid grabs the girl and hurls her around to face the brick. She stands, like Jackie, a couple of inches from the wall, her body facing the chipped, damp surface, her head still lowered. She looks like a guilty child, told to stand and face the corner. The English boy stands a couple of inches to her right, the gun now lowered, muzzle pointed at the spattered stalks of her calves. The Belfast man orders them to place their hands on the wall. Jackie complies, sees the intricate patterns of the brick, its ridges and furrows. He hears a car slew past the entrance to the alley, oblivious to the drama playing out just a few yards away, and the cry of a siren somewhere. He can smell the musty scent of the dust, still thick and dry, on the sheltered windowsill to his left and spies an empty beer bottle nestled next to the edge. Too far to reach before the trigger is squeezed on the Beretta and he feels the nip of a round pierce his back.

The boy says, 'Shouldn't we move?'

'The car'll be here soon,' says the hardcase. 'Just calm down, young 'un.'

Then another voice, farther off and with the thick slur of an accent, shouts a foreign word Jackie doesn't understand that sounds like, '*La bide*,' and another, '*Tour ve.*'

The girl yelps. All three men turn to her as her arm moves with speed, slicing up and out, the sleeve of her jacket drawn tight against her wrist to reveal the stiletto heel of her broken shoe. It drives hard and fast into Macrossan's face, his head jerking back to ride with the blow. He steps back a pace and the revolver clatters at his feet. The girl's momentum carries her into the kid and they both tangle in a mad dance before they fall hard.

Someone hits the slow motion button for Jackie and he and

the hardcase stare for a moment that seems to last a minute or more.

It's broken with a shout of, 'Fuck!' from the hardcase and a hissed, 'Shite!' from Jackie. The girl and the younger man are splayed on the wet concrete, the girl struggling to stand, feet scrabbling on the ground like a cartoon character, while Jackie lashes out, his right hand catching the hardcase on the thigh. He moves, adrenaline surging, launching himself at the revolver on the ground, waiting for the flat crack of the Beretta and a hot pain in his back. As he stumbles, landing on one knee and grasping at the Ruger, he hears another curse, west Belfast invective ripping through the damp shadows. He thinks the hardcase forgot to take the Beretta's safety off. He hears the click, sharp as a slap, as he takes the weight of the Ruger in his hand and barrels into the girl, shunting her forward in a stumbling run.

The kid, Padraig, is still shrieking; the hardcase is silent, and Jackie knows a shot will follow any second. There are other, foreign voices, too, from further up the alley towards Brewer Street. As he breaks into a stooping run, grabbing hold of the girl by her collar and hurling her across the alley, three sharp cracks explode behind him and he hears the snap of a bullet punching through glass. In a few strides he's behind two industrial rubbish bins and the girl is huddled next to him, breathing hard. The Security-Six .38 has the heft of a full cylinder in his hand and he praises whoever might be up there in the heavens, smiling down on him. The revolver is the same as the model he carried in uniform, back in the day. No safety, wood grip, and a big, fat red insert on the front of the barrel to line up in the back sights. It's a beast of a handgun.

Three more rounds slice the air and the metal of the bin gives a muffled grunt, iron absorbing the bullet; the other two hit the wall above them, coughing up dust and fragments of brick. The hardcase is firing wild but Jackie knows they have to get moving again, can't allow the gunman to suppress them with further fire. He hears more shouts from the mouth of the alley and realises he's holding his breath. Cursing, he forces his body under control and kneels on one knee, peering around the bin. Breathing steady, keeping his body over his toes to control recoil, he sees the hardcase crouched next to a rusting office cabinet and the kid, Padraig, kneeling next to him. They're less than twenty feet away. Jackie squeezes the trigger and the white noise of the adrenaline coursing through his system is shattered by the roar of the revolver, the .38 bucking twice in his grip, muzzle flash spitting fire in the murk of the alley. The boy makes no sound but his body lurches, two .9mm rounds punching him centre mass, and slumps against the wall.

The shouts from the mouth of the alleyway are silenced as he wrenches the girl up and hauls her across the alley, making ground towards the entrance and crossing to the same side as the hardcase. Now there is no sound but the shuffling of the armed man a few feet away. They drop behind a stack of vegetable boxes, no cover at all, and Jackie pulls the girl upright, taking her gaze from the mouth of the alley. He glances behind them at the entrance to Brewer Street and sees a man sprinting off to the left in the direction where he bumped into the girl. Another man is standing in shadow close to the wall holding something, his body no more than an inky smudge against the glow of the streetlights.

As Jackie begins to run, he hears the scrape of shoes, knows that the hardcase has also set off. Jackie again flings the girl in front of him, freeing both his hands to grip the Ruger. As he scuttles at another diagonal across the alley, moving precious yards closer to Brewer Street, he fires once. The bullet is wild but, he hopes, distracts his opponent. It seems to work. The hardcase fires three shots in a heartbeat, then another as he follows them. The girl lands hard against the angle of a power-box on the same side and yelps, arching her back as Jackie falls awkwardly against the wall in front of her. He glimpses the hardcase slam into the wall on the same side fifteen yards behind. Jackie and the girl are both panting hard. Her eyes are locked on the entrance to the alley, now just twenty feet away, and the man who still stands there in shadow. There are three shots left before the Ruger becomes a useless ornament; the Beretta, he thinks, has five.

Shouts go up from windows nearby, and Jackie hears a scream coming from the street beyond. He tries to map where they should run once they reach Brewer Street, tries to calculate the fastest route out of Soho.

The girl inhales sharply. There is a wild panic in her and Jackie takes her shoulder in his grip, kneading the flesh there. He lifts her head and looks into her eyes. They focus on his and he says, a whisper, 'It's okay.' And he means it.

The man at the mouth of the alley is gesturing in the murk, waving for more men to come. The hardcase is waiting, snug in his cover, for Jackie and the girl to move. Her arms and legs have a skin of dirt, her face is haggard. The clothes are, like her limbs, filthy. He runs his hand across the brick behind her head, then smears the dirt across her face, darkening her alabaster skin more, then gives himself a coating.

'Listen to me,' he says. 'I want you to run. Run like this.' His hand strikes a diagonal slash through the air between them. He must get her to move fast. He doesn't want to give the hardcase time to reload, or reinforcements to arrive. 'Then, like this,' he says, 'into the centre of the alleyway.' His fingers point to the mouth of the alley, equidistant between the two walls and the shadow on the right. Then he raises the gun to point at the shadow.

He says again, 'It's okay.'

She doesn't like it, but she's smart and knows they can't stay where they are. Also, he thinks, she has seen and suffered enough to not care, just a little, if she lives. He resolves to ensure she does. He lays his hand across her waist for a moment, like starter tape, finds his breathing again, then nods and takes his arm away. And then she's gone, sprinting across the concrete, the filth on her limbs and face a ragamuffin camouflage. He gives her a second, then steps out to see three more flashes and hear the dull, wracking cough of the Beretta, and squeezes off two shots. They're good, the big red insert steady between the back sights, his centre of gravity sure, his breathing strong. The roar of the revolver is a lion's answer to the sharp bark of the semi-automatic, the muzzle flash making a negative of the alleyway in front of him. Then he turns and runs to the opposite wall, the girl sprinting for the centre of the open end of the alley and Brewer Street. As Jackie's shoulder hits the brick, the man at the entrance to the alley steps out of the shadows to grab the girl. Jackie uses the wall to steady himself and aims once more. The Ruger spits fire and the figure reels back, as though belted on the chest.

As Jackie takes off, following the girl, two more rounds hit an air-conditioner to his right, a foot away, and he knows the hard-case isn't hit. Jackie made the rookie error: aiming for the muzzle flash and not the body behind it. He knows he has missed but he's in Brewer Street, the glaze of the streetlights in the film of rain like a blaze after the murk of the alleyway, the girl sprinting ahead of him. He glimpses three men running from the direction where he met her, shouting and cursing, and sees the man he hit lying, staring at his upraised hand in silence. People are on the street, a girl in front of a massage parlour, two men leaning out of a sex-shop doorway, a small scrum of men in front of the gay pub. And, with the girl, he runs, still clutching the empty revolver and praying that no one has the presence of mind to follow.

Harris sees the black silhouettes gather around the fallen man at the mouth of the alleyway and shoves the Beretta deep in his pocket. He runs over to Macrossan and finds him propped against the wall like a baby who can't sit upright.

'You stupid wee shite! You stupid wee fucking edjit!'

He drops to his knees and rips the kid's shirt open. He sparks his lighter in the gloom and sees blood and two small wounds, like oversize cigarette burns, on the kid's scrawny chest.

A couple of figures begin walking into the alleyway. Harris sees the glint of something sharp and metallic and realises there's only one round left in the Beretta. They're Albanians from the club on Brewer Street; on the same side as him, but he knows the blood of one of your own can cloud judgement and blur lines. So he swears at the kid again and pulls the Beretta, ready to drop at least one of them if they don't listen to reason and try to hack him to pieces. He's furious in his fear. And in his shame. Harris knows he froze, unnerved by London and this Brit shithole, Soho. And he knows he was outgunned, outfought, by the bastard from Belfast. The largest shadow takes on features, a blue-grey definition in strip lighting which has appeared in a first-floor window. Harris sees a scowl of controlled violence.

Then the Hyundai comes to a shrill halt at the mouth of the alleyway. They all turn to the figure of Morgan, unfolding himself from the driver's seat, striding down the alley and taking one of the men by the throat and pinning him to the dirt-encrusted wall.

Jackie begins to struggle as the adrenaline subsides and he realises he is chasing a much younger, lighter girl through the urban tangle of Soho. Despite its reputation for nightlife, it isn't a well-lit quarter and the girl is like a flickering icon on a dim screen as she flits through the streets, taking random turns. They draw looks from the few people strolling on the rain-glazed pavements. Jackie is desperate to catch her and try to learn something of the violent mayhem he's been dropped in. He wants to help her, protect her. But, with her in the lead dashing crazily ahead, they are becoming utterly lost.

Then he catches a lucky break. She turns into a narrow passage he recognises. It's L-shaped with a courtyard in the centre – he spoke to some homeless people huddled against one of the walls in the central space just an hour ago. As she enters the courtyard, the girl hesitates, unsure of how to escape the square patch of cobblestones boxed in by preserved stable doors, Victorian brick and gas lamps. He comes at her from an angle to cut the distance between them and collides with her, writhes with her in mid-air, fighting to land on his back and take the impact as her scream turns to a grunt. A bundle of rags shifts, stirred from a ragged sleep, as Jackie and the girl collapse on the cold, wet stone. He takes a hard landing on his left shoulder and she, winded, starved and exhausted, surrenders to his rough protection.

CHAPTER 14

Monday

Less than twenty-four hours, thinks Laurence Gilmore. Less than twenty-four hours of Jackie Shaw on the streets and it's already turned to shit.

They'd been settled in with a decent brew and a night of soaps on the telly, the analysts doing their thing in the next room, when the news report had come on. A gun battle in Soho, a man and woman reported fleeing the scene, the woman in some distress. Possible casualties but information was scant at the present time. Burton had shifted in his chair and said, 'Couldn't be your man, could it?' and Gilmore had said, 'I'd doubt it: London's a big place and he isn't armed.' He'd tried calling Shaw's mobile a couple of times, getting voicemail after a series of rings and something had begun worrying away at the back of his mind.

Then Burton had checked in at the office, NCA Organised Crime Command, and told him the Met were expecting CCTV footage from a PR company and restaurant which had operational cameras at the location. Gilmore had asked him to call back with updates as the night wore on. He hadn't called Thames House. He couldn't bother his superior with pure supposition and he wasn't inclined to share his unease with Stuart Hartley.

When Hartley himself called Gilmore's phone – 'just checking in' – Hartley had kept it simple and professional but Gilmore could hear the strain in the other man's nasal whine. Then Hartley said, 'If this all goes south, who's going to take ultimate responsibility?'

'If it goes all the way south, Shaw, I'd have thought. It won't be a happy ending for the poor bastard.'

Gilmore had killed the call with the pompous old git, inventing a report that one of the analysts was hounding him to look over and approve. He and the Met lads, Burton and Powell, had supped their tea and watched TV and digested Chelsea's recent results and if the Mancs were coming back into form.

Powell hauled himself off the sofa with a grunt and made for the toilet as Burton fiddled with his mobile, looking for further reports on the shooting in Soho. Gilmore rubbed his eyes and stood, stretching. He had just decided to call Jackie Shaw again when his own mobile, sitting on the coffee table, began its shrill ring. He lifted the slender tablet and slid his finger across the screen to answer the call – a call from Shaw's mobile – and everything changed.

Less than twenty-four hours, thinks Laurence Gilmore. Less than twenty-four hours of Jackie Shaw on the streets and it's already turned to shit.

#

Harris chains another cigarette and takes a deep drag, his right foot beating a tattoo on the carpet. He sits on a hard wooden chair in the corner of a stark, barren room, exhausted plaster hanging from the walls. Like something from fucking Dickens, he thinks, if he'd written about skag and crack fiends.

Morgan has seen this before, the shame and anger of a man who froze in combat. He can see the resentment seethe in Harris with every crinkling drag the Irishman takes. The Albanians can see it, too, and that's bad. It's weakness, and reflects on Morgan. Morgan eases past the men guarding the doorframe and takes a seat at a scarred wooden table in the centre of the room with Bashkim and Agon. The lower-ranking Leka stands by the wall with another gorilla in regulation black leather jacket and an industrial strength gold chain slung around a bull-neck. A lot of angry egos in a small, enclosed space, he thinks.

The flat is nestled half a mile from the strip club in the cubbyhole of Wardour Mews, a small lane with a dead-end and tunnel-like entrance. The flat has a couple of bedrooms, furnished with simple metal bedframes and pummelled mattresses, fucking spaces for the girls from the club to earn on their backs rather than prancing in their thigh boots. There is a begrimed bathroom at the rear of the flat, a foul toilet crammed next to a cracked sink the colour of cheap tobacco and a stained bath, now containing the unconscious and blood-soiled body of Padraig Macrossan. Morgan knows death, and he recognises it lying crumpled in that filthy tub.

Bashkim is sizing up Harris and leans, conspiratorial, over the table to Morgan.

'Your friend,' he whispers, 'is a cunt.'

Morgan smiles and shakes his head from left to right, the Albanian gesture for 'yes', his eyes locked with Bashkim. The Albanian smiles back, a vacant grin. 'No offence,' he says.

Morgan places his palm over his heart and says, 'None taken.'

The *Krye* of Soho places a Turkish cigarette in his reedy lips and his second-in-command, Agon, passes him a silver-plated Zippo. As he lights up, Bashkim says, 'My man is critical, shot through the lung. A good shot in daylight, a lucky shot at night.' He turns to look at Leka and the doorway beyond. 'Your boy, Macrossan: I do not think it looks good.'

'The kid came up against a professional. That's what happens when you send a puppy to a dogfight.'

'Or a pussy,' says Bashkim.

Harris looks up from studying the fag ash on the carpet. For a moment his foot stops tapping. Morgan focuses on Bashkim's grey eyes, the colour of dead skin. He says, 'I am very sorry for your loss, and for bringing this carnage to your doorstep. Had I been there, I would have counselled caution and contacted you before acting.' He places his hand on his chest again, then flat on the table, feeling the thin ruts on the surface, in front of the mobile phone and wallet in the centre of the wood. For a moment they all stare at the phone, taken from the mystery man – Policeman? Gunman? Killer of Albanian gangsters – like a Ouija board piece about to spit out a message from beyond the grave. Then Morgan looks over at Harris, still sucking on the cigarette. 'You saw the guy,' he says. 'Recognise him?'

'No. The accent was definitely Belfast, but softened up, like. I'd say he's lived away from Ireland for a while.'

'Could he be security forces?'

'He wasn't looking for us or the girl and he wasn't armed, although he knew how to handle a gun when he got his hands on one, and he wasn't bothered about following a Yellow Card either.'

'Yellow Card?'

Harris exhales a dense stream of smoke from his nose and stubs out his fag on the windowsill. 'Brits' rules of engagement in Ireland.'

Morgan says, 'The average cop in London wouldn't be that adept at handling a firearm, and SC&O would have been armed when you searched the bastard.'

Agon reaches for a Turkish blend and Morgan despairs at the damage his lungs are suffering in the cramped room. The *Kryetar* says, 'What was he doing in Soho?'

'He was showing around a picture of our target. It looks like the girl was an accident,' says Morgan. 'He stumbled into her, frightened her somehow, she drew attention to the two of them. Harris and Macrossan got involved and your boys pitched in. Then it all went, what we used to call, FUBAR.'

Bashkim pointed to the mobile. 'Anything on that?' So my girl was coming home, he thinks.

Leka takes a step forward and says, 'One number only, in the contact list. He hasn't dialled it or texted, although he received a call this afternoon and two more in the last forty minutes. That's it. No names. Nothing except the photo of this man, McLelland.'

'And the wallet?'

Morgan picks up the weathered leather. 'A licence with an address in Edinburgh; thirty pounds in cash; a blank hotel room key-card; an Oyster Card for the tube.' He turns the wallet over in his hands. 'Whoever he is, he seems professional and travels light. We checked the address in Edinburgh, found a phone number. A woman called Morag Freidman lives there now. The issue date on the licence is six years ago: he's moved on and not bothered updating it.' Morgan places the wallet back on the table and says, 'Jack Shaw.'

Silence settles again, a stillness broken by a groan from Macrossan in the next room.

Leka says, 'The alley is clean. We got the boy and our man, Gjon, out and away before the police showed up. We are lucky. It is dark. Any witness would have struggled to make out features and the cars we used are already on their way out of London. We are covered and the club is one of several in the area. The police will scout the area, but we are clean.' He bows, a fractional movement but there nonetheless, to Morgan. 'We have you to thank for your presence of mind.'

Morgan returns the bow. He had seized the Albanian by the throat out of anger at Harris's blundering and the boy's incompetence, and knew that the Albanians had killed for far lesser slights against their own. But it had galvanised the men there, forced them to act. And now the police, setting up their tents and pulling on their forensic suits, have a couple of bullet cartridges and the bloodstains of two men. And the Albanians had not taken offence, or chosen not to, so his throat would not be cut.

Instead, he will finish the job. He will work with the *Krye* of Soho and this fucker who blew away the kid in Kew. So Morgan picks up the mobile, looking from Leka to Agon, to Bashkim. He holds the gaze of the most powerful man in Soho for a moment, then looks at Harris.

'Let's make a phone call,' he says.

#

The girl sits, a small, impenetrable grime-encrusted figure. Immovable. Jackie brought her to the safety in numbers of Leicester Square where, confronted by the flock of post-theatre crowds, he could see the panic rise in her face like a hot flush. He took her by the arm in one fluid motion, almost lifting her off her feet, and led her to a place where they wouldn't stand out from the crowd, a place where no one would give them a second thought. Chinatown.

The febrile pulse of Chinatown funnels crowds of people down Lisle Street. Tourists, hawkers, the gay set, youths at work and play, people braying and shouting, weaving and brazen with drink. Girls totter on spiked heels over the cobblestones. Chinese flit from restaurant to restaurant carrying various ingredients and there is a sour-sweet fruit and vegetable stink that reminds him of seductive nights in Asia, heavy with promise. A few couples stroll and a lone reveller is regurgitating his Kung Pao Chicken next to a fortune-teller's locked doorway.

Jackie and the girl huddle below scaffolding clinging to the back of a Leicester Square cinema like a metallic vine. Jackie reaches out a hand to her, just shy of contact; Beatrix stares past him to the restaurant opposite, somewhere else entirely. Those out for fun make a determined effort not to see the two of them, dirty and frayed, another couple of victims of London's insatiable appetite, crouched in a fire escape doorway. Jackie and the girl need to move, to get the hell away from here and contact MI5, Gilmore or Hartley, and run to the security service safe-house near Victoria. Grab a police officer and work their way up to Five from there. But instead, the girl sits, small yet unyielding, delicate yet intransigent.

He's at a loss. He won't bully her: she's been through enough. He can't leave her. She's a loose end, and loose ends are liabilities. She also knows the trigger-men: her eyes said as much when she saw the hardcase back at Brewer Street. So he reaches out to her, his fingertips just short of touching her streaked, bare forearms wrapped around her knees.

'I want to help you,' he says, and knows it sounds forced. What help can he, dishevelled and anxious in a dirty coat and jeans, a plum-coloured bruise flowering on his cheek, offer her? He finally places his hand on her arm in a slow, gentle movement and her eyes focus for a moment on his. He says, 'I'm sorry.'

'Why?'

Her eyes are still staring beyond, as though he were a ghost.

'For scaring you back there.'

'And saving my life?'

'I think you've got claim on that one: your trick with the stiletto heel?'

He smiles, testing the waters now that she's talking to him. In answer, her face is an impassive mask. He shuffles an inch closer to her.

'We can't stay here. Sooner or later, someone will think we don't look right and we don't need any attention.' He's trying to keep his voice down but the flat, constant rasp of big-city background noise makes it difficult. A siren whoops in protest somewhere. He feels the empty revolver in his waistband and a stab of regret at his jibes at Gilmore's Met colleagues. He says, 'We can go to the police, get some help. Then you'd be safe.'

'No,' she says, a spark in her eyes. 'No police.'

'But you'd be safe.'

'Are you a policeman?'

'No. But – '

'I didn't think so. If you were a policeman, we would both be dead. A policeman wouldn't shoot like that: too many rules. So police cannot make me safe. I have been fucked by policemen here. They do not pay money and they do not look at my face when they are fucking me. They are friends with the bosses.'

Jackie feels sick. He realises his hand is now on the girl's arm for support as his body slumps. He is so tired. He shifts the weight on his haunches and says, 'Which country are you from?'

'Why?'

'It might help me understand what's going on. The men who were at the end of the alley shouted in a language I didn't understand.'

'They shouted "*lavire*: whore" and "*buce*: bitch".' She sounds defiant, almost proud. 'It is Albanian.'

He looks at this pretty, delicate girl, and the harsh words are like slaps. She's too young to be truly beautiful but, one day, she will be. Her English is excellent, educated, her accent soft, like a hint of fragrance. And yet she wandered the streets of Soho alone at night. Dangerous men called to her.

'Do you work for those men?'

Her face flushes. The corners of her mouth turn down, two faint lines creasing her cheeks on either side like ripples. 'Work? What I did was not work and it was not *for* anyone. I existed; I survived. That is all.'

Jackie looks hard into the girl's scowling face. 'That's over,' he says. 'There are people who can help, but I need to contact them. Not police. They're in Victoria.'

At last she looks at him and says, 'Is that near Kensington?' Her small face is still knotted in anger. 'I must go to Kensington.'

'Not far, but we have to move. I can get you to Kensington, I can help you. But we have to move.'

'And no police?'

'No police.'

He wants to ask what is in Kensington, but they've been here, in Chinatown, for too long. She stares at him for seconds that feel like an age, then shrugs and springs upright, standing with an ease that makes him feel old.

'Okay,' says Jackie. 'We can talk as we walk. My name is Jackie.'

She doesn't reply.

#

A body, thinks Harris. You are just looking at a body. Nothing new, you've seen plenty before.

Padraig Macrossan, folded into the bath, seems to be deflating, collapsing in on himself with each shallow, laboured breath. His eyes are closed but the lids spasm like a dog having a bad dream, and his shirtless chest rises and falls with strained, irregular gasps. The rounds were hollow points, and the two chest wounds, craters of viscera, have tiny bubbles of blood percolating in them. The bullets are still in there somewhere and it looks like at least one of them has done its terrible work on the right lung.

Harris exhales, wishing there was a stream of tobacco smoke rushing from his lips. He's glad the kid – no, the body in the tub – is unconscious. He clears his throat and tells himself he isn't in the mood for the useless wee fucker's shite. He tells himself the kid fucked up and now he's a liability, simple as. Then he closes the door behind him and walks to the edge of the tub, laying toilet roll on the floor to kneel on. The room is coated in dust, the bath flecked with grime, like the wall of an old steam-train platform. He kneels and straightens his upper body and waits for the kid to exhale with a throaty wheeze, then places a cushion firmly over the blue-grey face and pushes hard against the coarse, frayed fabric.

#

'You have a lost a man.'

Morgan takes a sip of coffee. 'So have you.'

Bashkim rolls another cigarette in his thick fingers, examining the tip. 'Maybe. Gjon looks bad, but I have seen worse. In Kosovës, I once saw a man lose a large piece of his skull to a sniper. Three months later he re-enlisted, determined to find the sniper and exact revenge.'

'And did he?'

'It doesn't matter. The point is, it drove him on and he lived to fight another day.' He takes a drag on the cigarette and glances back at the closed door, lowering his voice. 'When this is over, I can deal with the Irish cunt. He should pay for losing the boy and, if it is God's will, Gjon.'

'He came up against a professional. This man, Jack Shaw, must have had some training. He handled the Ruger with some skill.'

'And this Irish cunt is an experienced terrorist, no?'

Morgan snorts. 'And what does that mean? He had the stones to walk up behind someone and pull the trigger before they knew he was there. Or shoot some poor bastard with his hands tied.' He takes another swig of coffee. 'This is all over, he's yours.'

The door opens. Harris stands clutching the cushion, now smeared with an ugly copper-brown stain, in his right hand. 'Done,' he says. He shoves the cushion into a plastic bin-liner and re-takes his seat, lighting another cigarette.

133

Bashkim's lieutenant, Agon, says, 'What now?'

Morgan puts the coffee mug down and folds his arms. 'You can deal with Macrossan's body?'

Agon smiles.

'Then we go on as planned. Harris and I will scope Ferguson. He's probably under the same protection as McVea, but we'll check his home address. Tomorrow. Now, we need to rest.'

Harris, sullen as a scolded teenager, says, 'And the wee bitch?'

Agon looks at Bashkim. 'We'll look at the sister's house tonight. We can put men on it immediately. This man is with her now, somewhere in London, and I think she will go back there with him.'

The *Krye* of Soho gives a short twist of the head in assent.

CHAPTER 15

Tuesday

London has always been chaos. Buildings rammed into slim apertures, sometimes bent and warped to accommodate the precious sliver of Zone One real estate. Brutal concrete office structures share the same, exclusive postcode with Regency or Georgian townhouses. Chaos, like the thoughts ricocheting around in Jackie Shaw's head.

His anger rises like hot bile as he thinks what these dangerous men have put the girl through. He seethes at the little boy shot on the bridge in Kew. And now a dull ache begins to knead his guts as the adrenaline drains and the thought settles that he may have taken two lives back in the alley in Soho. He knows the fear will come next: of the consequences; of another corner of his soul eaten away; of himself. At last, there will just be harrowing emptiness. To occupy his mind, he frets over the girl. She's wearing his coat, after much protest, in the early-hours' chill. Jackie stole a pair of shoes for her from a young woman, inebriated and passed out on Great Windmill Street, up the side of the Trocadero. He was surprised at his indifference to the drunken girl.

He tries the number again.

The Belfast hardcase should have searched him. The kid, Padraig, had been terrified and ran his fingers over Jackie in a panicked rush. More haste, less speed. The kid had found the phone and wallet, the two items of bulk in the coat, but missed the slim, folded map of London and left a couple of creased twenty-pound notes and two quid in change in Jackie's jeans pocket. But his wallet is gone and now they can't go back to the hotel in case the men have somehow traced the key card.

Public telephones had proved to be almost as rare as police officers on the streets. He'd spotted two uniforms at the Lilly-whites entrance to Piccadilly Circus underground station. Any other cops had been safely sealed inside a patrol car, flickering by in the late-night traffic. The phones around Leicester Square were as dead as the flowers in the borders of the central plaza and the girl wouldn't go near the curving bank of telephones in Piccadilly Circus Station after they spotted the two coppers. Jackie wasn't too worried: he'd call Laurence Gilmore and the MI5 man would sort things out. Cold had dug in as they walked on Piccadilly. The streets became sullen in their silence. Great edifices of empire: exclusive members' clubs, banks, the Royal Academy of Arts, the Ritz. The only life on these streets in the wee small hours was the occasional lost soul in a sleeping bag huddled in a doorway; he saw a snoring pile of blankets under a window display of dainty, expensive Japanese sweets. Near the Ritz, he spotted a red phone box on Arlington Street and slung a pound coin into the slot.

Now he hits redial and waits, watching the girl as she stands next to the box, arms wrapped about her slender frame as though wearing a straitjacket. She had given him few answers as they walked, just occasional short, abrupt facts peppering her silence. Abduction, trafficking, abuse. And she survived it all; endured and then lashed out and saved them both in the alley. She has great strength. Does she need him? Can he trust Gilmore to help her? Protect her? When he looks at her through the smeared glass of the phone box, wretched and shivering, swallowed by his coat, he knows he must do something. Some-thing to help her and something to balance his own ledger of darkness and violence.

Jackie wills the number at the safe-house on Gloucester Street to connect. The number that should bounce from the phone at Gloucester Street to a secure line on the MI5 system. The line to Gilmore. His life-line.

He hears the recording again: 'The number you have dialled has not been recognised.'

He's been screwed. They are on their own.

#

Gilmore sits at his desk in Thames House and picks a small thread from his shirt. He'd begun his career with GCHQ, done a spell in operations and been bored out of his mind by the job and the location. To him, Cheltenham was nothing more than a giant, gentrified retirement home. After a couple of years, he'd answered an interdepartmental memo and applied for second-ment to the security service. A year and a half later, he'd completed a permanent transfer and bought a shoe-box in Charlton, south-east London, that he spends as little time in as possible.

Until recently, he'd never heard of Stuart William Hartley. The man was a singular type of civil service animal, those unre-markable characters who, by virtue of their mediocrity, golf partners and whisky-tasting societies, rise through the ranks to a position of seniority. They possess a rapacious hunger for what meagre power the service can afford them. It is this, more than salary scale or title, which Gilmore thinks Stuart Hartley enjoys about the job.

Hartley had cut Jackie Shaw loose without compunction or conscience. There was no malice in the order, just a callous dis-regard. After the reports of the shooting in Soho had come in, and the Met had studied the murky video footage from the al-leyway, they were left with scrappy reports and grainy footage of an anonymous man and woman who had fled the scene. But it was the phone call that had done it, a call from Shaw's service-issue mobile. A name, P. O'Neill, spoken with an Irish voice so harsh you could graze your ear on the receiver. Gilmore had been silent throughout the ten-second call, then contacted Hartley on a direct line. Hartley had ordered all communications with Jackie Shaw cut, the safe-house cleared and Shaw disavowed. The name, P. O'Neill, had been a codeword used by PIRA back in the day for phoning in bomb alerts and claiming murders. Alive or dead, Hartley said that Shaw had been compromised; cut him adrift and save any potential damage to the service. Order a notice with the Met to pick him up on sight, treat him as a hostile, incarcerate him without legal recourse until someone could figure out what to do with him. It was domestic rendition by any other name.

So the flat in Gloucester Street had been gutted, the rooms swept and all materials relating to Jackie Shaw's involvement with the Seven Skins disposed of.

Much like the poor bastard himself, thinks Gilmore. If he's still alive.

#

This man, Jackie, who still doesn't know her name, is furious, striding from the phone box on this grand, echoing avenue. The street is deserted at this hour, much like the grand boulevards of Tirana. Before the phone box, the man had been all concern for Beatrix, had been fierce in his desire to protect her. She balled her small hands in fists at his arrogance: like she was a mission he had to see through, as though, if he lost her, he lost something much more. She was not his damsel in distress and he was not her white knight, saving her from the dreaded Kulshedra. She has learned that life is no fairytale. But now he walks, silent fury driving long, quick strides, and she struggles

138

to keep pace with him. He swears and curses and his accent has become harsher, more lilting and yet rougher. He has stopped treating her like a fragile prize and seems to think she is the heroine of another folk tale, *The Girl Who Became a Boy.*

Beatrix wants to trust this man – she doesn't want to be alone any more. They have been thrown together by circumstance, but why would he want to help her? Why not cut her loose and run? And his voice is so similar to the angry one, Harris, who shot the old man a couple of nights ago; so long ago. In Soho, this man used her as a decoy, tossing her into the exposed space of the alley to draw the other killers out and gun them down. He used the gun with skill and confidence, a man who knows violence. Then, after, he had clung to her like an abuser consumed with guilt for the pain of his victim. Now, the dark core of his eyes tells her the killer who worked so efficiently in the alleyway is back.

The shoes cut into her heel. Typical, she thinks. He has managed to steal shoes from the one girl in this vast city who has smaller feet than hers. They are walking away from the bright lights to a stretch of road with a broad, black expanse of park on the left and she has to skip to keep up with him. She is tired now, so very tired, and her nerves are frayed like the edges of the tapestry that hung on her grandmother's wall when she was a small child. Images of her mother and father, like old photographs, flicker in her mind and she breathes deeply, clenching her jaw. Her mother, giddy and proud as she took her to the airport at Tirana. Her father, the masculine smell of his shirt as she snuggled at his chest as a child; the rough graze of his stubble when he kissed her cheek at the door, the last day she saw him. But first, Flori. She must see Flori.

No, she doesn't trust this man, Jackie, but she doesn't want to be alone. She wants to stop him and take a moment, just a moment, to draw breath but he moves on and she knows from his scowl that, behind his eyes, he is somewhere else, blinded by anger. The city is so huge, beyond any human scale, and she is afraid they are drifting in this ocean of buildings, further and further from Kensington and Flori. She trips and pitches forward. Her knees land hard on the pavement and she yelps.

Then he is beside her, his face pale and anxious, hand reaching out to her. He is talking in a rushed stream of words. He is back: his eyes are now piercing her with fear and concern. She wants to hit him hard in the face, to beat the dumb look of concern out of him. Beatrix sweeps her hair back from her face a little too hard, yanking the matted locks in her fingers and grunts. She has known him for a couple of hours and is already exhausted by his moods. But she has had enough of drama and confrontation for now.

She says, 'I'm fine.'

'Your knees. You've skinned them.'

Her knees have two vivid scraps of virgin skin peppered by the dirt and grime of the pavement. His damned hand is hovering above her shoulder and she wills him to touch her. She wants someone to touch her without anger or greed or lust.

'Help me up,' she says.

His shoulders drop, his face softens in the streetlight and he places a coarse hand under her arm. She feels his strength.

'This place,' she says, pointing to the black sweep of the park on the left, 'does it lead to Kensington?'

'Green Park. It leads to Buckingham Palace. This road leads to Kensington.'

'So, we stay on this road.'

'Okay. In about thirty minutes or so, we'll be in Kensington. There is another, bigger park near there where we can rest for a while. Then I'll help you do whatever you need.'

She nods, stares at him a moment, and sees loneliness – God knows she recognises a lonely man after whoring – and hurt, too. She realises that he looks at her like no man has since she arrived in this country: as someone with a past and a family, a person.

She says, 'My sister lives in Kensington. Her name is Flori and she does not know that I am in London. I must warn her that I have run from those men in Soho. They might come for her, for revenge on me through my family.'

'Then let's walk,' he says.

They set off at a slower pace, his hands rammed awkwardly in his jeans pockets. She stops him and smooths the slight snag of his sweater over the butt of the empty revolver tucked in his waistband.

'Jackie,' she says, 'my name – my real name – is Elira. I am from Tirana, Albania.'

He smiles a sad, uncertain smile.

They walk on, side-by-side, in silence for a time.

CHAPTER 16

Tuesday

Morgan says, 'Every cloud, right, Harris?'

They turn onto Great Western Road, Harris struggling to keep pace. He manages a hoarse, 'What?' before a wracking cough seizes him by the throat. Too many fags, he knows, but now is hardly the time to knock them on the head. Not with the stress he's under.

'Now the targets are blown, the cops have placed Ferguson under protection. He's a stationary target, instead of cruising in his taxi. Easier to hit.'

'But,' says Harris, timing each clause with a rasping breath, 'he's under protection.'

'So, we look at the playbook again. How did you guys do it back in the day, huh? Bomb or up close with a bullet. Ever been to South Armagh?'

'Business or pleasure?'

'People go there for pleasure?'

It is the first time Morgan has come anywhere close to making a joke, and it takes Harris a moment to recover. Morgan reads his gawp as confusion.

'Did you ever operate down there?'

Harris says, 'Belfast mostly, some stuff in Derry. And one job in Tyrone.'

'You know, some of the Brits didn't rate the IRA in Belfast; they thought they were cowboys. The real deal, they said, was out in South Armagh, South Down, the border country.'

'Yeah, yeah,' says Harris, squeezing words in between gasps. 'Bandit country.'

They near a pub and, beyond, a small bridge over a canal. The traffic is building as the roads and streets of London begin shuttling people around the city, a sprawling network of arteries pumping the human life-force of a massive organism around its clogged system. It's a clear day, early morning sun already burning off the slick sheen of last night's rain. Harris, up and about on three hours' sleep and a nightcap of Dublin's finest, craves a coffee and another nicotine hit. The cars, the taxis, the buses, all conspire to drill a rushing hum of background noise into his skull. He sees faces in the window of a double-decker, a miscellany of colours and nationalities. As they slide by, his imagination, usually dulled by drink and a life lived hard, conspires against him and short glimpses of the wee boy on the footbridge compete with Macrossan lying in the bathtub in his mind's eye. He wants to go home to the simplicity and purity of Belfast. The us-and-them dichotomy, so entrenched, so familiar. So safe.

Morgan stops walking a few yards short of the bridge, the pub on their left and a low-level block of flats in the distance to their right on the other side of the canal, shiny and new-looking in the early morning light. He sprints across the road to the edge of the bridge; Harris negotiates the traffic and joins him a full minute later. Morgan points to a clutch of trees some five hundred yards further down the canal on the far bank, diagonal to where they stand.

'Our boy lives over there somewhere, behind the greenery, in a typical four-storey council block in the housing estate.'

'Probably still in his pit, lucky bastard,' says Harris. 'Maybe he's having his first wank of the day, before he makes a cuppa.'

'If he's jerking off, I hope he closed the door. I figure there'll be a two- or three-man protection detail with him in the flat. Possibly some surveillance outside, too.'

'Armed.'

'Oh yeah. Maybe not Specialist Protection Units, but someone, somewhere will have a weapon.'

Harris reaches into his jacket pocket for his pack of cigarettes but Morgan walks on until he is standing in the centre of the bridge studying the view. Harris looks to the heavens for help or patience, reckons he's burned his bridges in that department, and spits over the edge into the murky water. When he joins Morgan, he sees a tall shard of concrete piercing the morning sky. The tower-block stands isolated, thirty-one floors tall, looking worn and unloved behind the trees.

'A good dose of Semtex'd bring that eyesore down.'

Morgan smiles, a first, and something cold creeps through Harris. He realises that the man is enjoying himself, and the thought almost unsettles him more than the shoot-out last night and the death of the young 'un. More than the man who bested him and escaped with two bodies lying in his wake.

Morgan says, still staring at the tower on the other side of the canal, 'Hell no. That right there is concealment and cover.' He turns to look at Harris, his eyes dancing. His fingers stroke something slim and cylindrical hanging on a chain around his throat, the tip just visible above the neck of his T-shirt.

'I'm gonna Cold Barrel Zero our boy, Ferguson. I'm gonna snipe the son of a bitch.'

#

Elira is still asleep. Jackie checks his watch and sees that it's just past five-thirty. They both slept deeply, despite the chill, huddled together near the Serpentine Pond in Hyde Park. He's stiff and, while loath to wake her, must stretch his limbs and shake some life into them. And they should get moving. He puts a hand on her shoulder and nudges her gently.

'What time is it?' she says.

'Breakfast time.'

Forty-five minutes later they are sitting on the steps of the Albert Memorial, gazing across Kensington Road at the orange tier-cake of the Royal Albert Hall. Elira has washed the filth of last night from her face, legs and arms in the Round Pond, near Kensington Palace, although her clothes are still crumpled and soiled. They have cheap coffee and a croissant each, bought from a chain café nearby, the girl eating in small, bird-like pecks. Jackie wolfs the pastry down and takes a sip of bitter coffee.

'It's beautiful,' she says, nodding at the hall. 'This park, too.'

'Yep, London has its moments.'

'What is this?' Elira's thumb indicates the ornate canopy behind them, a golden Prince Albert sitting beneath, radiant.

'It's a memorial – a statue to remember someone. He was a prince, married to the Queen of England.'

'What is its purpose?'

'I suppose it's just there to remind people of him.'

She looks intently at the croissant, plucking slivers of pastry with her slim fingertips. 'So all the people in their cars, and taxis, and buses who drive past here, and all the people on bicycles and walking, they all remember this prince? If he is so easy to forget, he doesn't deserve that thing.'

'Yeah,' says Jackie, smiling. 'To be fair, he's been dead for over a hundred and sixty years. He got a clock where I'm from, in Belfast.'

'That is more practical. At least it is some use to the people now.'

'We still managed to cock it up, though. It leans to the side. Maybe the boys who built it were liquored up.' He is about to tell her that, when he was younger, it was a famous stomping ground for prostitutes out scouting for trade with sailors from the nearby docks. Then he remembers where he met her, and her former employers.

'That, over there,' says Jackie, pointing across Kensington Road, 'is a concert hall named after the same prince.'

She looks at the Royal Albert Hall, then back to Jackie, her small chin jutting a little as she peers upwards, and says, 'A clock is better.'

#

Fifteen minutes later they are standing on Launceston Place. The street slices Kynance Mews in two, the entrance to the cobblestone side-street heralded by a stone arch on either pavement.

As they walked from Hyde Park, Elira told Jackie all she could: the gang, the brutality, the enforced prostitution; Flori's work in the diplomatic and executive sector, interpreting for Albanian and Arab politicians and moguls when they visit London; and the killers who assassinated Len Parkinson-Naughton in a dusty alleyway in the City of London. She gave him names: Macrossan, Morgan and Harris. Jackie thought of a little boy lying on a footbridge in Kew.

Harris is a Player. The accent, the look, the feral intelligence, Jackie has seen before in loyalist and republican killers alike back home. The younger man, Padraig Macrossan, is an anomaly. English, at least in accent, anxious and scared. He seemed to be a regular in the gay pub, known and liked by the staff, and Elira had told him how Macrossan had botched the Parkinson-Naughton hit. In Soho, Jackie could see the kid had been frightened of the gun in his hand; but he'd been more frightened of the man beside him, Harris. The third man, Morgan, is another mystery. The only one of the three that Jackie hasn't seen and who is , according to Elira, economical with language. She said his accent was more rounded, smoother than Jackie's or Harris's, and he had a tattoo with the letters 'SS' in what sounded like the double-sig rune in Armanen form: the Waffen SS symbol from Nazi Germany, beloved of right-wing nutcases the world over.

Elira told him how the third man, Morgan, had arrived at the Gentleman's Club one morning five days ago. She was brought from a brothel and handed over to him. The gang *Kryetar*, Agon, had warned the man that his 'goods' were not to be damaged, then took a handful of her hair in his fist and warned her in Albanian that she was to follow the man's instructions. She thinks she was chosen as she spoke good English and the old man, Parkinson-Naughton, liked small, fragile girls that he could dominate. And the *Krye* of the gang, Bashkim, had tormented, abused and manipulated her to such an extent, they thought she would be total in her compliance.

She had been blindfolded, bundled onto the floor of a car, and driven for a long time. The man, Morgan, had played loud music, heavy metal. Then she had been led from the car to some steps and onto a strange, moving surface: a boat. Finally, she was placed on a bed and the blindfold removed to reveal a small room with shuttered windows. The three men stood before her and the young one, Macrossan, looked scared. But the men left a bag of clothes on the bed, the clothes she wore now, and left. They brought her meals and coffee but kept the door locked. She could hear blurred murmurs coming from rooms nearby, but only learned their names as they shouted to each other outside the door. She heard other sounds, too, children playing and people chatting easily somewhere outside. There were footsteps above and once, a loud, stuttering engine, another boat passing.

Then she was blindfolded again and led outside, back up the steps to another car. After some time, her blindfold was removed. The sky through the car windows was darkening. The man, Morgan, told her that she should wait alone in a bar to which they would take her. They would be watching her from outside. They showed her a photograph on a mobile phone of an older man and instructed her to make conversation with him, flirt, and be sure to leave the bar with him. Then she was to lead the man to a passageway. If she did not do this, the men would inform Agon and she would be punished upon her return to the gang.

She never considered running. She was utterly lost in London and the gang's domination was complete. She was convinced there was no life for her beyond the *Fis*: the family. Bashkim was her surrogate, abusive father.

The older man had come into the bar and she had approached him. She was nervous, eager to please. Would the old man like her? Could she get him to leave with her? Would he allow himself to be led?

She didn't want the gang to hurt her again.

But she saw the hunger in the man's eyes as soon as she spoke to him. She said, 'He held himself upright, pompous and foolish, telling me stories I couldn't understand.'

She had thought Morgan and the others wanted to threaten or cajole the old man. Perhaps he owed money or could be blackmailed. But when Morgan had seized her in the passageway, wrenching her from the old man's grasping tongue in her mouth, she had seen the gun. Then the younger man, Macrossan, had ruined the old man's ear and the angry man, Harris, had shot the old man in the head. The three killers were bickering.

'And something snapped in me,' said Elira. The final thread that gave a semblance of sanity to her world, and she had run. The terror of drifting through a midnight London, the cold, dismal wait near her sister's flat, and her dejected return to Soho had followed.

Jackie sat for a moment, then said, 'A man, a man I don't know called Samuel McLelland, is being targeted by Harris,

Macrossan and Morgan. It's my job to search for this man before they get to him.'

He spoke of the list and how he had connections with people – not police, but government people – who had tasked him with finding and protecting McLelland. 'McLelland is homeless,' said Jackie. As he talked, he thought of how hopeless his task was: finding one man in the vast sprawl of London. When she asked why he had been tasked, he told her he had worked for the government people before.

Now, he says, 'We're alone: the government people have cut me loose. They won't help. The Metropolitan Police don't know about my involvement with the government people beyond a very small, specialist group. If we go to the regular police, they will arrest us because of the shooting.' When he mentions the violence in Soho his shoulders sag a little.

Elira looks at him, her eyes darting in her small, serious face. 'You are a good man.'

'No,' says Jackie, 'I'm not. I try to be a better man, but then I end up fighting, or hurting, or killing someone. People get hurt around me.'

'Sometimes good men must do bad things. It's the way of things.'

He thinks she sounds old, not like a young woman in her twenties.

'My father told me that,' says Elira. 'He is in politics.'

'Jesus,' says Jackie, his face a mask of mock horror. 'If I'd known that, I'd have left you back in the park.'

She freezes for a beat, then smiles. It is a shy, young smile, and, for a moment, he sees the young girl who should be drinking and flirting with boys at university.

Jackie looks at the granite arches which herald the entrance to the mews. The area is neat, well-tended. Elira's sister, Flori, must have an elite clientele in her interpreting business. Home security would be good in this neighbourhood. They walk to the archway and look down the western side of the cobblestone mews. A slapdash line of brick, two-storey residences, some painted in pastel colours. A cosy, Hollywood vision of London, the cobblestone lane stretches to a dead end five hundred feet ahead. Some of the facades are bearded with thick ivy.

Jackie unfolds the street map and studies it for a moment. Queen's Gate, a large road, is a five-minute walk away.

'Stay here and watch the house,' he says. 'Try to look casual, like you belong here.' He looks at her rumpled clothing, the miniskirt, and realises how ridiculous he sounds. Still, the street is quiet. Not the kind of area that would see a lot of traffic. 'Stand in the opposite archway and I'll be back in ten minutes or so.'

'What if something happens?'

'Do nothing, just watch and use the archway for cover. I'm going to find a newsagents. I'll be right back.'

'You want a newspaper? To read about the shoot-out last night?'

'No,' says Jackie, 'a packet of cigarettes. I quit smoking years ago. Time to take it up again.'

CHAPTER 17

Tuesday

The street is quiet when Jackie returns, thirty minutes later. He's worried that Elira might have given up on him and bolted, but she is leaning against the granite arch opposite the entrance to the side of the mews which houses her sister's place. She looks nervous and conspicuous.

'You okay?' he says.

'You took a long time. I thought, maybe, you won't come back.'

'I had a quick look around the immediate area. No one suspicious but there is a police presence near the main road, a few cars and uniforms. I had to take a different route back here.'

'Are they looking for us?'

'I doubt it. If you're in the UK illegally, no one can identify you, and the men who killed Parkinson-Naughton won't go to the police.' Elira looks unconvinced, but Jackie can see in her eyes that she wants to believe him.

On the way back to Launceston Place, he called Derek Bailey from a public phone box, telling him about the SS symbol on Morgan's arm and asking him to reach out to some of his more extreme associates and try to get more information on the man. He told Bailey the name, the Function, somewhere in Maida Vale, which the old man on the street had given him, and Bailey had promised to look into it. Finally, he'd given Bailey a brief rundown on Elira: no name, no details. Bailey had sounded doubtful and nervous but suggested bringing her to him for protection. Jackie didn't trust Bailey as far as he could throw him, but said he would be in touch again.

Now he says, 'Okay, I want you to walk down to the wall at the end of the mews and back again. When you pass Flori's place, check the door for her apartment number: is her flat upstairs or down? Is there a bell? Maybe a small box in front: does it have a screen or a logo? Is there a small light flashing?'

'Can't you come with me?'

'You have a reason to be here, Elira; I don't. If your sister is at home and sees you out the window, problem solved.'

Her face darkens, two patches of red, like angry welts, bloom on her cheeks.

'You think *they* are there,' she says. 'That they have killed Flori already and wait for me.'

'No, but we have to be ready for that, just in case.'

Her eyes shimmer.

'I don't think Flori is dead,' he says. 'She's more useful to them alive. They can use her to get you back. But we can't take chances, so I need to see what the entrance looks like, what kind of alarm is there. Okay?'

Elira looks through the arch to the narrow strip of cobblestones beyond, picture-perfect two-storey mews cottages on either side. He can see her jaw working beneath the pale skin of her face. Then she walks off without a word, strolls under the arch and makes her way to the end of the mews. She is back by his side a couple of minutes later.

'The windows look dark, like there is no one at home. Her apartment is upstairs. The downstairs neighbour is also in darkness. The ivy on the walls is very thick, so I almost missed it, but there is a box below the upper window, probably an alarm. Also, there is a keypad next to the door with a small screen. The screen is dead now.' She looks away. 'Blank, I mean.'

'Good. I'm going to pass your sister's place. You stay here. When I light up a cigarette, I want you to walk up and buzz the video screen next to the front door. Okay?'

'Okay.'

Jackie walks along the mews. As he passes Flori's place, he glances at the door. There's a small window with frosted glass set in the blue-painted wood, a couple of pots with plants on the ground next to the shallow doorstep. He walks another ten yards and unfolds the map, looking around as though lost, then retraces his steps until he is standing next to the ivy which covers Flori's place, out of sight of the property's windows, and takes one of the leaves between his fingers. It's dry to the touch. He begins tearing the leaves from the vines, working fast. No one is walking in the mews, but there are plenty of windows and he knows that curious eyes could be watching him from any of them. When he has a bunch of ivy leaves in his hands, he stuffs them into his pockets then takes the packet of cigarettes and box of matches he bought on Queen's Gate road and lights up. The smoke burns and claws at his throat, and he's amazed how familiar it feels after all these years.

The small figure of Elira crosses Launceston Place and flits through the granite arch at the entrance to this western stretch of Kynance Mews. As she nears the door to her sister's residence, Jackie whispers, 'Look through the glass. Can you see anything?'

Elira peers through the frosted windowpane then murmurs, 'There is a small yellow light flashing on the wall near the door.'

'Like the colour of a traffic light?'

'Yes.'

Amber. Back at Garbella Hill Farm, amber indicated the alarm system was disabled. Jackie hisses, 'Press the call button on the keypad.'

A muted electronic buzz sounds.

They wait for seconds: silence. The screen remains a lifeless grey. Jackie gestures for Elira to step back and then takes a gentle but firm grasp of the door handle and turns. The door opens with a soft click and swings inward to reveal an empty square patch of carpet with a door on the left, the ground-floor flat. Facing the front door, a flight of steep carpeted steps leads up to Flori's flat.

Jackie lifts a plant pot and brings it into the small hallway then upends it, sending soil and plant tumbling on the carpet. He takes another pot and rips the plant from the soil and tosses it on the floor. He works fast, ushering Elira into the hallway and closing the front door with another soft click. He empties some soil and, satisfied that the remainder is dry, shoves both batches of leaves into the pot. He stubs out his cigarette and rips the paper open, sprinkling the tobacco onto and among the leaves. He repeats this until only half of the cigarettes are left in the pack, then tears a corner from his streetmap. Jackie twists the paper into a long, rough cigar-shape and lights the end with a match, then uses the glowing taper to light the tobacco and wedges the burning paper in among the leaves. He blows until the leaves and tobacco begin to smoke.

Jackie whispers to Elira, 'Wait here.' Then he makes his way to the top of the stairs, leaving the pot of smouldering leaves at the halfway point while carrying the empty pot to the top. He places the empty pot upside down on the carpet in front of the door and retrieves the smoking pot full of burning tobacco and leaves, placing it on top of the upended pot. He opens the letter-box flap set in the flat door and wedges it open with the box of matches. The door to the flat opens inwards, and he stands with his back flat against the wall to the right of the door, next to the hinges, wafting the smoke in the letter-box flap with the map.

The smoke is billowing from the pot as he gestures for Elira to join him at the top of the stairs. As she sidles up to him, her small body hard against his in the narrow space, they hear voices from within the apartment. Jackie arches his eyebrows and mouths, 'Albanian?' Elira nods. He listens for a moment longer, the voices rising in pitch and volume, then holds up three fingers. She nods again, her hand over her mouth and cheeks puffed out as she tries to stifle a cough in the thick smoke. Jackie's eyes are beginning to sting; he pats the empty Ruger in his waistband, willing those inside to open the door.

They hear the clamour of an argument build, the smoke now filling the small landing and beginning to tumble down the stairs and then, at last, a click. The door is flung open and Jackie kicks the pots hard, sending them toppling into a slim man standing in the doorframe with a pistol in his hand. The man begins to fold as Jackie grabs his arm and hurls him, like a dancer sending his partner into a pirouette, towards the stairs. The man pitches over the top step. Jackie hears the clack of a suppressor shot and a bullet tears into the ceiling above him.

He peers through the smoke, not as thick in the flat as he'd thought, and sees a second man standing, legs apart with the long snout of a silenced semi-automatic held in both hands. The shooter is no more than six feet away. Jackie launches himself, low and straight so that his body is almost parallel to the ground, at the man's groin and connects with full force. Both of them sprawl on the carpet, the gun sailing out of sight. They begin scrabbling for purchase on one another, desperate to find a grip with one hand and sending in punches with the other. Jackie smells the smoke and the heavy musk of body odour from his opponent, hears the hissed obscenities in Albanian. He feels a sharp sting as a ring catches his eyebrow with a glancing blow. Someone is shouting. Jackie's legs are scything through the air, grazing the carpet as he struggles, and he finally pulls the revolver from his waistband and clouts the Albanian across the face with it. The man's head bounces off the carpet with a soft thump and Jackie presses the muzzle hard into his temple, shouting, 'Enough. Don't fucking move!' The man, a red cloud spreading in his left eye, is dazed, his head pinned to the carpet by the heavy revolver. Then Jackie sees the feet of the third man and looks up to face a revolver levelled at his nose, almost point blank.

He doesn't wait for oblivion, doesn't pray for his eternal soul or plead for his life. Instead, he flinches at the flat, harsh bark of a shot. The body in front of him jerks. Then again. And again. The man topples, rigid as a tree at first, then crumples in a heap, bleeding on the expensive wool carpet. Jackie hauls himself up on one knee, the muzzle still hard against the temple of the man on the floor below him, and turns to the door. Elira stands, wreathed in fading smoke, grasping a Beretta Px4 Storm handgun in her small hands, her legs splayed wide on the carpet. She looks like a pretty, petite scarecrow cloaked in the ivy-smoke, the gun heavy and dragging her arms downwards, locked in her grip. Jackie stands, dragging the Albanian he was fighting with him, and puts the man in an armlock, bending the wrist in on itself, the gun still against the man's head.

Elira looks at the bleeding body on the floor and says, in a small voice, 'Is he dead?'

'If not, he may as well be. What about yer man on the stairs?'

'I think his neck is broken. This is his gun.' And with that, Elira drops the pistol on the carpet, walks to a chair against the wall near the door, and sags into the leather. The man in the armlock spits something at her in Albanian but she doesn't react, staring at the body behind them. Jackie gives him another clout with the empty revolver, just for good measure, and takes in the apartment. It's all restrained, tasteful furnishing in one, central living space. The salmon-coloured carpet is now tarnished with blood. The flat is more like a hotel suite, and probably costs a small fortune to rent.

Time is critical. The shots were loud and this is a quiet district. The police could be charging up the stairs at any moment. The flat downstairs looked empty but could have a frantic resident dialling emergency services as Jackie stands panting. There is one dead Albanian on the stairs and another on the carpet chasing hard on his friend's heels to Hell. The problem right now is containing the sprightly fucker who belted him with a ring, now swearing at Jackie instead of Elira after that second smack with the revolver. He kicks the man's legs out from under him and the Albanian lands hard on his hip, a sliver of spit flying from his pursed lips. Jackie keeps the revolver trained on him as he collects the gun with which Elira shot his mate. He picks up the injured man's pistol and suppressor and then, just to piss him off, shows him that all six cylinders of his own revolver are empty. The man stares at the carpet in disgust, shaking his head, before Jackie kicks him, waving with the suppressed handgun, another Beretta Px4 Storm, to indicate the man should roll over onto his belly. Once flat to the floor, Jackie removes the man's shoes, pulls off a sock and shoves it deep into his mouth. Elira is sitting like a puppet princess with strings cut, legs sloppy, dress dishevelled.

Then Jackie turns back to the man and fires a round from the suppressed Beretta.

CHAPTER 18

Tuesday

Elira is staring at him in horror and he turns from her eyes, now huge in her small-boned face. The man on the carpet has been screaming into the sock stuffed in his mouth, a hoarse screech dulled by the soaking sock. A small, smoking hole smoulders above the gangster's left knee and Jackie swallows hard. It's so easy with a gun, he thinks, so detached. But now he won't have to worry about there being any fight left in the Albanian. And he has some real threat to work with.

He turns the man onto his back and slaps him across the face, then puts his index finger to his lips. The scream breaks down into a series of ragged grunts and, when he pulls the sock out of the mouth, the man swallows hard and strains to keep quiet. His face is pale and slick with sweat.

Jackie says, over his shoulder, 'Translate if I need you, okay?'

There is silence behind him.

'Elira,' he says.

A small voice says, 'Yes,' from far away.

#

Elira stands up. She had thought she wanted to kill them until she saw the life punched out of the man sprawled dead on the floor. The angry clack of the gun, the terrible spastic jerk of the body and the final crumpled fall, as though the life was seething from the man like air from a tyre. It was so easy. Just pressure on the trigger and it was done: the ugly, sordid thing in her hands hurling the bullets out, doing the dirty work.

She had thought Jackie was different and then she saw his face, so focused, so possessed by the violence that she fears him again. She fears his past – what he must have been through – to have become this person.

And now, here they are.

Jackie is dragging the wounded man to his feet and taking his weight as he slings an arm over his shoulder and leads him to the chair she sat in moments ago. Jackie is saying something and it's like they are underwater, his words are dull and obtuse. He is speaking English and she is Albanian and – damn him! – why can't he speak her tongue instead? Why is English so widely spoken and not Albanian? Who made the Americans and the British so damned important? And then he is in front of her and he raises his hand and she prays he doesn't slap her because he has been kind to her and she is so frightened by the man he was just before and she wants to believe that people can still be good. His hand comes down softly on her shoulder then makes its way to her cheek where it rests.

'It's okay. You're okay,' he says. 'We're okay.'

She wants so badly to believe him. Then he pulls her head gently to his shoulder. Elira lets him and, just for a moment, allows herself to be lost to him.

#

He understands where she is right now, and that it'll get worse. When Jackie first killed a man, it hadn't hit him immediately. It was when a quiet moment came that the earth tilted and, somewhere inside him, a dark veil was drawn over his world. It had felt like the worst all-night shift, the worst jet-lag, the worst hangover of all time on top of a terrible regret. Not for the man he'd killed, but for the part of himself that was gone forever. He drives the shadowy forms of two men lying in a Soho alley and the broken body on the stairs from his mind. No time for guilt: he'll live with it later. He holds Elira for a moment, to let her know it's okay for now, then he pushes her quietly back and she lets him like she needed to breathe anyway.

He says, 'I need you to translate. That man was a threat.' He points to broken form in the the chair. 'He'll live but now he can't walk and he's scared, which means he isn't a threat. But he may not speak English.'

She walks past Jackie and stands before the man, his face the pallor of an old egg, clutching at his thigh above the bullet wound and straining like he's trying to shit. She feels less fragile. She has something to do. She's in control.

Jackie walks over and stands next to her. He says, 'What's your name?'

The man looks up, eyes swollen and bloodshot. Elira repeats the question in Albanian. He barks a reply.

'He called me a bitch and said he will fuck your mother.'

The sharp report is sudden; she jumps. A hole appears in the armchair, just to the right of the injured leg.

Jackie says, 'You want to keep that leg you'll answer my questions. So far it's soft tissue damage. Sooner or later I'll put one through your kneecap. I'll blow your fucking ball-bag off, you say another word about my ma.'

Elira begins to translate, then hesitates and turns to Jackie. 'What is soft tissue? Ma is mother? And ball-ba – '

'My name is Kreshnik.'

Jackie and Elira look at each other. The man's English is clear, his accent mild. Elira turns and walks out the door to an adjoining room.

Jackie says, 'Where's the girl's sister?'

'We have her.'

'She's hardly been in the kitchen the whole time, making a cup of tea. Where do you have her?'

'I don't know. I am just a foot soldier. Agon and Leka came here with us and took the girl. She was in bed. We had orders from Bashkim, the *Krye,* but me and the other two here, we were told only to help Agon and Leka take the girl and wait for you.'

Jackie takes aim again, slow and deliberate.

'Please, we were told to talk to you and take the whore back to Soho.' He nods, conspiratorial, towards the door through which Elira disappeared. 'The *Krye* can see you are a dangerous man. He thought it best to contact you through us, on the phone.' The wounded Kreshnik struggles to pull a mobile from his pocket, the leg of his jeans now soaked with a dark, widening stain as his thigh bleeds into the denim.

Jackie says, 'Now you're talking.'

He takes the mobile and spots a framed photograph on a small table next to the sofa in the centre of the living room. There is Elira, younger, smiling, and, next to her, another girl. This girl was closer to womanhood when the photo was taken, with the same delicate features and a knot of auburn hair tied up in a makeshift bun. The two are unmistakably sisters. Kreshnik recites a number to dial on the mobile.

#

Laurence Gilmore says, 'Anything on the girl?' and bites down on a snack.

'Slight, young. No one got a good look, we don't have any information to go on beyond ropey descriptions from a couple of punters outside the gay bar up the street.'

'What about the other shooters?'

DC Don Boxton sighs on the other end of the line. 'Same story as last night. Two men down the bottom of the alley, one of whom seemed to be badly wounded. Another shot at the mouth of the alleyway. All three disappeared. Someone turned up in a Hyundai and whisked the lot of them away.'

Gilmore had met Boxton on a training course hosted by the Security Service for Met officers tasked with Organised Crime and Special Branch liaison. A soft-spoken Welshman in his late forties with a thick head of jet-black hair, a long, thin face and used-car salesman pencil moustache, the detective had approached Gilmore after the last seminar, asking for advice on a counterfeit credit card operation being run out of White City that he suspected might have links to a crime syndicate in Eastern Europe. The two had adjourned to a quiet pub and so had begun a clandestine relationship of information sharing. Neither overstepped lines when it came to offering intelligence – Gilmore hasn't told Boxton about Shaw's remit from the Security Service – and both treasured the other as a source of agency knowledge on the ground.

Gilmore knew that CCTV footage provided little help in identifying those involved in the Soho gun-battle, although Hartley had circulated a full intelligence package on Jackie Shaw to the Met, working with the NCA to ensure officers on the ground were keeping a look-out for him with a view to immediate arrest and isolated detention. The girl had the police flummoxed and the disappearance of the other gunmen had brought enquiries to a grinding halt. Boxton said everyone was now waiting on forensics in the hope they might provide new lines of enquiry.

'No progress on Shaw, then?' Gilmore looks out of the window at the flat, churning river.

'Nothing. We received a call from Kensington station to say they may have a shooter in custody so we set up a cordon in case there were others in the area: Elvaston Place, around the Thai Embassy. A complete dud.' Boxton snorts. 'Some dickhead pulled a stop-and-search on a punter because he fitted the profile for gun crime in the city. The "suspect", one Adam Keegan, is a motor mechanic from Clapham. And he's black.'

Gilmore guffaws, then hopes the bitterness in his laugh hasn't seeped down the line. He pictures the DC in a huge office in New Scotland Yard with a low ceiling and banks of workstations with harassed, bored or frustrated detectives drinking coffee and tapping biros on desks as they try to remember what they were supposed to pick up in Tesco on the way home. He says, 'Do you think the shooting could be connected to any of the local businesses in Soho?'

'That's always a possibility. You've got a few Turkish dealers in the area, a couple of Jamaican-run pubs we know are fronts for drug business, the Albanians running riot and, of course, the local colour. I'd say not much happens in Soho without the Albanians' say-so these days, but they tend to keep the violence behind closed doors. They have a club nearby, the Gentlemen's Sporting Club. We had a look around last night but, aside from the cum-stains on the floor, it was clean.'

'So you're ruling them out?' Gilmore says.

'I wouldn't say that. They certainly have their share of homicidal maniacs, but the likes of last night is bad for business, and they're all about business. This seems a lot more impulsive. If I didn't know better, I'd say it was the bloody Pikeys.' There is a pause before Boxton adds, 'But then one of yours, this Hartley bloke, gives us a Jackie Shaw and I think it's probably a whole lot messier than that. That's it: nothing on the other three shooters, or the girl. Just pick up Shaw, who has past links to Irish paramilitaries and organised crime. I mean, what's that all about?'

'Trust me, Don, you don't want to know. Thanks for the chat.'

'No, I don't think I do want to know. You can return the favour when I'm in need, eh?'

'Most definitely, cheers again.' Gilmore kills the call. Then he pulls the files on Jackie Shaw from his days in Belfast on the Ulster drive of the system, both old and those from the not-so-distant past. He suspects he'll find the information in both to be as bloodstained as the cold concrete in a Soho alley in the wee small hours of this morning.

CHAPTER 19

Tuesday

London spreads before them like a bric-a-brac maze and Harris feels the wind whip at his face as they look down on the four-storey housing block, thirty-one storeys below. He grips the railing and peers over the edge of the roof of Trellick Tower.

'Are you going to hit him with a head shot?' he asks.

'Centre mass,' says Morgan, answering without really listening. He is squinting down a pair of binoculars at the squat rectangle of Holmefield House below, just one link in a winding chain of such buildings, the canal snaking past on their far side.

'I got to hit him with a cold bore at about three hundred feet without a spotter to help me factor in wind. I can't risk aiming for his head in case the barrel pulls on me, so I got to go centre mass. Also, this is a pretty tight angle to hit him at. There's a building facing Ferguson's flat but this is better: it'll take longer for the authorities to spot where the shot came from and it's good for exfiltration.'

Harris lights up a cigarette and blows a stream of smoke over the edge of the roof. Morgan catches the tobacco scent in his nostrils and looks from the binoculars to his companion with disdain. 'You ever do any sniper work?'

'Me? Nah. I like to get up close, you know?'

'What about all that "Sniper at work" road-sign bullshit on the news from Ireland?'

'South Armagh stuff. We couldn't risk civilian casualties in Belfast.'

'Like I said,' says Morgan, returning to the binoculars. 'Bullshit.'

It would be so easy, thinks Harris. Just pitch the arrogant Yank fucker over the edge of the tower-block roof. Watch him flail his way down thirty-one floors and explode on the pavement below. But the pay-cheque is too good and the job is only half done. Since the wee lad, Padraig, got himself killed it's just the two of them. For now, he needs this wanker. Besides, Alex Morgan represents the money.

Morgan says, 'Think of a line from nipple to nipple, then a line from each tit to the base of the throat and that's where I'll aim. Front if possible, back if I have to. We're looking at a much lower elevation than this, fifth or sixth floor facing north-west.'

Harris takes another deep drag on the cigarette, checks Morgan is still focused on the binoculars, and blows the smoke from the side of his mouth so that it clouds around the lenses. A small notch begins working at the angle of Morgan's jaw but he keeps it professional and says, 'That's where you come in. You find and secure the flat I choose in this tower and hold it until this evening. I'll get the rifle from the client, zero it in somewhere north of London. Fire a couple fouling shots to smooth out kinks in the barrel. We'll take him tonight.'

'What kind of rifle are you going to use? Armalite?'

'No good. I want bolt action if I have to shoot with a cold barrel. Less chance of the shot going astray.'

He looks at Harris and gives him a wink. 'Don't worry, Conal. I'll nail him for us.'

Then he walks across the rooftop towards a service door with Harris behind, miming blowing holes in his back with his fingertips.

#

The voice is deep and throaty, like its owner has made a career of late nights smoking roll-up cigarettes and drinking hard liquor. It's like a man could be mired in the voice and slowly sucked under until suffocated. Elira stands a few metres away, out of earshot.

'The sister is alive, which is more than I can say for a couple of my men. That's all you need to know.'

'Is she unharmed?' says Jackie.

'She is alive, among the dead.'

'What the fuck does that mean, Gandalf?'

'She still has a life. It's up to you whether she gets to lead it.'

'I can find you. I can go to the club in Soho.'

'And do what? You are one man. Your companion is a scared little girl. *My* scared little girl. If you were with the authorities I would be out of business by now. Instead, you ran. You have no options.'

'I could kill you.'

The voice of Bashkim, *Krye* of Soho, tightens for a moment. 'Fuck you.'

Jackie looks at Elira, focused on the front of a cottage on the eastern stretch of the mews, on the other side of Launceston Place. They are standing on the street in a fresh morning breeze, watching Flori's address to see if any police turn up; the injured Albanian is secured in the apartment. It has been ten minutes and so far they have seen an old lady walk a corpulent dachshund and a man in a sharp suit hurry out a door. Elira is wearing a pair of her sister's jeans, trainers and a simple sweat-shirt, her hair scraped from her face and tied back in a pony-tail.

The call has been business-like, almost civilised, up to this point. Bashkim and Jackie exchanged names, made arrangements for the gang to pick up the injured Albanian and his dead colleagues in a car park in Hampstead. Elira had found the car keys. Flori's Volkswagen Tiguan was parked in a row of garages nearby, the address written on the key fob.

Jackie says, 'If I agree, what happens to Flori?'

'Upon completion, she is released. She won't talk to the police: she is Albanian. She loves her parents and understands what we can do.'

The downstairs neighbour is not at home. The wounded gangster is tied to the chair with a T-shirt secured around his bullet wound, held in place by a belt. The pistol suppressors seem to have done their job, despite the racket the shots made in the flat. There's no sign of police.

'What about Elira?'

'She is a problem. We have made a lot of money from her in a short period of time. I have enjoyed fucking her myself.' A smile creeps into the voice. 'My God – the things I did to her. She is my property.'

'Not any more.'

'This, I think, is true. She defied me. I think she has little left inside her, and that makes a woman reckless. Dangerous. You can have her, although I want you to think of my cock in her ass when you lie with her. Or, you can dispose of her.'

'Funny, she told me you were hung like a half-chewed hangnail,' says Jackie. 'I'm in. But Elira stays with a friend. You will never see her again.'

A sniff of contempt. 'No matter. Call this number in two hours and I will give you an address. Go there.' Bashkim's voice thickens further. 'You tell her that her sister is alive by my grace. Her parents know nothing of this, yet. If she ever speaks of me, or betrays the *Fis*, I will make them suffer before I kill them.'

Then, silence.

Jackie slips the Albanian's mobile into his jeans pocket and turns to Elira. They'll return to the flat, look for cash and sort out the injured man and the two bodies. Then there's Bailey. Jackie will give him a call.

As he pulls the girl gently from the wall, something malignant gnaws at him. It's a wicked feeling, a feeling that he wants to destroy and maim. A bloodlust. And he realises that he hasn't hated anyone the way he hates the men ranged against himself and Elira for a long, long time.

#

Mahdi Farah had always been a good boy. He toed the line drawn by his father, Liban, studied as best he could and tried with all his heart to please his mother, Ruqia. Then his friend, Jongdo, from Ruttlefield Comprehensive School, had got an X-Box for his birthday and Mahdi had begged his parents to buy one for him, too. After a set of excellent exam results, they relented.

Now, with a maths test a couple of days away, Mahdi is in his bedroom taking out bad guys with an M16, all played out on the TV on the dresser at the foot of his bed. He will study, he really will use the revision day given him by the school, he just needs to clear this level first and save. Then he'll turn to the textbook and three months' worth of notes scattered on the floor and get back down to it.

His father is sleeping in another bedroom. A shift worker at Paddington station, he got home from work at six-thirty and, after a hurried kiss from his wife and a sandwich, he collapsed into bed, popped in earplugs and drifted off into a dreamless sleep.

Ruqia, loyal wife and devoted mother, is sitting at her desk in another school, George Dunlop Academy, marking essays while the class of fourteen-year-olds spread in rows in front of her slog their way through three pages of *Measure for Measure*. She makes the most money in the house and is proud that she has come from a refugee camp in Yemen to be an English Literature teacher with a reputation for a dynamic approach in the classroom and a good rate of academic achievement for her students.

She does worry about Mahdi and that infernal game console, though.

She would worry a lot more if she knew that Conal Harris is making his way to the door of the family's flat on the sixth floor of Trellick Tower, ready to secure the space as a base for Alexander Morgan to set up his sniper rifle and execute Patrick Ferguson, six hundred yards away in Holmefield House.

Harris has slipped through the entrance and past the concierge by doing nothing more than timing his approach to the front of the building to coincide with an elderly woman carrying shopping bags. As the woman struggled at the door to the building, he'd slipped between the bollards in front of the entrance and pushed the door open for her. He'd repeated the courtesy at the second door across a small entrance hall. Then he'd made his way to the lifts, offering a cursory nod to the concierge, held the doors for the elderly lady and punched the button for the eighteenth floor, then the sixth. It had been the same earlier with Morgan: wander in, exchange a pleasantry with the concierge and blether some nonsense as they called the lift. Look like you belong, people assume you belong.

As he stepped out of the lift and said goodbye to the lady he saw fire-doors and a long corridor. He'd never been put away during the struggle, never served time in the Maze or Crumlin Road prisons, but he imagined those corridors might have looked something like this. Now, as he passes flat after flat on his way to the third from the end, he thinks of all those men, full of piss and vinegar, locked away for years. Years of their lives lived in a small concrete cell, and for what? At least now his killing is an honest living.

He reaches the door and knocks. There's no answer.

He tries again. Waits. Nothing.

Third time's a charm, he thinks. If there's still no answer, he'll break in. Doubtful this place will have a security system and he doesn't want to spend much longer out here in the corridor. He knocks again and hears footsteps approaching the door, unhurried. The light behind the peephole dies for a moment and he knows he's being watched, then the door opens a fraction and, past a taut chain, he sees a black kid with a modest afro in some cartoon T-shirt. It throws him for a second. He thinks of the wee boy on the footbridge at Kew and for a crazy moment he thinks this is his ghost, come to seek vengeance.

Then he realises the kid is a young teenager rather than a child, and he batters the edge of the wood with his shoulder so the chain snaps like a tendon and the kid is knocked on his arse. Harris strides into this stranger's home, pulling the handgun from his jacket pocket as he does so. The boy's eyes go wide and his mouth follows suit and Harris belts him across the face with his left hand. He hauls a dark green balaclava over his head and grabs a handful of the kid's wiry hair. Crouching low, getting in the boy's face, he smells sweat, hormones, and crisps.

'Are you alone?'

The kid gapes, gone from the verge of a scream to struck dumb with fear. Harris releases the kid's hair, takes his chin in his hand and spits, 'Are you alone?' This time the kid shakes his head and his eyes mist, the first fat tear teetering on the edge of a lower lid.

'Who's here?' says Harris, bringing the gun up in preparation. He snaps again, hushed, 'Who?'

The kid's voice is a cracked whisper. 'My dad, asleep next door. He works at night. He wears ear plugs when he sleeps.'

'Your mother?'

'Out all day, at work.'

'Let's get your da up, will we?'

Harris takes the kid's arm in a firm grip and drags the boy to his feet. He judges the kid to be around fourteen and says, 'What's your name, son?'

'Mahdi.'

'That some Arab name?'

'Somali.'

They reach a door painted powder blue and Harris eases it open to reveal a bedroom, simply furnished, with a man sleeping on his side in the large bed. The man faces away from the door. Harris leans against the doorframe and nods towards him.

'Get your da up, Mahdi.'

The kid walks over to the man and gently shakes a coffee-coloured shoulder. After a few moments the body stirs and the man looks up at his son. Harris sees the face in profile, the confusion in the interruption to a deep sleep. Strong lips set over large teeth and the look of a man who is comfortable in his own skin. Harris hates him instantly. The father and son speak in Somali and then the man props himself up on his elbow and looks over his shoulder, locking eyes with Harris. There is no fear in the expression.

'You and your son are going to stay here with me for the day,' says Harris. 'Another man will come and join us. He'll have a rifle and he's going to kill someone, shoot a man from your window. When it's over, we'll leave and your family can get on with your lives. Mahdi has seen my face, briefly, but I'm sure he has a very bad memory.'

There is a ripple of anger across the man's composed features when Harris calls the boy by his name.

'But you give me any trouble,' says Harris, 'I'll kill you and your boy, and leave youse to rot in this flat. You understand me, you black bastard?'

CHAPTER 20

Tuesday

It was smooth and simple. A call to a mobile number from a public telephone; an address in Hampstead and a locker number in Euston station; a set of keys inside; go to the address, the basement of a modern-looking office space. Within, in a packing case nestled in the corner of a featureless basement room, is a Sig Sauer SSG 3000 sniper rifle with a detachable suppressor, a box of .223 Remington rifle ammunition and a set of car keys, vehicle registration on the fob.

He checks the rifle over and takes a firing pose. Satisfied with the weapon, he replaces the slender black killing machine in the case, along with the cigar-like suppressor and .223 ammo, and carries the case out to the building's underground car park. He finds the car and places the case in a hollowed-out section of the boot of the Vauxhall Insignia. Then he pulls out onto a nondescript Hampstead street, heading north to the outskirts of the city to play with his new toy.

#

Elira drove the Volkswagen to the front door while Jackie waited in the flat with the Albanian. With one of the back seats down, they could fit both bodies in the rear, wrapped in Persian rugs. It was a struggle and he waited for a police car to draw up to the mews at any moment, summoned by a suspicious neighbour, but none came. Thank God for London's millionaire homeowners, he thought, with their second houses, empty for most of the year, and quiet little flats for extra-curricular, extra-marital activities. After a scout around for money and snacks, Elira sat in the other back seat with the bodies, the wounded Albanian up front in the passenger seat while Jackie drove. After twenty minutes, they stopped and bought a pre-paid mobile phone for Elira.

Thirty minutes later Jackie pulls over to the kerb in a quiet residential street, the wounded Albanian asleep next to him. He needs to talk with Elira before driving on to the car park in Hampstead and he gestures for her to get out, then eases out of the Tiguan and locks it. He steers her to a traffic island in the centre of the street with a small patch of grass flanked by three trees and a weather-blistered wooden bench squatting under a brooding willow.

Jackie says, 'You're quiet.'

'I killed someone.'

They sit in silence for a full minute. Then Elira says, 'You are going to leave me.'

'Yes, because I'm going to help you. We went through this at Flori's place: if I do what they say, they will leave you in peace and your sister will live.'

'That is bullshit and you know it.'

He sighs. 'Yes.'

'So don't go. Stay with me. We can find Flori together. That *kafshë* in the car can tell us more, we can rescue her.'

'*That's* bullshit, and you know it.'

Elira wraps her small body in her skinny arms and drops her chin onto her chest. She isn't crying but tears aren't far away. They sit in wordless impasse, Jackie keeping an eye on the slumbering Albanian in the car twenty yards away, Elira fixed on the scrabbly tufts of grass and a couple of empty beer cans at their feet.

'Back at Chinatown, you said you knew I wasn't a policeman,' says Jackie. 'You were right and wrong. I was, years ago, in my hometown of Belfast. I worked undercover, trying to stop a gang who were terrorising the local community and planning political murders. It was dangerous. I was stressed, frightened: not sleeping, drinking and smoking too much, getting into brawls. I was becoming one of them. Then they tried to kill me. Thought I was an informer. They never realised I was actually a copper.' He's still focused on the Albanian slouched in the passenger seat of the Volkswagen across the street. 'I got out and left the country, though not the police. I went as far from Belfast as I could: Hong Kong. I was a cop there for a while, before the handover.' He turns to see if she is following him, but her head is still down, her eyes hidden by her tumbling hair.

'Last year I went home, for a funeral. My father's. The two leaders of the gang found me. They were locked in a feud but they still didn't know I'd been a policeman. They thought I was a genuine gangster who'd been an informant, whisked away by the authorities when my life was in danger, and one of them contracted me to kill the other. If I didn't, my sister and her family were dead. Then the other contracts me to kill the first.' He shakes his head. 'Honestly, you couldn't make it up.'

Jackie pauses, looking up at the pale blue sky infused with a chemical filter of London pollution. From behind the cloak of her hair, Elira says, 'And did you?'

'Kill them?' He swallows, pushing something back down into his core. 'They weren't men to be reasoned with.' Elira sweeps her hair back and looks at him, her eyes questioning.

'Let's say I destroyed them.'

'But you are working for the law now.'

'It turned out that people who work for the government, security services, knew what was happening and sat back, letting me do all the work for them. The same people who got me involved in all of this; the people I called from Piccadilly, who've abandoned us.'

'This is true?'

'Every word.'

'What did you do after Hong Kong?'

'A lot of things you don't need to know about and I don't need to remember. The point is, I was a policeman, not a killer, and I never really lost that copper's sensibility. Every day, I wish I'd never taken a life, but I do what has to be done. As a cop, I wanted to stop bad people doing bad things to good people. Last year, it was all about protecting my sister's family.' He puts a hand on hers, almost obscuring it. 'Now, I will do whatever I have to, to protect you and your sister.'

Her head tilts a fraction and Elira says, 'How well do you know this man you are taking me to?'

'Not well. He was a policeman in Belfast, like me, though different. I think he knows some bad people here in London. But I don't think he's involved with the men who kept you on the boat or the Albanian gang.'

'And what will you do?'

'I'll do what Bashkim wants until I find an opportunity to stop him and get Flori away.'

A tear comes, then her shoulders spasm as she fights back the first sobs. Through snatched breaths, she says, 'Can you do that?'

'I don't know.' Jackie smiles. 'But God loves a trier. I just hope I won't be meeting Him anytime soon.'

\#

Derek Bailey had sounded pleased to hear from Jackie on the phone: he said he'd tried to reach Jackie at the number given to him at St Katharine Docks and started fretting when he couldn't get through.

He gave Jackie an address in Islington. The street was nondescript, in Upper Holloway, all roomy red-brick terraces that could have been a residential street in any British city. The kettle is coming to the boil as Elira positions herself in the corner of the front sitting room, back to the wall.

They had left the Albanians and the guns including the empty Security Six revolver, in the car near Hampstead Heath and taken the train a couple of stops to Upper Holloway station, then walked to the house. Bailey led them through a small hall and into a sitting room with a coffee table, sofa, old TV and a wooden chair in the corner. Now Elira sits stiffly in the chair and the two men walk through to the adjoining kitchen, leaving the door open.

'Drop in your hand?' says Bailey.

'Aye,' says Jackie. 'Milk, no sugar. Elira?'

She jumps. When Bailey offers her tea she asks for coffee instead and he has to strain, craning his neck, to hear her.

'Not a bad wee place,' says Jackie. 'Are you living here on a security guard's wage?'

Bailey, dropping a tea-bag into an Arsenal mug, says, 'It's a mate's. Guy who was in the Met. He inherited the place from his folks, no mortgage to pay, and then got a job as a security consultant out in Dubai. He's raking it in.' Steaming water follows the tea-bag into the mug. 'When I told him I was coming down to the Big Smoke to look for work, he said I could stay for reduced rent.' Bailey grabs a jar of instant coffee. 'What's the story with the wee girl?'

'She's a friend, her name's Elira. Albanian. Been through a lot, but she's tough. Still, don't be offended if she's a bit stand-offish. I don't think trust comes easily to her.' Jackie runs his fingers around the rim of a wooden fruit-bowl next to the kettle, filled with takeaway menus, coins and assorted bric-a-brac: keys, paperclips, buttons, a couple of sweet wrappers. He catches a distinctive scent when he leans over the bowl to push the contents around with a finger: the musk of neglect, the lingering smell of fruit and something else more fragrant. He pauses. His tongue feels stupid and swollen in his mouth. Like Elira, trust doesn't come easily to him these days, and Bailey isn't exactly a trustworthy man. But they are alone and vulnerable, and there may be enough goodwill from the RUC old-boy connection for Bailey to give a helping hand. With a sigh, he tells Bailey about the Albanian gang and Elira's slavery, of how her sister has been taken and he must work with some very bad people to get her back.

'You think the sister's still alive?' Bailey's tone suggests there's more chance of Northern Ireland winning the World Cup.

'What can I do?' Jackie looks at Elira and wonders, if he were twenty years younger, could they be together? Would she love him? Could they build a life together?

'You could walk away,' says Bailey. 'You're free, no ties, no responsibilities. Just quit.'

'I have to go with Edmund Burke on the triumph of evil on this one.'

'And you're the good man? Here's another one for you: "A conscientious man would be cautious how he dealt in blood".'

The drinks made, Bailey walks into the adjoining room, gives Elira her coffee, and returns to the kitchen.

'What are you asking me here?' says Bailey. 'You turn up with some wee girl, full of stories of gangsters and shootings and the rest; you don't think that's a bit heavy? I'm not sure I want to get involved in any of this.' He sighs and shakes his head. It looks like a performance.

Jackie feels irritated but holds his peace. 'Sorry to be keeping you away from your coffee morning, Derek, but I didn't know who to turn to and what's going on here just isn't right. I got the impression from the three stooges you were drinking with in the Lily Bolero, maybe you weren't a stranger to trouble. All I want is a place to draw breath and a bit of information: any progress on the guy with the tattoo, the Nazi symbol, like two lightning strikes? The one with an accent I told you about on the phone? The way I heard it described, it sounds mid-Atlantic.'

Bailey frowns as he takes a chug of tea.

'I know a few guys with that kind of shite on their arms. March-on-Tower-Hamlets, mighty-white, ex-skinhead bollocks. They're all English, though, and sound it. You don't have a physical description?'

'Not much. Tall, in good shape. Clean-cut with short hair but not cropped.'

'Hang on, it rings a bell now,' says Bailey, taking another gulp of tea as though for inspiration. 'There was a big lad, a Canadian, who was hanging about the usual far-right circles for a while. Name of Chas Turner.'

'He has the tatts?'

'He's from Vancouver and came to London with his job. Actually a bit of a high-flyer, works for some brokers in Canary Wharf, but he's a true-blue homicidal maniac on his days off. Says Vancouver's full of Asians. Says they're ruining the city. He talks about going up a bell tower some day and picking people off.'

'Is he a marksman then?'

'Strictly your Guns N' Ammo type. I don't think he was ever in the Army or that, but he used to belong to a gun club back home. Drove over the border to the States to buy rifles, I think.'

Jackie sips his tea. It's strong and bitter, like his father used to make.

'What about the name,' Jackie says, changing tack. 'The Function? Somewhere in Maida Vale?'

Bailey frowns.

'Maida Vale. There's a Function House Hotel, has a decent boozer attached.'

'Did yer man Turner ever drink there?'

'He may have done. It's not that far from Hampstead, and Chas had a flat there for a while. He was shacked-up with a Dutch girl was dancing in some dive in Soho. An "exotic dancer", if you know what I mean.' He finishes his tea with a slurp and sets the mug down.

Jackie is quiet for a moment, digesting the information. There is a clock on the wall of the kitchen with a pendulum, and the steady tick-tock is like a platoon marking time on a march.

'What happened to your phone?' Bailey asks. 'I tried to call you a couple of times and got nothing.'

'Dropped it. Had a couple too many and went arse-over-tit down the steps of a pub.' He knows it's weak as water the moment he mumbles the explanation. But Bailey accepts it, smiling to himself and shaking his head.

'Mate,' he says, 'I didn't peg you as a drinker: takes one to know one. You weren't too eager to get your hands on that Guinness in the Lily Bolero. You do have good reason to drink, though.'

Jackie looks at Elira again. He thinks of the men he shot in that Soho alley – it had been so simple. A gun, a trigger, a target. Loud, angry rasps of rounds driven through the muzzle: the target drops. Done. What frightens him is he could do it again. After listening to the thick poison of Bakshim's voice, he could do it again, God help him.

Bailey puts a hand on his wrist and Jackie snaps backwards.

'All right, big lad, all right,' says Bailey. 'I'll help you out, if I can. This can be an unforgiving city and a man needs all the back-up he can get here.'

Jackie, riled by his thoughts, says, 'Like those Nazi bastards in the pub?'

Bailey's face hardens but the hand remains on Jackie's wrist. 'Listen, we got a handshake when the Constabulary was taken apart. "Thanks for being the bait in the trap for thirty years, lads. Thin Green Line and all, but youse can fuck off now". Police Service of Northern Ireland.' His mouth twists as though he's taken a shot of distilled vinegar. 'Try saying that with Gerry Adams's dick in your mouth.'

'Way of the world.'

'So if a fella can put a couple of pounds in his pocket by having a drink and doing business with some right-wing dickhead, then mine's a double.'

Then Bailey raises his hands in supplication. Jackie puts his empty mug on the kitchen counter and folds his arms. He doesn't like it. Then again, he doesn't like Hartley and his Spooks. Or the scum he's about to work with on the Ferguson hit. But there's something he needs to know. 'Did you ever know a guy called McVea? James McVea?'

'Wasn't he a midfielder for the Crues?'

'He was RUC, did some work with the Army intelligence boys out at Thiepval Barracks years ago. Smart money says he helped the Prods put the finger on a few republican movers. Maybe fed intel, set up a couple of hits. Restriction Orders to keep Security Forces out of the area when hits were going down. He was probably complicit in some Yank IRA fundraiser's murder, too.'

'So? When was his knighthood?'

'McVea is in London. You knew a few other boys from the force: did you ever come across him?'

'Another drop?' Bailey turns away and starts refilling the kettle. 'McVea, you say? Never heard of him.'

'Are you sure about that, Derek?'

'I never heard of him,' says Bailey. He steps up, his eyes drilling into Jackie, his nose a couple of inches away and his shoulders set back. He looks like a boxer who knows his opponent is out of his depth and going down.

Jackie holds his stare and says, 'All right.'

Bailey squares up for another beat, then his body seems to decompress. 'So, your man McLelland,' he says. 'Last anyone heard, he was sleeping rough somewhere about White City, living under the Westway elevated flyover somewhere. Does a bit of work here and there on the estates, picking up litter, that kind of shite.'

'Can you get word to him that I'm looking for him?'

'I can try. Do you have a mobile number I can get you at? One that works this time?'

Jackie takes a pen and begins scribbling the number of the Albanians' mobile down. 'Thanks,' he says.

'What the fuck,' says Bailey. 'We're a dying breed, right? If we can't help each other, no other fucker will. I just hope you aren't getting me into some really evil shite here, Jackie.'

The kettle growls as the water begins to boil.

CHAPTER 21

Tuesday

He looks at his watch. Elira should be somewhere around Oxford by now. Seeing her off was his last action before leaving for the estate in north-west London and Trellick Tower, looming ahead like an H. G. Wells alien giant astrode the city.

He'd needed to get Elira out of London. Bailey had been calling an acquaintance, trying to chase up more information on the SS tattoo. When Jackie punched in the postcode for Garbella Hill Farm on the Satnav, satisfied that Bailey was busy and her destination would remain secret, Elira had looked uncertain and he worried that he'd lost her trust again. As he spoke in a hoarse whisper, Elira had frowned, her mouth set. She had nodded when he described the horse paddocks and the open fields and the security of the cluster of buildings in the remote, hidden dales of the Cotswolds. He called her with the Albanian's phone and told her to keep the number in call history and not pick up if she got a call from it again; he'd memorised her number and would call from a public phone when the time came. She hadn't argued or pleaded, but had thrown her arms around his neck and whispered in his ear, 'Be careful.' Jackie had wanted to give her something, a token to hold onto, a promise. But he had nothing.

Instead, he had led her to the hallway and handed her the car keys and Satnav. As he fished in his jacket pocket, the coat hanging over the end of the banister at the foot of the stairs, he had pushed his sleeves up, revealing the blistered scar on his forearm where a tattoo had been, back when he was undercover.

Elira had reached out and touched it with the tips of her fingers, running a broken nail over the knotted ridge where the damaged skin ended. She had looked up at him then, some meaning in her gaze that he could sense, heavy and urgent, but not understand. He'd mumbled something about a hangover from his days undercover and then, to close those piercing eyes, he'd kissed her left eyelid.

'I'll finish the job and kiss the other one when I get back,' he'd said, feeling foolish.

He had watched her pull out of the street in Islington, anxious that she could make the drive safely alone, and told himself that he could do no more. Bailey hadn't asked and Jackie wasn't about to tell where she was headed. Instead, the two men had shaken hands and parted with a nod.

He approaches the concrete housing block of Trellick Tower via the Golborne Road, an iron railway bridge up ahead and the tower on the other side, teetering on the edge of the estate. He thinks of another railway bridge and the life bleeding from the young head of Christopher Martins. The bullet was fired by one of the men he is to meet. One of the men he is to abet in another murder, this time of Patrick Ferguson.

He rolls his shoulders and loosens up.

Time to go to work.

#

Elira's home, Tirana, is tucked below the great bulk of the mountains, bulging like biceps from the edge of the city. Here the land is gentle, rolling, green, unchanging. The roads are good but she was nervous on the motorway. When she reached Oxford, the city seemed an endless series of interlocking roundabouts but, finally, she is on the A40 and headed further into the Cotswolds. Near the village of Burford, she leaves the A40 and drives at slower speed through a tangle of ever-narrowing roads until she is on a lane leading to a cluster of buildings, Garbella Hill Farm.

She has trusted Jackie Shaw. It was not easy, but when he said he would protect her and her sister, she had to believe him. And perhaps he can do it. After her time as a whore she knows when a man is lying; she looked into Jackie's eyes and saw a ferocious sincerity.

The farm buildings seem huddled at a distance, a rolling hill to their north, paddocks to the west and south, and a lane threaded away from them to the east. She joins the lane at a fork after passing through a gate and driving for a hundred yards or so along a tarmac driveway. There is a flag flying next to the lane to the east, a design she doesn't know, and the track becomes pitted and scarred as she nears an open concrete space in the centre of the buildings, slick with a thin veneer of muck.

A bitter-sweet memory: Elira and her father, mother and sister at stables in the Albanian countryside. Riding lessons.

She believes that she has left a shadow of herself in each of the places rooted in her memory. Each one is a small piece of her, specific to time and age, who lives on in that moment, frozen in time like a photograph. It is how she has coped over the last months, taking comfort in the thought that younger, untainted Eliras are living their lives forever carefree in the pockets of happy memories which appear, like unexpected relatives at Christmas, on the doorstep of her consciousness. By this reckoning, she thinks, when a woman is old and tired, little strips of her have been shed over many years in many memories, and so the aged live more in the past than the present.

A girl of about Elira's age appears from a squat brick building, a wide smile on a pretty, smooth face under unruly blonde hair. She is wearing riding boots, jodhpurs and a grey jumper which has seen better days. Elira pulls in next to a Range Rover and steps from the car. She is grateful that she could change into Flori's clothes at the flat in Kynance Mews, although she still feels awkward and grubby next to the simple warmth of that smile and the open-faced country prettiness.

'You must be Elira,' the girl says. 'I'm Kelly. Jackie called to say you were coming.'

Without a word, she takes Elira by the hand and leads her towards an open door and the pleasant kitchen within. Elira breathes deeply of the country air and its sweet purity.

#

He knocks on the door of the flat, identical to the others on the long corridor, and blinks when a delicate, oval face peers through the crack between door and frame.

Jackie says, 'What's your name?'

No reply.

Jackie clenches and relaxes his fists: he doesn't like being exposed here in the corridor. He keeps eye contact with the boy and gives one, quick wink. The smooth, dark face retreats an inch. Then, 'Mahdi.'

'I'm Jackie. I'm here to talk with the men who invaded your home.'

On hearing the word 'invaded', the eyes soften and, for a moment, it looks as though the boy will cry. Then there is the sound of a chain sliding off a lock. The door opens and Jackie steps through into a narrow hallway. The fear and tension is like heavy sweat in a locker room, almost palpable. He says, 'How many are here now?'

'One.'

They walk through to the living room and a panoramic view of the London skyline, spoiled only by the bruised and swollen face of a man with strong African features sitting slumped in a chair and the pall of smoke surrounding another man wearing a balaclava with a pistol dangling from his right hand, seated in a chair opposite. As Jackie enters, the handgun centres on his heart.

'What happened to him?' says Jackie.

The man says, in a Belfast accent, 'He was a bit groggy when I got here. Needed waking up.'

Harris, thinks Jackie. He turns to the beaten man and says, 'Are you Mahdi's father?'

The man grunts an affirmative. 'Liban Farah,' he says.

'I'm sorry you and your boy have been subjected to this.'

Harris drops his cigarette in a mug and stands.

'I was fucking talking to you,' he says, a flicker of spittle sailing through the smoke as he gestures with the pistol.

'Nobody's stopping you,' says Jackie, still looking at Liban Farah, leaning to turn the man's head and assess his injuries. He says to the injured man, 'It hurts, but there's no permanent damage that I can see, Mr Farah.'

'You look at me when I'm talking to you, cunt.'

'You'll be Harris,' says Jackie. 'I recognise your voice from Soho. Bashkim told me to meet you here and, no doubt, you're expecting me. I know what you and your mate are going to do and, apparently, I have to help you.'

'Else that tasty wee tart's sister never plays the violin again, eh? I got the call to expect you. Can't say I'm happy about it.'

'The boy I shot in the alley, the youngster who was with you, is he still breathing?'

Harris shakes his head, taking another cigarette from the pack with his left hand.

'Did he shoot the wee boy in Kew?'

'Some fucking chance. He couldn't even shoot his load with a hooer.'

'It was you?'

187

Harris lights the fag one-handed and draws deeply on the filter. 'Not my proudest moment, but there you are. I got the job done in the end, anyway.'

Jackie, taking his jacket off, says, 'You enjoy that cigarette. They say those things'll kill you.' He sets the jacket, folded, on the sofa. 'Not that you'll live that long.'

There's a spark in the clear, grey eyes and Harris's knuckles whiten around the grip of the handgun. The cigarette hangs from his lip like a splinter and he takes a step forward slowly, quietly furious.

'Get the rest of your clothes off. I want to be sure you're unarmed, you black bastard.'

The boy, Mahdi, lets slip a sharp breath and Jackie thinks, looking at the boy's dark glare, that anger prompted it rather than fear.

Harris sees it, too, and laughs. 'Don't you worry, young 'un, that's what we call police back home. See, wankers like this specimen here' – he stabs at Jackie with the gun – 'wore dark green uniforms, near black, like. So: black bastards.' He takes deliberate aim at Jackie's temple and stares, his mouth twitching into a slanted smile, like a knife slash across the balaclava. Jackie begins undressing, slow and deliberate.

'I knew a boy,' says Harris. 'One of you.' His mouth puckers at the thought of his old enemy, the RUC. 'Campbell, his name was. Family man, you know? Couple of brats, nice-looking wife. He was on a dawn house search in Creggan, up in Derry, back in the eighties. The bastards turned up in force, RUC and Brits, kicking the door down, fucking the house up. It was a fella called Brennan's place. Used to source bomb-making materials for the Derry boys in Donegal and bring it over the border in tractors. So the Brits were standing about with their dicks in their hands as always, waiting to get shot, and the peelers were turning the house over.'

The boy and his father watch Jackie, their faces unreadable.

'Some of the wives were civil, making youse cups of tea when you raided the house. But not Bridget Brennan. See, I was fucking her while I was up there for a while. Her oul' boy, Tony, was a tool. Anyway, your man Campbell had some sweeties on him and he saw the Brennan kids standing there in their jammies and he went over and knelt down and gave them sweets. He told them the peelers and Brits wouldn't be there long and they were just trying to protect the kids' daddy, stop him before he hurt another kid's daddy.'

Jackie stoops to pull his jeans off, leg by leg.

'Bridget was livid,' he says. 'Some RUC bastard with his hands on her kids. And worse, the younger one, Tara, took the sweets and thanked Campbell for them. So, next time she was bouncing up and down on top of me, she asked me to have the Army council sanction a job on Campbell. Three weeks later, me and my team were looking down at Campbell in his bed with his missus lying next to him. She screamed and the kids came into the bedroom. A fella called Gimpsey had his gun on Campbell and I knelt down and said to the brats, "Don't worry, kids, your daddy did some bad things and I'm just here to make sure he doesn't hurt anybody else." Then I handed them sweeties.' He sniffs. 'Wee shites wouldn't take them. Anyway, I stood up and shot him six times, the wife shrieking and the kids wailing, "No, don't shoot my daddy! Don't hurt my daddy!" Then I went down the stairs, out the door and drove to Bridget's house. Shagged her senseless, so I did.'

Jackie stands naked. He knows the story is to wind him up, get a rise, but the effort is wasted. He's heard it all before. He's been at crime scenes where those same wives and kids are still screaming or, worse, catatonic.

Harris's eyes narrow like slits in the skin of an armoured car and he presses the muzzle of the handgun to Jackie's forehead.

Jackie feels the pressure of the hard metal on his temple, says, 'Do you want me to turn around and make it easier for you?'

He glances at the father and son. The boy is panting softly. There is a sad look on his father's battered face. Harris takes a step back from Jackie, his arm extending but the cool weight of the muzzle never leaving Jackie's head, butting his skull like a boxer in a clinch. Jackie breathes shallow but slow and determines not to blink. Not to flinch.

\#

Kelly likes the girl, Elira, but she is troubled by her melancholy. Elira has told her nothing other than that she is from Tirana, Albania, and that she has parents there and a sister in London. She's pretty in a tragic way and Kelly wonders how the girl met Jackie and how deep their relationship goes.

Kelly has always liked Jackie. He's a mystery to her and, like the girl, he carries a sense of gravitas, perhaps too much knowledge of what the world can do to people. She's caught him looking at her and knows he finds her attractive. Most of the men on the farm do, hardly surprising considering the ratio of male to female employees. Jackie is handsome in a dark, troubled way, but he can be remote, with a cruel look in his eyes.

As she shows Elira her room, she watches the girl empty her pockets on the bed. A few coins, car keys, and a small mobile phone. After a pause, the girl grabs the mobile and grips it tightly in her right hand. Then Kelly leaves Elira to freshen up before dinner and her introduction to the others on the farm. As the door settles into its frame, Kelly supposes Jackie's number is recorded on the mobile and she wonders, if she called him, where he would be and what crusade he might be on for the delicate, damaged girl from Tirana.

#

A smooth voice says, 'Put that goddamned gun away.'

The man walks into the space like the floor has an electric charge running through it, his body loose but controlled, ready to act. His eyes and mouth are set firm in the black balaclava.

He says, 'You're Jackie Shaw. Bashkim told me you'd be joining us.'

Jackie nods slowly, the muzzle of Harris's gun pushed into the skin of his forehead.

'The gun,' says the man. The command in the dark, malt eyes is unmistakable. Harris lowers the pistol with an insouciance so mannered it sweats with effort. The man says, 'My name is Morgan.'

Jackie takes the newcomer in; the mid-Atlantic honey of the accent is of a US citizen who has lived in England for some time. He wears a hooded top, open, with jeans and casual boots. He takes the hooded top off, folds it and places it on the sofa, re-vealing a pale blue T-shirt. The clothes are simple and cleave to the wiry frame without drawing attention to the wearer. Morgan is carrying a long object in a slender sports-bag. It could be fishing rods, or a folded tent, but Jackie can see the weight of the rifle in the tension of Morgan's arm. Bashkim had explained on the phone that Morgan was going to snipe Ferguson. Things begin to click. He looks at the small cylinder on a chain, outlined by the tight cut of the T-shirt just below the neckline.

'Is that your Hog's Tooth?' he says, nodding to the necklace.

The American sets the long bundle on the floor. 'And what would you know about that?'

'That bag doesn't hold a bunch of roses; you're American,' he glances at Morgan's forearm, all sinew and lean strength. 'And that double "S" tattoo stands for Scout Sniper, US Marine Corps, right?'

Harris looks confused. Morgan turns to him and says, 'It's a bullet.' He pulls the necklace out from under his T-shirt, a long, smooth bullet hanging from the chain. 'They give it to you when you graduate from Scout Sniper school. Beats a certificate.'

'I was British Army for a bit,' says Jackie. 'Did some training with some of your lads. The rifle in your bag; the tattoo. And the Hog's Tooth. I could see it through the T-shirt.'

Morgan says, 'You're a regular Sherlock, aren't you?'

Harris stews. The father and son sit silent. Morgan gives a short nod of his head and thinks that Jackie Shaw is no fool. And Jackie wonders how the hell Harris knew he'd been in the RUC in the first place.

CHAPTER 22

Tuesday

Morgan is terse, direct, professional, using an economy of words and displaying a sharp intelligence for the business of killing. There is an obvious friction with Harris. Maybe the professional soldier sees the Irishman as an undisciplined cut-throat. Perhaps Harris sees Morgan as an archetype: the arrogant Yank, the Patton-figure who rolls in and talks big, takes the credit. They rifle through Jackie's jacket and jeans pockets, not bothering to confiscate the small change and his street map. They take the Albanian's mobile phone from him. He tries not to look at the father and son sitting in the corner as he dresses again, their eyes huge and staring from stoic faces, like their strong features were carved from walnut wood.

'You're here, alive, because you have the girl,' says Morgan. 'All Bashkim's talk: "She's yours. You can have her. She means nothing to me". It's bullshit; I can see it. He wants her back. And, apparently, our client agrees to your involvement.'

Harris is fiddling with a cigarette, tapping the filter, turning it end-over-end in his fingers. Jackie wishes he'd light the damn thing and be done with it: the man's fidgeting sets his nerves on edge. Morgan holds the mobile in his hand as though weighing it and says, 'She's on the other end of this, right?'

'Check call history: it's wiped. She won't call. I told her to wait for me to contact her on another number. She's been through the wringer, and she's smart.'

'Well, she's still alive. That says something.'

'And the sister?'

Morgan says, 'I don't know about the sister.' When Harris's head snaps up to look at him, he says, 'A man deserves to know the circumstances when he's going to do some killing.'

Then he lays it out. Jackie will be the trigger-man for the Ferguson hit. Morgan had been ready to take the target out with the rifle until Bashkim called with new orders, fresh from the client himself. Jackie considers asking who the client might be if not the Albanians, but knows it's a dead end with a professional like Morgan. Anyway, the two killers may not know.

'I reconnoitred Ferguson's place before I came here from another building across from Ferguson's flat. A thermal imaging scope showed two men in the space with the target.' When they feel the time is right, he explains, Jackie and Harris will approach Ferguson's flat on foot. When they reach Ferguson's floor, Harris will don a balaclava. Jackie will not cover his face. There is probably a man outside the door to the flat: they'll neutralise him and use him to gain entry. If he refuses, Harris will use a small amount of C4 to blow the lock on the door. Then, while Harris holds the bodyguards at gunpoint, Jackie will shoot Ferguson dead.

As a plan it doesn't have much finesse, but the job of killing is blunt and cruel. In the end, it always boils down to an individual with a finger on a trigger, or a thumb on a detonator, who is willing to dismiss the moral and emotional cost of the act and apply the pressure necessary to kill. Just a couple of pounds in exchange for a life.

They assure Jackie that Harris won't kill the officers guarding Ferguson, merely take them out of the game. What 'take them out of the game' means is left unsaid. They don't want to raise the stakes any higher with Met or security force fatalities. Dead cops means tighter security, perhaps even witness protection for McVea. They don't mention McLelland, the vagrant. They tell Jackie they'll use him on the McVea job, too, but he knows that only Bashkim and his obsession with Elira, and the mysterious client, are reining Morgan and Harris in. He'd have been dead within seconds of walking into the flat if they knew her location.

Elira. He'll do this for her and her sister. He says, 'How do you know Ferguson isn't wearing a vest?'

'Didn't show up on the scope on my recon,' says Morgan. 'I got a good look at Ferguson and his sweater is tight: no sign of any armour bulking it out or a dampening of heat signature. If he was wearing a skin, I'd have picked it up: I know what to look for.' He snorts. 'The security services over here won't bother to give him armour with a two-or-three-man protection detail. They're too fucking cheap. Still, I'll be monitoring things from up here, through the scope. If I sniff a vest I'll let you know.'

Harris grunts, 'Best go for his head, anyway. That's where I'd be aiming, if I was shooting you.'

'The back of it, of course,' says Jackie.

Morgan says, 'I keep your phone.'

The father and son look on. The boy looks from Jackie, to the phone, then hangs his head. His father nudges the boy in the ribs and Jackie sees the youngster's eyes drift off, to follow the father's gaze to the clock on the wall above the door to the hall. It's only then that he spots a woman's umbrella tucked into the hat-stand next to the front door and a warm, genuine-looking female face framed in a colourful headscarf in the family photographs arranged on a dresser.

#

The girl is sharp and, somewhere beneath the sullen armour of her silence, Kelly thinks a bright, fiery spirit burns. It's there in a loud, braying laugh at an offhand joke; a breathless rush in her speech when they discuss the horses; a light in the eyes when she talks about her hometown. Then the dark glare will settle on her brow again and she will be somewhere else, living – or reliving – a life Kelly can't hope to understand.

So, when Kelly leaves the girl in the kitchen to go and check on a couple of the mares, she isn't fazed to find the chair next to the heavy wooden table empty upon her return. She calls, her voice light and tinny in the empty room. She knocks on the toilet door next to the kitchen, again calling, 'Elira.' She takes the stairs two at a time, unease kindling in her stomach like the warm glow of the vodka she sips to take the edge off a hard day on the gallops.

The yard is deserted, the stables, too, save for the horses themselves, fussing softly.

Back in the kitchen, the only trace of Elira she can find is a half-drunk cup of tea and the crumbs of a plate of biscuits the girl had demolished as they chatted at the table. And the mobile phone Elira had been cradling, like a holy medal, as they passed an hour at the large slab of wood in the centre of the tiled kitchen floor. Kelly picks the phone up from the table and checks the contacts directory, empty. There is one number in call history. Kelly is uneasy, and doesn't quite know why. It's something in the girl's way, in her empty stare, in her damaged smile. It's something in the girl. And now the girl has gone, which frightens her.

The other staff are busy, running errands, making deliveries or shirking chores. The boss, Mack, is in Wales at an auction and won't return for another couple of hours. Kelly is alone.

Kelly doesn't see the small, handwritten note on the floor under the table. A note Elira left for her. A note that slipped through the slats on the top of the rough wood table.

The number on the mobile, she thinks. It must be Jackie, and Jackie will know what to do. Dark, troubled, capable Jackie. So she punches a key and listens to the hollow trill of the dial tone.

The sun hangs low in the sky, lazy and bloated as they walk to the path which skirts the canal beyond, snaking through Paddington.

Harris feels good. He's taken off that fucking balaclava for a start, and a sports bag hangs from his shoulder containing C-4 explosive, blasting caps, wire and detonator. He has his handgun, a Makarov, in a shoulder holster and a snub-nose Colt Detective Special revolver in his jacket pocket, three rounds in the chamber and his finger on the trigger. The bastard, Shaw, walks a little ahead of him; the revolver is pointed at the fucker's spine. Three rounds: enough for Shaw to finish Patrick Ferguson. Harris will give the ex-peeler the gun just before they enter the room, then cover the two men who are baby-sitting Ferguson while Shaw shoots him down. He breathes deeply, taking the scent of the trees, big-city corruption and the heady, springtime musk of possibility deep in his lungs. For the first time in a while, he doesn't crave a fag. This evening, he knows, he'll get a hit from a different drug.

Tonight he'll take a trophy he hasn't nailed for twenty years.

Harris is wearing an earpiece, and the sickening, slurred tones of Morgan have just finished spreading the good word. Once Shaw has pumped those three rounds into the body of Patrick Ferguson, Harris has the go-ahead to put the black bastard down, just like old times.

Tonight, Conal Harris is going to bag himself a peeler.

#

Two men, Morgan had said, his cheek pressed against the stock of the rifle, eye squinting through the sniper scope. There were still two men with Patrick Ferguson, both sitting in the living room with the target. Jackie knows from experience there's probably another in the corridor, bored out of his mind, outside the door. He had done a couple of hospital stints, when still in uniform, in the RUC. Once, he'd guarded a fellow officer who'd been mangled in a carbomb and a couple of times he'd baby-sat a nationalist politician, in for two separate bouts of drink-related health problems. It had been endless cups of tea, the odd flirt with the nurses and a few stolen moments with a paper-back.

The men inside with Ferguson, probably Met, are on protective detail in a pair. There'd be tea and boredom, but also chat and banter, maybe with Ferguson himself. All distraction, all factors to blunt their edge and give him and Harris a few precious seconds to take command of the situation. As they approach a gate on their left, a couple of barges hard against the bank of the canal on their right, Harris spits, the wad of phlegm landing just short of Jackie's boot.

Jackie turns to give the pinched, hard-bitten bastard's face a stare but Harris is now looking at the surface of the canal, opaque water smeared green by the reflection of the trees on the bank. 'We could have brought the fucking boat up here.'

'Surprised you'd need one. Being the perfect killer, I'd have thought you could walk on water.'

Harris scowls and says, 'Get over the gate.'

Trellick Tower still glares down at them, a solid mass of pastel blue in the haze of late afternoon. Jackie knows that somewhere in that hulking stack of humanity, Morgan has his sniper scope trained on him, insurance that he'll follow the killing through. He leaps for the top of the gate, a solid sheet of iron, finds purchase, and hauls his body over the top.

\#

Morgan says, 'He's over the fence.'

The American describes Shaw standing in a dusty yard, deserted save for himself.

'He's standing, looking around. Looks benign enough.'

The two Somalis sit glowering in the corner, the father slumped and broken in a chair, the boy at his feet. Morgan doesn't approve of unnecessary violence but in this case, he must admit, Harris's sadistic tendencies have made life easier. The boy is scrawny, busy tending to his father, no real threat. The man's arm looks broken. Morgan has tied them together with a plastic cord and secured the father's arm to the chair, like a dog tied to a post.

He settles against his sights again, adjusting his eye relief and going through a slow rotation of his shoulders. His concentration had been broken by the buzz of Shaw's mobile phone. He'd picked up and spoken to a young English girl – *Did he know Jackie? Old friends, and who is calling? Kelly? Well, Kelly, Jackie is busy right now, gone out on an errand and forgot his phone. Elira has wandered off? Just sit tight and I'll have Jackie call you back when he returns.*

Morgan called the client and relayed the caller's number to be traced. The location would be established and the girl secured. And Harris would kill Shaw, the fresh corpse of Ferguson just feet away. Whether the authorities believe Shaw is the hitter or not is immaterial: it's about misdirection and muddying the waters.

The rifle is good, but he's only lived with it for a matter of hours and hasn't had a chance to 'weld' his eye, finding a favoured spot at which he places his cheek on the stock, shot after shot. No weld means lack of consistency, and he isn't helped by his positioning. He sits, hunched on the sofa, his shooting platform a coffee table. In front of him, the wall-to-ceiling sliding door is open and he is sighting through the metal slats of the balcony railing. He should be lying prone, he should have a spotter, shouldn't have to deal with the occasional grey, vertical blur of an iron railing. The balaclava is itching, making it difficult to get comfortable with the sight. Why did that Irish asshole choose wool?

Come on, Alex, he thinks. Remember the Corps. Improvise, Adapt and Overcome.

He breathes out, slow and controlled, and concentrates on targeting Jackie Shaw's brain stem, imagining a bullet tearing through it.

#

In his earpiece, Harris hears, 'He's stationary.'

He leaps for the crest of the gate and can't find purchase at the first attempt. There's a loud clang as the revolver in his pocket collides with the metal and he curses, imagining Shaw and Morgan smirking. Once over, Harris slips his hand into his pocket and aims the Colt at Shaw again, hissing, 'Get a fucking move on.' They step over the low brick wall in front of the yard and are confronted with the concrete façade of Holmefield House.

From the air, the apartment complex would resemble two trains, following the parallel curve of Hazelwood Crescent and Kensal Road, four short blocks of Brutalist concrete joining the longer wings like rungs on a ladder. Harris and Shaw stand on Kensal Road, to the rear of the complex. Harris places a boot on Shaw's hip and gives him a vicious kick forward. The lower floors of Trellick Tower, off to their left, are now obscured by Holmefield House and Harris knows, until they reach Ferguson's place, Morgan won't have sight of them.

Now he is in control.

Now he has this ex-peeler, black bastard's life in his nicotine-stained hands.

They enter the block of flats through a simple wooden door opposite a tall Victorian building with the legend *Cobden Working Men's Club and Institute* worded in tile on its front.

Is that what we are? thinks Jackie. Working men? He almost envies Harris and Morgan: at least they know why they're killing. They're grafters, taking lives for money. He killed for survival, but it still doesn't sit right. What is survival if you have to live with this guilt around your neck? And now he'll kill again, to save Elira's sister.

Another kick to his back propels him through the door and they are inside the housing block, in a deserted corridor smelling of bleach and fresh paint. He hears a TV bleating somewhere. As they walk down the passage, he sees a flight of stairs to the right with thick wooden banisters.

'Up to the second floor,' says Harris.

And so they climb.

#

Ruqia Farah pulls into the car park behind Trellick Tower and gathers her handbag, a file, and a plastic bag full of homework to be marked. Always nice to finish early, even if some joker set the fire alarm off and sparked an evacuation. Liban should be awake by now, hopefully with the rice on the boil, ready for her to put the beans and meat together. She hopes Mahdi hasn't been snacking through his studies and resolves to introduce the blanket ban on soft drinks in the house that she had discussed with Liban.

Ruqia locks the car and begins traipsing wearily across the open concrete to Trellick Tower and her family, happy and thankful for their lot, a small but clean and comfortable flat in the soaring tower, overlooking the great sprawl of London below.

CHAPTER 23

Tuesday

Harris finally gives him the Colt as they stand at the top of the staircase, peering around the corner at the corridor and Ferguson's apartment, five doors down. Jackie notices that Harris's neck is flushed, an angry crimson against his pale skin. The Makarov is aimed low at Jackie's groin.

'Three bullets for Ferguson. You walk in front of me, you enter the flat first. I neutralise the guards, you kill him, we go.' Harris's face is pinched and his voice rises. 'But first, we need to take care of the cunt at the door.'

The man standing in front of the door to Ferguson's flat is in the classic bouncer pose, hands clasped in front of his crotch, pulling the arms of his light jacket tight. It's difficult to see an earpiece and mic from this angle and distance.

'You take him out,' says Harris.

There is no doubt in the words, and no room for questions. Jackie nods and takes the snub-nose in his hand, the stump of a barrel pointed at the floor. He turns it over once then tucks it into his waistband, the metal hard against his spine.

He says, 'Give me a cigarette.'

Harris's neck goes a deeper shade of furious red and he is about to spit some invective when Jackie says, 'Now. We don't have time to slap our dicks about.'

Harris glowers, takes a packet from his pocket and hands it over. 'Give me a lighter.'

Silence. Harris's eyes are as black as the muzzle of the Makarov now aimed at Jackie's face in the dim light.

Jackie says, 'Pretty-fucking-please.'

'I'll light it for you.'

'I'm not going to smoke it,' hisses Jackie. 'I'm going to walk down the corridor trying to light it. It draws the guard's focus away from my face to my hands and gives me something to do as I approach him.'

Jackie takes a cheap plastic lighter from Harris and pops the unlit cigarette in his mouth. He stoops, loosening up his rigid limbs as though drunk, and shuffles into the corridor, heading for the grey door set in the wall ahead to his right, last in the row, and the walking dead man behind it.

#

Morgan can see the target from the waist up through the window, like a negative of a moving image in the thermal scope. Occasionally, one of the bodyguards drifts into view, glancing out at the street through the grime-stained window, his body mass almost merging with Ferguson's slim frame in the scope. Morgan shifts position a fraction, a dull pain beginning in his lower back as he hunches over the rifle.

'Mahdi,' he says, still focused on the scope, 'how many people are on the street?'

The boy is quiet for a moment, then Morgan hears him straining at his bindings to get a better view of the street six floors below. Mahdi says, 'A few people are walking. Two women with shopping bags, another with a baby. There are two teenagers standing in front of the building entrance, just talking.'

'Mahadsanid.'

The boy doesn't respond to the thanks, but his father says, 'Af Soomaaliga maad ku hadashaa?'

'A little,' says Morgan. 'I picked up a couple of phrases here and there when I served in your country, back in the nineties. It's a beautiful place.'

'Yes,' says the father. 'My son has never been to Somalia. I pray that, someday, he will.'

'Well, you never know,' Morgan says. Ferguson has moved closer to the window of his flat and Morgan can place the crosshairs between the target's shoulder blades. 'Look at the two men who were here with me. They come from a beautiful place that was busy tearing itself apart just about the time I landed in Mogadishu. Now it's hosting MTV awards and G8 summits.'

'But those men hate each other.'

'That's the Irish for you. They do love to hold a grudge.'

'Our people are no better. Pride. Intransigence.'

'Can make for great fighters.'

'It makes for martyrs, and widows and orphans. I will not have my son follow that road.'

Morgan licks his lips and hears Harris whisper through his earpiece that Shaw is approaching the door of Ferguson's flat. He says, 'You're right, sir. You should listen to your father, son.'

The father says, 'Mahadsanid.'

Morgan says, 'Adigaa mudan. You're welcome.'

The boy remains a wraith in the background, haunting Morgan with his stony silence.

#

The protection officer notices him and rolls his eyes.

God knows how long he's been standing outside that door, thinks Jackie. Dealing with nosy residents, smart-arse kids and deadening boredom. The shuffling drunk who can't master the motor-skills to light a cigarette is just the latest in a string of irritations, no doubt. The good news is there are no signs of body-coms. The man muttered something when he clocked

Jackie, but it looked more like a whispered moan – 'for fuck's sake' – than any relay to the officers inside. Jackie covers the lighter with his cupped left hand as he sparks it over and over. He looks up and smiles a stupid, lop-sided grin, prompting another curse from the protection officer, now only a couple of feet away.

The officer decides to pre-empt any attempt at conversation.

'I don't smoke, I don't have a light and I don't have a couple of quid for you to go and buy one. I'm waiting for someone and I'm not in the mood, so fuck off.'

'Not very civil, mate,' says Jackie, in an excruciating attempt at a Glaswegian accent. He puts his hands up, palms out, the cigarette now lit, his lungs flooded with the harsh burn of the smoke for the second time today. 'Panic's over, anyhow.' He takes the cigarette in his left hand between thumb and forefinger and points it at the man, then tucks the lighter in his right-hip pocket and leaves his hand there, inches from the grip of the snub-nose. He leans towards the officer a little, sloppy, offended, but unthreatening.

'Just for future reference, mate...' he says, then flicks the cigarette in the man's face, the glowing tip exploding like tracer fire as the officer recoils. Jackie has the revolver in his hand, his arm moving in an arc from pocket to waistband to ramming the muzzle in the man's distorted mouth. His left hand pins the officer to the wall by the throat. He pushes in close, his voice a frantic rasp. 'Keep quiet. No noise, no movement.' He glances to his right and sees Harris begin scurrying towards them from the staircase, hauling the balaclava over his face. 'The man who's with me would love an excuse to kill you. Don't give him one.'

The officer's eyes are wild. Jackie lowers his voice. 'Calm down. Just breathe and calm down.'

Then Harris is next to them, ducking under the peep-hole in the door and shouldering Jackie out of the way, the bag bouncing off his hip. He pats the officer down, pulling a handgun from a shoulder rig and shoving it in his jacket pocket, then clamps his palm over the man's mouth and says, 'Tell them to open the door.' When he takes his hand away, the officer's fear hangs in the air, a musk of sweat, adrenaline and terror.

Jackie says, 'What's your name?'

Harris spits, 'Shut the fuck up,' then turns to the officer and rams his left forearm hard against his throat. Harris produces a flick knife. It snaps open and he holds it to the man's face and says, 'Tell them to open the door.' The officer, his throat still straining against Harris's arm, stares at the blade, dumb.

Jackie says, 'Do it. He'll blow the lock if you don't. Just call for them to open the door.'

Harris mutters to himself, 'No time for this.' Then he slaps his left hand over the officer's mouth and stabs him twice, driving short thrusts into the man's side. There's a sound like someone crumpling wet paper and the blade emerges from flesh with a thin film of blood. The man's eyes clench, his face goes pale.

Jackie hears a thin, strangled, high-pitched sound. 'For fuck's sake,' he says, 'you'll kill him.' The corridor is still deserted but they need to secure entry now. If a civilian wanders into the scene, there'll be more bloodshed.

'Tell them to open the door,' says Harris.

Somewhere, they hear an echo, the hollow shuffle of footsteps.

Jackie reaches over and begins rifling through the officer's pockets. He finds a wallet and flips it open as Harris mutters an obscenity. Among the cards and receipts there is a small photograph of a woman and two children, a girl and boy. He holds it up to the man's face, just as Harris had done with the blade, and says, 'You want him to find your family? You want him and your kids in the same room?' He shoves the photograph and wallet back in the officer's jacket and says, 'Tell them to open the fucking door.'

The man looks at Jackie and nods.

Mahdi is angry with his father. He is angry that he would talk with this man who has invaded their home and brought violence to their family. And he's frightened. His fear drives his anger, the two emotions goading one another.

The man, Morgan, has changed his position. Mahdi can feel his father's body stiffen next to him in anticipation of something very bad. He turns to his father, the calm, care-worn face now bloated with the beating from the man, Harris. He thinks of the Irishman's furious eyes, the sharp cheekbones, the animal sneer as he charged the door of the flat. He can't believe they'll let him live now he has seen that face.

Liban's eyes, the right pupil almost covered by the swollen eyelid, glance at the clock again and then settle on Mahdi. 'Ina,' he whispers, 'my son.' His voice is weak and his tongue sounds swollen and heavy in his mouth. His split lips barely move. 'Waxaan dareemayaa in aan waxba.'

I feel nothing.

His eyes flit to his left arm, still tethered to his son's by the plastic cord. Mahdi has heard that paralysis in the left arm is a sign of heart failure and his gut contracts. He's heard stories about Mogadishu and the refugee camp where he was born but can't remember, and through it all his mother and father survived. He's never considered that his father might die, nor his mother. Now, that reality has come upon him. The thought chokes him and he realises he hasn't taken a breath for many seconds.

His father whispers, 'Gacantayday la jebiyey. Waxaan dareemayaa in aan waxba.'

My arm is broken. I feel nothing.

'Jebin aan suulka. Xudunta. Maroojin.'

Break my thumb. The cord. Twist it.

Mahdi nods, the movement barely perceptible, and begins twisting his father's joint as tears sting his eyes. The snap is short and harsh, like dry wood splintering. They turn to Morgan. The sniper is engrossed in the view in his scope and Mahdi starts twisting the cord and his father's limp, useless hand and wrist. The cord gives a fraction, bites hard into the flesh before moving another tiny degree towards the broken thumb. And beyond the door, in the corridor outside, there is the measured step of a woman returning early to her home after a day's honest work, unaware that her husband and son sit a few feet away from the violence and death she had fled so many years ago.

#

The wounded officer knocks on the door.

It opens a crack, but it's enough. Jackie is up front, the wounded officer behind him and, covering them both with his Makarov, Harris. Jackie pulls the revolver and places the sights on the second protection officer's forehead, standing in the flat behind the door, then drives his heel hard into the wood, battering the man's face with the edge of the door so hard it splinters. He hears Harris grunt and the first officer with the knife wound comes clattering past him, struggling to stay on his feet as though flailing on ice before colliding with the now-falling second officer. Both collapse on the floor of the hallway as the last officer reacts. He is standing at the threshold of the living room, at the end of the short hallway, and has his weapon half-out of his shoulder-rig before a deafening flat thunder-clap explodes and the man drops to one knee, his expression incredulous. Harris glides past Jackie, fluid and agile. He stabs the officer who opened the door with three sharp thrusts in the lower stomach then makes his way to the third man who is staring at the small bullet-hole in the groin of his jeans.

208

Jackie says, 'What the fuck?'

Harris says, 'They're still breathing, aren't they?' as he wrenches a handgun from the shot man and shoves it in his waistband. 'Get the other fucker's weapon and give it to me.'

The officer who opened the door is pale, shock sucking the colour from his face as Jackie removes his pistol and checks the small, seeping slits in his stomach. Jackie turns back to Harris to find the other man's Makarov covering him.

Harris says, 'To me.'

Jackie tosses the gun to Harris who holds it in his left hand. He says, 'Get it done.'

Jackie walks past Harris, his limbs suddenly heavy, and a figure comes into view. A shrunken figure in a long-sleeved sweatshirt and jeans. The face is plain with a thin nose and two dark, deep-set eyes, like raisins set in dough. Then the wide mouth opens a fraction and emits a small sigh as Patrick Ferguson meets his executioner.

#

The commotion in his earpiece tells Morgan they're in the flat, but when he sees Ferguson through the thermal scope, backing up towards the window, a pale stain spreading on the leg of his jeans, he places a little pressure on the trigger.

He's ashamed for this man who once did hard and dangerous things for a living and now pisses himself in fear, in his own home. Morgan knows he could have become the same after leaving the corps: soft, maudlin and sentimental, robbed of purpose. He settles in a little closer to the rifle. Yes, it's the right thing. To use his skills, to serve a different master and – yes – make a little to put away on the side for when the time comes to drift away on a sea of booze and easy women in the Caribbean, or Pacific.

The voices in his head, babbling from the earpiece, swell and coalesce. Morgan sees a tattoo peek from the collar of Ferguson's sweater as the man backs up further towards the window, his neck now clearly visible in the scope. It's a flat, solid shape and he wonders what the rest of it looks like. Perhaps some tribal shit, or one of the Yakuza-style works of art he sees on the subway back home. The earpiece is still alive with seething, chattering voices.

'Do it!'

'Shite.'

'No! No!'

'Shut the fuck up.'

Then Ferguson steps back until his head and shoulders are pressed against the window of his flat and his arms raised, his hands above his ears. And at that moment, a thick clutch of fibres sprout from Ferguson's tattoo like pubic hair, and Morgan sees a small seam around the shoulders in the thermal image. A strap. It isn't a tattoo: the fucker is wearing body armour. He's seen it before, in Iraq, the Blackwater guys in their Goldflex and Airfree: ultra-thin vests the DOD wouldn't stretch to for the Marines. And then, as his finger begins to exert a smooth pressure on the Sig Sauer's trigger, all hell breaks loose.

CHAPTER 24

Tuesday

It's all sound and fury, a cacophony of moaning and whining behind him, Harris's shrill bark goading him on like a boot in the back and Ferguson before him, tears in his eyes and piss on his crotch, hands raised. Jackie advances, gun raised, and Ferguson retreats until his back touches the windowpane and there is nowhere to go. Someone, surely, has heard the commotion, has heard Harris's shot, thinks Jackie. The police must be on the way. He can't kill this man. He despairs of Elira and Flori.

The snub-nose is light, the three bullets chambered and waiting for that pound or two of pressure to release them, to hurl them through the air, then skin, flesh and tissue. So he does.

He whirls around, the room a blur, until he is facing Harris.

Harris screeches, 'What the fuck?'

The room seems to compress, the walls and furniture wrapping themselves around the men. Jackie can hear Harris's ragged breathing, sees the sweat patches on his T-shirt as Harris raises his gun, and senses the confused terror of Ferguson behind him. Then Jackie fires, revolver bucking in his hand as the sharp roar of the shot fills the air. The muzzle flash is a furious amber flare. Harris is punched backwards, his eyes wide. Jackie pulls the trigger again, sure in his position, his eye on the target, centre mass. The hammer drives home and again the air is filled with the deafening bang, the muzzle spitting fire. Harris takes the bullet in the chest, his own gun firing three rounds, the sharp bark of the Markarov bouncing around the walls. Jackie fires his last round, the Colt flaring again, the bullet hitting Harris above the heart. The man jerks once more before he goes down, firing two more shots before landing in an awkward heap in the doorway.

Something hard and angular connects with Jackie's left shoulder. It's as though something huge and invisible has just punched him hard, setting off a bomb beneath the skin. His body rebels: too little food and sleep; too much violence. His legs give and he doesn't know why and he drops to the floor. Lying on the carpet, he cranes his neck and sees Harris slumped and, as he twists his head backwards, Ferguson on his arse, upper body propped against the wall, head hanging with his chin on his chest. A thin seam of blood is tracing a line along Ferguson's jaw from somewhere in the back of his skull.

Jackie's ears are ringing. He doesn't feel any pain but has a dim recognition that he has been shot. There are fading sounds: men scrabbling to their feet, or whimpering. He hears someone rushing to the door of the apartment. His body feels heavy. He can see a fabric of cracks in the plaster of the ceiling above his head. Someone holds a palm full of pennies up to his nose and then he realises he can smell blood and his left shoulder is wet. There is the smell of Ferguson's piss and, just before he passes out, the heady musk of strong deodorant and the stale reek of tobacco.

#

The cord tethering Mahdi to his father jerks and comes away as the man, Morgan, grunts a profanity and they hear the scrape of a key in the door lock from the hall. As Mahdi is freed, Morgan squeezes the trigger of the rifle, a harsh clack snapping around the living room. It's joined by the light call of his mother, the front door opening with its customary whinge, and his father's frightened call.

212

Liban Farah tries to struggle from his chair as Morgan realises someone has opened the door. The American drops the rifle, its stock hitting the table as he reaches for his jacket on the sofa next to him. Mahdi's mother, Ruqia, strolls up to the threshold of the living room and stops dead, her warm, lidded eyes and easy smile frozen. Her features distort and collapse as she sees the intruder in her home. Her eyes are drawn to the movement of her husband, his brutalised face set with a terrible purpose, his useless left arm hanging at an obscene angle.

Morgan is pulling a handgun from the jacket on the sofa. Ruqia Farah, the rock of the household, screams. The sound is more terrifying than any sight or sound Mahdi has experienced in his sixteen short years, and it shocks him to action. As Morgan raises the gun Mahdi howls, a raging cry that fills the room. The terrible sound seems to grip Morgan's arm and he freezes, the gun not fully levelled at Ruqia, the muzzle aimed at the carpet at her feet. The American swivels, bringing the pistol to bear on Mahdi as the young Somali launches himself, covering ground faster than the professional killer can aim.

His mother screams again, incomprehensible, insensible. His father bellows, a roar that belies his frail frame and the room is a spinning barrel of tumbling sound, Mahdi running, his momentum driving him into Morgan as the killer fires. The flat report of the gun slams into the walls with the bullet and kills all other sound for a second. Mother and father are out of sight, and now it's just Mahdi and Morgan, tumbling over the coffee table, the rifle clattering ahead of them onto the balcony. The older, stronger man clouts Mahdi with a wild punch across the back of the head but the teenager is lithe and fast. He's on his feet while Morgan is still crouched. The younger man shoulder charges, the American losing his footing again and tripping on the rifle at his heel. Morgan's shoulder collides with the balcony railing with a dull ringing sound. Mahdi leaps. He feels barely contained by his body, adrenaline surging, his arms shaking. Then he is crumpling. Morgan's legs scissor his ankles, and Mahdi falls, his body carried forward by his momentum. His face batters into the iron balcony railings.

He has a fleeting glimpse of London spread before him, a vast circuit-board of concrete, brick and greenery. Then his head snaps back and there is a stinging sensation in his cheek and his eyes fall on Morgan, the balaclava gone, lean face set, lips sucked between his teeth, fist raised for another punch. Mahdi's focus is clear despite the battering, and he sees the room spin before him again through the open windows as he is whirled around, his back to the city, the railing pressing hard against his back. He sees the table is upright but askew, the sofa upended. And his father, still tethered to the chair he has dragged to the window, has the rifle in his good hand. He can barely hold it, never mind raise it, and his face is awash with pain.

Another blow connects with Mahdi's temple. The hand clenched around his neck tightens and he feels his throat closing. He flails as though trying to snatch some oxygen from the air. A low heat ignites behind his eyes and he claws at Morgan's hand. Another sharp punch snaps his head a fraction sideways, jolting his brain as the killer's grip stops him riding with the blow. He feels stupid, his movements awkward despite the rising pain and appalling knowledge that he is going to die.

Mahdi closes his eyes. At his back lies London, cold, remorseless, relentless. The city will churn on. But he is so sad that he won't see his parents again. As he thrashes his last, he loves them like never before.

The thick thud of the rifle stock on the American's head comes from a place far away. Mahdi opens his eyes in reflex as Morgan's grip tightens in a spasm, then slackens as the killer stumbles, still upright but suddenly inert. The second crack of the rifle on Morgan's skull is sharper, like a metal pipe on a block of wood, and it sends the American into the railing as Mahdi collapses below him, gasping. Through the spastic twitch of the man's legs Mahdi sees his mother, her cheeks glistening with tears, the rifle still in her hands, the barrel gripped by her slender fingers. His father stands by her, his face a mask of swelling and bruises, his expression unreadable. His mother raises the rifle again, swinging it backwards behind her head in a crazy arc, her brow knit. The sight is terrifying. Mahdi can't, won't let her kill this man, she's too good for that. So, with a blistering fire in his throat and chest, he struggles to stand, gripping the railing behind his back, awkward and clumsy. His legs fail him for a moment, find their strength, and he rises. His shoulder catches Morgan in the groin, driving him upwards and pivoting the wiry American over the balcony railing and into the London air, six floors above the hard concrete plaza below.

There is no scream, only silent seconds before a small sound, like crockery breaking, echoes around the concrete forecourt. Then the wailing and shouting of those below, in the tower, on the street, begins. Mahdi's father looks smaller, fragile and vulnerable. His mother still clutches the rifle as though for support, her expression blank.

Mahdi turns and, the air filling his searing lungs, his eyes focused on the small, cracked marionette six floors down, joins those below in their screams.

#

This is dangerous, thinks Elira.

She walks along the pitted track after an aimless wander through the fields, an open theatre of large, rolling hills, lazy and long. They are a patchwork of green grass, yellow rapeseed and the burnt oatmeal brown of arable land.

Elira rubs her eyes. She'd wandered for a time and found a

thick-waisted yew tree, a clot of gnarled roots erupting from the earth at the base of its trunk. She'd sat under the canopy of leaves, where the dirt at its base met the grass of the surrounding field and, exhausted, laid down her head and drifted into sleep. When she awoke, stiff and chilly, she thought of blurry eyes and the cold London morning, waking in the park with Jackie before sipping coffee on the Albert Memorial earlier today. Stretching, she'd begun the trek back to Garbella Hill farm.

The sky is a massive blanket of blue, deepening in intensity as it yawns towards the land below, occasionally striped by thin slivers of brilliant white cloud. It's a sky to dream under, and there lies the danger: she dares to dream.

The land is clean, her lungs full of the scent of animals in the fields, the tang of the rapeseed, the earth beneath her feet a tapestry of hoof-tracks. London is behind her and she wants to – has to – believe that Jackie will be back. With Flori. He is her hope, a hope as delicate and fragile as the floating spider-webs of cloud above. She trudges along the track, her trainers slipping and tripping through the ruts below, a drystone wall on her right. If there is a man who can win through, she thinks, Jackie Shaw is as good as any. He's angry, and men can achieve much through anger. He is angry at Bashkim and the others, the men who killed the little boy on the bridge. Maybe he is angry with himself, for not being the man he wants to be; the man, in his mind, he should be.

She sees again the huddle of headstones at the side of the lane and knows she is nearing the farm buildings again. The horse graveyard is foolish to her, sentimental English folly. She has been away from the farm for well over three hours. The girl, Kelly, will be worried, despite the note she left. Elira feels guilty but had craved the quiet and open space. She pats her pockets to check if she has a key for the front door and realises that her mobile is not there. Lost in her wanderings, she hadn't noticed that she'd left it on the kitchen table. She quickens her stride and a small nub of panic begins rubbing against her spine. The mobile is her connection to Jackie. And the number of the mobile belonging to the *Fis*, recorded in the call history, the only number.

The movement behind the weather-bleached headstone is little more than a fleeting impression in her peripheral vision, but it registers in her troubled mind. A shaved head ducks behind a granite cross. There's another movement, this time behind the wall ahead, and to her left, the sound of something settling against the rough stone and a grunt. To the right, over the wall beyond the graveyard, lies a flat expanse of land. To the left, more of the same and far off, behind a tree-line, a road. She can hear the hum of a vehicle as it passes far up ahead, scything through the empty landscape.

They have come for her. The *Fis*. She might be a valuable commodity or costly liability but to these men, foot soldiers of the 'family', she is nothing more than a whore. A silly little bitch to be used and abused and, when spent, jacked up on cheap heroin and cast aside on the street, or retired to the bottom of the Thames. She is weak and foolish, a hysterical woman; not a mother or sister and, thus, inferior.

So, she plays to type. As she takes a faltering step on the track, the ridge of her trainer slides at an awkward angle on the hard, pitted dirt. She yelps, high-pitched and sharp, and falls to her knees. Crouching, she massages her right ankle, glancing at the mound of graves. Another shaved head dips behind a headstone. She looks at the flag flying above and then stands and gingerly takes a step to the wall on her right, her hands behind her. Hobbling over, she rests against the rough stones for a moment, then launches herself at the wall opposite, her slender frame covering the width of the track in seconds. As her hands slap on top of the wall and her arms take the strain, she hears an oath. The man she heard grunting behind the wall is already lunging towards her as she scrambles over the stones into a field of coarse, matted grass and she brings all the power she can muster into swinging the stone she picked up on the track, the size of a large bar of soap, hard onto his temple. The man stops, a dumb look of confusion on his face as she swings the stone again. His head drops to the wall before impact, so that his skull is sandwiched between the stones and Elira's blunt weapon. There is a thick slapping sound and something gives way in his skull. He collapses, clutching at the stone wall for support and Elira hears a clotted gurgle. It is then, when she sees the bloodied, ruined face, that she realises it is Leka, the *Mir* responsible for the girls in the brothel. She runs, dropping the stone with a heavy thud.

She's lucky. Leka is the only man on this side of the path. Another three were hiding in the horse graveyard on the other side of the track, and are now clambering into the field. Her slender frame gives her an advantage in the chase but the surface of the field is uneven and the grass tangled in places in thick, grasping knots. Her trainer is snagged and she goes to her knees. But her ankle is uninjured and she can get to her feet. The men are more than ten yards behind her, shouting and cursing. No one has drawn a gun. The tree-line is getting closer but the progress is arduous. The men are slowing, too. Their shouts recede, more desperate as she nears the tree-line, and then she is feet away from a cluster of bushes and a massive, squat beech. Peering through the foliage, she sees a shallow bank which dips, then rises again before the strip of road.

'Don't! Please, don't!'

The shout, frantic with fear, comes from her right and she pauses, the English accent halting her in her tracks. Her three pursuers are still sweating and heaving across the last stretch of the field.

'No!'

And there is Kelly, Agon's fist buried deep in her blonde hair, her neck exposed to the mild evening air like a lamb for the slaughter. Agon holds the bursa knife less than an inch from the skin, the long, curved handle at an angle to the blade.

He says, 'Elira.'

This man who has beaten her, spat on her as she lay in agony after Bashkim had punished her, has never used her name before.

'This girl,' he says. 'Do you want her to die?'

I'll run, thinks Elira. The girl is already dead: they won't let her live after she's seen them. But her skinny legs will not move, no matter how hard she wills them and, as the three men labour from the field and take her arms in a painful grip, she cannot avert her eyes as Agon slits the young Englishwoman's throat.

CHAPTER 25

Tuesday

Jackie is in a pub. He's been hitting it hard and a hangover is creeping across his head and body before he's even sobered up. The sharp spice of whiskey stings his nostrils. Then his exhausted mind ascends to consciousness and he opens his eyes. Conal Harris, eyes red and hungry with drink, a stained T-shirt and faded black jeans hanging from his skinny frame, is standing in front of him. He's shaved – with broken glass if the number of nicks and cuts on his face is anything to go by – and is sucking on a cigarette. Jackie is naked, tied to a wooden chair. His arms are stretched behind his back and secured to the hard wood with a thick, biting rope, his bare feet cold on the stone floor. There's a dull ache in his left shoulder. His clothes, stained with blood, lie crumpled in a heap a couple of feet away.

'Wakey, wakey,' says Harris. 'Remind me to get your lottery numbers. You are one lucky bastard.'

Jackie stares at the floor, slick with an odorous slime, tufts of straw scattered here and there like hair that's been ripped out at the roots. The wide, bare walls around them are Cotswolds stone, splattered with dim Rorschach blots of moisture. He's in the stinking husk of a barn. By the honey-hue of the stone it's in the West Country, but it's nothing like the well-kept buildings of Garbella Hill Farm. A pitted, rickety-looking wooden table is tight against the wall halfway down the space to his right, a glass and bottle of Jameson on top next to a brick-shaped package wrapped in foil and a bullet-shaped steel flask. A sturdy-looking chair, like the heavy-duty oak one Jackie is strapped to, is wedged under the table.

'So, this is the afterlife,' he says. The fug in his mind is slowly dissipating, to be replaced by a thrumming headache.

Harris says, 'All good things come to he who waits. You'll get there soon enough.' He chains another cigarette. 'I shot you. Lucky for you, you'd pegged me first, threw my aim off. Bullet went right through your shoulder instead of your chest.'

'You don't seem any the worse for wear.'

Harris smiles and it's all wrong, as though his face has been broken and rearranged out of whack. He puts the fag in his mouth and pulls up his T-shirt to reveal a torso all sinew and tight-packed muscle, a series of large welts splayed across his stomach and chest. Whatever body armour Harris had been wearing was top notch: ultra-thin for Jackie not to have noticed it. The big question burrowing through Jackie's headache like a buzz-saw is: why am I still alive? Why didn't Harris finish me off on the floor of Ferguson's flat?

'This hurts like a bitch,' says Harris, fingering one of the welts. Then he punches Jackie hard on his wounded left shoulder. A bonfire of pain flares and Jackie cries out, a ringing howl in the empty barn.

'So, here's the craic,' Harris says. 'Patrick Ferguson's dead. He was wearing a vest, too – great minds think alike, eh? But I didn't have an ex-US Marine staring at me through a sniper scope. Morgan tagged him in the head. Then the silly Yank fucker got himself killed, tangling with the blacks in that flat. He went off the balcony, six floors down. Years in the Marines and he's done in by a fucking family of Africans.'

'How do you know?'

'One of the boys who picked us up and brought us here watched him do a triple somersault from the sixth-floor balcony.'

'What time is it?'

'Why, is there a good film on the telly?' Harris looks at his watch. 'It's about eight p.m.' He sneers, spits, then stares into space for a couple of beats. 'Morgan was a twat,' he says with a whiskey slur. 'Still, he finished his shift before he clocked off. McVea's dead, too.'

'How?' Jackie's voice sounds cracked and far away through the pain.

'Same as Ferguson: Morgan sniped him. Shot him through the heart as he left his home for a shift at his restaurant. The two goons with him didn't know what had happened. It was done before you and me set eyes on each other. Then Morgan came over to Trellick Tower and met up with us.'

After Morgan took out McVea, thinks Jackie, Ferguson must have been given a vest for protection. And he had driven the poor bastard back against the window, giving Morgan the chance to take his shot.

Harris says, 'Now, here's the good part. A few yards from here, in another building, the Albanians have your wee friend. The tart.'

Jackie sharpens up, fast. The thought of Elira in the hands of the gang clears the debris from his mind.

'Yeah,' says Harris, nodding. 'God knows what they're up to in there.'

'How did they find her?'

Harris comes close and leans forward, hands on knees for support. The booze on his breath seeps into Jackie's nostrils. 'There's a wee girl you sent her to stay with. A wee blonde doll worked at some stables near here. She used the whore's mobile to call you, but Morgan had your phone. He sent the details to the Albanians and here we are.' The pleasure lights up Harris's face. 'The boys tell me she was a pretty wee thing, that English bird. Even now, with her throat cut. Shame I never got to meet her.'

Jackie remembers Kelly on her horse with her careless laugh and fresh good looks; he thinks of her pale, unblemished throat;

then a crimson, jagged tear slashed across skin; Elira, stripped, in a building next door. His face reddens and he shakes his head to clear the flickering images and tries to think. How had the gang traced the phone so fast?

Harris says, 'Alone at last. You and me, we have all the time in the world.' He takes the fag, now smoked to a stub, from his mouth and, with care and deliberation, grinds the burning tip into the bullet wound in Jackie's shoulder. The searing pain erupts like a firefight in his flesh, shredding nerve endings and forcing a low, strangled grunt from Jackie. Harris steps back, tuts and says, 'You wanna watch that doesn't become infected.'

Channel it, thinks Jackie, use the pain to focus.

Harris wore a balaclava to obscure his face and left Jackie a convenient patsy for the hits. Hardly believable for men like Laurence Gilmore, even his MI5 cohort, Stuart Hartley, but enough to misdirect, confuse and delay investigation. But he was alive because he had hidden Elira, harboured her at Garbella Farm. Now they had her, Bashkim would be satisfied, the loose ends tied up. Except him.

So why is he still breathing?

'I was in the nutting squad for a bit,' says Harris. 'Back in the day. I didn't root out the touts, or the Brits' or peelers' sources, but I dealt with them once they'd been taken.' He begins unthreading his leather belt from the loopholes of his jeans, his fingers slow and clumsy. 'There was a bit of room for interpretation, like, but IRA command liked to talk about the Three Degrees. First off, you'd hand out a good hiding with hurley sticks. Second, you strip them bollock naked, men or women, stand them in water, and run a live wire over them. If they're still alive, or haven't confessed by then, the poker or gas ring comes out.'

The burn in Jackie's shoulder is now a cold fuse of fear creeping towards his groin. He's afraid, very afraid. But he's alive.

There must be something Harris and the Albanians want from him, but no one seems in a rush to force him to talk. Is Elira suffering the same kind of treatment? Or worse? He tries to concentrate but it's a losing battle. He knows there is much pain coming, and there's nothing he can do to stop it.

'Some of the lads used cigarettes,' says Harris. 'Some used kerosene, pouring it over an arm or a leg and lighting it. Then, finally, the blindfold and the bullet in the head.'

The belt clears his narrow hips with a violent tug.

'A Yank journalist interviewed me once, in a pub in west Belfast. We were having a couple of drinks and he said he was going to write a novel someday.'

Harris wraps the pointed end of the belt around his right hand, the buckle hanging by his knees.

'So I asked him what it was going to be about. "Stick to what you know," he says.'

Jackie's jaw aches and he realises he's been grinding his teeth.

Harris says, 'I reckon that applies just as well here, right? You fucking black bastard.'

And he brings the belt down hard and fast.

#

The breath is driven from her like air through tongs as Agon's fist buries deep in her stomach. Elira is alone with him in a small, bare room. A single bulb on a rusted lamp-stand throws a sickly light across the walls, speckled with a garish flower pattern and creeping damp.

She thought he would throw her to the bed. She has seen him watch her in the club and thinks he would have taken her before, if she were not one of Bashkim's favourites. But he rasped the name Leka, and the beating began. Had she killed Leka, the weasel-faced sadist who managed the girls in the Soho stable, with the stone? Was he downstairs, his wounds tended and drinking strong liquor? Or was his body in the cold night air, lying in tarpaulin under the thin scattering of stars?

She doesn't care; it doesn't matter. She has attacked one of their own and she has to pay. The only thing keeping her alive is that they have to take her to Bashkim, so that he can deliver the final sentence. The end is not here, in this sordid little cell of a room.

Agon grabs a fistful of her hair and hauls her upright then snorts, his face stretched tight with the effort, as his fist drives into Elira's stomach again. And again, the air is driven from her in a rush that sounds like a short, wistful sigh.

#

Laurence Gilmore feels the eyes on him as he approaches the cordon in the small plaza at the foot of Trellick Tower. He owes DC Don Boxton a bottle of single malt for keeping him in the loop, giving him the tip-off on the disaster at the housing estate before it makes its way through the usual, tortuous channels from New Scotland Yard to Thames House.

The uniforms are mildly curious. They've seen it all, have spent hours shuffling from foot to foot around the perimeters of the sad, blue crime scene tents. They're probably taking bets on which he might be, NCA, Special Branch or MI5.

CID are more hostile. Gilmore heard that the first men on the scene, two uniforms patrolling the nearby estate, finished their burgers while waiting for the Duty Officer and the rest to show. The DS had vomited on arrival while the uniforms were licking ketchup from their fingers.

There's the odd stifled laugh as a copper cracks a joke, and the photographers are having a cup of tea while the video team are upstairs in the flat, poring over the Farahs' home with their lens. Gilmore has already been there. The sniper rifle was still in the living room, yet to be removed while SOCOs stripped any available forensic material from it, but the boy and his parents had gone. First to hospital, then to a spartan, indifferent interview suite where they would answer gentle questions from the investigating detectives, family liaison officers on hand.

Initial statements had been taken and inquiry teams were working around Trellick Tower and Ferguson's flat, gleaning whatever they could from witnesses.

The McVea hit earlier was a clean affair. A sniper shot, two protection officers on hand in a quiet street, the body dead in a doorway and no passing civilians nearby. The bullet would be a good match for the rifle upstairs. No doubt, the finger on the trigger was now broken and cold under the blue canvas SOCO tent a few yards away.

'Black bastard'. That was what the Irishman said. It had stayed with the family, the racial connotations. Gilmore understood. He'd been on the receiving end of worse in the service from senior officers, no less, and the sting of the words never lessened. But the disappeared Irish killer had put the slur in the context of the Irish Troubles. Some of the older police on the perimeter of the scene mumbled uncomfortably when the subject of Ulster was broached.

There had been a decent description of Jackie Shaw. The other two men had covered their faces with masks but the boy had given a rough sketch of the Irish hood when he broke into the flat. The kid and his father had remembered names: Morgan, the dead man lying inside the tent; Shaw; Harris, an angry, violent bully.

The Irish hold a grudge, Morgan had said. The murders were all classic IRA hits. Point-blank shooting, a bomb, a sniper. Not contained in that insanity across the water but, once again, scuttling free on the streets of Britain.

'It won't do, will it?'

He turns at the voice, the lisp of the weird, projecting teeth.

'All these bloody Irish running around London, playing cowboys and Indians as if it were twenty-five years ago.' Hartley tuts and shoves his hands deeper in his suit trouser pockets. 'The body in the tent is American. The tattoo: US Marine, Scout Sniper. He had a 7.62mm NATO round on a chain around his neck, now wedged in his windpipe thanks to the impact of the landing. They call it a Hog's Tooth, presented when they graduate from Scout Sniper School.'

Gilmore says, 'You checked Wikipedia on your mobile.'

'Better. Perry here served with the Royal Marines and did a short course with the Yanks.'

Behind Hartley, in a casual jacket and jeans, stands a wiry man with a haircut so neat he could be a Lego figure. One of Hartley's boys.

'You know,' says Hartley, 'you almost sound like Shaw. That's exactly the kind of jaded crack he'd make.'

'Sorry, just a little tired. When did you get here?'

'About thirty minutes ago. Bennett is on site, from Organised Crime. And some mob from Special Branch. They've all been told our lot are to monitor the situation only, no boots on the ground so to speak.'

'Right,' says Gilmore. 'And Shaw?'

'What about him?'

'The security detail on Ferguson stated he turned on the other killer and fired on him. The man, Harris, put him down with a shot to the shoulder and a back-up team arrived and extracted Harris and Shaw from Ferguson's flat.'

Hartley looks at the ground for a moment, his jaw working with impatience. 'You've been busy, Laurence. Have you been over to Ferguson's flat?'

'I spoke to CID over there. I think Shaw was coerced into participation in the Ferguson hit and turned on the killers.'

'And is most likely dead.'

'We don't know that. Why not just put a bullet in him there and then? Why extract him? Who pulled them out and why didn't they finish off the wounded protection detail?'

'That,' says Hartley, rolling his weight from the balls of his feet to his heels, 'is not your concern. Providing a positive ID and a profile on the man splattered over this plaza is. Get onto Six and have them liaise with Langley; GCHQ to contact NSA; give Carter a call at the Bureau. The man is American, so surely one of their embarrassment of agencies can give us some intel.'

'And the man with Shaw – Harris? We have a name but no ID on him, just a hazy description from a terrified kid. The father can't give us anything as the Irish thug was wearing a balaclava.'

'Old habits die hard,' says Hartley, a smile on his lips that never makes it to his eyes. 'I'll get on to Belfast, see if we or the PSNI have anything to help in that respect.'

Gilmore lets a silence pass between him and the older man for just long enough to allow a crease of discomfort to creep across Hartley's brow. Then he says, 'And Shaw? He probably saved the lives of the protection officers. We cut him loose and now we write him off, is that it?'

'He is not a priority,' says Hartley. 'Ensuring that no more violence taints the good name of the capital is. ID the dear departed under that tent and this Irish maniac, and we get a step closer to finding Jackie. Find this man Harris, and we find Shaw. As I told you, I will contact Belfast.'

Laurence Gilmore turns to the tall, flat monolith of the tower-block and mutters, 'This is a sham.'

'Dictionary definition, "A thing that is not what it is purported to be",' says Hartley. 'Rather sums up our profession, wouldn't you say?'

'It sums up this investigation.'

'And why would that be? What exactly is bogus?' Hartley

places his right hand gingerly on his breast. 'If you, Mr Gilmore, are privy to information not known by the police and security services, I would remind you that you are bound by law to divulge said information, immediately.'

'I know nothing other than what I have learned from speaking to police here, at the scene, and studying Shaw's file.' Gilmore's voice is as flat as the body splayed across the concrete under the crime scene tent.

Hartley, his expression just as dead, says, 'Very well. Perry can drive you back to Thames House if you don't have a car. You'll just catch supper in the canteen if you hurry. Now, Mr Gilmore, go and do your job.'

#

Jackie's body is an inferno. The pain engulfs him. Everything aches but his left shoulder is worst of all. When Harris brings the belt down, the metal buckle gouging flesh, the leather strap is like an electric shock searing through the burning torment. Jackie screams. Each roar of fear and agony is a release so he screams again and again, after each blow. A clammy film of sweat coats his body. It eats into his wounds and stings to the point his nerves are shredded.

Harris, breathing heavy, face flushed, pours a measure of Jameson and takes a stoic sip. There is a hint of disappointment in his slouch.

Probably savoured the thought of putting the hurt on a peeler from home, thinks Jackie. Now the reality hasn't lived up to expectations and he's sluicing the disappointment away with booze.

And, still, no questions. Plenty of pain but this is no interrogation. If it were, Jackie knows, he'd break. Harris has the time and the means. In the old days, perhaps, he'd have had the conviction in a cause, too.

229

Harris says, 'You know, your shoulder looks bad.' He walks over and pours the rest of his whiskey over the wound, igniting another blaze in Jackie's shoulder. Then the cigarettes are out again, one of them wedged in the tight slash of a mouth.

A match flares and something kindles in Harris's eyes.

The tip of the cigarette glows a fierce red in the gloom of the barn and, with unhurried care, Harris grinds it out on Jackie's right leg, a bare inch from his groin.

CHAPTER 26

Midnight

His mother is shrivelled and sunken in the coffin, the white polyester lining shining under the lights in the cramped sitting room. Jackie calls out to her, begs her to see him with her egg-white eyes, grant him some comfort from the pain, but her head lolls slowly away from him. There is another flare of pain and he opens his lungs with a furious obscenity and his old partner, Gordon Orr, is there, gently rebuking him for his language. A wave of nausea washes him away and a hard slap jolts his face to the right and he sees Elira, small and hopeless Elira, in a squalid little room, two men, huge and powerful, standing over her. They turn to face him and he sees they are two boys he went to school with, Billy Turner and Joshua Hobson. Smiling, they turn back to the girl, now his sister Sarah. Sarah as she was when they were kids, sitting on the swing in the Ormeau Park and folding in on herself as the bigger boys gloat and goad, although he can't hear their words. Then his father is there, frail and slow but gentle, always gentle, holding a glass of the hard stuff. He offers it to Jackie, tells him it will soothe him, will dull the pain and help him breathe. And he is tempted, so tempted, to take it. He hasn't touched a drop for years, has seen the booze eat away at his da like a slow-acting cancer until there was little left but a shell. But Jackie wants to slice his body open and escape it. Escape the pain. He is so tempted to take the drink.

Harris holds the glass of whiskey in an outstretched hand, waving it in front of Jackie's nose. And Jackie is back in the fresh hell of reality.

He says, his voice very far away, 'No. Thanks.'

'You were away with the faeries there,' says Harris. 'I used up a couple of fags on you. But there's not much use in torturing a man if he isn't compos mentis. Like poking a dead animal with a stick.'

'Well,' says Jackie, shifting position, 'you're very good at it.'

'Practice makes perfect.'

Harris downs the drink and staggers to the table, setting the glass on the battered wood with a heavy finality. He picks up the brick-shaped package and weighs it in his hand, then begins to unwrap it with the slow, deliberate care of the inebriated. He peels back the layers of foil to reveal two thick, weighty sandwiches and lifts one with resignation. A gravedigger's piece, they'd call it back home.

'Fucking egg. I told him no egg.' Then he shrugs, takes a bite and leans back against the table. Harris munches on his food and Jackie waits for the pain to subside to a level where he can think of something other than a white-hot poker searing his flesh. After a couple of minutes he says, 'This couldn't be easy. Doing this to another human being.'

'You'd think, wouldn't you?'

'How many did you nut back in the day?'

'Honestly, I don't remember. It was like Stalinist-fucking-Russia at one point. Follow the party line, or else. If you had a cousin who worked in civil service, who pissed in the same urinal as a peeler on guard duty at City Hall, you were a tout in some of the boys' eyes.' The man looks spent, almost disconsolate.

'Back in the day, who did you hate more, the Brits or the RUC?'

'Me, personally? Probably youse, the peelers. I knew the Brits were just doing a job. Most of them didn't want to be in Ireland. But your lot? You were true believers. Born and lived in the occupied six counties, had families. Called it your home.' Harris

232

spits, then reaches into the shadows and produces the bullet-shaped metal cylinder. He unscrews the tip and pours hot, steaming tea into the cap. 'But a Brit was a higher-priority target. Harder to hit, made more headlines. The media didn't give a shit about the locals. And, true to form, the English threw you lot into the firing line ahead of their own. You had less equipment, you were easier to access, you were at the frontline at any riots, first and last out the doors of the station on foot patrol. The London government used you like cannon fodder, just as they have the Irish in all their colonial wars.'

'Careful, now. You're starting to sound like you sympathised with us.'

'Hardly,' says Harris, bloodshot eyes downturned to take in the remains of his first sandwich. 'Back then I hated youse with a passion. I didn't lose anyone personally, none of that. I just hated youse because you were authority, and trying to stop us. You had a crown on your cap badge. I didn't even care about the Prod thing that much, unlike most. But it gets to a point, you know, when you just don't feel it so much any more.' His hand falls to his side. 'And, anyway, we won.'

Silence.

Jackie's body is a burning, seething, stinging creature out of control: he would claw it to shreds if his hands weren't tied. And he's angry. Angry at his pain, his nakedness, this psychotic bastard in front of him. Killing doesn't come easy to him, but he would tear Harris limb from limb given the chance. He's been stripped down to his soul. He wants the agony to end; the suffering, self-hate. And he wants to live. He wants to kill Harris.

He says, 'What do you want?'

Harris puts the tea down, stretches and says, 'Something you can't give me.' He takes a step towards Jackie. 'The other fella, he wants to talk to you. Ask you questions and all.'

'The other fella?'

'Morgan called him the client. I call him a future partner. But I asked him, as a favour, to give me some time with you. Soften you up a bit, like. Never had the chance to play with a peeler before I killed him.' Harris pulls a knife from his pocket, shaped like a cut-throat razor with a curved handle, longer than the blade that unfolds from it. His grip on the weapon is so tight Jackie can see the delicate thread of cartilage around the whitened knuckles.

'I thought you could give me back something. All those years ago, I had a purpose. It was exciting, scary sometimes. I felt elated, like, every time I saw a bomb go off or shot someone.' Harris's forehead knots in an intense frown. 'That wee lad, Macrossan: it's funny, every time I close my eyes, I see his stupid fucking face staring up at me before I put the cushion...' He snorts. 'That was your fault, too. Fucking bollocksed the wee lad, didn't you, with his own fucking gun. Fucking peelers, always pushing. Pushing until I push back.' He's nodding, working himself up, like a boxer psyching himself for another round. 'I wanted you to take me back a bit, to the good old days when I did this shite for more than money. When I had principles.'

A poem floats to the surface of Jackie's mind, from a collection his sister sent him when he lived out in Hong Kong.

He says:

> *"'Two wee girls*
> *were playing tig near a car...*
> *how many counties would you say*
> *are worth their scattered fingers?'"*

Harris gives a slow hand-clap, a sloppy grin on his face. He pulls a cigarette from the pack in his pocket and shoves it between his lips, a practised movement with one hand, the other still holding the knife.

'Aye, very good.'

'And the wee boy on the bridge in Kew?' says Jackie. 'Or the girl, Kelly? What's worth killing them?'

'You're hardly in a position to be asking me questions. You're not in uniform now.' Harris edges closer to Jackie, the slim blade keen in the flare of a cheap lighter as the cigarette catches. 'Here's another poem for you, from that Prod fucking cuckold –

"Hurrah for revolution and more cannon-shot!
A beggar upon horseback lashes a beggar on foot.
Hurrah for revolution and cannon come again!
The beggars have changed places, but the lash goes on."

'Well, I'll tell you, I'll be a beggar no more. I'm paid well for what I do.'

There is a light in Harris's eyes.

'You,' he says, the knife tip a couple of inches from Jackie's face, 'you're a bonus, big lad. I haven't recaptured that oul' magic yet; they say you can never go back, but I'm willing to give it a good oul' try. If at first you don't succeed, eh? What do you say, mucker?'

Then the blade works its way into Jackie's shoulder wound and the agony shreds his body again.

#

He has no idea how long it lasts; time has lost all meaning. There is only the here and now. Jackie, the smeared walls and sullied floor, the blistered wooden furniture, and Harris. The chair he is tied to is heavy, its legs weighed down by ironwork on their ends, but he almost tipped it over, collapsing onto his crumpled clothes nearby as he jerked in spasms under the knife.

Now Harris looks exhausted and has begun lacing the

235

remains of his tea with the Jameson. Jackie shivers, his body slick with sweat and blood. Then the large metal door at the end of the barn thunders as someone kicks it outside and Harris saunters off to answer. The great iron plate grinds in protest as it lumbers open, a shaft of brilliant light flooding through the open entrance. There is the low purr of an engine and figures flit between car headlights now streaming into the barn. The curtain of night is drawn beyond. Jackie hears voices, another Belfast accent, and an angry, incomprehensible bark. Harris points at him, challenging the silhouette of a heavy-set man. Another slight figure stands to their right.

The shivers get worse as the night air finds Jackie, the cuts on his flesh stinging with each convulsion. Harris strides over, the other figures hanging back.

'Your wee girlfriend's going back to London. That fat Albanian bastard's waiting for her in Venice.' There's a shouted reprimand from behind and Harris points at Jackie and snarls, 'Ach, sure, he's dead anyway.' He turns back to Jackie. 'My colleagues here, the *client*,' he says, voice heavy with cynicism, 'want to talk to you. Looks like I've had my fun.' He lights up another fag, bloodied red hand cupping the cigarette, and mutters, 'And done the donkey work.'

He appraises Jackie with disgust, as though for the first time, and marches from the barn. The heavy-set man closes the large iron door after him, the sound of the revving car outside competing with the grinding protest of the metal. The figure and his slighter companion approach.

Jackie says, 'All right Derek? Wondered when you'd show your face.'

'Jackie.'

Derek Bailey stands, his shoulders slouched, his hands deep in jeans pockets. Jackie shudders, pain washing in and out like a tide, but he's calm, more centred. The companion, a man with pinched, mean features in a parka jacket and faded black jeans, lights up a fag. He spits an insult in Albanian.

'Well, this is awkward,' says Jackie.

The Albanian picks at a fingernail.

Bailey says, 'You don't have to worry about Harris. He's away to London with the Albanians and Elira, furious that he couldn't finish you off. You won't have to suffer his treatment again.' He looks uncomfortable with the other man standing behind him, twenty feet away.

Jackie says, 'I won't be doing much of anything again, will I?'

'When it comes, I'll make sure it's quick and painless.'

'It's a bit fucking late for that.'

Bailey looks from the pile of clothes on the floor to Jackie's naked, tortured body. He clicks his tongue.

Jackie says, 'You told Harris and Morgan I was ex-RUC. That's how Harris knew when I met him in Trellick Tower. I suspected you were involved from then, but I didn't really believe it until I saw you in the open doorway there. I thought you were dodgy, but this?'

Bailey looks sorry and it might be genuine. 'I need to know something.'

'Fire away.' Jackie winces, his jaw set as though he is staring into a fierce gale. 'You can always ask. All that time your man Harris didn't ask me a single question. Go ahead and make the last couple of hours worthwhile.'

'I need to know what you know about me and Harris and the Albanians.'

'I know you're all fucking parasites. Murdering, pimping parasites.'

Bailey walks to the table and drags the battered wooden chair across to sit opposite Jackie. The scraping of the oak on stone is a banshee scream in the cavernous space of the barn. 'I am sorry you've been treated this way. You were in the job, same as me,

237

and I wouldn't give you up to the likes of Harris lightly. But commerce makes strange bed-fellows, and I need him.' He crosses his legs, placing his thick, blunt hands in his lap. 'If you don't answer me, I can make things much harder on you. There's still this boy,' he gestures over his shoulder, 'and two more of Bashkim's lads in the farmhouse outside, and they can hurt you in ways Harris couldn't imagine. You don't have to keep a civil tongue in your head, but you do need to answer my questions.'

Jackie smiles, dry lips cracking. 'There's change in my jeans over there for the fucking swearbox.'

'Who are you? I mean, who *are* you?'

'Jackie Shaw, ex-Army, ex-RUC, ex-Royal HK Police Force, and the rest.'

'Let's bypass the CV. Who do you work for now?'

'I don't.'

'You were just looking for an old buddy, aye? McLelland.'

'Spot on.'

'Bollocks.'

A small tic appears, a staccato twitch in Bailey's cheek, as though someone were tugging at his face with a string. 'You worked with Gordon Orr. I checked. Left the job after some bother with the UDA. You never knew McLelland. You were undercover for a long time, couldn't have known him. He was in a different division and only Orr and top brass knew you were RUC at all.'

Jackie sighs. 'I was contacted by the security services. People started dying, people with a history in the security forces back in the day. McLelland was on the list but nobody knew his whereabouts because he was on the streets. They asked me to try my hand at finding him.'

'And you came to me. Why?'

'You were on their radar. They thought you were involved in dodgy organisations, far-right nonsense. The theory was you might be able to reach out to McLelland.'

Bailey puts his hand to his cheek to still the twitch. His eyes have a hunted look and his voice is a whisper. 'Who put you onto me?'

'I told you, the security services.'

'This isn't America, we only have a couple of agencies at the sharp end. Which service, exactly?'

Jackie closes his eyes and lets his head roll back until his face is tilted to the ceiling.

'If you don't tell me,' says Bailey, 'I'll have Mergim here get to work on you. Then I'll phone London to make sure Elira gets a reception all of your making.'

'MI5.'

Bailey eases his bulk forward until he is perched on the edge of the chair and leans close. There is a reek of beer and onions, and the sour bite of body odour. 'Like I said, I checked you out,' he says. 'I want details. And if you don't talk to me, I'll have someone pay a visit to that sister of yours, when she gets home from her holidays.'

#

Elira lies on the floor of the vehicle at the feet of three men, one of whom rests his boots on her ribs as if on a foot stool. She is less than human, nothing to them.

But not to Agon, sitting up front. She can tell from his quiet snarl as he talks with the Irishman that he is in a murderous mood. He had no love of Leka but the man was a brother, a *Mir* and, therefore, family. If Leka is dead, that cannot be let go. Bashkim might want her back but she cannot be allowed to live if she has killed a *Mir*. And, besides, she has crossed them, dishonoured them and, in their twisted code, betrayed them. So she lies, her stomach still aching from Agon's beating, on the floor with their cigarette butts and reconciles with the fact that she will die.

She isn't frightened. Perhaps, there would be a relief in death. Elira had stopped living her life on that day of pain and shame in the Parisian apartment when the men had taken her because, simply, this was no longer her life to live, but Bashkim's to dictate, control and end. Jackie Shaw had opened up a sliver of hope, but that was over.

Elira's fear now is for Flori.

The car hits a pothole and the wind is driven from her for a moment. The man who is resting his boots on her side grumbles in Albanian and places them on the floor, toe-caps tucked under her.

She glimpsed Jackie Shaw before they bundled her into the car. In the barn, on a chair, in the centre of the floor in a pool of liquid. He was naked and she felt ashamed to see him that way. Great swathes of ugly red welts covered his body. He was coughing and spitting onto the floor at his side.

He is probably dead already. Like her and Flori, come tomorrow he will be no more than a memory.

CHAPTER 27

Wednesday

Bailey continues to question him. Jackie answers because they have Elira and he is too tired to lie.

They cover Hartley and Gilmore; the search for McLelland, the chance meeting with Elira and the firefight in Soho. Flori's flat and the housing estate in Paddington. Bailey shakes his head and his broad face seems to sag. He places his hands on his thighs and makes to haul his bulk to his feet, the weight of the world on his shoulders.

'Wait,' says Jackie. 'Do us a favour, for old times' sake, the job, whatever.'

Bailey eases himself back in the chair and raises an eyebrow.

Jackie says, 'What about McLelland?'

'Already dead,' says Bailey. 'He was the first to go.'

'Him and the rest, it wasn't about collusion, was it?'

The big man is silent for a moment that stretches into a minute. He searches Jackie's face. Then his pinched mouth and strained eyes relax and he says, 'No, it wasn't.'

'But they were involved in the old days, weren't they? Parkinson-Naughton, McVea, Ferguson, Bannister, our man McLelland? Even the woman, Dodds? They were all security forces. MI5, Military Intelligence, RUC. They had the means.'

Bailey looks like someone has just shoved an album of embarrassing family photos in his face. He leans back in the chair. 'What do you want me to say? Yes, there was collusion with loyalist killers. Yes, they were involved. We did it quiet, under the radar: Parkinson-Naughton kept it off the books. Harris knows they were involved. Is that why they died? No.'

'What about you?' Jackie says.

'It was a long time ago.'

'It was assassination.'

'Fuck off!' Bailey springs forward on the chair and stabs a thick, rigid finger in Jackie's face. 'Like you never thought about it? Pass a name and address off to some cowboy with a "For God and Ulster" tattoo and a semi-automatic in the coal shed and Bob's your uncle, one less Provo in the world.' He licks his lips, swallows hard. 'We all worked together, on and off. I did some intelligence, logistics support so the loyalists could take a few people out for us. Sometimes they got them, sometimes they fucked up and shot somebody's da driving a taxi for a living.'

Jackie says, 'I lived undercover with east Belfast UDA. Prevented some violence and not much else. I was compromised, had to be pulled out. But there was a Provo commander, a top man. For once, the loyalists had come up with a workable plan to hit the bastard: tit-for-tat for the Ravenhill bombing. Don't know if you remember it.'

Bailey nods.

'I knew about the plan, thought it over, agonised a bit, got drunk. You know I was working with Gordon Orr; I didn't tell him about the hit at first. I just sat back and hoped maybe somebody would actually carry it out.' Jackie flexes his wrists a little, the bite of the rope binding him to the chair outclassed by the lacerations and burns he suffered at the hands of Harris. 'I never slept well while I was undercover. But, in the end, I told Gordon about the Cochrane hit and at least the little kip I got was with a clear conscience. And I told Gordon Orr every scrap of intel I picked up from then on. I didn't need that shite on my ledger. I was a fucking policeman.'

Bailey's nose wrinkles and his wide mouth purses. 'It was a war, and we weren't allowed to fight it. Fucking Yellow cards before you could fire on a terrorist. We were considered a rogue

242

unit, had to hide our work from the Army, Political, the Constabulary. Meanwhile, I've boys making pistol signs with their fingers at me on roadblocks. Kids writing police fatalities like football scores on gable walls. Fuck that.'

'And yet, here you are, working a good cop/bad cop routine on me with Harris.'

The Albanian in the background glances at his watch. Bailey opens his mouth, ready to justify and rant, then seems to lose momentum. He looks old. 'There's collusion for you, eh?' he says, coughing up a laugh as dead as the light in his eyes.

'And what about the English girl at the farm? Did she deserve to die?'

'That's on you, brother. You put the Albanian's girl with her.'

'Her name's Kelly,' says Jackie, his teeth gritted. 'She was young, wanted to be a vet, had a younger brother. She made the worst tea I ever tasted and had one of the best laughs I ever heard. Guileless, you know? You only hold onto a laugh like that if you've no harm in you.'

Bailey's voice lowers. 'She's in the car outside. We'll take her body south, near London. I'll be sure she's buried properly.'

'You're a real Christian, Derek, cheers.'

'Look, there was many's a wee girl just like her back home.'

'And you were trying to protect them from the likes of Harris,' says Jackie. 'Now you're working them, making money off their misery.'

Something changes in Bailey. He looks imbalanced, as though dizzy, about to fall off the chair.

Then the big man recovers, turns back to the waiting thug and says, 'A minute.' He leans close to Jackie's face. 'Dodds had a nice car and a flat in Chiswick. McVea lived in a semi-detached in zone two, on a cook's wage. Ferguson, Bannister – shit – even Parkinson-Naughton, all lived beyond their means. Me, I was happy getting by. I never wanted this.'

The words sound hollow and, for a moment, it's Bailey who looks as though he has been pounded on and tortured for a couple of hours.

'And McLelland. He was the first we took out, because he was the main man. He got close with Parkinson-Naughton, back in Belfast. He was smart, could see how the pompous oul' bastard thought: public school education, through the Eton and Oxbridge mill to a decent mid-management position in MI5 admin. While his contemporaries were calling the shots in Five and Six, or off on glamour postings like Moscow and Washington, Parkinson-Naughton was stuck shuffling papers in Lisburn in our dirty wee conflict.'

'So, McLelland played him?'

'McLelland played him. Turns out our Len was partial to scrawny wee tarts. McLelland had something on Parkinson-Naughton and he used it to get the old fart on board. When you work in the intelligence sphere, you get to know a lot of very bad people.'

'Just look at my present company.'

Bailey's eyelids flutter. 'McLelland left Northern Ireland at the end of the nineties. He'd pissed a lot of people off on both sides. He was well trained, aggressive, amoral and out of work. He came to London, looked up Parkinson-Naughton and used him to establish contacts in London. Organised crime, street-level thugs, pushers. Ferguson, Dodds and the rest followed like rats to the piper. Co-conspirators, all with their dirty little secrets back in Belfast. When the ceasefires held and Sinn Féin got into government, they all got a bit restless, in case anyone opened the book on their past activities. Me and the other RUC boys moved over here to distance ourselves and everybody made good money in drugs, McLelland running the show. He was of no fixed abode. Difficult to trace, easy to move unhindered through London.'

Jackie winces at a sharp jab of pain in his wounded left shoulder, and sees Bailey grimace.

The big man says, 'It was all going great, a bit of pocket money for everyone while they worked the day job, putting up a decent front. I got into it through my connection with McLelland. I phoned him when I moved over here and he met me in the Lily Bolero.' He raises his eyebrows and the corners of his broad mouth turn down. 'Then they got into the girls.'

Jackie looks at the Albanian leaning against the table.

'Your mate over there?'

'Aye. Parkinson-Naughton met them through business contacts.'

Jackie says, 'I don't see where your buddy Harris fits in.'

'McLelland and the rest were getting sloppy, arrogant. I reached out to Bashkim and his boys. Said I could help in a takeover if it was a joint venture. I contacted old names I knew from both sides back home. You know,' says Bailey, 'old enemies are new partners now. They sent Harris and Morgan over to take out the lot of them and make it look political. Some fella in a Kilburn republican club put Harris in touch with the young lad, Macrossan. He'd a hard-on for the whole "cause" shite, thought it was legit dissident stuff. He knew London.'

'Morgan was American.'

'The money. The backing comes from the States. New York. Some from Brighton Beach, a lot from Woodside and north Bronx. Irish-American interests who funded the Provos back in the day.'

Bailey looks on edge but there's relief in his eyes, as if this is a confessional.

Jackie says, 'And I stumbled into the whole shebang.'

'Unlucky. I told you to look for McLelland around the City, but you went traipsing into Soho. Too bad you bumped into that wee girl. The rest is history.'

Jackie shakes his head. It hurts. 'There was a name on the list on the memory stick. At first, I thought it was my codename, when I was Special Branch: Katana?'

Bailey lurches forward, almost head-butting Jackie, says, 'Keep your voice down.' He's panting, his face flushed like a slapped arse. Jackie stares for a moment. The Albanian has moved off the table and is watching them both. Bailey leans heavily on his knees, ready to rise.

Jackie says, desperate, 'And Maida Vale? *Function*? Is it a pub?'

There is no reason for Bailey to tell him any of this. But he sees himself through Bailey's eyes – a broken, hollow man, vulnerable and naked, tied to a chair in a barn surrounded by armed killers – and thinks there's no reason not to tell him. He's beaten.

The ex-policeman says, as if in agreement. 'I don't know why I'm telling you all this.'

Jackie says, 'Guilty conscience?'

Another flash of something stirs behind the big man's eyes. 'You were RUC, and you deserve to know more about why you're going to die tonight.' His voice is a rasping whisper. 'It's *Junction*, not function: Junction House, in Maida Vale.'

'A pub?'

'A building. Probably a lock-keeper's house or something in the past.'

'There's a canal?'

'Regent's Canal.'

Jackie remembers Harris on the approach to Ferguson's building, the canal running alongside them as they made their way to Holmefield House. That waterway runs east to a pond near Paddington station, a small wooded island in the centre. Little Venice. He remembers Harris's complaint, that they could have saved trouble by bringing the boat up to the estate where

Ferguson lived, and his mention of Venice as he left this torture chamber, bound for London.

'Is the houseboat there?' says Jackie.

Bailey blanches and stands. He turns and follows the Albanian, who is already making his way to the iron door.

'What about Seven Skins?'

At the entrance to the barn Bailey looks back, a broad silhouette against the dark blue ink-wash of the night outside.

Jackie shouts, 'The wee girl's name is Shepherd, Kelly Shepherd. At least let her parents know she's at peace.'

Then the door is hauled closed again and Jackie is alone.

He shifts in the wooden chair, his body protesting with bursts of pain in his sides, his shoulder, his legs, his groin. The chair is so heavy, and the metal fixtures on the legs give it further weight.

But it isn't bolted to the stone floor.

He pivots, rocking back and forth, slowly at first as his wounds fight back against the motion. Then, as he detects some small, almost imperceptible give, he shifts his weight with more energy, breathing hard, expelling the agony through gritted teeth.

Time passes. Seconds, minutes: he has no idea. At any moment Bailey and the Albanian could return and his fate would be sealed. Desperation sets in and he's on the verge of crying out when the two legs on the right side tilt, the left struts lifting off the ground. They return to the slick floor with a slap and now the right legs are free from the ground. He arrests his momentum as much as he can manage in his damaged, weakened state then sets his shoulders low. Willing his aching frame, he hurls his body to the right. The chair tilts and Jackie fights the reflex to correct the momentum, feeling the legs list crazily. He's suspended for a moment, his body weightless, the pain gone. Then he topples and falls hard on the slick stone floor. His arm lands badly between the wood of the chair and the filthy ground. There is a surge of agony and his mouth is wrenched wide in a silent scream.

The pile of his clothes is brushing against the hair on the crown of his head, and he begins digging his bleeding elbow into the ruts and crevices in the stone floor, sometimes slipping on the film of slime which covers it. He smells piss and animals and every second is filled with the torturous wait for the slow roar of the iron door as Bailey and his killers roll it back. Maybe they'll laugh at him and his pitiful attempt at escape. Then they'll see the clothes, search the jeans and find the cigarette lighter he pocketed after Harris gave him a light in Holmefield House.

If they haven't taken it from the pocket already.

Now Jackie is on top of the jeans. He contorts his hands, splaying the fingers, searching for a grip on the denim which lies crumpled, half bunched at his shoulders and half under his armpits. He finds purchase and slowly, ever-so-slowly, drags the jeans down his back until he can feel the ridge of the pocket. Were they careless as they hauled his unconscious body into the barn? In their confidence, did they bother to search his pockets? Fumbling in the pockets he finds a wedge of crumpled paper: his London street map. Surely this means they stripped him without searching, he thinks, confident he was no longer a threat, trussed and naked on the chair. He almost cries out when he feels the faint plastic lump of the cheap lighter in the coin pocket. He is just probing the pocket with his fingers when he hears voices outside the barn. Angry, bitter, full of recrimination. Most of the talk is in what must be Albanian. Occasional outbursts are in accented English. Then Bailey's Belfast curse cuts in. There is something about Elira, how she attacked one of the men. He hears a name, Leka, and understands that she bashed this man's head with a stone. As the voices drift round the exterior of the barn, Jackie tries to imagine the slight girl he hurled across an alleyway in Soho beating a grown man insensible. Then Jackie remembers her face when she shot the man in her sister's flat. That vacant, damned gaze is still in his head when there is a thunderous clamour from the great iron entrance to the barn. He closes his eyes, ready and yet not ready for death.

The voices fade and there is quiet, save for the dying echo of that angry kick to the metal door.

He takes another moment, then pulls the lighter from his jeans pocket with straining fingers. He uses the ground to manoeuvre the cheap plastic into his palm, then sparks the flint and feels the glowering warmth on his wrist. The flame burns Jackie's skin as it devours the ropes which hold him but it's nothing to the torture of the past hours. In what seems like an age he is free of the chair and zipping up the jeans. He leaves the stained white T-shirt and judges that he's been alone for ten minutes or more. They must return soon. He searches for a weapon. There's nothing. The flask of tea on the table is light and mostly plastic. The chair and table are sturdy and he can't break off a leg in his weakened state. Scanning the rear inner wall of the barn for something to use, he sees a small hatch set into the stone. He's seen the like before on Garbella Farm. A feeding hatch.

Jackie falls to his knees at the wooden door, not much larger than a TV screen, and fumbles at the edge. He wills the latch on the outer edge to be unlocked and finds the wood give. Prone, jeans smeared in the thin muck of the floor, he hauls himself through to the crisp, vast night outside.

Sounds become sharper. The car, an asthmatic cough, an irritated tutting. There's the edge of a strip of yellow light to his left. Peering around the corner of the barn he sees it comes from a window at the rear of the farmhouse, ten yards away. Ahead is a low stone wall and a huge, flat expanse of fields. A murky sky stretches above, pockmarked by cloud, and a rolling line of black hills lies in the distance, drawing a dark, careless border between land and sky. Jackie knows those hills, recognises the loaf-shaped silhouette of a familiar ridge. Garbella Farm is about two miles off to the north-west.

He slathers soil and mud over his torso and jeans, rude camouflage for his flight. He's a child's nightmare vision, the bogeyman, hunted eyes staring from a sweat-streaked mask of filth. He is about to climb the low stone wall when a voice says, '*Janë të vdekur?*'

A stab of pain in his throat is joined by a chorus of sharp aches across his body. A man stands two feet away, clutching a knife like that which Harris used. The face is a dark tapestry of shadows, the eyes like shining black buttons in the night. The man makes no move but stands inert, rooted to the spot.

'Are you dead?' The accented English is similar to that of the other Albanians, the voice as bland as a flat-line on a heart monitor.

Somewhere in the farmhouse, a voice barks, 'Leka!' Then, '*Qij!*'

Jackie whispers, 'Are you Leka?'

The face, still sheathed in darkness, says, 'You know I am. Which are you? The Englishman in Hackney? The Jew in Highbury? The woman in Kilburn? You look like the Jew. I killed you for a long time, with a machete.'

'The Jew, yes,' says Jackie. He can see that this man, Leka, is no longer Leka. The darkness which coats the man's face is not only shadow, but a rich mottle of dried blood from a head wound. The hair is flattened and matted, the right side of the head a glistening mess. Elira's work. Trauma has scrambled brains, thought and speech. Is he seeing past victims? Jackie doesn't care, he only wants to keep him quiet.

The rumble of the iron door being rolled aside in the barn drifts towards them. Voices shout, '*Mut! Leka! Qij!*'

'I have to go,' says Jackie.

'To the underworld, yes. To the cedar in the circle.'

'The circle?'

'To Lebanon. So many souls there.'

Bailey's voice pierces the chill air. 'He's gone! Fuck!' followed by a cacophony of curses and grunts. Jackie places his foot on the stone wall. Leka says, 'I am sorry that I killed you.' He takes a faltering step forward, like a marionette on tangled strings. 'I killed so many.'

Jackie spits a frantic hiss. 'It's okay. I have to go. To Lebanon.'

Torches begin darting around the walls of the farmhouse. He hears arguing, but also the sound of footsteps. He hauls himself on top of the wall. Before he drops to the field on the other side, Leka holds the knife out towards him, like a toddler offering a toy. 'I will mourn for you, and the others,' he says. Jackie takes the knife with a nod. Then he is half running, half stumbling across the dark, rugged surface of the field.

He hears shouts and men calling Leka's name. The car drives off with a rasp of shredded gravel. The sound of boots scrabbling over the stone wall follows. Jackie reaches the eastern edge of the grass and finds a ditch skirting the field with a stream running through it. He drops into the shoulder-high channel and lies against the bank.

He hears two hunters, torches darting across rough grass. They are tentative and swear with frustration at minor stumbles. Jackie begins edging north along the stream, away from the buildings, his movement slow so the ripples in the water will be quiet. He sees a shape ahead. A dead sheep, lying in the channel. He peers above the lip of the bank and sees the two men are fifty feet away. Something glints in their hands. Now they split, one making off to the western perimeter, the other to the east, and Jackie.

He crouches, slipping his hand into the freezing water and under the sheep carcass. It hasn't been dead long, doesn't stink of decay. Leaning his weight against the animal, he slices hard into the belly. It's exhausting work, the tough meat and sinew fighting the blade every ragged inch, and he hears the Albanian shout across the field to his comrade. The man is close, maybe less than twenty feet away. After precious seconds, Jackie pulls the blade free and drags the entrails from the sheep, forcing them down into the stream to kill any steam and stifle the stench. Then he lies in the freezing water, intestines lapping against his back, and curls into a foetal position, dragging the sheep carcass over his own, ravaged body. He hears grass shifting with the stride of boots and the heavy breath of a man. Torchlight dances across the bank and he prays the hunter is too cold and weary to search with care. He can't take one man, never mind both.

Jackie feels a great weight descend on him, fatigue dragging him down so that he seems to be melting into the freezing water around him. The pain of his wounds is fading as the frigid stream serves as anaesthetic and, incredibly, he finds himself fighting sleep. He battles to remain conscious, sifting through fragmentary images in his mind: Elira, Harris, Bailey, the dark figures hounding him in the field above, the broken Leka. Then, there's nothing. No breath, no sound, no light.

He eases the heavy carcass from his body and uncoils in the water. The agony reignites as he edges his head above the ridge of the ditch and scans the countryside. The men have gone. He works at the sheep carcass, his fingers traitorous with numbing cold, his breath coming in short, angry rasps. When he's done, Jackie lobs a tattered blanket of hide, wiry wool on one side and raw, bloody skin on the other, onto the grass above, then digs his fingernails into the cold, damp soil and drags his body from the ditch. A handful of grass scours the hide, then Jackie wraps it around his shoulders. He takes a deep lungful of West Country air and begins a slow, painful trek to the north-west and Garbella Hill Farm.

CHAPTER 28

Wednesday

Elira wondered if they were nearing London when the men put the hood over her head. Her world went dark, and the musk of sweat, alcohol and tobacco smoke was muted by the coarse burlap.

Time stretched and contracted. The sweating fear of what lay ahead, where she was going, what was happening to Flori and Jackie, was almost unbearable. Then a mobile phone chimed and Harris answered. He listened in silence, then exploded in a torrent of abuse and fury. She heard him say, 'Bastard! Shaw!' and she knew Jackie was alive. In a heartbeat, her world tilted and she wanted to live.

At last, the light dims and the people carrier comes to a stop.

The doors open and her arm is seized in a rough grip. Something sharp brushes her skin. Elira panics, claws at the sacking and is punched hard across the back of her head. She is hauled out of the car, the sound of the men's chatter caroming through the echo chamber of her skull. Then her world lightens from black to sombre grey shadow as the sacking is removed and she sees dust and grime-encrusted brick walls and thick, iron struts peppered with bolts. The ground is sandy dirt punctuated with discarded cans and bottles. She feels afraid and small. The sour memory of a room in Paris rises in her mind like an acid reflux. The Irishman looks at her like shit on his shoe and jerks his head at the others who advance on her, huge in the bleak, dim space. They are rough as they strip her down to her underwear. But they do not touch her once stripped. Instead, a wiry man with a long, veined neck throws a white plastic suit at her, like those scientists wear on TV, and barks an order to put it on. The men do likewise, pulling on rubber boots once finished, and their clothes and shoes are folded and placed in backpacks, which they sling over their shoulders. The Irishman bundles her clothes in with his.

They lead her to a circular metal plate set in a patch of concrete. A squat man, thick patches of sweat already darkening his suit, hauls it open to reveal a funnel plummeting into the dark, iron rungs set into the side. Harris and two others descend into the murk, then Elira and, finally, the long-necked man.

At the bottom, they begin walking. The gallery floor is strewn with pebbles and she almost goes over on her ankle as she slips on a stone. The scrawny man behind her curses, his voice tinny in the enclosed space, and catches her. The torches illuminate patches of wall, sickly yellow-orange brick, smothered in places with a grey, calcified sludge. There is an insidious undercurrent of sewage-stench. The gallery narrows as they progress, so that the squat man fills the space in front of her, the torchlight creating a stark spotlight on the stone ceiling above and ahead.

Elira hears the splash of footsteps in puddles before her own boots are dashing water against the walls, then wading through ankle-deep sludge. The gallery opens out into a broad tunnel running across its mouth, the brick replaced by coarse stone sluiced with sewage. The tunnel is semi-circular, perhaps eight feet high, and she can see weak shafts of light punctuating the dark at irregular intervals up ahead, where daylight seeps through ventilation shafts. London grinds on above. She has no idea what time it is.

Harris says, 'Let's get a move on.'

And as they wade through the city's waste, Elira thinks of her sister, prays she is still alive, and, despite the fetid squalor of her surroundings, again dares to dream.

The cobalt blue canopy of the night had segued into an azure sky as Jackie neared the farm. All was still, the only sound the occasional snort of a horse in one of the stables, but he knew that in a short time, before the first chill flush of dawn brightened the sky, the stable-hands would be up and about to begin their morning chores.

Ian Sparrow, the keeper, lived in a small annex on the western reach of the farm buildings. In his late fifties, Sparrow was a lean, delicate-looking man with an aquiline nose and deep-set eyes whose frame belied strength of spirit and body. Jackie had seen him talk down some of the younger locals, flush with Dutch courage, in pubs throughout the villages. As he knocked on the door, he prayed that Sparrow would hear him out, not call the police at the first sight of him. When he opened the door the keeper stood silent for a long moment. Caked in mud, lacerations across burns across welts on his chest, arms and stomach, Jackie gripped the doorframe, swaying, then collapsed into the small living quarters.

A short time later, he was sipping strong tea as Sparrow fiddled with a needle and thread. He had offered the hard stuff but Jackie declined. They sat at the sturdy country-style table in the kitchenette. As the needle pierced his flesh, Jackie sucked in a lungful of air, grunted through clenched teeth. The older man muttered to himself: he'd done this in the Army a couple of times, and once for a farmhand who got a bit too familiar with a mare in season, but he'd been younger then with a steadier hand. Jackie gave Sparrow the bare bones of his story, facts without too many specifics as to who was involved – Harris, Bailey, the Albanians. Sparrow said he was no expert, but it looked as though someone had treated the bullet hole before he was tortured. Jackie told him about the Junction House in the

Little Venice area of London, in Paddington. That he suspected Elira had been taken to a houseboat there: he remembered her telling him of the sensation of being on water and the sounds of everyday life outside where she'd been held by the three killers. Then Sparrow told him that Kelly was missing and police had been at the farm. Kelly hadn't told anyone the girl was coming and no one knew that Elira had been there. Jackie held back on the fate of the young Englishwoman. The man had a daughter of a similar age in Yorkshire.

Sparrow finished the rough stitches, and the gouges and slashes from Harris's knife were closed, like ugly seams in the fabric of Jackie's skin.

Jackie said, 'I need the shotgun.'

Ian Sparrow looked at the bloodied needle in his fingers with a frown like a father whose worst fears have been confirmed.

He said, 'Jackie,' and seemed to think it was enough.

'Say someone stole it. I was never here.'

'Why *didn't* you bloody steal it?' Sparrow considers the table top for a moment and says, 'Don't you think you need to go to the police?'

'No way. Any sign of police and Elira's dead.' He thought of the gun battle in Soho, Trellick Tower and Ferguson's assassination. 'Anyway, they might not be too keen to hear what I say now, and I can't waste time explaining myself. That's why I couldn't take the risk of someone seeing me at the farmhouse.' An understatement, he thought, and spread his arms wide. 'Look at the state of me. I needed rest for a minute or two, to get patched up.'

Sparrow put the needle on the kitchen table and threw a couple of painkillers next to it. 'Who are you going to use the gun on?'

'Maybe no one. It's not about people dying, it's about saving the girl Elira and her sister. Christ, Ian, she saved my life.'

256

Sparrow walked to the sink and began filling a glass with tap water. 'Say she isn't dead already. I served nine years in the Army, a few months in your neck of the woods, and I never killed anyone. I saw enough to know that what you're going to do won't happen without someone being killed.' He returned to the table, sat down and handed the glass to Jackie.

Jackie downed the painkillers. 'Yes, these guys aren't to be reasoned with, Ian. People might die. But the right people. The people who killed Kelly.'

He hated himself as he watched Sparrow's face crumble, the lips buckle. The older man turned his head from Jackie and seemed to stare at the far wall. Was Sparrow seeing Kelly in his mind's eye or his own daughter? Then Jackie hated himself more as he realised he hadn't thought of Kelly until now. What did it say about him, that death had become so accepted, almost mundane, in his world?

Twenty minutes later he stood in the shower, the jet of steaming water sluicing the blood and dirt from his battered body. His hot tears mingled with the piping spray. Each heave of his shoulders sent convulsions of pain through his body and took him back to the scarred wooden chair in the squalid barn. Took him back to his shame at his nakedness; the awful terror of being at the utter whim of Harris.

Jackie screwed his eyes tighter and uttered a prayer for Kelly. He prayed that Elira and her sister were still alive, and that he might have the strength – God help him – to save them. And he prayed for his own immortal soul.

When he opened his eyes again, he was sprawled on Sparrow's bed, a black cotton T-shirt, weathered dark blue jeans and black trainers laid out for him. His body was a work of art in the mirror, shades of blue, purple and grey. His face had one small, faint stroke of dark blue where Harris had punched him back in the Soho alleyway.

He dressed, catching his breath with each thrust of pain, and returned to the kitchenette where Sparrow was screwing the cap on a flask. 'Not a bad fit for a fat bastard,' he said.

Jackie tried to summon a smile. 'How long was I out?'

'About three hours. I found you slumped in the shower, unconscious. Here, strong coffee.'

'I can't wait, Ian. I have to get to London, now. Christ, she could be dead already.'

'You couldn't operate without rest. Your body has taken serious punishment. It'll take a hell of a lot longer to repair than a couple of hours, but that kip was a bonus. If you tried to get her back in the shape you were in this morning, you'd both be dead by now. Come on, I'll drive you to the outskirts of London.' He smiled, 'I'm too old for silly buggers, so no heroics for me. You'll have to cope with the bad guys on your own when you get to the city.'

Jackie put a hand on the older man's shoulder. 'Thanks, Ian,' he said. 'There's one more thing: can I make a phone call?' As Sparrow handed him a mobile phone, Jackie prayed that someone – the right someone – would pick up on the other end.

The shotgun had been propped against the table.

#

Now they are parked next to Hanger Lane underground station, a twenty-minute straight shot on the Central Line to Paddington. Jackie has the cheap, pre-paid mobile phones kept on the farm wedged in the pocket of a jacket Sparrow took from the stables. The Beretta shotgun is in a long canvas bag.

During the drive, Jackie could see this wasn't coming easy to Sparrow. The man didn't give much away, wasn't a talker, but it was clear in his grim, silent concentration on the road ahead that he was struggling with his decision to help. The news about

Kelly had pushed him over the edge. So many times, death lit the touch-paper on a much bigger bang. To take Sparrow's mind off the situation, they'd talked about work, mutual friends, their regiments, on the drive. Then about Little Venice and the Junction House. Sparrow had explained that Regent's Canal meandered through Paddington, then Camden, and on to King's Cross, Islington and beyond. He'd spent a few weeks on a retired military friend's houseboat, berthed near Camden, a few years back, and they had made their way to Little Venice on a lazy Sunday afternoon.

'Pretty transient lifestyle,' said Sparrow. 'You have to keep moving, you see, can't stay in one place too long. They call it "continuous cruising". One day here, another there.'

'Doesn't anyone have a permanent mooring?'

'Some. "Residential mooring", they call it. But it costs a fortune to get one, like everything else in London.'

Jackie had thought an organised crime gang could afford it.

Now Sparrow looks at the UFO-shaped tube station and says, 'I can't believe I'm doing this.'

'Doing what? You had to drive to London for personal reasons. If a traffic camera picks up a passenger, the image will be vague; it could be anybody. An acquaintance, even a hitch-hiker.'

'And the shotgun? The mobile?'

'Somebody nicked them. You didn't check this morning, so you couldn't have known.' Jackie puts a hand on the man's arm. 'Most people would have called the police as soon as they saw me and sat back. You stepped up. You're helping save two girls' lives. And no one need ever know your part.'

Sparrow's smile is desperate. He says, 'Just don't ruin my clothes, all right?' Then he rests his forehead on the steering wheel and says, 'Kelly. My God.'

Jackie steps out of the car into a crisp London afternoon, a trace of cloud straddling the pale blue sky. His body screams in protest and his movements are stiff and laboured after a couple of hours in the car. He moves like an old man. The look on Sparrow's face makes him feel older, and for a moment the insanity of what he's doing hits home. Then he thinks of the pain and horror Elira has endured, that she saved his life and he thinks the real insanity would be to do nothing. He leans into the back seat and withdraws the long canvas bag, then thanks Ian Sparrow again. For a brief moment Jackie worries that his friend will panic and call the farm, blow things wide open.

No, he thinks. He's sorry to have dragged Sparrow into the affair, but he has faith. Ian's an old soldier, he knows what needs to be done.

Then Jackie shuts the passenger door and enters the squat, circular facade of Hanger Lane station, leaving the old soldier and his conscience behind.

CHAPTER 29

Wednesday

The knife blade is a long, cold razor against Elira's throat.

'You talk, you die. Understand?'

Some time ago they split to the right onto a side channel from the main underground tunnel and have now come to another crevice. The sewer has tomb-like chambers branching off to left and right and the gang now gather in one of them. She can see iron rungs set into the walls, leading upwards like a spine of staples. They have walked for a long time, driving the stagnant water ahead of them, and her legs ache. For the last fifteen minutes they have waded on a slight downwards slope. She tried not to breathe deeply, to keep as much of the stench from entering her nostrils as possible, which made the effort of walking more strenuous. Sometimes they made their way down wide-cut concrete steps, the effluent cascading like a fetid water-feature.

'You strip and change in the side-gallery, like us,' says Harris. 'Then we go up. You stay quiet, you follow me, and maybe you and your sister will live.'

Her limbs are heavy. She dreads having to climb the rungs. It is an age since Elira has closed her eyes and slept.

The side-gallery opens out into a space that can accommodate all of them in a huddle. They undress awkwardly, limbs jabbing one another, taking care not to touch the walls, spreading large strips of sacking to act as mats for their feet. It is a bizarre sight, she thinks, almost comical. When she is almost naked they show no interest in her body. They are not clients. She is merchandise.

The squat man ascends the ladder while two others fold the sacking and place it in plastic bags to be brought with them. The suits and rubber boots go in another two bags. Harris follows the thick-set Albanian, then Elira is shoved towards the rungs and begins climbing. They pause as the cover above is removed and a shaft of pale light scythes across the walls. Then they resume their climb. She reaches the opening of the shaft and draws in a deep lungful of cold morning air. Harris grabs her arms and hauls her out into a dense copse of shrubs and small trees on a steep slope. About fifteen feet below, a concrete path cuts between the thicket and a canal. Behind, the shrubs and trees rise steeply to a ridge and, beyond, Elira hears the heavy drone of city traffic.

The Irishman says in a harsh whisper, 'I don't like doing this in daylight. It's the first and last time.'

'I agree,' says the squat man. 'But Bashkim wants to see her.' He shoots a contemptuous look at Elira.

'It would be so easy,' rasps Harris. 'Cut her throat and leave her here, just another dead slag in this English shithole.'

The other men emerge into the wan light, the sky consumed by a mass of concrete-coloured cloud. When all are concealed in the shrubbery, they replace the cover. Two men make their way up the embankment to their rear; another picks his way through the bushes in front. Harris and the squat man remain with Elira. She feels the tip of the knife between her shoulder blades; the shallow breathing of the men guarding her; the low, assertive thrum of the city as it ebbs and flows around them. She has just begun to think about Flori and Jackie again when a mobile phone buzzes and the squat man fishes a Samsung from his pocket.

He studies the screen, says, 'Go.'

She is propelled through the bushes. Harris keeps her upright, the steel grip of his thin fingers digging into her arms. Then she is stumbling from the shrubbery onto the concrete path bordering the strip of water. A long, flat boat is moored against a moss-covered jetty to the right.

A jogger disappears around the bend of the canal to the left. Small jetties and the gardens of tall townhouses line the far bank. A long, brick wall curves to their left on the near side, swallowed by trees at the bend. To the right, dog-walkers stroll a hundred yards away, beyond the dark shadow of a brick bridge. A metal plate bolted to one of the outer struts on the bridge reads *Regent's Park Road 15*. It's a pretty scene, an urban oasis of calm and reflection.

The knife digs into her lower back and Elira is led onto the deck of the houseboat, through a low door and into its quarters.

Inside, she glimpses the knife as Harris folds the blade back into its curved handle: an Albanian bursa knife. He produces the burlap sack from his backpack.

'You don't have to do that,' she says. They are the first words she has spoken since the farm.

'I don't *have* to do anything,' says Harris. 'Now put the fucking sack over your head before I swap it for a plastic bag.'

Her world goes dim and hot again, and she is led through doors and thrown onto a wide bed, the sack wrenched down on her head and tied with a loose cord. Her hands are also tied, her feet left free. She sits on the edge of the bed and hears the accent, like Jackie's, and the voice, so different from his soft lilt.

'Wait here and don't move.'

Then she hears the door slam shut and a stuttering engine cough to life, and the world beneath her feet begins to pitch and shift.

#

Jackie looks around the tube-train carriage and wonders how many of these people have a guilty conscience.

When much younger, he had a Catholic girlfriend. She and her friends were convinced that Protestant boys and girls were at it like rabbits thanks to their loose morals and sinful contraception. Catholics, she said, had too much guilt to enjoy sex.

She didn't have a clue, he thinks. Presbyterians might be taught to pray on their feet to their maker and answer to no man, but that direct line to the Father Himself meant confessing your misdeeds direct to the stern parent. You had to face your God and ask for forgiveness, and a couple of Hail Marys wasn't going to cut it. Be sure your sins will find you out.

Notting Hill Gate is four stations away en route to Paddington and the usual horde of tourists hasn't spilled into the carriage yet. Instead, mothers are wrangling kids. A couple of students scrutinise a book and mobile phone respectively. A man in a boiler suit flicks through a *Metro* newspaper, heavy metal toolbox wedged between his boots.

The tube pulls in at White City, the sunlight above, filtered through the glass roof and shredded by iron roof supports, spilling slats of light across the platform. The passengers shuffle like cards in a pack. The others in the carriage have bags containing personal effects, groceries, working materials. Jackie sits with a 12 gauge shotgun. He feels like the crazy who walks into a shopping mall with a gun and a chip on his shoulder, tearing into the regular people living their lives around him.

As the train pulls out of the station bound for Shepherd's Bush, he tries to imagine Elira among the people scattered around the car. He tries to picture her in jeans, a blouse and a simple jacket, reading a book or eyes glazed in a daydream. He tries to see her as casual, nondescript.

He can't. Nondescript isn't a word that lends itself to Elira. Perhaps that was her curse, that she could never be a face in the crowd. She has looks, a melancholy, a spirit, that are exceptional. And she has been touched by another world that the people here have only read about in their newspapers or seen on the news. He wonders if there is any way back from that world, for her or himself. And he prays she is still alive.

Please God, he thinks, let her be alive.

#

She knows Bashkim is nearby when the level of activity on the houseboat intensifies. Men speak in brittle, rushed snatches, orders and rebuffs. They speak Albanian, and she hears them refer to her with slurs and insults. Only the Irishman, making an occasional comment, sounds relaxed. He is the object of barbed comments in her mother tongue, too.

Then all goes quiet and the boat shifts in the water as people clamber on and off. Her breathing is amplified in the hot, scratchy burlap. There are heavy steps on the corridor leading to her cabin. The door opens and a broad shadow passes in front of her. Then the cord is loosened and a delicious rush of cool, clean air brushes her face as the sack is removed. Her hands are freed by a broad-shouldered, barrel-chested man in a too-tight jumper, the sack slung over his shoulder. The man says nothing but tosses toiletries and a clean towel on the bed before leaving the room and closing the door.

She stands up, uncertain for a moment, and walks back and forth in the space. Her legs ache. The cabin has a double bed with a small bedside cabinet, a chest of drawers, a glass shower cubicle and a built-in wardrobe opposite the bed. A floor-length mirror covers the door. A blind is drawn over the window above the head of the bed. She summons the courage to look at herself in the mirror. A scrawny, hollow-eyed wraith, grit and sweat-streaked grime smeared across her face, stares back.

The cubicle isn't much larger than an upright coffin, and she bangs her elbows off the plastic walls, but the shower is heaven on

265

earth. They want her clean and presentable for Bashkim. The small cubicle, the steaming water sluicing the filth away, the stinging caress of the spray massaging life back into her tired limbs, and the soft roar of the jet enclose her in her own world. When she emerges, the carpet is soft and spongy under her feet. All is quiet. Fresh clothes have been laid out for her: white underwear, a white blouse, denim knee-high skirt and flat-soled shoes. Simple clothes, far removed from the seedy, fetishistic rags forced upon the girls in Soho and the other satellite clubs and brothels of the *Fis*. Good labels from America and Italy. Perhaps she has been afforded a degree of respect, the only girl to have run from the *Family*.

More likely, they are her funeral robes.

#

Paddington station is a microcosm of London, a collage of surfaces, textures and people glued together in one teeming mass; so many races, nationalities and beliefs. Jackie thinks Belfast could have done with some of this diversity years ago. He walks through the forecourt, his body aching. The long canvas case is just one of many items being hauled, carted and wheeled through the great station. Like many other central areas of London there are few visible police but he knows cameras keep vigil and hears the distant whine of a siren outside. He keeps his head lowered. Only when he doubles back to the exit leading to the path running along the edge of Paddington Basin, the canal which will lead him to Little Venice, does he realise he could have exited the station at its northern end and avoided the concourse. A small doubt scratches at the back of Jackie's mind: *London is not your city, you're lost here.*

He mutters an obscenity and studies the map on the mobile phone screen. He grips the Samsung in his right hand, the handle of the long canvas bag in his left.

The canal towpath is lined with over-priced restaurants and chain cafés, all concrete and steel, facing re-purposed warehouses across the thin stretch of green water. Then the houseboats appear, sprawling, multi-coloured, hugging the side of the waterway. Some are chipped and bruised by years on the city's waterways, some fresh and pristine, sitting end-to-end, hugging the banks like a guard of honour lining the canal. Jackie walks under a low brick bridge and the strip of water widens into an algae-speckled pond ringed with tall, Regency houses. Browning's Pool on the map.

Little Venice.

The scene is pretty, prim, almost pastoral. Regent's Canal branches from the pool. On the mobile's map, the canal runs north-east from Little Venice, long and straight, slicing through Maida Vale. The Junction House is on its northern bank, where the canal begins its journey wedged between Blomfield Road on the northern side and Maida Avenue on the southern bank. Jackie cradles the canvas case for a moment, the weight of the shotgun inside calming him, giving meaning to the festering pain in his body. He realises he's adopted the posture of a soldier carrying his rifle on foot patrol. Self-conscious, he holds the bag by its handle again and begins scouting around Browning's Pool. His breath whistles through pursed lips and he mutters to himself, scolding: *Calm down; more haste, less speed.* But Elira is near. *Must* be near – he can't think otherwise and he prays that she is still alive, that she still has time while he searches and wanders – and where *is* the fucking Junction House? Why can't he see it?

What the hell will he do when he finds it?

Ten minutes later he is standing at the entrance to Blomfield Road, next to the Junction House, the canal stretching ahead of him below street level on the right. The towpath is quiet. He scans the houseboats.

There are so many.

So, so many and he has no idea in which he might find Elira. His eyes dart across the multi-coloured boats in panic, and his imagination begins conjuring up terrible scenes of Elira dead, or worse. So, so many boats. The long, red boat next to the Junction House is named *Sanchez's Delight*. Next sits *Windsor Dream*. And then, sandwiched between *Hana Banana* and *Anlaby*, lies a long, deep red houseboat named *Katana*. His pulse spikes. He pants in short, loud breaths. His legs are hollow.

He walks onto Blomfield Road past the Junction House. A small iron gate next to the House leads down to the concrete towpath and the boats moored alongside. A man sits at the bow of the long, cigar-shaped *Katana*, the houseboat tied to a large metal bollard at the stern with thick rope. Jackie winces as he drops to his haunches, unzipping the canvas bag. The torture has left him with a fluctuating pain. It's bred a rising fury in him. He felt it build on the tube journey. He fought it down at Paddington as he searched for the canal.

Now, he thinks, it's time to let the rage take over.

CHAPTER 30

Wednesday

Elira heard Harris leave after a muted debate about twenty minutes ago. She is sitting on the bed taking a mental stroll from her parents' house to her favourite coffee shop in Tirana, focused and calm, when Agon opens the door of the cabin and Bashkim enters.

It occurs to Elira that she has never seen Bashkim, the *Krye* – the Godfather – open a door for himself and, at that moment, despite how he dominates the physical space, she sees him as a spoilt child. Petulant, capricious, self-obsessed and attended by a literal army, every whim catered for. A needy bully who demands respect because he has so little for himself. When he takes a girl, she is expected to be vocal. Elira had never played the game and, as a result, she fired his passion. Bashkim was never as virile as when he punished.

She can see the hunger in his eyes as he stands, damp patches under the armpits of the shirt straining against the violence packed in his huge frame. His tie is loosened, his sleeves rolled up.

'Vajza ime,' he says. *My girl.*

He towers over Elira, gazing down at her as she sits on the bed, the disappointed patriarch, his pantomime-sad smile voracious.

Elira says nothing.

'You were special,' he says, nodding. 'Not some snotty little orphan or mongrel country girl in need of a scrub and a haircut. You were class and men paid for that class. They wanted to own

269

it, to dominate it. And now,' he waves his hand dismissively and looks at the window, blind still drawn, 'you are nothing.'

Her voice is small but clear. 'No.'

His wolfish smile widens, cruel but pleased.

'You dare to defy me?' The tone is not angry but expectant.

She doesn't answer, but her eyes never waver from his.

'You are right. You are not nothing,' says Bashkim. 'You are filth. Shit. Lower than the scum on the water this boat floats on.' He crosses his arms. 'You ran from me and you let this man, this Shaw, take you away. Leka is an idiot now because you struck him with a rock.' He is working himself into a rage, his eyes widening. 'You put your sister in danger and you probably let Shaw put himself in you. You bitch!'

The beginnings of an erection swell the crotch of his trousers.

'I am the *Krye* and you defied me! Only I had the right to have you for free. Only I could take for free what the sad little fuckers who come to my girls pay for. After I saw you, no other man could have you in the *Fis*, not even Agon. And you let a low, Irish potato-fucker have you.' He spits on the carpeted floor.

Elira says, 'You did not *have* me, and neither did he.' She puts her hands to her bony chest. 'I am not some animal you can trade and put to work. How dare you be so arrogant. You *had* me? Never.'

The *Krye* steps back. The space is small and his back is pressed against the chest opposite the bed. Elira feels like she is growing in size, taking back territory. 'You think because I feared you that you owned me? Pathetic! Yes, you put yourself in my body, but you might as well have been lying with a corpse. *I* was not there. I was with my sister, my mother and father, in another place deep inside. In my being I was in Tirana, living my life while your fat, slovenly body sweated and laboured in your sad little fantasy. That I felt anything, that you even existed, is a joke.'

270

Bashkim is stunned. A scolded little boy.

'This man, Jackie Shaw, has not tried to sleep with me,' says Elira. 'He has been too busy tearing through your men, humiliating you and your hired assassins. He sees me as a woman, not some beast to be worked and punished as he sees fit. And he is alive. I heard the Irishman, Harris, say so and I see the fear in your eyes.'

She smiles. She is right.

'If you hurt me again, he will kill you. If you hurt my sister, he will kill you. He is a good man. But you,' her mouth creases in contempt, 'you are not even a man: you are irrelevant. When I take stock of my life, I consider the things that are important. The people I love, what I hold dear, the places and experiences that made me. You are not even a consideration. You are the waste that is left when all that matters is considered. *You* are shit.'

She realises that she is standing now, a foot from Bashkim, looking up at his pale, horrified face. She turns her back on him then sits on the bed again, her face turned to the side. 'You are nothing.'

For a moment the head of the *Fis* stares at a point somewhere above her head, at the window above the bed. His features have collapsed, his mouth is wet and working silently. She can see a thin gloss on his eyes. Then the dying, dark embers of his glare rekindle. His eyes become heavy and hooded. Bashkim's gaze falls to bore hard into Elira. His right hand disappears into his pocket and emerges holding a mobile phone. He punches the keys with his big, brutal fingers and raises the mobile to his ear.

The *Krye* once more, he says, 'Shkoni në Liban. Vrasin motrën.'

Then, frustrated, in English he says, 'Go to the Circle of Lebanon. Kill the sister.'

Elira sighs. Her body becomes heavy, yet empty, as though sinking through the bed, through the wooden hull of the boat to the dark, clouded bottom of the canal. She looks up at the man who has blighted her life for what seems like an age as though from a great depth. Then a broiling rage surges through her, rocketing to the surface. No fear, no pain, just fury. She bolts upright from the bed. Her scream seems to soar above the city itself as she shrieks, 'Ju maskara!'

A second later her scream is answered by the bellow of a gun, then the panicked cries of men on the boat. Bashkim flinches. Elira smiles. She knows that Jackie has come.

#

Training, craft, caution, all abandoned. Jackie hears the scream and runs at a crouch to the top of the short flight of steps leading down to the towpath, and the *Katana*. He takes the steps two at a time, ten yards from the boat when the man on deck realises what is happening, struggling to his feet. Jackie snaps the Beretta's stock to a firing position and pulls the trigger, three shots punching recoil into his shoulder, three rounds punching holes in the man on deck. The man spasms, then slumps against the bow window. Another man emerges from the narrow door on the deck clutching a handgun. On the move, Jackie fires another three rounds, the sharp blast of the report in his ears. Splinters explode from *Katana*'s hull as the first round goes low. The second blows a hole in the man's left thigh and, as he folds, the third drills a hole in his crown.

As the body tumbles over the side of the boat, hitting the path a couple of feet from the spent cartridges, Jackie reloads. The movement is fluid, his breathing even. He doesn't break stride, now alongside the *Katana*, a couple of steps from the bow, the dead shooter at his feet. He feels outside himself, beyond himself, adrenaline coursing through his body, his only thought to get to Elira. So it takes a moment for him to register the sharp crack of a pistol shot and the brief whisper of air on his wrist as a bullet skims his right hand and bites into the wooden hull beside him. He ducks and spins then scuttles to the stern of the boat, another round from the pistol skipping off the concrete at his heels as he creases up, trying to hide behind the bollard, *Katana*'s rope wrapped around it. His senses ignite: he smells the musk of the canal water; the dust skipping off the concrete as another bullet searches him out; he sees the flaking paint on the hull and the open-mouthed horror of a couple of pedestrians on Warwick Avenue bridge; his ears ring with the shotgun blasts, but he still hears a handgun chattering angrily as this unseen man fires another two shots, one careening off the bollard. Jackie is trapped. The light is fading, but not fast enough to give cover.

He curses himself for rushing in. The shooter must be in the shrubbery of the bank a few yards ahead of the boat, off the path. Jackie could reach out and touch the hull of the *Katana*. There is a large window at the stern, opaque in the low light. Then a screaming, feminine voice calls his name. Elira.

He takes a fast, hard gulp of air. The shooter on the bank has gone quiet, waiting for him to make a move; perhaps advancing through the shrubbery towards him. Jackie wrestles with his growing panic, forcing his body to answer to his will, slowing and controlling his breathing. He releases a long sigh, then launches himself up and over the low lip of the houseboat's hull. Three shots ring out from the bank. He lands on his back on the narrow deck at the stern, right arm clutching the Beretta, level with the bottom of the window. Another shriek from Elira. A blast. The window shatters, shards of glass fly outwards, showering him. Through shredded blinds he sees Elira splayed on a bed, her hands clasped over her ears, eyes screwed shut. A big man stands at the foot of the bed. The man snatches a sawn-off shotgun from a wiry, frightened-looking companion standing in an open doorway. He grasps the weapon in large, meaty hands and lets fly. The roar ricochets off the walls as Jackie, spread-eagled on the deck, fires twice into the cabin, one-handed, the fingers of his left hand gripping the rim of the deck as his right clutches the shotgun. The blasts bellow over one another and he sees the broad gut and barrel chest of the big man flower red. The man falls back against a chest of drawers and drops to a sitting position.

In the quiet that follows, Elira stares at the man, alive but struggling with shallow, laboured breaths. She turns to his thin companion, frozen in the doorway, then Jackie. The dying man's weapon lies under his bulk on the blood-stained carpet. The scrawny man, unarmed, runs from the cabin, slamming the door behind him. Elira stands on the bed and reaches out to Jackie. Neither speak as he hammers at the jagged glass in the window frame with the stock of his Beretta. When he reaches for her to pull her up through the frame onto the small deck at the stern, she turns to the large man, his chin disappearing into rolls of sweat-slick fat.

She says, 'Unë jetoj dhe ju nuk janë asgjë.'

Then Jackie hauls her through the frame.

Elira kneels on the deck as he peers over the roof of the houseboat and sees the shooter from the bank now creeping along the rim of the shrubs at the edge of the towpath. The man sees him and fires two shots, one wild, as he breaks into a run. The second tears into the roof of the houseboat, sending a fine spray of dust into Jackie's eyes. He ducks behind the cabin and blinks, kneading his eyelids with his palm. When he looks over the roof of the boat again, the man has fled.

Elira kneels on the narrow deck, hands over her ears. Jackie takes out a mobile phone and she hears the click of its camera. He fiddles with the phone for a moment, then takes her arm and eases one of her hands from her head. He says, 'How many on the boat?'

'I don't know. They had a hood on me most of the time. But Harris has gone. The man who ran from the cabin is Agon.'

The drone of a helicopter drifts across the city towards them. Elira cries out, 'Your side!'

A red flower is blossoming across the left side of his shirt and under his torn jacket. Four jagged shards of glass spear his flesh, barbed tails sticking out through his clothes. Elira goes to remove them but Jackie says, 'No.'

She looks shocked. He says, 'I don't want to get blood on you. Take this money and mobile phone and dial the number in the directory, the only number. Someone I trust will meet you at an underground station on the outskirts of London and keep you safe until I'm done. When you call, ask to speak to Lily and give your name as Garbella.' His voice is a hoarse whisper and he swallows to wet his parched mouth. He places a mobile and a clutch of sterling notes in her hand.

'My sister,' says Elira. 'They're going to kill her. But it doesn't make sense. Bashkim gave the order on the phone. To go to Lebanon, to a circle, and kill Flori. First in Albanian, then in English. It must be Harris. But Lebanon? I don't understand. She could be dead already.'

'Calm down. I know where Harris is going. I'll stop him. Where's Bashkim?'

'In Hell. That's him in the cabin.'

'I can get to your sister and I can stop these men but I can't do it with you,' says Jackie. He hopes the words sound more convincing to her than they do to his own ears. 'I can't do it if I'm worrying about you. Please, run. Call my friend and be safe. Go, run up the path to where the water goes under the next bridge. Climb up to the Edgware Road and away. Hurry, before the police turn up.'

Elira says, 'One thing: they brought me to the canal underground through a long tunnel, like a river under the city. We came out onto the canal at a bridge with a sign, Regent's Park 15.'

She stands up, the two of them pressed together by the narrow deck, and kisses him on the cheek. Her lips barely touch his skin as the dusk closes about them like a velvet shawl. Then she hops from the houseboat to the towpath, light and agile, clutching the mobile and makes to run up the canal in the direction of Camden. Jackie sets the shotgun down and begins easing a shard of glass from his side, a dull ache throbbing as adrenaline drains. Sirens are whining, drawing nearer. On the path, Elira takes off at a jog, her figure a flitting silhouette in the deepening gloom, when Jackie remembers the man from the cabin. Agon. As though on cue, the man steps out from the door at the bow of the *Katana* and raises both arms, pointing a handgun at Elira's back.

Elira runs towards the tunnel where the canal passes under Edgware Road on its way to Regent's Park and Camden. She's ten yards away, not far enough to be out of range, and Jackie's cry is caught in his cracked, dry throat. He begins to reach for the shotgun but can't take his eyes from the man at the bow. The shots are flat snaps, two in quick succession, and the scrawny man seems to cave in. In the gathering darkness, Jackie sees Elira run on. White specks dance above the bushes at the top of the bank to his left on Blomfield Road. After a moment, he realises they are the light checks of Metropolitan Police officers' caps. The white turns blue as the flashing lights of squad cars come to a sliding halt and a helicopter searchlight dances to the south-east over Paddington. These past days there's barely been a Bobby on the streets, thinks Jackie, and now they're setting record response times.

He lies flat on his belly and takes the shotgun in his hands. Then he eases his body, nerves screaming with pain, over the side of the *Katana* houseboat and descends into the black void of the canal.

CHAPTER 31

Wednesday

Elira hears two short cracks behind as she sprints towards the black mouth of the tunnel under the road ahead. Men shout, panicked; she hears screams from the street, from neighbouring houseboats lining the canal; the muffled clatter of a helicopter drawing close. As she nears the tunnel and the steep path leading up to the Edgware Road, figures appear from the houseboats. People are stooped and hesitant, but no one approaches her, no one tries to stop her. No one wants to get involved.

There are lights in the windows of a café above the tunnel, the patrons' silhouettes, half standing at tables and staring out at the drama. She runs through an open gate leading from the towpath and up the slope to the Edgware Road.

At the top, she almost runs into an old man with a small dog worrying and yapping at the noise and confusion as the helicopter chops the air above, its searchlight twitching across the canal. More cars are arriving, radios crackling and police officers bluffing in their calm and authority, marshalling the curious away from the immediate scene. The old man is blocking her way off the slope and she makes to sidle past him as he stares at the chaos around the far end of the canal.

'Are you all right, dear?' His hand is a claw, his grip surprisingly strong on her wrist. Elira almost drops the mobile phone Jackie gave her. She stares at the old man, skull-eyed, as he continues to gaze at the cluster of police. The dog sniffs at her ankles, then takes an accusatory step back and growls. The old man is entranced by the pulsing blue lights of the police cars.

Still staring at them, he repeats 'Are you all right?' Insistence in the question. And suspicion?

Elira looks at the canal, at the uniformed men galloping down the embankment to the *Katana*. She glimpses bodies in the flash of cameras and a man in a heavy jacket is berating a couple of armed police next to a Range Rover.

'It's terrible,' she says. 'Some kind of shooting. My friend is in the café.' She pulls her hand free as calmly as she can manage and points to the brightly lit windows above the tunnel. 'I want to see her, let her know I'm okay.'

The old man's rheumy eyes settle on her. 'Yes,' he says. 'You should find her before you talk to the police. I should think they'll want to know if you saw anything.'

'Yes,' she echoes. As she walks away, fighting the impulse to run, the old man begins hobbling towards a tall police officer unfurling a tape, ready to seal off the road.

The Edgware Road end of Blomfield Road is blocked by three police cars, blue lights gliding across the small crowd of curious onlookers now huddled at the side of the café. Two policemen stand in front of the crowd in conversation with a couple of women pointing at the canal. Another officer stands next to a car muttering to a colleague and another is running to a fourth car parked ten yards away. Traffic grinds by, people walk past, wrapped up in texting or the drama of their own lives. The old man is still hobbling over to the policeman now tying the tape to a lamppost.

Elira walks towards the café. A peripheral light catches her eye and she realises she has turned the mobile phone screen on by accident.

'She can get through, why can't we?'

A hard voice, English and entitled, one of the women gesticulating with the officers next to the café. A policeman turns around and looks at Elira.

'We bloody live here. If she can wander around in your bloody crime scene, why can't we go to our house, indoors and out of your way?'

The policeman turns back to the woman whose companion is nodding her head in violent agreement. Desperate, panicked, Elira hits dial on the mobile. Her hands are shaking and it takes a moment for her fingertip to register on the touchscreen. The old man is reaching out to the officer with the tape, calling to him in a tremulous voice. The policeman in debate with the angry woman looks harassed and says, 'No one should be behind these cars, madam.' The old man stumbles, setting off a fresh round of yapping from his dog. The harassed-looking officer says, 'Christ, there's another one. Oi, Charlie!' The tall policeman with the tape stops unfurling the blue and white ribbon and looks up. The harassed officer says, 'Get that gentleman out of the street, sharpish.' Then he turns his back on the gesticulating woman and studies Elira. She thanks God for the gathering dark, and for the fluorescent blue of the police lights painting over the scarlet of her cheeks.

The policeman's stare drills into her and the crowd seems to go quiet in anticipation, eager for more drama. She takes a step towards them all as though someone were reeling her in on a line, her legs hollow. A vibration makes her start and she almost drops the mobile: the call is connected. A ringtone drifts from the crowd. The angry woman pulls a phone from her pocket and checks it, then crosses her arms in fury. The harassed policeman waves Elira towards him, gesturing for her to hurry. The ringtone stops. The officer's colleague is studying her now, too. He opens his mouth, bad teeth splitting a professional scowl.

'There you are! I was worried sick. Thank God you're okay.'

A small woman with big hair steps forward from the crowd to stand next to the policemen. She looks in her late fifties and, despite her diminutive size, seems to obscure the angry, gesticulating woman. 'I'm so sorry, officers,' the little woman says, 'this is my girl.' She beckons Elira over. 'Not my daughter, but my girl, Garbella.' Her smile is warm and reassuring as she gives Elira a hug.

Elira says, 'Lily.' She hopes the officer can't hear the doubt in her voice.

The policeman with bad teeth says, 'Explain.'

The little woman's smile is gracious and open. 'My name is Lily Dunstable. I'm a host mother for foreign students who come here to study English. Garbella is staying with me while she studies at Clifford's Nest language school, in Paddington. We were just having a coffee and she popped out to take a photo of the houseboats on the canal when all that trouble broke out. I was worried sick: she's only A1 on the CEFR scale, if that.'

A flicker of confusion crosses the policeman's face. His colleague looks bored, his eyes glazed over.

'Sorry, teaching term. Anyway, I'll get her home to Wimbledon now, if that's okay.'

Bad-teeth says, 'We might need to talk to her,' but his voice has lost its aggression. 'A-C-what-did-you-say?'

'A1 on the CEFR scale, dear,' says the little woman. 'It's a language scale of competence used in Europe. Garbella is at the lowest level for English, bless her. Can barely string a sentence together beyond stock phrases.' Elira glances at the old man with the dog in conversation with the policeman holding the tape, the officer stooping down, frowning, as he struggles to understand the man. The little woman says, 'It looks like all the action was at the other end of the road. Anyway, if you have a Latvian translator and plenty of time, you can interview Garbella, here.'

The two officers look at each other. The crowd is restless again and the angry woman says, 'What about us?'

The policeman with the bad teeth cocks his head and says, 'Go on, off home.'

As they scurry past the café, the angry woman says, 'Bloody foreigners.'

The little woman leads Elira across the Edgware Road and turns right, walking so fast that Elira is panting to keep up. They stop after a minute and the woman produces a mobile phone.

'Lucky you called me when you did,' she says. 'Well done, dear. We'll go to Edgware Road station and take the tube home, then I'll make you a nice cup of tea. Jackie said you were a beauty, and he's right.'

'Jackie.'

'Oh yes, dear. You were to call me and say, "Lily" then I should answer "Garbella". All very cloak and dagger.'

'You are Jackie's friend.'

'You could say that, yes. I only met him a couple of times but he knows my brother very well. Jackie phoned me this afternoon and told me to wait for your call but I couldn't just sit there at home. A young girl shouldn't be running around alone in London, so when he told me he would be going to get you from Little Venice I came down here and had a coffee, waiting for you. When all that shooting started I thought I'd never find you. Then my phone rang and I saw your mobile was lit up, so I used the password and you replied.' She turns the screen to display a photo of Elira crouched on the back of the houseboat. 'I received this photo while I was waiting.'

Elira says, 'You told that policeman the name of a language school. What if they check?'

'Clifford's Nest school? They're welcome to: I own it.'

The woman rubs Elira's arms and smiles again, a warm, bright smile to get lost in. She says, 'Jackie told me what happened to you, how you came to England. That's over now. Come on, let's get you home and wait for him to fetch your sister.' She makes it sound as though he is strolling around the corner to get Flori from a friend's house. Elira likes the thought; she likes this woman.

'Thank you,' she says. 'I'm sorry, what is your real name?'

'It's Betty, dear. Dunstable was my married name, although my Clifford passed away ten years ago. I go by my maiden name now, before I was married. It's Sparrow, Betty Sparrow.'

#

Gilmore has his coat in his hand before he replaces the receiver on the phone in Thames House. The office is quiet, his colleagues gone home for the night, so no one hears him mutter, 'Shaw. Has to be Shaw.'

An Albanian, Don Boxton said, the DC bellowing down the phone over the background noise of the office at New Scotland Yard. Bashkim Jusufi. A known Albanian organised crime boss shot on a houseboat at Little Venice. A known Albanian organised crime boss with a club in the very street in which Jackie Shaw shot two missing people in Soho.

Gilmore has one foot in the corridor en route to the stairs and Regent's Canal when the lift doors slide open and Christopher Howell-Barraclough shuffles through, accompanied by Morris and another, unfamiliar face. Howell-Barraclough, Director General, a year off retirement and the inevitable knighthood, raises a withered hand. Morris, his Deputy, says, 'Just a moment, Laurence.'

'Is there a problem?'

Howell-Barraclough does his best approximation of a human being and says, 'No, no problem, we simply need a quick word.' Then he musters a game but unsuccessful attempt at a smile.

Morris, acutely comfortable within his own, lizard-like skin, makes no such effort. 'The fifth floor – now, please. We can take the lift together.'

The unfamiliar face, probably a legal advisor, remains silent. The three of them stand, uncomfortable yet superior, looking offended at the lack of reaction from Gilmore.

An invitation to the fifth floor, the mandarins' realm.

The fifth floor, the highest echelons of the service.

For an officer of Gilmore's rank, it can only mean he is being summoned above to plummet downwards at speed.

#

Jackie lost the shotgun in the canal. He sits in the back of a taxi, his clothes wet, chill in his bones. The heater in the cab is stifling and pain nips at his warming limbs, growing in intensity. He's glad of it. It keeps him sharp.

The driver, Middle-Eastern, doesn't talk. He had a studied ambivalence to the dishevelled appearance of his fare when he picked him up. There is only the soft purr of the engine as they drive through Hampstead and the blur of light sweeping past the windows from houses, shops, other cars. It gives Jackie time to think. He doesn't want to.

Elira is free but he's locked in his own head, his conscience rattling the bars. Four more dead at the *Katana*. Three more men he's killed. Jackie closes his eyes. Waves of illumination wash across the darkness of his mind's eye as the cab passes streetlights, affording glimpses of the dead.

A ripple of light: a man deflates against the stern of the *Katana*, his shirt shredded and crimson.

Another: a man falls, leg jolting with the impact of the first round, head punched into his neck by the second, collapsing onto the towpath.

'Enough of this bullshit,' whispers Jackie.

More sweeping light: Bashkim, a big man, eviscerated by the shotgun blasts, Elira looking on.

He says, 'Bollocks.'

The driver says, 'Sorry?'

'Nothing.'

Before he opens his eyes, the view almost unchanged in the sprawl of north London at night, he sees a wee boy on a footbridge in Kew. And Harris. He will not let Harris kill Flori. Please, he begs his maker, let her be alive.

As Jackie had clung to the hull of the houseboat the gun had slipped from his fingers, stiff and clumsy with cold. He had edged along, gripping the rim of each painted hull, heading for the tunnel under the Edgware Road, praying no one would notice him. He reached the tunnel entrance, took a couple of deep breaths and swam into the dark.

The going was hard.

When Regent's Canal emerged into the London night again, he hauled himself onto a stretch of the towpath and took long gulps of air, the chill harsh in his throat. Before making his way to the street, he pulled his sleeve down to cover his palms and eased each ragged blade of glass from his flesh, moaning softly. He took off his jacket and turned it inside out so that the black lining was on the outside, then pulled it back on and reverse zipped it to his neck.

Now he sits, battered, in the back seat of the cab, praying that Elira is warm and safe. Praying that Harris was far away when he got the call and that Flori is still breathing.

It had been the map that provided the spark. He'd unfolded the London street map on Sparrow's kitchen table, smoothing out the creases. His eyes were drawn to the two red crosses he'd sketched back in the hotel room, talking with Laurence Gilmore on the phone while he plotted his route for the night he'd trawled the hostels and streets in search of McLelland. The crosses, like spindly grave markers, spread over Hampstead Heath and Islington. Jackie had run his index finger down each stem while Sparrow watched. Then he'd traced the rough crossbars with his fingertips. They splayed outwards to east and west but almost met in the centre, at the small, mushroom-shaped patch of greenery of Highgate Cemetery.

Jackie had remembered the chill when he'd found the cemetery on the map the first time. Scraps of memory began to flit through his mind. The clock in the kitchen in Islington where he'd spoken with Bailey after the fight at Kynance Mews, a tree in a circular trench on the face. Bashkim's phrase on the phone about Flori: *She is alive, among the dead.* And Leka, head bashed in, speaking riddles, zombie-like, to the ghosts of men he'd killed: *the underworld*; *the circle*; *Lebanon*; *so many souls.*

He'd asked Sparrow, 'What do you know about Highgate Cemetery?'

Not much. But the search on the mobile provided plenty. The cemetery was divided into east and west, split by Swain's Lane and straddling the boroughs of Camden and Islington. In the West Cemetery stood a large stone façade, built to resemble a scene from Ancient Egypt. This Egyptian gateway led to an avenue lined with tombs and, beyond, a circular trench, more tombs set within the stone walls and, on the raised island in the centre of the trench, a huge Cedar of Lebanon.

The Circle of Lebanon.

Flori has to be there. Somewhere in the circle, in the cemetery, alive among the dead.

The taxi pulls over to the kerb at the lower end of Swain's Lane, the steep gradient sweeping up before it, as a fine drizzle coats the city. Jackie pays the driver with soggy sterling notes. Immune to the random insanity of London, the driver accepts them without question. As the cab pulls away, Jackie rubs his side. The wounds are tender. His left shoulder aches. He's tired of fear and pain. Time to inflict some on those who deserve it.

He walks to a public phone across the street and makes a thirty-second phone call, checking in with Sparrow. More than enough time to end Flori's life, but needs must. Then he begins to jog up the steep incline, the road curving in a lazy arc to his destination, a set of monumental gates and the towering Victorian-Gothic façade of Highgate Cemetery. The tall, stone church-like façade of the West Cemetery, all Hammer horror, appears on his left. No one is around. He remembers the Google map he studied and knows there is another entrance two hundred yards ahead, at the north-eastern corner of the cemetery. He jogs on.

Now the lane is dark, sided by a brick wall on the left and a high wooden fence on the right. Tall trees form a skeletal canopy above. Streetlights shed vague smudges of light on the road ahead and a cold, white blaze is thrown across Swain's Lane by a modern glass and steel building, more San Fernando Valley than north Camden. The building is set partly in the cemetery itself and Jackie sprints past the bright illumination it throws. He reaches the northeastern corner of the West Cemetery and a simple, ten-foot-high iron gate. Beyond the bars, a path stretches into the grounds. A small gatehouse is inside. There's no sign of a guard and no light within the cemetery grounds besides moonlight, shredded by low-hanging branches, on the gravel path ahead. Headstones and plinths line the path on either side like a dark, immovable honour-guard.

Jackie checks that Swain's Lane is still deserted, then takes a firm grip on the railings and hauls his body upwards with a groan. His feet gain purchase on a horizontal bar midway up the gate and he pauses, breathing hard and praying that no one will amble along and spot him. Then he bends his knees and launches himself, his inner thigh snagging on the fleur-de-lis heads of the railings, mercifully rounded at their tips. He is suspended for an awkward moment before collapsing over the gate to land in a sprawl on the gravel path inside, the breath driven from him with a grunt. After ten seconds he stands, stiff and sore, and hobbles into the undergrowth.

His clothes had dried out some in the taxi but they're getting heavy with damp in the drizzle that now drapes the city and

Jackie rubs soil over his jeans to darken them, then spits on his palms and slathers his face with the musty earth. He checks his pockets to ensure the blade folded into its long handle, the knife Leka gave him when he escaped the farm, is still there. He looks at the clutter of plinths and sarcophagi ahead, erupting from the earth like crazy, rotting teeth, and begins picking his way through the graves.

Time is all-important, each second another window for Harris to kill Flori, but the going is laboured. A tangled carpet of ferns and bracken blankets the headstones in the inner cemetery, a confusion of graves, some canting at mad angles. Great, flat slabs of stone, grave markers wiped almost clear, form steps through the undergrowth, the moonlight catching granite amid dark thickets of overgrown grass. His footing betrays him in the shambles and he collapses, his left elbow scraping stone. He lies still, heeding the silence and again praying that he isn't too late. Looking around, he sees a brilliant floodlight a distance off. The modern house on Swain's Lane, its façade set within the cemetery itself. Grasping tendrils of tree roots reach across the ground around him, clutching at the earth before enfolding a ruined plinth in their skeletal fingers. Jackie curses them for tripping him, and the dark for hiding them.

His eyes have adjusted to the dark now, however, and he sees ivy swallowing many of the headstones. He passes a cluster of them in various states of collapse, like dominoes frozen in the act of falling, and the ground flattens and clears. A path appears and beyond, a black, gaping void set in a huge stone wall flanked by two towering obelisks. A high, jagged archway yawns between fat, stone papyrus columns. The Egyptian gateway – a dark, Victorian imagining of the land of the pharaohs. The entrance to the Egyptian Avenue and, beyond, the Circle of Lebanon.

Muffled voices in conflict, angry but indistinct, drift from within the impenetrable dark. Harris and Flori are somewhere in the obscure gloom beyond. Judging by the voices, they aren't alone.

Jackie crosses the path in three strides and enters the Egyptian Avenue, a hundred feet long at a slight incline, with heavy tomb doors set in the high, oppressive walls. The rain is solidifying into a decent downpour now, the angry voices dampened by its hiss. It streaks the soil on Jackie's face. At the end of the avenue is another arch and, beyond, he sees a huge shape. Distinct against the cloud in its sheer, dark mass, the ancient cedar stands, raised, in the centre of the Circle of Lebanon.

Jackie winces with each soft crunch of stones underfoot as he creeps towards the circle. The voices grow louder.

'You fucking edjit! You fucking edjit!'

'For fuck's sake!'

He steps out of the shadows to face Derek Bailey and Conal Harris.

CHAPTER 32

Wednesday

Jackie walks into the sunken circular avenue of connected tombs to a scene from a Victorian-Gothic horror. A stone wall curves away to either side, lines of heavy tomb doors set within ornate stone entrances. An LED torch on the ground throws giant, twisted shadows on the inner and outer walls of the curved trench and Bailey and Harris stand to the left and right, their faces lit like ghoulish masks. On the gravel path at their feet, a small female figure is sprawled, the glittering rain dancing around her in the light of the torch. Flori.

She wears tight jeans tucked into boots and a simple sweater. Her hair, a forest of loose curls encrusted with mud, covers her face. There's an ugly stain on the sweater and a narrow thread of blood flows to the rain-slick stones of the gravel path, shining in the torchlight.

Bailey and Harris are frozen like guilty children discovered at mischief. They gape open-mouthed. Bailey has wiped blood on his blue raincoat and there is a small tear on the sleeve of Harris's leather jacket. The door of the tomb to Harris's left is open, the torch on the path lighting a cracked inner wall, pale grey bricks showing through seams in the stone. Jackie can't see a weapon. He touches his pocket, feeling Leka's knife folded and snug inside. Pain seems to gnaw deeper into his shoulder when he looks at the girl. He's glad her face is covered. He doesn't want to see her eyes.

Instead, he stares at Harris. 'Congratulations,' he says. 'That's the second woman you've murdered in the last few days.'

'I've killed a lot more than that. But I didn't – '

Bailey says, 'Listen – '

'And you,' says Jackie, 'you're worse. This animal is just doing what comes naturally.'

Harris says, 'That's enough,' and begins slowly moving his hands to the back of his waistband.

Jackie steps back, away from the torchlight, and puts his hands in his pockets. He looks at Bailey and says, 'To impress Hartley? Or is it Gilmore? How much do MI5 pay these days, anyway?' He begins to unfold the knife blade, one-handed, in his pocket.

A shadow bobs at Bailey's throat as he swallows.

Harris's eyes narrow. His hand rests somewhere at the small of his back. He says, 'MI5? What the fuck's he talking about?'

Bailey doesn't take his eyes off Jackie, and he doesn't say a word.

The blade grinds against its handle in Jackie's pocket. His fingers slip, slick with sweat and rain. He studies Harris's face. Did the murdering bastard notice the movement? Can he see Jackie's fidgeting in the shadows?

Harris looks at Jackie but says to Bailey, 'I asked you a question.' He pulls a handgun from his waistband and covers Jackie and Bailey, swinging the pistol like a scythe. He steps forward, his feet straddling the body on the ground, small in the torchlight.

Bailey takes a deep breath, as though he's about to dive to a great depth.

'Go on,' says Jackie, 'answer the man.'

The blade is almost free, its tip at the mouth of the pocket.

'Fuck it,' says Harris. 'My-Aunt-May-she-called-me-in...' pointing the gun left and right.

Jackie nicks his finger as the blade comes free with a final wrench. He flinches.

Harris fires two shots. Jackie scrambles forward, his feet spitting wet gravel. Bailey goes down and lands on the dead girl's twisted foot as Jackie barrels into Harris. His hand is clear of his pocket and clutching the knife, arm moving in a sharp arc, stabbing at Harris's side. The first thrust skewers the leather jacket and comes back out clean. Harris fires a wild shot. Jackie thrusts the blade again. He feels shirt and flesh give and hears a bellow of anger and pain. They land hard on the gravel and he stabs a third time, the knife driving into skin and grinding against a rib. Harris bucks and flails in a blind panic and an arm batters Jackie's wrist as he withdraws the blade. The knife sails through the lashing rain and clatters somewhere in the dark beyond the torchlight. Jackie can smell stale tobacco and booze on Harris's breath. They thrash and scrabble, sending stones skittering in all directions.

Jackie's blood is up, adrenaline surging, fuel for his rage. He thinks of Christopher Martins, Flori and God knows how many in the past. No more. He clutches at Harris's right elbow, forces the gun above the killer's head and digs his knees hard into the gravel. Then he hurls himself, his head like a jackhammer, and butts Harris full in the face, cartilage snapping as the killer's nose caves in. Harris screams and fires two more shots wild. Flori's body twitches as a stray round hits.

I'm winning, thinks Jackie. Then the gun fires again, close, muzzle flash blinding him, heat scorching his cheek. He remembers the cigarettes, the belt buckle, the barn. Harris still has the pistol. Jackie's lost his weapon. Up close, any one of these shots could find its mark and Jackie would join the dead girl, bleeding on the gravel. Flight gives fight a swift kick in the bollocks and he lurches towards the arch of Egyptian Avenue like a drunk. He hears the frantic crunch of feet on gravel behind.

Harris roars, 'You fucking black bastard! You cunt!'

Then Jackie is running. He clears the avenue and sprints

across the path into the mess of graves in the ramshackle inner cemetery, so dark after the stark glare of the torch. He threads his way through and over the tangle of headstones, ferns, ivy and tree roots, not looking back, waiting for the crack of another shot. He hears a thrashing through the undergrowth and the scrape of boots on the slabs of grave markers behind him. Jackie prays Harris hasn't picked his way through this section of Highgate before, that he has that edge, at least. Breathing hard, he runs his hand over his face, wiping the rain from his eyes, straining to see the dim light from the house set just within the cemetery grounds. In seconds that seem like hours he spies the glow from the floodlights. It silhouettes the grasping trees off to his right. And he stumbles, cries out, and falls. Harris staggers into view, high-stepping over a thick, snaking tree root. Slim, straight prongs catch the light low to Harris's left, like splintered outsized needles rammed in the wet earth. Broken iron railings.

Harris levels the handgun at Jackie's stomach and says, 'One bullet left. But I've a second magazine in my pocket. Don't you worry, I'll take my time with you.'

Then Jackie, his legs like pistons, hurls himself forward, his head low and arms outstretched. He hears the sharp roar of a final shot and something nips at his arm, then he crashes into Harris, driving him backwards and down. Jackie pivots as they land hard. Harris's body cushions some of the impact. Jackie rolls off him onto a pitted stone slab and groans, winded. He lies, waiting for the rasp of a west Belfast accent, the click of nine rounds inserted in the pistol, a final blast of heat and noise and a white descent into death.

Killed in a graveyard, he thinks, how fucking apt.

Instead, he hears a wracking cough followed by a wet, fragile wheezing. The railings surrounding the crumbling grave slab are hidden under the body of Conal Harris, shivering in the pale light, blood running from his mouth to his ear like a crimson chain. The spears of iron haven't gone through his body, but its weight is still driving them onward, through his back, his broken spine and splintered ribs. His eyes are staring at the heavens, full of pain and horror and confusion. If he's lucky, he'll pass out before shock and blood loss take their final, terrible toll.

Jackie winces and covers his aching shoulder with his right hand for a moment. He pulls at the neck of his jacket and T-shirt, breathing out as the cool balm of the night's rain soothes his wound. The left arm of his jacket is torn and he feels a stinging sensation: grazed by Harris's last bullet. His side is tender with lacerations and he runs his fingertips over the cuts. Then he gives the dying Conal Harris one more look before leaving the man alone in his terror and agony, among the dead.

CHAPTER 33

Wednesday

When Jackie returns to the Circle of Lebanon, Bailey has struggled into a seated position against the stone wall of the circular trench and is staring at the delicate female body on the gravel path, his arms folded in his lap. His chin is slumped on his chest, blood soaking into the stubble, his shoulders rising and falling as his lungs fight the good fight to keep him alive. He's been shot in the left breast and the gut. His mobile phone gleams in the light of the torch, still throwing its glare on the surroundings, beyond his reach.

A long, slow, painful way to go, thinks Jackie, dropping to his haunches. He takes a fistful of Bailey's hair, pulling his head back. The man coughs and looks up with bloodhound eyes. The gore on his chest, face and stomach is dark crimson in the stark light.

Bailey says, 'I'm going to die, aren't I?'

'Looks like it.'

'What about Harris?'

'Saint Peter's locking the pearly gates to keep him out as we speak. He'll be roasting nicely in the other place in a minute or two.' Jackie lets Bailey's head drop back on his chest.

He places a hand on the tangle of hair covering the dead girl's face. Strands shine in the rain, despite the mud. He closes his eyes for a moment and offers a silent prayer. Then he sweeps the hair gently back, forcing some, matted with wet earth and blood, away from the cheeks peppered with gravel, to reveal the sleeping beauty. She looks more beautiful than he could have imagined. Her features seem more mature, the refined nose and generous mouth. Her face has taken on a tint like tarnished marble. He's cleared some of the mud to reveal the blonde curls beneath. Kelly Shepherd is peaceful in death.

He says, still stroking strands of hair from the smooth forehead, 'Thank you.'

'You arrived just in time.' Bailey swallows. It looks a minor victory, his chin heavy on his heaving chest. 'I brought her here, let the other girl go. Told her to call the number you gave me. Then I put a bullet in this wee doll's body, made it look like I killed her, covered her hair with mud and draped it over her face. And waited. Lucky Harris turned up on his own. He'd never seen the girl, Flori.'

Jackie remembers the rushed phone call before he and Sparrow left the farm for London. In the barn he'd sensed Bailey's guilt and regret, his need to confess, his shame. He had prayed the man was in the Islington house, that he'd pick up. He had prayed that Bailey would listen and that Jackie could reach him, that the ex-copper would take the chance to do some good. Bailey had answered. He had listened. When he spoke, there was an eagerness in his voice to help, contrition. At that moment, the policeman was back. But Jackie had still doubted: would Bailey really follow through? Now, he says, 'Not much of a plan, eh?'

'My head must've been cut even trying it.' Bailey coughs, gives a sharp cry of pain. 'I don't think Harris swallowed me being a killer. I was so fucking nervous I dropped the gun and he grabbed it, shoved it in his waistband.' Another rattling cough.

'Then I turned up.'

'Aye, just in time to get me shot.' A wheezing laugh.

'Sorry,' says Jackie. 'I tried to buy time, distract Harris so I could get my knife out. The MI5 thing seemed a good idea.' He looks at the entrance to the tomb. 'Is this where they kept her?'

'Aye.'

Jackie can't comprehend the terror. Entombed and alone, in the dark with no sense of time or place. The ceiling of the tomb is blackened by damp. The thick iron door is swung inward. He sees a camping bed and a bucket in the corner. The entrance is set deep and sandwiched between the doorway and the pediment which crowns it is a plaque, the name scoured from the stone.

The tomb on the right has a similar plaque bearing the name Charles. To the left, George. To the left of that, Henry. A castle is carved above each name.

Jackie says, pointing, 'These tombs...'

Bailey attempts to lift his head and Jackie hauls him into a more upright position, tilting his crown to rest against the stone wall.

'Aye,' says Bailey. 'Something look familiar?'

'The castle.'

'Enniskillen Castle, back home. These boys were soldiers a long time ago.'

'I saw this castle on the wall, above the mural in the Lily Bolero pub. The Inniskillings.'

'The Inniskilling Dragoons. Cavalry regiment, fought in the Crimea.'

'The Skins,' says Jackie. The regimental nickname. 'How many soldiers have tombs here?' He knows the answer before it's given.

'Seven.'

'Seven Skins.'

'Aye.'

'And new girls were kept here?'

'Sometimes. Only in this one. We used to stash drugs in them at first, mostly heroin.' His head bobs like a baby. 'McLelland used his various addresses as halfway houses for newly smuggled girls. He'd the bright idea of using this place, too. Dodds managed the wee girls, and a right hard-nosed bitch she was, too. The others did a bit of ferrying, McVea and Ferguson, the odd security detail.' Bailey winces and looks up to the heavens. The rain is easing. He closes his eyes for a moment. Jackie slaps him hard, beads of rain flying from the man's face. The blood-shot eyes go wide and stupid, like he's just been woken from a deep sleep. Then he sees the blood across his belly and says, 'Shit.' He looks like he's about to cry.

Jackie says, 'You told me McLelland did some security guard work around here.'

'Yeah. He did a bit here at the cemetery, when they still had guards. After a while, a guide told him about these tombs they nicknamed the Skins, because some volunteer at the cemetery was an ex-serviceman and up on his regimental history. Six of the tombs had caskets, but one was empty. A pauper, a soldier who was literally blown to bits at Balaclava. The lad was highly decorated so an officer paid for the tomb in tribute. There were no remains to bury. The tomb just sat there, empty. The perfect hiding place.'

Paid for by a real soldier, for a real soldier, thinks Jackie. Not a thug, or a criminal, or a bent copper, or a terrorist. And these parasites had desecrated the memory.

He says, 'And the houseboat?'

'Some old guy McLelland met when he was slumming it on the streets told him about the River Fleet, how it ran under the city, under Highgate. Dodds came up with the idea of the house-boat on Regent's Canal and the Fleet became a supply route to move the drugs – even the girls – when he thought there was too much risk above ground.'

Jackie shakes his head in amazement. 'How did you end up with MI5?' he says.

'How did you know?'

'At Ferguson's flat, whoever extracted me and Harris didn't kill the security detail. Conscientious for a gang of killers.' He stands and walks a couple of yards to Bailey's mobile and picks it up. 'And back in the barn, you used a phrase: *We're not Americans, we only have a couple of services at the sharp end*, something like that. Hartley said the exact same thing to me when he brought me on board this whole sorry mess. That's a spook talking.' Bailey's chin sinks lower into his chest. Jackie lifts it with his fingertips. 'But the house in Islington where I brought Elira; that's what sealed it. There was an empty fruit-bowl in the kitchen with sweet wrappers in it. They smelled of menthol: the same wrappers and smell as Hartley's red sweets. He'd been there.'

Bailey's eyes are heavy-lidded, his mouth slack. He says, 'I got scared when the Albanians came sniffing.' Jackie has to lean close to hear him. 'I knew of this guy, Stuart Hartley, through Parkinson-Naughton. They'd crossed paths in MI5. I reached out to him and he recruited me as an asset, told me to work with the Albanians and the people from Belfast and their American backers, who wanted to move in. Then we set up the hits and the police started paying attention. I thought it would fog the investigation if we made it look political, republican. Hartley told me you'd been brought in as a free agent. That I shouldn't give you anything solid, but you wouldn't be a threat to me.'

'What happens now McLelland and the rest are gone?'

'The girls come from the east, with the drugs. They work in London, sometimes Belfast or Dublin, and a few go across the Atlantic with the odd shipment of Turkish heroin.' His eyes close. His head lolls to the side.

Jackie says, 'And there you go, and here we are.'

He stands with a heavy grunt. His nerves are screaming blue murder and he takes a moment to wait for the burning pain in his thighs and calves to lessen before calling 999 on Bailey's mobile.

He asks for police and says, 'There are three dead bodies in Highgate West Cemetery. No, it's not a fucking joke. They're all above ground. Two have been shot and one impaled.'

He kills the call with his thumb and begins dialling another number as he shuffles towards the Egyptian Avenue, wiping rain from his eyes. He looks back at Bailey, sitting next to Kelly's body on the gravel path, his back against the wall and his head still slumped on a chest that has stopped heaving.

#

Highgate High Street, with its bespoke delis, organic cafés and butchers selling pheasant and game, is quiet. Jackie drops onto a bench in the square at the top of Swain's Lane, the High Street behind, and rests his elbows on his thighs, his head in his hands. There are no sirens, but the dark chuckle of a helicopter drones nearby. He sits for what seems like a long time.

When he looks up, Stuart Hartley is standing over him. Three men are ranged behind Hartley in various poses of studied menace, about twenty feet away. The red and blue strobe of emergency service vehicles pulses from Swain's Lane.

'Fancy seeing you here,' says Jackie.

'Jackie boy,' says Hartley, like a proud parent. He sits on the bench. 'Thanks for the call, although you could have been more discreet: Bailey's mobile? Thames House switchboard got me at home just as Mrs Hartley was about to begin a diatribe about my spending too much on a particularly rare single malt.'

They sit side-by-side, watching the helicopter's searchlight in the middle distance. At least the rain has stopped. Hartley gestures for Jackie to stand and one of the body-guards pats him down. The bodyguard takes Bailey's mobile phone and rejoins his colleagues in their silent vigil. Jackie sits again.

'There's a gun,' he says. 'In the cemetery, near one of the

bodies. Harris. The Met should find it. And your man Bailey is down there. A nasty-looking knife somewhere around his body, too.' He turns to Hartley. 'You used me. Again.'

'Pray tell?'

'The shite about my RUC call name on the list, *Katana*. It was bollocks from the very start. Even at GCHQ I knew it was ridiculous, but you pressed the right buttons. Provos taking out security force personnel, death lists. Any ex-RUC man's nightmare. And my trouble in Belfast last year: of course you'd hold me to account on that, even if it was done in your name.'

'And the child, don't forget,' Hartley says. 'You may have a gift – and a hair-trigger – for violence, but I know there's a bleeding heart beneath that homicidal exterior. I simply exploited your weaknesses. It's my job.'

'You had Bailey, a man on the inside with Harris, Morgan, Macrossan and the Albanians. You wanted someone else to take out Harris and Morgan once they'd finished the killing so your man could pull the strings unhindered.'

'Yes, Bailey was my man. Only I and the higher-ups know he worked for us. He told me the name of the young man you shot in Soho: Padraig Macrossan.' Hartley licks his lips. 'I was forced to bring you in on this by my immediate superiors. Take it as a compliment. I didn't agree, for what it's worth, and coerced you in Cheltenham because I was ordered to do so. I told Bailey to feed you a couple of titbits to keep you busy and out of the way. But you have a very real talent for mayhem, Jackie.' Hartley pulls his woollen overcoat tighter. 'You blundered into that squalid little alleyway in Soho, and that was the end of Padraig Macrossan.'

The three bodyguards have moved closer. They could be Albanian gangsters, in their leather jackets. Jackie looks to the sky.

'Padraig Macrossan,' says Hartley. 'An idealistic young man. A young man whom no one knows is dead. His poor mother will think he's a missing person. His body will never be found. I pulled his P-file when Bailey gave me his name. It had redacted material. After his death, I could lift the restriction order on that material and recover the data from the computer drive. It was examined by the ranking officer in this whole, sorry episode.'

'That would be you.'

'Indeed. Turns out young Padraig was a good student, a keen sportsman and an active dissident republican sympathiser. A young Englishman with a fetish for Irish terrorism. Oh, he had no truck with *us*, not really. It was the Protestant Irish he hated. But he was approached by Laurence Gilmore at one point with the intention of grooming him as a possible asset, hence the P-file. It never got beyond the initial approaches: Macrossan never knew the security service was interested in him.'

'It's hardly Gilmore's fault that the young lad went on to be part of this shambles,' says Jackie.

'Quite right. He didn't even know Macrossan was involved. However, Gilmore broke one of the cardinal rules of our profession: never become personally involved with your mark. Seems Laurence fell for Macrossan's boyish charms and, a couple of Shirley Temples later, spent the night in a Premier Inn with him.' Hartley produces a handkerchief and sneezes. 'Every cloud and all that, eh Jackie? You performed a public service, blundering into that firefight. Thanks to you making a martyr of the young man, I discovered Macrossan had had a casual fling with a Crown agent. In disposing of him, you protected the integrity of Her Majesty's intelligence services.'

'Medal's in the post, aye?'

'Quite.'

'And Gilmore?'

'Soon to be enjoying a new position at a listening station somewhere on the North Yorkshire Moors. Once I had a word with the higher-ups, common sense prevailed and he was deemed an overly-ambitious, power-hungry Mission Leader. A liability whose past sexual relations and lack of self-control threatened the safety of assets, and to discredit the security service.'

'Christ,' says Jackie, 'are you all at it, clambering over one another's backs for the next opening at the Mayfair Club? If you're protecting the country, God help us.'

'Your self-serving cynicism isn't very endearing, Jackie.'

'I'll work on it for next time I'm used as a pawn in MI5 office politics. Gilmore was a threat to you at Thames House. You exploited my involvement in a gunfight to remove someone you thought was an obstacle to your career. A fucking power play.' Jackie shakes his head. 'And you cut me loose after the shooting, for fuck's sake.'

'You were a liability at that point, out of contact. Utterly deniable and, yes, I took advantage of circumstances and shut the operation down. A calculated risk on my part. I was concerned when Bailey couldn't get hold of you after the Soho incident, but I knew you'd contact him eventually. You had nowhere else to turn.'

'You let them take me, torture me.'

'Don't be so bloody dramatic. By that stage, Bailey was with the Albanians almost constantly. We couldn't communicate; events were beyond my control.'

Jackie winces, a spasm of pain reminding him just how out of control events had been. 'I suppose this is a real result. Harris is dead, Morgan, too, and none of it with your official knowledge.'

'I told you back at GCHQ, I couldn't have UK special forces running around the streets of the capital. But I had you.' He leans back on the bench, licks his lips and places his hands on his lap. 'The names on the list were dropping like flies, clearing the way for Bailey and, once you uncorked the bottle, I had to disavow you, let you run and see what happened. And I saved your little girlfriend's life. Or rather, one of these gentlemen behind me did. Back at the *Katana*, when she was running along the towpath.'

'You were there?'

'God, no,' says Hartley with a dramatic shudder. 'We knew about the houseboat through Bailey and it was moored a two-minute drive from Paddington Green police station. Two of my men were on stand-by there in case you turned up. When the shooting began, they got over there in time to pick off the fellow who was about to pop your little friend as she ran off. One of the top men in the Albanian organisation, as it turns out: a lieutenant called Agon Ruçi. It caused all sorts of ructions with the police at the scene. You should be thanking me.'

'Thank you for putting a vulnerable young girl and myself in harm's way with a violent gang of criminals,' says Jackie. 'You're a real gent, Stuart.'

Hartley looks up in exasperation, calling on help from the heavens. The helicopter is still chattering somewhere above.

Jackie says, 'A young girl's dead, lying down in that cemetery.'

'There are often casualties, you know that.'

'The girl is English, Kelly Shepherd.'

Hartley raises an eyebrow. 'I was under the impression she was your little playmate's sister.'

'Your man Bailey switched the bodies. Elira's sister is in the wind, best forgotten.' Hartley purses his lips. Jackie says, 'Explaining Kelly's body is a mess I'll leave you to clear up.' He shifts on the bench. 'What about Christopher Martins?'

'There are variables in any operation.'

Jackie snaps, 'He's a child, for Christ's sake.' The body-guards twitch.

Hartley says, 'The boy is alive, albeit on life support. Considering the violent, capricious nature of those involved, I'd say the level of damage limitation was acceptable.' He wipes his nose with his linen handkerchief. 'For God's sake, grow up. Do you know how many kids are knifed or shot or beaten on the streets of London in a year? The young boy in Kew is regrettable, yes. But in a year – a month – he'll be a statistic. The destruction of Conal Harris, Padraig Macrossan and Alexander Morgan prevents more of those statistics: that's what you should focus on. Stop being a bloody policeman and try thinking more like…' His voice trails off.

'Like you?' says Jackie. He is about to lose it. To yell, maybe swing for Hartley and break his nose all over again, whatever the consequences.

But what's the point? Stuart William Hartley will never change: amoral, self-serving, narcissistic, manipulative Hartley. He'll no more accept and understand the terrible consequences of his operations than a parasite will regret sucking the life from its host. Jackie says, 'Where did the list come from?'

'Some idiot in Belfast who probably carries notes around reminding him to change his underwear. One of your countrymen shoved it in the shotgun, thinking the cache was bound for Harris and co, not that they needed a shopping list. Another traitorous little bastard grassed the arms stash to PSNI who, unfortunately, were rather too scrupulous in their search.'

'Where do we go from here?'

'I go on the shortlist for the position of Director of Standards. We recruit Bashkim Jusufi as an asset in the London underworld.'

'He's alive?'

'Yes, you can strike him off your tortured conscience. Intensive care, of course; a shotgun blast will do that. But he'll pull through. We have an officer on-site at the hospital at present. I dare say Bashkim won't be too pleased at my man shooting his top lieutenant, mind you.'

'He's beaten and raped. He's ordered executions, ruined lives, pushed heroin.'

'And he's badly injured, his organisation in disarray. Vulnerable. The other jackals pushing drugs and women in London will be clambering over themselves to tear him apart and swallow up his Soho business: the perfect time to persuade him we can provide stability and a measure of security; in return for intelligence, of course. Despite the antics of the fundamentalists, we still retain a wide remit for organised crime in the UK. The service has a considerable stake in the National Crime Agency.'

'You should be locking him up and throwing away the key.'

Hartley shakes his head, the disappointed mentor. 'Come now. You've taken a couple of lives yourself.' He takes a crumpled bag of boiled sweets from his pocket, offers one to Jackie, who refuses, and pops a menthol-scented, cherry-red pellet in his mouth. 'Bashkim is a high-value asset, a major player in serious crime, not to mention a link to the maniacs in Ireland. You know how we operate, Jackie. We're about containment and intelligence. He stays in play, with our blessing. The American agencies will keep an eye on the funding over there. Shame about Bailey, but that is what it is.'

'And the girl, Elira?'

'Bring her in. We'll put her under protection; you, too. You can both disappear.' The thin slit of Hartley's mouth seems to tear as it twists into a leer. 'Together, if you'd like. Set up and play house somewhere.'

'No,' says Jackie. He looks at his tainted hands, turns them over. 'Here's how it works: the girl gets a UK residency visa, if she wants it, and is left in peace. Her sister, too.' He smiles, beginning to enjoy himself. 'You can correspond with her at this P.O. Box.' Jackie hands Hartley a sheet of folded paper. 'She'll get any messages you leave. Also, you find her mother and father, in Tirana. Give her the opportunity and means to contact them. You make sure Bashkim leaves them be.'

Jackie looks into Hartley's small, mean eyes. 'I am left alone, immune from any prosecution for my actions over the past couple of days, and any past trouble. And I never hear from you again. No more contact. No more work for you. Ever.' He breathes deep and sucks up a wave of pain. 'You have the Albanian shut down the trafficking side of the operation. The drugs are what they are, but the girls get an out.'

Worth a try, thinks Jackie. You don't ask; you don't get.

Hartley crosses his legs, amused. 'Are you dictating terms?'

'No, I'm blackmailing you. This conversation is being recorded by a friend of mine who is positioned nearby with a camcorder and remote microphone. He has already contacted the press to inform them we are here, so it'd be best to wrap this up and get out of here, I think. He hasn't given any names but if I, or the girls, are in any way harmed, the recording goes to the media and New Scotland Yard. Hell, the Archbishop of-fucking-Canterbury and His Holiness in Rome. If any ill luck should befall either me or the girls in the future, the recording goes to the media. It's really that simple. You go on to be Director-fucking-General for all I care. Me and the girls live our lives. Understand?'

Hartley's eyes are small, polished black beads in the light and shadow around the bench. The High Street is deserted, the suburbs tucked up for the night. But a microphone is hidden in the hedge to the left of the bench and Ian Sparrow is somewhere nearby. Judging by the abject scowl on Hartley's face, he knows it isn't a bluff and can't take the chance in any case.

Hartley swallows hard. 'It's been a pleasure,' he says, a faint tremor in his voice. For a moment, he looks old and fragile. Then he clears his throat and says, 'Come and see me if you ever want a job. You show great aptitude.' He stands to go.

Jackie looks him up and down, sits back on the bench and says, 'If I ever come to grief because of you, at any time, you're ruined. Now fuck you, Hartley. And fuck off.'

CHAPTER 34

Later

Jackie sips his coffee and remembers.

He remembers sitting outside cafés in other great cities – New York, Hong Kong, Tokyo, Budapest – watching and dreaming while the world spooled by, as he takes in the bustle of Covent Garden. He studies the massive portico of St Paul's Church, with its huge, jutting pediment, like a pillbox guarding the path to Heaven, and remembers spending an afternoon with an old girl-friend here when he was in the Army. He remembers gawking at the price of a beer near the Royal Opera House, back when he visited in his twenties, and a trip here with Ian Sparrow when he was still working at the farm.

Jackie remembers the wounded self-pity on Hartley's face as the bastard slouched away from the square in Highgate that night, flanked by his goons, the two-tone staccato wail of an emergency service vehicle drifting up from the city sprawling below Swain's Lane. He remembers taking the remote mic from the bushes and meeting Sparrow in the car on Hornsey Lane, Sparrow assuring him he got it all on the camcorder.

Jackie remembers arriving at Sparrow's sister Betty's house later that night. The look on Elira and Flori's faces as they sat together in the spare bedroom, their soft, quiet intimacy. They'd seen him and wept, overwhelmed. He'd had a couple of days with the sisters, nursed by them with a ferocious intensity. Elira had sat with him and touched the wounds on his shoulder and side, speaking in Albanian, her voice a soft incantation. And then she left, a soft, sweet kiss planted on his cheek and a letter in a simple cream envelope placed in his hand. She and Flori sat together behind Sparrow as he pulled into traffic to drive them to the countryside and the safety of a holiday cottage in Devon. He read the words on the envelope: *Për kalorës time të bardhë. To my white knight.* Betty had shepherded Jackie back into the house and made him a cup of strong tea.

He takes another sip of bitter coffee.

The file photo of little Christopher Martins is a constant memory. So is a beautiful, still face in the Circle of Lebanon and the mad swirl of violence that day.

If only Elira hadn't left the mobile on the table. If only Jackie had told her to wait for his call to the landline at the farm.

If, if, if...

He finishes the dregs at the bottom of his mug. Covent Garden's plaza is packed, tourists gawking, Londoners shopping, chancers hawking. It's a crisp, bright day, the kind of day that always seems to exist in the Hollywood London, where everyone that matters lives in a handsome townhouse and foppish Englishmen muddle on through. He's about to summon the resolve for another negotiation to obtain a simple white coffee when the man exits an expensive clothing boutique thirty yards to the right on King Street. Two bruisers are with him, struggling to look comfortable in their tight-cut expensive suits, flanking their master as they walk in the direction of Charing Cross Road.

The man in the centre is bold, enjoying the stroll, his chest high and proud in the tailored, woven herringbone Savile Row two-piece, face stern and confident. He looks like a man who belongs, and to whom the city itself is in thrall. A man safe and secure in his fiefdom.

Jackie knows the route, has seen the man, always accompanied by the heavies, stroll these streets many times in the last months. Jackie has established a pattern and identified a blind spot: the narrow, cobbled alleyway off Rose Street, passing a quiet pub with a metal gate set in the wall leading to Lazenby Court. A quiet urban lane in the bustling West End en route to Soho. A place where a mugger or gangster might, if he worked fast and had the edge of surprise, make quick work of the two bodyguards with a blade. Then the assailant could take a few more seconds with their master. Deliver a message and give him a good look at who was ripping the life from his guts with the knife.

Jackie stands and pushes the small table away, patting his pocket, feeling something slim and metallic nestled there. Then he strides across the plaza, maintaining a discreet distance but never taking his eyes off the two bodyguards and their boss, the *Krye* of Soho, Bashkim Jusufi.

ACKNOWLEDGEMENTS

My thanks go to: David Cameron for his time and suggestions; Desmond Egan for his generous permission to quote 'The Northern Ireland Question', from his wonderful collection *Elegies*, published by The Goldsmith Press, Newbridge, 1996; Robert Dinsdale, my editor at Silvertail, for his expertise; Shona Andrew, for a striking cover; Humfrey Hunter at Silvertail, for continued support and a lovely pub lunch; Christopher Zuk, for many great nights out, and technical advice; my beautiful wee daughter, Hana; and my wonderful wife, Tomoe.

AUTHOR'S NOTE

In the course of writing *Seven Skins*, I made the trip to London for some research: there are many great pubs in the city, and I and my liver took my fact-finding mission very seriously. There is not, however, a Lily Bolero pub in Aldgate. Highgate Cemetery West is as described, and a fascinating place for a guided tour: I had the cemetery in mind as a location thanks to its cameos in several Hammer and Amicus horror films and it didn't disappoint. The Egyptian Avenue, towering cedar and Circle of Lebanon are all there in their Victorian gothic splendour. The seven tombs of the Inniskillings – the Seven Skins in the Circle of Lebanon – are not. They exist only in a dark wee corner of my imagination. Finally, in Cheltenham, I have no idea whether GCHQ has a 'sparse, windowless room containing a table, two chairs and a thin, musky stink of damp' on the first floor, although I wouldn't be surprised. While I highly recommend a pub crawl around London or a tour of Highgate Cemetery, I wouldn't advise turning up at Government Communications Headquarters to find out, either.

Printed in Great Britain
by Amazon